GW00502096

THEATRES OF FEELING

Theatre and theatregoing was central to the cultural life of later eighteenth-century Britain. In this engaging work, Jean I. Marsden explores the playhouse as a source of emotion during a period when the ability to feel demonstrated moral worth. Using first-hand accounts, reviews, and illustrations to complement the drama of the era, Marsden examines why both critics and audiences elevated the theatre above the pulpit and how they experienced the plays and performances they witnessed. Tears and even fainting fits were a common reaction to powerful productions, and playwrights sought to harness this emotion. The book explores this intersection of text, performance, and affect in a series of case studies of plays exploring British liberty, empire and the evils of antisemitism. With a focus on emotional response, *Theatres of Feeling* delivers a new approach to dramatic literature and performance, one that moves beyond more limited studies of text or performance.

JEAN I. MARSDEN is Professor of English at the University of Connecticut. Her previous publications include *The Appropriation of Shakespeare: Post-Renaissance Reconstructions of the Works and the Myth* (ed. 1991), *The Re-Imagined Text: Shakespeare, Adaptation, and Eighteenth-Century Literary Theory* (1995), *Fatal Desire: Women, Sexuality, and the English Stage* (2006), and numerous articles or editions dealing with diverse topics ranging from Restoration and eighteenth-century theatre, children's literature, and Shakespeare, to the poet Anne Finch.

THEATRES OF FEELING

Affect, Performance, and the Eighteenth-Century Stage

JEAN I. MARSDEN
University of Connecticut

CAMBRIDGE
UNIVERSITY PRESS

University Printing House, Cambridge CB2 8BS, United Kingdom

One Liberty Plaza, 20th Floor, New York, NY 10006, USA

477 Williamstown Road, Port Melbourne, VIC 3207, Australia

314–321, 3rd Floor, Plot 3, Splendor Forum, Jasola District Centre, New Delhi – 110025, India

79 Anson Road, #06–04/06, Singapore 079906

Cambridge University Press is part of the University of Cambridge.

It furthers the University's mission by disseminating knowledge in the pursuit of education, learning, and research at the highest international levels of excellence.

www.cambridge.org
Information on this title: www.cambridge.org/9781108476133
DOI: 10.1017/9781108694629

First published 2019

Printed and bound in Great Britain by Clays Ltd, Elcograf S.p.A.

A catalogue record for this publication is available from the British Library.

Library of Congress Cataloging-in-Publication Data
NAMES: Marsden, Jean I., author.
TITLE: Theatres of feeling : affect, performance, and the eighteenth-century stage / Jean I. Marsden.
DESCRIPTION: Cambridge, United Kingdom ; New York, NY : Cambridge University Press, 2019. | Includes bibliographical references and index.
IDENTIFIERS: LCCN 2019008016 | ISBN 9781108476133 (Hardback : alk. paper)
SUBJECTS: LCSH: English drama – 18th century – History and criticism. | Emotions in literature. | Theater – Psychological aspects. | Theater audiences – Psychology. | Emotions.
CLASSIFICATION: LCC PR448.E46 M37 2019 | DDC 820.9/353–dc23
LC record available at https://lccn.loc.gov/2019008016

ISBN 978-1-108-47613-3 Hardback

For Lane

Contents

List of Figures — *page* viii
Acknowledgements — ix

Introduction — 1
1 Divine Sympathy: Theatre, Connection, and Virtue — 18
2 Dangerous Pleasures: Theatregoing in the Eighteenth Century — 41
3 Roman Fathers and Grecian Daughters: Tragedy and the Nation — 70
4 Performing the West Indies: Comedy, Feeling, and British Identity — 102
5 The Moral Muse: Comedy and Social Engineering — 137
Afterword — 166

Notes — 170
Bibliography — 203
Index — 216

Figures

2.1 'How to Harrow up the Soul'. *Theatrical Portraiture No. 6*, in *Attic Miscellany, Or Characteristic Mirror of Men and Things*, vol. I (1791). Courtesy of the Lewis Walpole Library, Yale University. *page* 53

2.2 Thomas Rowlandson. *Comedy in the Country, Tragedy in London*. 29 May 1807. Hand-coloured engraving. Courtesy of the Lewis Walpole Library, Yale University. 55

3.1 Johan Zoffany. *Roman Charity*, c. 1769. Oil on canvas, 76.3 x 63.5 cm. National Gallery of Victoria, Melbourne, Felton Bequest, 1932 (4614–3). 85

3.2 *Sarah Siddons as Euphrasia*. Hand-tinted engraving by Caroline Watson, from a painting by Robert Edge Pine. 1784. Courtesy of the Lewis Walpole Library, Yale University. 94

3.3 James Gillray. *Melpomene*. 6 December 1784. Hand-tinted etching. Courtesy of the Lewis Walpole Library, Yale University. 98

3.4 *The Mother and the Child*. Anonymous cartoon from *The London Magazine: Or, Gentleman's Monthly Intelligencer*, v. 42 (January 1773). HD P 270.1. Widener Library, Harvard University. 99

Acknowledgments

This book has been many years in the making, and it would not have been possible without the assistance of many individuals and institutions along the way. Fellowships from the University of Connecticut Humanities Institute and from the National Endowment for the Humanities gave me the release time that enabled me to write this book. My research was also supported by generous grants from the University of Connecticut Research Foundation and from the College of Liberal Arts and Sciences; Associate Dean for the Humanities Shirley Roe facilitated my travel to several special collections.

As scholars, we tend to live in the sometimes restrictive world of the mind, making the response of others to our work an invaluable stimulus and at times a necessary corrective. Much of the material included in this book has been presented in a variety of forms at meetings of the American Society for Eighteenth-Century Studies, the Northeastern American Society for Eighteenth-Century Studies, and the Southeastern American Society for Eighteenth-Century Studies. The colloquium "Enlightenment Changes" chaired by Peter Sabor and Fiona Ritchie at McGill University allowed me to test the early stages of my work on sympathy, and invited talks at the Southeastern American Society for Eighteenth-Century studies and the British Women Writers conferences gave me the chance to present more developed work on Murphy's *The Grecian Daughter* and on Sarah Siddons, respectively. Therefore, many thanks to Judith Slagle at Eastern Tennessee State University and to Kristine Jennings at Binghampton University. Presenting the Cardin lecture at the University of Hartford gave me the opportunity to discuss father-daughter relationships more generally; my thanks to Mark Blackwell for making that possible. Responses from these audiences both large and small have enriched my work.

I have been fortunate to have many colleagues who have assisted me with this project. Misty Anderson read the second chapter and provided copious, thoughtful remarks. Heather McPherson shared discussions about responses to Sarah Siddons, and Gordon Turnball was a fount of knowledge for all things Boswellian. Aleksondra Hulquist provided useful information on the world of affect outside of drama; my thanks to her for her comments on my theories on the operation of affect within the theatre. Joseph Roach and Bridget Orr read the manuscript in its final form and provided perceptive insights that assisted in articulating and sharpening the argument, especially in the Introduction. Although I never had the opportunity to meet him before his death, I am grateful to the late Michael Ragussis, who generously shared his work on stage Jews with me. In addition to these specific examples of scholarly generosity, I am indebted to many individuals for their help and encouragement. Laura Rosenthal and Deborah Payne gave unstintingly of their time as I worked through much of this material, each providing much needed support at various points of the project, while Diana Solomon and Aparna Gollipudi listened to me patiently and with good humor. Many others provided assistance along the way, including Brian Corman, Marilyn Francus, Lisa A. Freeman, Julie Hayes, Robert D. Hume, Kathryn King, Robert Markley, Jessica Munns, Fiona Ritchie, Peggy Thompson, Brett Wilson, and Kathleen Wilson. Chris Mounsey provided information on pantomime and gave a memorable tour of eighteenth-century sites in London. I would be remiss if I did not mention the redoubtable Vickie Cutting, who saved me from a variety of missteps.

A few friends deserve special recognition. For more years than I care to remember, Anne Goldgar has welcomed me into her home and introduced me to friends who have since become my own. She is a true member of the republic of letters. Michael Dobson and Nicola Watson extended hospitality on many occasions, contributing a wealth of knowledge on things literary and theatrical. My colleague Margaret Higonnet's unfailing kindness and intellectual generosity have been a constant inspiration to all who know her.

Although the world of eighteenth-century theatre was well outside their own, my colleagues at the University of Connecticut have provided me with much needed encouragement. In particular I would like to thank the members of the Transatlantic reading group, Anna Mae Duane, Wayne Franklin, and Liz Hart, who listened to and commented on early versions of chapters three and four. The give and take of these informal discussions helped me develop many of my ideas regarding the implications of popular drama and audience response. Cathy Schlund-Vials generously read several chapters of the project at an early stage while conversations with Margaret

Breen, Pam Brown, and the late Hans Turley enriched the project as it grew. Mary Udal provided friendship and concrete support from start to finish. Numerous classes of graduate students at the University of Connecticut have provided useful input; I am particularly grateful to my former students Dawn Goode, Jennifer Ryer, Jarred Wiehe, and the late Karen Cajka.

Throughout my research on drama and response I have been aided by many librarians and archivists in Britain and the United States. The wonderful staff at the Theatre and Performance Collection of the Victoria and Albert Museum Library assisted me in finding and photographing promptbooks and other materials related to performances of *The Grecian Daughter* and *The Jew*. Librarians at the Houghton Library helped me navigate the Harvard Theatre Collection while archivists at the Hungton Library helped in my search for extra-illustrated volumes and theatre manuscripts. Susan Walker, Cynthia Roman, and Kristen McDonald provided invaluable assistance in locating illustrations and images at the Lewis Walpole Library. As always, Richard Bleiler, Collections and Humanities Librarian at Homer Babbidge Library at the University of Connecticut, deserves special thanks for his tireless efforts to acquire materials necessary for my work and for helping me find my way through the intricacies of databases and special collections. During the past two years I have benefitted from the care Cambridge University Press has lavished on the editing and production of this book; my thanks to Bethany Thomas, Sharon McGann, Tim Mason, and Linda Bree. My wonderful copy editor Jacqueline French deserves special credit for her patience and unerring eye; I hope to thank you in person some day, preferably in sunny Italy.

An earlier version of chapter five appeared as "Richard Cumberland's *The Jew* and the Benevolence of the Audience: Performance and ReligiousTolerance," in *Eighteenth-Century Studies* 48, no. 4 (Summer 2015), 475–477. A portion of chapter four appeared as "Performing the West Indies: Comedy, Feeling, and British Identity" in *Comparative Drama* 42, no. 1 (2008), 73–88 and a discussion of the figure of Inkle from the same chapter as "The Problem with Inkle: A Study in Performance," in *The Oxford Handbook to the Georgian Playhouse 1737–1832*, ed. David Francis Taylor (Oxford: Oxford University Press, 2013), 692–696. My thanks to the publishers for republication permission.

Friends and family outside the world of academia have celebrated and commiserated with me as I worked. My thanks in particular to my mother, Ellen Marsden, and to Katie, Jeff and Daniel Nyswaner, all of whom never failed to believe in me and in the possibilities of the work. Thanks also to Captain Thunder, who provided his own unique support.

My greatest debt is to my husband, Lane Barrow, who has lived with this project from the beginning and read far too many drafts of the manuscript along the way; I could never have done this without you.

Introduction

> The heart knows nothing of heroics; it cannot feign.
>
> –Charles Dibdin, *A Complete History of The Stage* [1]

> Lessons for the Stage may be convey'd, in one respect, stronger than from the Pulpit, if the Audience were attentive as they should be at Church: For a Play well wrote, and well perform'd, where Virtue suffers, or meets its just Reward, must have strong Force upon the Mind, where the Eye is suppos'd to view the very Persons in the real Circumstances of History.
>
> –W. R. Chetwood, *A General History of the Stage* [2]

> I kept myself at a distance from all acquaintances, and got into a proper frame. Mr Garrick gave me the most perfect satisfaction. I was fully moved, and I shed abundance of tears.
>
> –James Boswell, *London Journal* [3]

Truth, explains Charles Dibdin, can be found in emotion. Emotion is transparent and immediate, without embellishment or guile; its source, the heart, constitutes an authority that not only does not but *cannot* feign. Writing about the playwright George Lillo's popular domestic tragedy *The London Merchant*, Dibdin both endorses emotion and links it inextricably to the theatre, where it exists as a good that can endure as 'heroics' cannot. Dibdin's words would not have surprised his contemporaries, nor would his connection of this truth-in-feeling to the stage. The theatre of later eighteenth-century England was a world of feeling, where audiences came to experience emotion and where playwrights sought to teach by speaking heart to heart. Emotion itself was a central topic within the plays, as characters displayed their worth through the warmth and sincerity of their passions. Just as the characters elevated true feeling above superficial art, the performance of these plays sought to evoke emotion within the breast of the spectator, emotion that would, in turn, promote virtue, both individual and communal.

While Dibdin, Chetwood, and Boswell each focus on different aspects of the theatrical experience, all three attest to theatre's ability to move and to the significance of theatrical performance both inside and outside the theatre walls. Attracting thousands of spectators daily, the dramatic productions of the later eighteenth century provide an important register of social and political change because of their unique position as a distinctly public and yet overtly emotional literary form, a conduit through which a nation's view of itself and its society was expressed. London theatres such as Drury Lane and Covent Garden attracted crowds that included royalty and tradesmen, apprentices and aristocrats, and the plays they staged generated a host of related publications including playbooks and reviews as well as poems, songbooks, and even paintings, making drama the most widely disseminated and influential form of literature of its day. Critics and moralists alike commended theatre's superior ability to instruct a broad audience; because of the intense emotions it excited and because of the public venue in which these emotions were experienced, it was hailed as a source of national moral authority. The emotion generated by the eighteenth-century theatre defined Britain's – or more properly Britons' – sense of identity and their vision of what they hoped to be. It reflected not an actual reality but the reality they desired to inhabit, a reality that incorporated their national identity as a moral community and as participants in a far-flung empire, thus reinforcing their vision of themselves and their values. Audiences applauded the performances they beheld and the emotions that they felt because these performances represented the truth they believed and the identities they sought to have.

Feeling alone was not sufficient, for when performed well, drama was freighted with moral possibilities. Writing fifty years before Dibdin, W. R. Chetwood praises the inherent virtue of the stage, elevating it above even the pulpit and privileging performance over sermonizing because of the force of its affect and the consequent power of its 'lessons'. Chetwood succinctly articulates the ways in which a series of interrelated entities provokes these lessons, beginning with the text brought to life through performance, 'where the Eye is suppos'd to view the very Persons in the real Circumstances of History'. In its form as a static lecture, the sermon cannot compete with embodied performance. Chetwood's comments represent the common association linking the stage with the church; both are communal spaces in which the congregation/audience is united through the 'force' of their response to the performance before them; as Brett D. Wilson explains succinctly, 'by *feeling* together, they feel *together*'.[4] The assumption that lies beneath Chetwood's association of theatregoing and religious experience is that, in the theatre, audience response leads to moral edification, an assumption radically different from the antitheatrical pamphlets of earlier generations.[5]

For audiences, achieving the proper response demonstrated personal merit as well as a certain amount of effort. In his description of seeing David Garrick perform Lear at Drury Lane, James Boswell provides a spectator's account of the theatrical experience, an experience that incorporates both the desire for emotional release and its fulfilment. At once candid and self-conscious, Boswell describes the practice of theatregoing as a complex process, one that involved a certain degree of careful preparation. To this end he explains that he arrived at the theatre two hours early in order to ready himself for the event and get 'into a proper frame'. His preparation was successful; as he notes, Garrick gave him 'perfect satisfaction'. What is perhaps most remarkable about this passage is the means by which Boswell calibrates this artistic satisfaction: deep emotion and its physical manifestation in tears. The link between emotion and theatrical success that Boswell describes is not only expected but even quantifiable; he not simply specifies that he shed tears but notes their 'abundance'. As a spectator, Boswell judges performance based on its visibly recognizable affect. In a broader sense, then, feeling is both expected and necessary. The plays of the later eighteenth century are frankly emotional because they needed to be. Their audiences expected and even demanded this of them. To remain unmoved represents a failure on the part of the actor, the playwright, and even the spectator.

Theatres of Feeling takes its inspiration from this repeated emphasis on emotional experience and its inextricable connection to the theatre of the eighteenth century. The passages cited above articulate the many facets of this coupling, from the certainty of Dibdin's association of truth and emotion, to Chetwood's link between the power of performance and moral edification, to Boswell's account of his personal experience within one particular theatre of feeling. In the fifty-year span that encompassed the writings of Chetwood, Boswell, and Dibdin, heartfelt emotion was accepted as a crucial component of human life. Man was not simply a thinking being but a feeling one, and too much thought in the absence of feeling was not simply distasteful but barren and potentially immoral. Entire nations could be implicated in a play's reception, for good or bad; writing of the reception of Richard Cumberland's reformist comedy *The Jew* (1795), one critic noted, 'we feel for the credit and advantage of our country, that [the play] was received with the warmest applause'.[6] In the later eighteenth century, emotion was not indistinct or amorphous;

it could be judged in terms of both its quality and its quantity, and these criteria were especially true within the walls of the theatre, where a play succeeded or failed based on the audience's response, and where audiences themselves were judged based on their ability to feel.

Theatre as Affect

This study seeks to consider audience response: the plays and performances that generated it as well as the nature of the response and its implications. In the eighteenth century, as in all other eras, examining the nature of emotion and response requires a recognition of the peculiar nature of performance and in particular of theatre. Theatre is unlike other forms of literary activity in that it is truly alive; it is three-dimensional and exists in real time. While the presence of the actor on the stage makes theatre physically embodied in a way no other art form is, it is nonetheless quintessentially ephemeral; it is impossible to recapture the details and impact of a performance after it occurs – a problem which is particularly acute when considering theatre before the advent of film. Studying the history of theatre and performance thus requires searching for traces of past experiences, glimpses of lost genius. It is a communal rather than an individual experience and cannot exist without an audience, just as it cannot exist without a performer. In this it could be said to be a collaborative venture between the actor who performs and the playgoer who responds. The two combine to create a symbiotic experience that is more than a sum of its parts, a response the eighteenth century understood as sympathy – a spectator's involuntary emotional reaction to what he or she sees upon the stage. This response cannot be codified; it varies from location to location, from day to day, and even from minute to minute.

Because of their contingent nature, assessing performance and response presents significant theoretical and methodological challenges, difficulties that even contemporary performance studies grapple with. At the most basic level lies the question of how to discuss and evaluate feeling. Because theatre is both intensely lived but always becoming past, determining the emotional response to theatre is challenging, and one of the goals of this study is to make visible these seemingly nebulous past experiences. Pondering the problem of assessing the past when looking back to the historical moment represented in method acting, Robin Bernstein asks, 'how can we historicize affect?'[7] If, as she suggests, historicizing emotion generated within the theatre over the course of the last five decades represents a challenge, how much more difficult is this process when the performance being considered and the affect assessed is centuries rather than decades in the past, at a time when performance could not be recorded and replayed.

Historicizing affect provides an important register of cultural developments, and because of this link between theatre and culture, explorations of performance as well as affect have turned to the work of Raymond Williams, in particular to his discussion of 'structures of feelings', as a means of approaching the complex operation of emotion and theatre. Williams's work has a strong affinity for eighteenth-century studies,[8] and his discussion of what he famously termed 'structures of feeling' is admirably suited to a consideration of the overtly emotional world of eighteenth-century theatre. It is a slippery term, as Williams himself admits, and he suggests as an alternative 'structures of experience' before rejecting that term because of its potential to imply past rather than present experience.[9] These 'structures' are, as Williams emphasizes, a process rather than an ideological system, growing out of lived experience, so that one of the crucial components of these 'structures of feeling' is that they are immediate, situated in a specific moment. As Williams explains,

> We are talking about characteristic elements of impulse, restraint, and tone; specifically affective elements of consciousness and relationships: not feeling against thought, but thought as felt and feeling as thought: practical consciousness of a present kind, in a living and interrelative continuity. We are then defining these elements as a 'structure': as a set, with specific internal relations, at once interlocking and in tension. Yet we are also defining a social experience which is still *in process*.[10]

Williams's focus here and elsewhere is on the affective; if we cannot pin down the notion of 'structures of feeling' and define it neatly, it is precisely because Williams rejects ideological certainties. Thought and feeling cannot be pried apart and codified; they are intrinsically interwoven, a 'continuity' that is 'lived and experienced' in a way that 'formally held and systematic beliefs' are not.[11] They are a 'structure' in the sense that they cannot be separated into neat and distinct components. In this manner, Williams rejects easy binary constructions such as thought and feeling in favour of networks characterized by connection, 'at once interlocking and in tension'. This lack of static fixed identity is key to Williams's description of the lived experience that structures of feeling represent as always in process.

Because structures of feeling centre on a network of affective relationships, the concept provides a useful means of approaching the 'interrelative continuity' that constitutes the lived theatrical experience. As Williams notes, 'there is frequent tension between the received interpretation and practical experience ... the tension is as often an unease, a stress, a displacement, a latency: the moment of conscious comparison not yet come, often not even coming'.[12] We see these tensions enacted repeatedly within the theatre, between spectator and performance, performance and text.

For Williams, the arts have a special relevance, for they demonstrate that 'the true social content is in a significant number of cases of this present and affective kind'[13] and are in this way the harbingers of social developments, experiences as they are actively lived rather than systematized. They are for him the epitome of the 'meaning[s] and values as they are actively lived and felt'[14] that compose these structures of feeling. As he notes,

> The point is especially relevant to works of art, which really are, in one sense, explicit and finished forms – actual objects in the visual arts, objectified conventions and notations (semantic figures) in literature. But it is not only that, to complete their inherent process, we have to make them present, in specifically active 'readings.' *It is also that the making of art is never itself in the past tense. It is always a formative process, within a specific present* (emphasis added).[15]

Williams makes the important distinction between the text as static object, a series of 'objectified conventions', and the process of making art, which is alive in the specific moment of its creation as well as in the specific present of our own experience with the work of art. His comments here are especially relevant for the study of theatre. As opposed to drama as text, the essence of performance is that it is always a formative process. As eighteenth-century writers such as Henry Home, Lord Kames understood, theatre is the most present of all the arts; performance is itself always in process, made and remade afresh with every staging.[16] Where performance studies often focus on the actual process of performance as embodied by the actor, *Theatres of Feeling* expands this focus to examine the affective relations established by the performance and the audience, where the audience is itself a performer, watching itself watching others. Thus Herbert Blau's statement that 'of all the performing arts the theatre stinks most of mortality' because an actor 'can die there in front of your eyes; is in fact doing so'[17] presents only half the equation. If the actor is in the process of dying, so too is the audience; the process of mortality connects them both. It is this unceasing process of mortality that, paradoxically, makes theatre so live.

The inextricable bond between performer and audience is trenchantly expressed by Joseph Roach, who directly addresses the relationship between celebrity and fan, performer and audience, a relationship he describes as characterized by vicariousness and what he terms 'synthetic experience'. As he explains,

> synthetic experience must answer the human need, regulated by both curiosity and fear, to experience life vicariously as well as directly. Vicariousness suggests the derivative nature of experience from some prior authority. The word *vicarious* is cognate to *vicar*, in the sense of one who serves as a substitute, agent or administrative deputy (as in 'Vicar of God' for the king of England as head of the church). Professional playwrights and performers manufacture and sell such experiences.[18]

Just as the celebrity needs an audience to exist, so too does the audience need the performer to create experience for them, something they encounter vicariously. In this sense, their experience is 'synthetic', not quite real. I would like to suggest a twist on Roach's words, a consideration of 'synthetic experience' as neither second-hand nor artificial but rather as synergistic, a collaboration between audience and performance. Eighteenth-century audiences eagerly 'experienced experience' when they attended the theatre; their experience was very real to them, but it was a composite response to the performance and to each other, magnified and reinvented in the communal space of the theatre. It thus exemplified Emile Durkheim's widely cited concept of *effervescence*, in which 'the very act of congregating is an exceptionally powerful stimulus. Once individuals are gathered together, a sort of electricity is generated from their closeness and quickly launches them to an extraordinary height of exaltation.'[19] A century before Durkheim, James Boaden described an audience watching Sarah Siddons dismiss an adversary with scorn, a moment 'which the audience caught as electrical'.[20]

The fact that the 'electricity' of communal response is linked to specific moments creates distinct challenges to the theatre historian in her attempt to historicize affect. How can we consider the nature of 'synthetic experience', of past emotion, when both the affect and the performance have vanished? How do we approach these questions of performance and response, the lived experience that is the essence of the theatrical experience? Having accepted that in the eras before visual or aural recordings we cannot recreate the actual lived experience, we must employ what might be considered a methodology of traces, probing archives for scraps of information that help piece together a history of performance and affect. Play texts on their own are not enough, although they provide invaluable evidence of the values that inspired authors and moved audiences. Because a play's text is fixed, a static document that in Williams's words consists of 'objectified conventions and notations', it cannot be relied upon to give a complete picture of the theatrical experience. In reading these texts, we bring our own expectations and biases just as eighteenth-century audiences brought their own very different expectations and biases into the auditoriums of Drury Lane, Covent Garden, and theatres across Britain and its empire. Textual analysis on its own is thus insufficient. Any understanding of theatrical experience must incorporate records of response: personal as well as published reviews; eighteenth-century theories of theatre as well as theories of emotional response, for emotion was frequently couched in terms of theatrical representations and response; records of performances; and even receipts. All of these pieces, no matter how fragmentary, provide glimpses of past performance and together can help recreate a sense of the theatrical experience of an age when drama in performance was seen as the most powerful of all art forms, the art that represented the most potential for good because of what Williams termed its 'present and affective nature' and Kames described as its 'real presence'.

Approaching Theatre as Affect

Response or affect is very different from what the eighteenth century termed the passions, the physical manifestations of emotional states such as anger, fear, awe, or astonishment. The proper portrayal of such passions on the stage and in the visual arts was discussed in treatises on acting and in manuals such as Charles Le Brun's widely disseminated *Methode pour apprendre à dessiner les passions* (1702, English translation 1734), with its illustrations of how passions could be recognized and portrayed. Writing about the passions and their place in the 'science of acting', Roach observes that in the eighteenth century discussions of the physiology of the passions 'became numerous enough to constitute a minor literary-scientific genre in which it seemed that ever more careful descriptions of outward expressions would somehow explain the inward nature of the phenomena'.[21] One outstanding manipulator of these 'outward expressions' was David Garrick, whose skilful embodiment of the passions was itself the subject of numerous illustrations and who used this ability to shift swiftly from passion to passion to entertain people both on and off the stage. (Denis

Diderot was so impressed by seeing Garrick's demonstration of the passions that it ultimately shaped his theories on acting and theatre.) Passions such as those demonstrated by Garrick were only representations, however; they might cause an emotional response in the viewer, but they did not, in themselves, constitute response.

When staged, the passions as conceived of by playwrights and embodied by actors operated to stir emotions in the audience, and the productions that Dibden, Chetwood, and Boswell attended specifically sought to arouse sympathy and move spectators to tears. New standards for the stage appeared and with them a new mode of drama that emphasized the representation of emotion and in particular that representation's ability to elicit a strong emotional response in spectators, one that often could be calibrated, as Boswell's was, through visible manifestations such as tears. This ideal resulted in modifications to the theatre repertoire as older plays deemed unaffecting vanished from the stage while others were reimagined and reshaped around contemporary models of feeling. In this manner popular plays from previous generations were reinterpreted, so that Lear can be seen primarily as a father rather than a king, an ordinary man driven mad by domestic betrayal. New plays by authors such as Richard Cumberland, George Colman, and Arthur Murphy shared the stage with Colley Cibber's moral reform plays as well as with domestic tragedies such as *The London Merchant*, the play Charles Dibdin praised for its true emotion and lack of heroics.

With this revisioning of the purpose of drama, the English theatre participated in a large-scale literary shift that occurred throughout Europe during the later eighteenth and early nineteenth centuries in which plays that provoked the kind of affective response applauded by audiences steeped in sympathy pervaded the stage. Even while English writers defined themselves against what they argued was the sterility of French classical theatre, they welcomed components of the French stage that blurred the lines between rigid categories of comedy and tragedy, such as the French *comédies larmoyantes* or tearful comedies At the same time, Diderot turned to the domestic tragedies of playwrights such as Lillo and novelists such as Richardson in championing a new hybrid form, the *drame bourgeois*.[22] While English writers did not always acknowledge their connections to the theatre of other cultures, this cross-fertilization demonstrates the increasing critical and popular taste for plays that rejected strict forms in order to stress the affective nature of drama.

Even though they were celebrated in their time, filling theatres night after night and remaining in the theatrical repertoire well into the nineteenth century, most of the plays written during the later eighteenth century have faded from theatrical repertoires and critical canons. Only a handful, the comedies of Richard Brinsley Sheridan, Oliver Goldsmith's *She Stoops to Conquer*, and the newly canonical *Belle's Strategem* by Hannah Cowley, maintain a place on the stage. Because the plays of this era do not adhere to traditional generic categories, scholars in the past have often found the plays difficult to deal with, typically identifying the plays of the post-Licensing Act era as 'sentimental drama' or 'sentimental comedy'. Dismissed as examples of 'cheap' sentimentality, a phrase which devalues – literally – works which participate overly in the generation of feeling within their audience, the frank emotionality of much later eighteenth-century drama has proved off-putting to many twentieth- and twenty-first-century critics. In a monograph devoted to sentimental drama, Arthur Sherbo provides a particularly caustic assessment, stating 'sentimental drama, like the heroic play, is a debased literary genre, incapable of producing literature of any marked degree of excellence. It is artificial; it exaggerates and distorts human nature and emotions; and it is conceived in terms of a view of life which is absolutely inconsistent with reality ... plays of artistic distinction and integrity cannot be called sentimental drama.'[23] For Sherbo, absence of literary value becomes the only means of identifying sentimental drama.

While Sherbo represents an extreme view, defining or even describing 'sentimental drama' has represented a kind of critical quicksand, and even the term 'sentimental' has proved problematic, shifting in usage, meaning, and popularity over the course of the eighteenth century (Lynn Festa describes it as 'the Scarlet Pimpernel of literary history'[24]). Sherbo's frustration highlights the limitations of trying to identify these plays as a specific genre, a critical move that involves evaluating them in terms of form by considering components such as structure, plot, characterization, or language. Using these components, they have frequently been found wanting in comparison to drama from earlier eras and seen as an indication of the growing power of the novel, an argument presented most succinctly by Laura Brown in *English Dramatic Form, 1660–1760: An Essay in Generic History* (1981). Like Brown, many twentieth-century critics agreed in finding the overtly emotional plays of the later eighteenth century simplistic in contrast to the interiority of the novel; the 'rise of the novel' resulted in the 'decline of the drama'.[25] The tendency to see emotive drama as simplistic arises from a tendency to consider drama primarily in terms of form; as Brown states baldly, 'the decline of the drama, then, is attributable to the particular nature of its formal history'.[26] Formalist strategies, however, are ultimately irrelevant when applied to the drama of the later eighteenth century. Because these plays are participatory events designed with the express goal of arousing emotion within an audience, they are quintessentially performative; they resist formalist approaches precisely because such interpretative strategies treat them as static objects rather than as experiences. Even sympathetic readers such as Frank H. Ellis run into difficulties when they endeavour to map the contours of sentimental comedy, a process that in Ellis's case leads to a description that fits almost every play staged in the eighteenth and nineteenth centuries.[27]

Considered within the context of an endorsement of feeling, the drama that emerged during the later eighteenth century can best be described as a mode, plays structured by affect, not logic, designed to create an emotional response based on a sense of fellow-feeling or identification. They focus on emotional connection between characters and with the audience. For theatre-goers such as Dibdin, Chetwood, and Boswell, response would trump form in any assessment of drama and its worth, and the terminology assigned to a form of drama would have seemed irrelevant when compared to the feelings it generated within the theatre audience. For this reason, grounding the plays in their era provides a link to response and to its causes, and some of the successful approaches to early eighteenth-century drama have shifted their methodology from an emphasis on form to one on function, as seen in Robert D. Hume's discussion of exemplary or humane comedy or Aparna Gollapudi's exploration of the workings of reform on the stage and in English culture in early eighteenth-century comedy.[28] Looking more specifically at ways of targeting political response, Brett Wilson considers the 'affective politics' used in early eighteenth-century drama,[29] an approach that explicitly links drama not with form but with the response it was intended to generate. Other productive approaches to later eighteenth-century drama have placed it within its social and political context, providing a necessary understanding of elements outside the theatre walls that shaped response within the auditorium.[30]

Sentiment and Sensibility

In contrast to our often negative connotations of the terms 'sentiment' and 'sensibility', these concepts were firmly embedded as a positive force in literary and moral judgements for much of the second half of the eighteenth century. While, the connotations associated with 'sentimental' shifted during the course of the century, the term 'sentiment' remained reasonably constant, referring to statements of moral feeling. For an eighteenth-century audience, sentiments were the specific elevated expressions voiced by characters within a play. (The character Sir Christopher Curry, for example, from George Colman the Younger's *Inkle and Yarico*, was much praised for his sentiments proclaiming British values: 'Men, who so fully feel the blessings of liberty, are doubly cruel in depriving the helpless of their freedom.'[31]) The satirical depiction of sentiments that opens Richard Brinsley Sheridan's *School for Scandal* provides a vivid illustration of the verbal nature of sentiment, as Sheridan depicts the duplicitous Joseph Surface dispensing trite platitudes as a cover for his villainous schemes:

JOSEPH SURFACE: Poor Charles! I wish it were in my power to be of any essential service to him; for the man who does not share in the distresses of a brother, even though merited by his own misconduct deserves–

LADY SNEERWELL: O lud! You are going to be moral, and forget that you are among friends.

JOSEPH SURFACE: Egad, that's true! I'll keep that sentiment till I see Sir Peter.[32]

Joseph's conversation with Lady Sneerwell reveals the insincerity of his sentiments; carefully constructed in advance, they can be stored for later use, somewhat like preserves or candied fruit. Purely superficial, they do not speak from the heart, as do the words of Cumberland's Belcour ('good heart'), a figure in *The West Indian* praised by characters within the play and critics in the audience for his sincerity. Despite Sheridan's overt ridicule of fine sentiments, his play hardly represents an attack on emotion as it includes one of the age's most common affective tropes: the famous screen scene in act four concludes not with the unmasking of Joseph's villainy but rather with Lady Teazle's moral reformation, a reformation prompted by heartfelt emotion:

LADY TEAZLE: Sir Peter, I do not expect you to credit me – but the tenderness you expressed for me, when I am sure you could not think I was a witness to it, has penetrated so to my heart, that had I left the place without the shame of this discovery, my future life should have spoken the sincerity of my gratitude.[33]

Lady Teazle's validation of feeling (Sir Peter's 'tenderness' has 'penetrated [her] to the heart') effectively trumps Joseph and his artifice. In the end, Sheridan's seemingly anti-sentiment play elevates sincerity and benevolence by rewarding those characters who demonstrate fellow-feeling: the Teazles, Charles Surface, and the crusty but warm-hearted Sir Oliver.

Sentiment is thus an expression of feeling, a verbal device designed to explicate emotion. In *School for Scandal*, Joseph's false sentiments inevitably fail because they are insincere, empty compilations of fine-sounding words unsupported by true empathy. In this sense, a text gains merit through its ability to generate appropriate feeling in its audience: Lady Teazle's response to Sir Peter's words and, implicitly, the theatre audience's response to Sheridan's play. This connection of feeling and language underlies Festa's definition of the related concept of sentimentality as 'a rhetorical practice that monitors and seeks to master the sympathetic movement of emotion between individuals and groups of people' and as 'a crafted literary form [that] moves to locate that emotion, to assign it to particular persons, thereby designating who possesses affect and who elicits it'.[34] Like sentiment, sentimentality is a literary device that links form and affect but on a larger scale, in the process establishing communal feeling and providing a means for making the audience 'feel together'. Festa's emphasis on the concept of sentimentality as a literary device by which a text shapes emotional response provides a useful alternative to formalist approaches that privilege text above response. The connection between text and response takes on an additional layer of complexity in the theatre with the incorporation of the actor, who becomes the means by which sentiment is conveyed and response shaped. In this sense, sentimentality in later eighteenth-century drama becomes a means of establishing a communal emotional response within the theatre audience.

Sentiment and sentimentality represent techniques designed to promote a sympathetic response in specific instances and on specific topics. However, they originate in language and are conveyed through specific narratives and performances. In human terms, the ability to feel, and thus be receptive to sentiment, constituted the other half of the equation. This crucial component of human nature when used more generally to describe individuals and populations was described as 'sensibility'. This was the self-defined 'Age of Sensibility', when sensibility was assumed to have if not virtuous properties in itself at least the potential for virtue. For much of the 1750s through the 1780s, sensibility was a positive quality, not simply indicating the ability to feel but imbuing these feelings with moral potential. In his *Dictionary*, Samuel Johnson defines it simply as 'quickness of sensation' or 'quickness of perception',[35] but a more fulsome exploration of the term appears in a work by a different Samuel Johnson, whose poem 'Sensibility' provides one vision of the way this 'quickness of sensation' works to enable all other virtues. In his words, sensibility is the 'priestess of the shrine' of the mind, controlling Study, Fancy, Wisdom, Benevolence, Friendship, Love and even Religion.[36] Sensibility as understood in this sense was a positive force to be encouraged whenever possible. Janet Todd describes the experience of sensibility in educational terms, as a 'pedagogy of seeing and of the physical reaction this seeing should produce',[37] and although when writing generally of the literature of sensibility scholarly studies have tended to focus on sensibility and narrative, for the eighteenth century, this pedagogy was located firmly within theatre walls. Because they provided a catalyst for the moral operation of sensibility, overtly emotional plays and performances were of value to the individual and to society as a whole.

By the 1790s, the understanding of sensibility as quickness of moral perception had shifted. New connotations of uncontrolled and uncontrollable passions began to take hold, fuelled by lurid images of the French Revolution which vividly evoked the downfall of an ordered and moral society, as rendered, for example, in Edmund Burke's famous depiction of the imprisonment of Marie Antoinette and her children.[38] Chris Jones notes, 'during the 1790s the attacks on the excesses of sensibility became more pointedly directed at its subversive and individualistic tendencies', stressing the perceived connection between politics and sensibility.[39] Gender represented another source of tension, with writers such as Mary Wollstonecraft and Maria Edgeworth decrying the increasing feminization of sensibility, seeing in it a tendency to associate uncontrolled emotion not just with mobs but with women. As Wollstonecraft complained, women are encouraged to become 'creatures of sensation' and cultivate 'an over-stretched sensibility' rather than an informed mind.[40] These assumptions inform Burke's endorsement of England's 'manly, moral, regulated liberty',[41] in contrast to the untested and suspect results of the French Revolution.

Despite the increased suspicion of sensibility, this distrust rarely extended to the theatre even though it was the site of displays of feeling enacted every night in the audience as well as on the stage. Excesses of emotion might be the object of scorn, but within the theatre they were rarely sources of anxiety, largely because, even though the theatre was an acknowledged site of powerful emotion, the sources of this emotion were carefully regulated. Because of the Licensing Act of 1737, all plays staged in London's patent theatres had to be approved by the Lord Chamberlain's Office before they could be staged, guaranteeing governmental control over the content of drama and through this oversight perpetuating a vision of the manly and regulated liberty that Burke so admired. A no less powerful form of regulation existed within the auditorium, as spectators watched each other reacting to the performance. The theatre was thus its own form of panopticon, where the object of scrutiny was the extent and propriety of emotion displayed by the audience.[42] While the performance of sensibility within this largely controlled space was potentially contagious and thus suspicious, as long as the emotions enacted endorsed communal values consistent with Britain's vision of itself as a moral society, they could be perceived as a positive and active virtue.

* * *

Theatres of Feeling seeks to integrate the affective response so expressive of this age of emotion with the venue which, in the eyes of the world, most perfectly provoked it. The study is thus constructed of two distinct but interlocking parts: one, the theory and practice of theatre as it was understood and experienced in the second half of the eighteenth century; and two, a demonstration of the ways in which these theories and practices were enacted in the theatre. To begin, Chapter 1 considers theatre's unique moral function as epitomized in its ability to elicit sympathy, using the works of Scottish Enlightenment figures such as Henry Home, Lord Kames, and Adam Smith, especially Smith's influential *Theory of Moral Sentiments*. The ability to inspire this connection represents the source of drama's moral impetus, a quality it holds distinct from other, more individually experienced forms of literature. As this chapter demonstrates, the stated goal of drama – and of art in general – was to prompt a sympathetic identification with the events represented. Chapter 2 explores the actual experience of the theatre, focusing on audiences' response to Sarah Siddons's performances in the years following her triumphant return to the London stage in 1782. As contemporary accounts indicate, audiences did 'sympathize' with the performances they saw, sometimes to the extent of fainting and falling into fits at especially emotional moments during performances.

The second part of the book turns to the plays that sought to arouse sympathy in their audiences and considers in what ways and to what end this wealth of emotion was directed. These plays and the emotional responses they elicited represent those 'articulations of *presence*'[43] Raymond Williams found so evocative in literature and art, 'where the true social content is in a significant number of cases of [the] present and affective kind'.[44] In this manner, they represent the actual physical representation of the 'latent feelings' that Williams describes. The final chapters look at the social tensions and experiences that prompted these intense moments of connection, those issues that were so 'present' to the audiences of the age. Chapter 3 ('Roman Fathers and Grecian Daughters') explores the ways in which emotion engenders political ideology by exploring the reification of the father–daughter bond as a means of investigating the social and political contexts of eighteenth-century serious drama. The focal point for the chapter is Arthur Murphy's *The Grecian Daughter* (1772), a play in which a daughter nurses her father with her own milk and thus saves her father and her fatherland.

The two chapters that follow turn to the more delicate issue of comedy and its representation of contemporary British society. Chapter 4 ('Performing the West Indies') considers Britain's preoccupation with its role as an imperial power as portrayed in two popular comedies, Richard Cumberland's *The West Indian* (1771) and George Colman's *Inkle and Yarico* (1787). These plays display England's vision of itself and its empire, using exotic characters such as the creole and the slave as a means of moving audiences and reinforcing an imagined reality in which models of commerce can coexist with the British ideal of liberty. The final chapter ('The Moral Muse') turns to the last decade of the eighteenth century, when the comedies promoting general benevolence fell out of favour, to be replaced by plays advocating social reform. The chapter focuses on one such play, Cumberland's *The Jew* (1794), and the ways in which Cumberland sought to awaken the 'benevolence of the audience' as a means of ridding Britain of the stain of anti-Semitism. Although it never achieved this goal, Cumberland's play succeeded admirably in arousing profound feeling, and the power of this collective experience was enhanced by a secondary response, the audience's self-congratulation on the virtue of their feelings.

The affective theatre of the later eighteenth century represents what could be called the theory of sympathy in action as spectators were asked to experience fellow-feeling and through that emotion be moved to a mingled sense of general benevolence and national pride. The plays that spurred such a response from their audiences depended for their success on the shared ideals and ideologies of their audience, and they failed if audiences were not moved. While dependent on their social and national context and on the age in which they were written and performed, the issues of text, performance, and response are not, of course, restricted to the second half of the eighteenth century. They are inherent in the way theatre operates, to what it is on its most basic level, and thus they have been considered in this light as far back as Aristotle. What differentiates the later eighteenth century is its fascination with – even obsession with – emotion, and in particular with the emotion generated within the theatre and the implications of this emotion and its passionate response to the double performance of feeling on the stage and in the auditorium. Emotion demands a context, and while we can never fully recapture the theatrical moment of the eighteenth century, we can trace its exuberance and recognize its power. All emotions, past, present, and future, are dependent on circumstance, and in this way the celebrated passions of the eighteenth-century stage can serve as a lens through which to view the values and visions of an age. More generally, looking back to an age that saw the theatre as a source of truth, of moral potential greater than that of the pulpit, as an enterprise that could touch the individual and unite the nation, demonstrates how theatre, both the ideal and the reality, operates within society. The implications of this search for meaning in the feelings of the past are not limited to the theatre of the later eighteenth century but illuminate the interplay of text, performance, and reception that make up the theatrical experience.

CHAPTER I

Divine Sympathy: Theatre, Connection, and Virtue

> Behold how Nature to connection tends.
>
> –Samuel Jackson Pratt, *Sympathy; Or, a Sketch of the Social Passion*[1]

> A man who enters the theatre, is immediately struck with the view of so great a multitude, participating of one common amusement; and experiences, from their very aspect, a superior sensibility or disposition of being affected with every sentiment, which he shares with his fellow-creatures.
>
> –David Hume, *Enquiry concerning the Principles of Morals*[2]

Samuel Jackson Pratt's words, part of a larger discourse on society and virtue, introduce a concept crucial to understanding the eighteenth-century perception of drama and its unique moral function: the importance of that connection known to the eighteenth century as sympathy. The ability to inspire this connection represents the source of drama's moral impetus, a quality it holds distinct from other, more individually experienced literature. The role of spectatorship in the formation of moral values was accepted as a given because of the emotional connection between spectator and spectacle. For these reasons, drama became a central element in discussions of ethics, in a near reversal of the response to theatre by moralists at the turn of the eighteenth century, when the licentiousness of the stage became a rallying cry for moral reform. As an introduction to the drama of the eighteenth century, I want to begin by establishing this theoretical context. How did writers, not only playwrights but critics and moralists, envision theatre? What should be its goals? By the mid eighteenth century, theatre's potential as a tool of moral amelioration in society was widely accepted. New discussions in moral philosophy, especially those prompted by Adam Smith's arguments regarding the development of moral values, endorsed its possibilities as a tool of ethical education. As the most communal and thus most social of all arts, theatre provided a venue for debates concerning social virtues, and, in turn, the terms of these debates provide insight into what would become significant developments in the form and even the perceived function of drama. Theatre's position in the social sphere, a position which made it peculiarly susceptible to evoking sympathy, also made it the entertainment most entrusted with moral edification.

Pratt's exclamation is only one expression of the eighteenth century's interest in the workings of what was seen as both an emotional and a moral state. Although present as a general concept in the earlier half of the century, the concept became omnipresent after 1750, appearing repeatedly in literature, philosophy, and even the popular press. In the eighteenth century, sympathy had a distinct philosophical, psychological, and even physiological meaning. At its core, as Pratt states, is the idea of connection between two entities. In the earlier eighteenth century, when discussions of sympathy were largely limited to sermons and to scientific or medical treatises, the term connoted a generally physical attraction, as between body and soul or between different organs in the body. The sense of connection is essential even in casual usages, for, as one doctor explains, 'sympathy . . . has nothing in it, and tends to nothing, but what is mutual'.[3]

This sense of mutuality, reiterated in Hume's comments on the theatre, would become the cornerstone of discussions of sympathy in the second half of the century. At that time, the understanding of the term shifted from emphasizing an internal or physiological tie to a contemplation of the ties between men and women within a moral society. If in earlier decades the essence of sympathy was the connection between two substances, to later thinkers its most important representation was a specifically human one. It was a pattern designed by nature and fulfilled in a moral society. Cited repeatedly as the source of all virtues, sympathy was lauded as 'the Social Passion' because it enabled humans to feel for each other, a reciprocal bond that made possible communal qualities such as charity.[4] Watching the distress of others and identifying with their plight, a tie commonly described as 'fellow-feeling', makes sympathy possible and prompts moral emotion. Connection is the crucial component: the connection between the spectators' experience and the experience they see represented as well as the relationship between this fellow-feeling and the practice of virtue.

As generally depicted, pity initiates connection, which in turn creates communal virtue with the whole sequence labelled the workings of sympathy. James Beattie, for example, describes sympathy as essential to the critic because it helps him empathize with others and thus understand the workings of literature. He explains the foundation of this process in 'On Poetry and Music':

> When we consider the condition of another person, especially if it seem to be pleasurable or painful, we are apt to fancy ourselves in the same condition, and to feel in some degree the pain or pleasure that we think we should feel if we were really in that condition. Hence the good of others becomes in some measure our good, and their evil our evil; the more obvious effect of which is, to bind men more closely together in society, and prompt them to promote the good, and relieve the distresses, of one another.[5]

Seen in these terms, sympathy is necessary for the moral functioning of society; without it, society lacks cohesion, becoming no more than a disparate collection of individuals who are unable or unwilling to unite for a common good. The Reverend Daniel Turner expands upon this point, arguing in more magniloquent words that sympathy rather than reason is the faculty that distinguishes humans from all other aspects of creation:

> For in how mournful a condition would human affairs be – unless the blessed operations of this fellow-feeling were universal? Had men no attachment to their brethren in distress – no pity to recompence those expressive symbols of grief, namely, sighs – groans – and tears, then were our circumstances in life little better than the brute creation. In such a case, nothing generous, benevolent, or divine, would exist among mankind. The bond of civil society would be dissolved; and the cement of souls, our nobler part be lost. It is Sympathy which joins the intellectual part of creation together – it is this emanation of the divine nature which rivets man to man, and renders each individual, instrumental in raising, and protecting, a beautiful and perfect whole.[6]

In an echo of Hobbes, Turner sees human existence as potentially nasty, brutish, and short, but only if it lacks sympathy rather than sovereignty. Divinely ordained, sympathy is inherent in human nature and ultimately makes society possible.

Theories regarding the operation of sympathy were commonplace by the later eighteenth century, but they were most famously articulated by Adam Smith in his *Theory of Moral Sentiments* (1759). Smith's first book, it was an immediate sensation. It went through multiple editions in the next decades, eventually being translated into both French and German. Edmund Burke reviewed the *Theory* favourably for the *Annual Register*, and both Gotthold Ephraim Lessing and Johann Gottfried Herder, among others, would cite it in their own works within the following decade. So synonymous was Smith's work with the very word sympathy that in later editions of his popular poem *Sympathy*, Samuel Pratt added a series of notes in which he explicitly connects his work with Smith's theories, carefully explaining in the process that he had not read Smith at the time he wrote the poem (thus establishing his own originality) but taking full advantage of the widespread popularity of Smith's work.[7] Following the success of the *Theory*, the workings of sympathy and its attendant virtues were nearly a national obsession in the later eighteenth century. Publications of all kinds were dedicated to the topic, from poems and moral tracts, to overtly 'sympathetic' travelogues (such as *A Tear of Sympathy!!! Or, Striking Objects of Travel, Antient, and Modern! In Italy, Prussia, Spain, Russia, &c.*, which charts the author's emotional response to the people he meets),[8] and even a short-lived periodical designed to excite sympathy in the breasts of its readers (*The Redresser, Or, Weekly Strictures of Simon Sympathy, Esq.*).[9]

The cornerstone of Smith's discussion of moral behaviour is a broadly applied theory of sympathy. He was not the first to use sympathy in order to explain moral principles; the term had philosophical currency throughout the eighteenth century. Hume, for example, had used the concept in his *A Treatise of Human Nature* (1739–1740) to explain the existence of moral approval (because we share feelings of pain and pleasure through sympathy, we approve of virtuous acts and disapprove of vicious ones).[10] While sympathy is not a central part of his later *Enquiry concerning the Principles of Morals* (1751), in that work Hume employs sympathetic connection as the means by which moral principles operate. As he comments, '[it] will readily, I believe, be allow'd, that no Qualities are more entitled to the public Good-will and Approbation of Mankind, than Beneficence and Humanity, Friendship and Gratitude, Natural Affection and Public Spirit, or whatever proceeds from a tender Sympathy with others, and a generous Concern for our Kind and species'.[11] As does Hume, Smith links sympathy to morality, but he expands its scope, using it as a founding principle for all moral behaviour; one observer likened it to the law of gravity in his moral system.[12] As Pratt was to note, sympathy's essential component is connection between one person and another who observes his emotion. As Smith comments, 'whatever is the passion which arises from any object in the person principally concerned, an analogous emotion springs up, at the thought of his situation, in the breast of every attentive spectator'.[13] This 'analogous emotion' is made possible through sympathy; as Smith explains, it is more than mere compassion or pity, rather it "denote[s] our fellow-feeling with any passion whatever."[14] Fellow-feeling enables us to judge others and ourselves because through it we appreciate virtue and abhor vice. Without the sense of connection provided by sympathy, we would not care about the actions of others, and humanity would exist in a brutish state much like that described by the Reverend Turner.

Significantly for the study of theatre, Smith founds his discussion of sympathy and its relation to morality on a theory of spectatorship. His opening paragraph stresses the pleasure one receives from observing another's happiness,[15] and he extends this image into his concept of the "impartial spectator," the "man within," whose metaphoric gaze watches and evaluates himself and others. The moral potential of spectatorship is a necessary corollary to his argument, for it makes sympathy and even virtue itself possible:

> In all such cases, that there may be some correspondence of sentiments between the spectator and the person principally concerned, the spectator must, first of all, endeavour, as much as he can, to put himself in the situation of the other, and to bring home to himself every little circumstance of distress which can possibly occur to the sufferer. He must adopt the whole case of his companion with all its minutest incidents; and strive to render as perfect as possible, that imaginary change of situation upon which his sympathy is founded.[16]

Spectatorship enables that 'imaginary change of situation' in 'all its minutest incidents' which in turn enables us to feel for others. This process of identification, Smith argues, is the source of human benevolence, for 'to feel much for others and little for ourselves . . . constitutes the perfection of human nature'.[17] Thus, because of the experience of sympathy, spectatorship can lead to virtue.

Visual experience, whether real or implicit, is the essential first step in the complex process of sympathetic identification. So widespread is this assumption that the language of spectatorship permeates discussions of sympathy as writers take for granted that sympathy begins by 'viewing' another's suffering. We are, as Turner says, 'spectators of his distress'.[18] A more complex view of the workings of sympathy, and one strongly derivative of Smith's theory, is articulated by Henry Homes, Lord Kames. In his *Elements of Criticism*, Kames depicts the experience of the spectator as essential for both morality and criticism. We see another's distress or happiness and are moved by it, a process that prompts another emotion which Kames terms the 'sympathetic emotion of virtue'. This unique feeling, which he describes as 'merit[ing] a deliberate view, for its singularity, as well as [its] utility',[19] unlike the other emotions and passions he describes, is a communicated passion dependent on either real or imagined spectatorship. We can kindle this sensation by watching another's virtue, thus experiencing sympathy through 'real presence'; we can even recreate this event in our imagination, in our mind's eye as it were, and thus experience what Kames terms 'ideal presence'. Kames finds spectatorship the only valid means of explaining this phenomenon: 'I perceive the thing as a spectator, and as existing in my presence. This means not that I am really a spectator; but only that I conceive myself to be a spectator, and have a consciousness of presence similar to what a real spectator hath.'[20]

Vision thus represents the important first step of moral action as watching others – or imagining ourselves watching them – enables us to establish a sense of fellow-feeling with them. Once vision establishes fellow-feeling, sympathy creates a recognition of virtue and ultimately prods us to moral action. As Pratt explains, the 'sacred force of heav'n-born Sympathy'[21] makes us virtuous in spite of ourselves:

> Spite of your arts, the sympathies arise,
> And aid the cause of all the brave and wise;
> Spite of your little selves, when virtue charms,
> To nature true, the social passion warms;
> Vain to resist, imperial nature still
> Asserts her claim, and bends us to her will.[22]

A less effusive but more concrete view of how sympathy creates moral action is expressed by Kames who explains more exactly how moral action follows from the experience of sympathy:

> We approve every virtuous action, and bestow our affection on the author, but if virtuous actions produced no other effect upon us, good example would not have great influence: the sympathetic emotion under consideration bestows upon good example the utmost influence, by prompting us to imitated what we admire. This singular emotion will readily find an object to exert itself upon: and at any rate, it never exists without producing some effect; because virtuous emotions of that sort, are in some degree an exercise of virtue; they are a mental exercise at least, if they show not externally. And every exercise of virtue, internal and external, leads to habit; for a disposition or propensity of the mind, like a limb of the body, becomes stronger by exercise.[23]

Sympathy creates the admiration of good which, by habit, eventually leads to active virtue.

These abstract discussions of sight, connection, and morality are intrinsic to the interpretation and assessment of literature of the period. Ultimately, critics agree, we can appreciate the fine arts only because we can experience sympathy. Our ability to connect emotionally with what we see or imaginatively with what we read (through Kames's concept of ideal presence) makes aesthetic pleasure possible because through this sympathetic response we connect with the work of art. This idea becomes a commonplace of later eighteenth-century literary theory. As critics attempt to explain the psychology of *why* we respond to art, they find an answer in the operations of sympathy and its attendant sense of fellow-feeling. Edmund Burke, for example, uses sympathy to explain our response to the sublime.[24] Similarly, James Beattie describes the arts and sympathy as necessarily linked: 'As a great part of the pleasure we derive from poetry depends on our Sympathetic Feelings, the philosophy of Sympathy ought always to form a part of the science of Criticism.'[25] This emphasis on a psychologically based aesthetic has various ramifications, from the increased importance placed on interiority in the literature of the age to the link posited between emotional response and morality as critics find literature's moral component dependent on its ability to generate sympathy. Understanding sympathy allowed the critic to understand the efficacy of the literary work.

It is an irony of literary history that while the increased importance of the internal and the emotional has become a commonplace in studies of the novel, the role of these issues in drama is frequently overlooked. In his description of the evolution of sympathy, for example, Jonathan Lamb identifies what he describes as four distinct categories of sympathy, one of which he designates 'the Theatre of Sympathy'.[26] While noting that his discussion has 'crossed into the territory of theatre', adding that it is 'worthwhile to recall how it has been supplying metaphors and illustrations for the discussion of sympathy',[27] he turns quickly from considering the importance of theatre when regarding sympathy to the novel, and his study contains no commentary on eighteenth-century drama, although he does refer frequently to works of fiction and poetry. Lamb is not alone in simultaneously acknowledging the importance of the theatre when discussing sympathy while bypassing a more detailed consideration of drama or performance. Almost inevitably, critical studies of sympathy use fiction as a means of explicating the experience they identify as being so inherently theatrical. In *The Surprising Effects of Sympathy*, David Marshall astutely assesses what he describes as the 'interplay of theatre and sympathy ... theories of acting as well as debates about the morality and effects of plays turn upon questions of identification, distance, and the ability of both actors and audience to perform acts of sympathy – just as discussions of sympathy turn on the theatrical relations that make the possibility of fellow feeling a problem of representation and aesthetic experience as well as a problem of moral philosophy'.[28] However, he immediately removes actual theatre from the discussion, using it instead as bridge to the novel: 'these are questions that are addressed by eighteenth-century novels, many of which are preoccupied with the theater of everyday life'.[29] Although both Lamb and Marshall cite Smith repeatedly in their works, it is worth noting that *The Theory of Moral Sentiments* never refers to a work of fiction.

This implicit assumption that fiction most vividly depicts the effects of sympathy would have surprised eighteenth-century readers and audiences, for in their eyes drama was the most overtly emotional of all literary forms and thus the most likely to spur a sympathetic response. For these reasons, drama, in particular the active performance of drama, became central to the theoretical discussions of the later eighteenth century in a way that fiction and even poetry did not. The influence of drama is evident not only in these critical studies but even in works as overtly philosophical as Smith's *Theory*. In *The Figure of Theatre*, Marshall correctly notes that today many scholars overlook the fact that Smith's 'impartial spectator is a *spectator*', adding 'what is at stake is the inherently theatrical situation that Smith describes when he pictures us appearing before each other as spectators and spectacles'.[30] The *Theory of Moral Sentiments*, however, is remarkable not only for theatre's influence on its general discussion of sympathy but also for its own debt to drama. Given his model of the emotional connection between the spectator and object, it is not surprising that Smith turns frequently to the theatre to illustrate his argument. Using our willingness to weep at drama as evidence, he finds our strongest expression of sympathy in our feelings towards those in 'distress'.[31] Hence his most potent examples are drawn from tragedy, most often the she-tragedy of a previous generation, plays known for their focus on distress. Where contemporary writers on genius turned to Shakespeare as their ideal, Smith turned for his examples to the tragedies of Otway, Southerne, and Racine. In the figures of Monimia, Isabella, and Phedra, he found the ideal analogue for his theory of sympathy. The distress suffered by these characters – and vividly realized upon the stage – provokes a response in the theatre audience, proving spectatorship is the source of this emotion, a direct corollary to his more general argument regarding the moral function of sympathy.

Like Smith, Hume turns to theatre to illustrate the workings of sympathy; however, he considers the broader experience of theatregoing rather than our response to specific characters. In a passage remarkable for its depiction of the communal experience of sympathy, Hume connects performance, spectatorship, and response:

> A man who enters the theatre, is immediately struck with the view of so great a multitude, participating of one common amusement; and experiences, from their very aspect, a superior sensibility or disposition of being affected with every sentiment, which he shares with his fellow-creatures.
>
> He observes the actors to be animated by the appearance of a full audience, and raised to a degree of enthusiasm, which they cannot command in any solitary or calm moment.
>
> Every movement of the theatre, by a skilful poet, is communicated, as it were by magic, to the spectators; who weep, tremble, resent, rejoice, and are inflamed with all the variety of passions, which actuate the several personages of the drama.
>
> Where any event crosses our wishes, and interrupts the happiness of the favourite characters, we feel a sensible anxiety and concern. But where their sufferings proceed from the treachery, cruelty, or tyranny of an enemy, our breasts are affected with the liveliest resentment against the author of these calamities.[32]

Hume stresses the mutuality of the theatrical experience: the actors need the audience in order to be fully animated and raised to enthusiasm; the playwright, no matter how skilful, needs the actors to communicate the passions of his characters; and the spectators need this magic combination of play and performance in order to sympathize with characters in the drama. By the final paragraph, the single 'man who enters the theatre' has become one with the audience he observes, participating in the event 'where any event [that] crosses our wishes' affects 'our breast'. The mutuality thus depicted is not insular; in Hume's representation, it stretches beyond the walls of the theatre. By becoming part of the sympathizing multitude, a spectator – even of other spectators – experiences 'a superior sensibility or disposition of being affected with every sentiment, which he shares with his fellow-creatures'. Thus, the theatrical experience, as represented by Hume, becomes a powerful source of 'superior' sensibility and connection with our fellow-creatures, contributing ultimately to the elevated moral principles of benevolence and justice. Hume makes no similar claim for any other art.

Other writers concur in finding drama the art that most directly excites sympathetic emotions. Kames notes that 'it is present distress only that moves my pity',[33] an observation that provides the fundamental explanation for why drama, and in particular serious drama rather than comedy, becomes the cornerstone for literary discussions of sympathy and morality.

In no other form of art is distress so distinctly 'present' than in drama; it is not fixed in time, as with a painting, nor diluted through the act of reading, as with fiction or even the silent reading of a play. James Beattie makes a similar point in *Essays on Poetry and Music*, as he endeavours to delineate which arts are the most affecting and why, concluding that 'Distress that we see is more affecting than what we only hear of'.[34] As Beattie and Kames indicate, the *performance* of distress is key. No other art form provided such rich opportunity for experiencing sympathy and all its manifold benefits. Kames adds, 'of all the means for making an impression of ideal presence, theatrical representation is the most powerful. That words independent of action have the same power in a less degree, every one of sensibility must have felt: A good tragedy will extort tears in private, though not so forcibly as upon the stage.'[35] In the terminology of eighteenth-century aesthetics, theatre stands alone in its ability to move and thus also to shape those who encounter it. It is unique in that the audience experiences it in real time; they truly are the spectators of the distress represented, an experience that is profoundly emotional and morally compelling.

Morality and the Stage

With sympathy understood as the source of all social virtues, moral philosophers as well as critics elevate those arts able to evoke the appropriate emotional response. This standard of value institutes a new hierarchy of the arts, one in which those works most able to elicit sympathy are most deserving of praise because they directly promote morality. As Kames explains, such literature actually creates virtue in its audience,

> A pathetic composition, whether epic or dramatic, tends to a habit of virtue, by exciting emotions that produce good actions and avert us from those that are vicious or irregular. It likewise, by its frequent pictures of human woes, humanizes the mind, and fortifies us in bearing our own misfortunes ... a work of this kind, has our sympathy at command, and can put in motion the whole train of the social affections.[36]

Experiencing the woes of others through the vehicle of art excites emotions that in and of themselves lead to good actions. Even the very sensation of sympathy constitutes an exercise of these emotions, making the practice of good habitual so that even if the work itself does not directly lead to a good act, its overall effect is to train the spectator to practice good. Just as exercising the body leads to physical fitness, exercising the moral faculties through sympathy generated by art leads to moral fitness.

The assumption that sympathy was not only a necessary part of aesthetic but also moral response prompted different criteria for judging the work of art and in particular a complete rethinking of the form and function of drama. Where Smith takes the theatrical experience of spectatorship and uses it as a means to explain how human sympathy contributes to moral principles, drama critics invert the paradigm. In critical studies, the internal workings of sympathy become the means first of explaining why art affects us and second of evaluating its value. As detailed by writers such as Kames, the performance of distress leads to active virtue through the mechanism of sympathy; the more powerful the effect, the greater the potential for good. As a result, for playwrights, critics, and audiences, emotional response was the key not only to good drama but to the moral function of theatre as well.

With moral philosophy underlying eighteenth-century theories of the theatre, writers turned to a more affective standard for judging dramatic worth. For example, rather than simply citing pity, which had been the traditional explanation for an audience's emotional response to tragedy, writers after mid-century theorized a series of complex psychological steps of which the most important was the establishment of the sympathetic bond between audience and character. The importance of establishing a sense of 'fellow-feeling' is crucial to arguments regarding drama, for such fellow-feeling is the source of the morality which eighteenth-century critics claim for the theatre as it prompts us to imitate the good we see and avoid the vice. Because of the centrality of these claims, even familiar critical standards are reinvented to fit under the aegis of the fellow-feeling that sympathy promotes. As Kames notes, for example, Aristotle's *catharsis* is simply the expression of sympathy at work: 'Our pity is engaged for the persons represented, and our terror is upon our own account.'[37] Crucially, the end result of the process is not simply emotion but moral action. This argument becomes the foundation of later eighteenth-century defences of the theatre; it not only redeems theatre against the charges that it was at best an idle pastime and at worst corruptive but even promotes it to the level of a positive social good. Because the act of spectatorship encourages the audience to participate in virtuous activity, writers can argue directly for the morality of the stage.

Proponents of the stage repeatedly stress theatre's potential for moral edification, even comparing it with the pulpit in terms of its role in promoting public virtue. Some writers elevate theatrical performances over churchgoing precisely because of the vividness of the experience (a claim that, not surprisingly, incensed clergy). This idea is vividly expressed by W. R. Chetwood in the passage cited at the beginning of this book: 'Lessons for the Stage may be convey'd, in one respect, stronger than from the Pulpit, if the Audience were attentive as they should be at Church: For a Play well wrote, and well perform'd, where Virtue suffers, or meets its just Reward, must have strong Force upon the Mind, where the Eye is suppos'd to view the very Persons in the real Circumstances of History.' If the actors themselves are virtuous, he adds, the effect will be stronger still.[38] Where the clergy can only narrate the fate of virtue or vice, the stage can actually represent this fate in action, presenting events to the eye of the spectator. The author of the aptly titled *Theatrical Entertainments Consistent with Society, Morality, and Religion* (1768) explains: 'Virtue is never so highly exalted, as when the affections of the heart are engaged on her side: without them, she produces only a lifeless apathy; with them, the most exalted impressions of which our nature is susceptible.'[39] Virtue remains a latent quality, 'lifeless' and 'apathetic', without the catalyst provided by emotional engagement.

Pamphlets attacking the stage did appear, but with the stage elevated in moral purpose, expressions of antitheatricalism diminish, and one of the most noticeable features of the general reception of theatre during the mid to later eighteenth century is the relative dearth of English diatribes against the theatre. The antitheatrical pamphlets that had proliferated in the years around the turn of the century subside by the middle of the century, and the majority of the attacks that were written can be traced to a group of conservative Presbyterian clergymen who considered plays and diversions unchristian in and of themselves. As Lisa A. Freeman observes, these attacks had their roots in a 'fundamental change in the nature and quality of public culture itself',[40] away from the Church and into the public realm of the universities and the secular 'pulpits' of the theatres. Unlike Jeremy Collier and his followers, they do not debate the pernicious effects that spectators might suffer by watching immoral images. Instead, their most common objects of attack are the immorality of such diversions, the distressing and ungodly number of suicides represented in tragedy, and, most particularly, the immorality of the actors, whom they see as completely and incorrigibly corrupt. (*The Stage the High Road to Hell* advocates that the English follow the example of the French and not allow actors to be buried in sanctified ground.[41]) A particularly magniloquent piece of such anti-thespian rhetoric appears in the Reverend Adam Gibb's attack on playhouses and players:

> It is agreed on by sober Pagans themselves, that play-actors are the most profligate wretches, and the vilest vermine, that hell ever vomited out; that they are the filth and garbage of the earth, the scum and stain of human nature, the excrements and refuse of all mankind, the pests and plagues of human society, the debauchers of mens minds and morals, unclean beasts, idolatrous Papists or atheists, and the most horrid and abandoned villains that ever the sun shone upon.[42]

Like a number of other Scottish clergymen, he felt particularly affronted that a fellow clergyman, John Home, author of the popular tragedy *Douglas*, should have turned to such an ungodly activity as playwriting. The success of *Douglas* in 1756/1757 sparked another rash of pamphlets attacking and defending the theatre, once again written largely by Scottish clergymen.

Where earlier attacks on the theatre were taken seriously by playwrights, even if they disagreed violently with Collier and his followers, these later assaults were largely ignored by mainstream writers. The few responses that were written take advantage of the assumed link between sympathy and the stage to rebut charges of immorality. The author of *Theatrical Entertainments Consistent with Society, Morality, and Religion* uses the affinity between sympathy and active virtue to respond directly to *The Stage the High Road to Hell*. If we accept the argument of *The Stage the High Road to Hell* that attending the theatre causes our passions to be inflamed thus prompting us to behave in lustful and vicious ways, he argues 'we must suppose the passions implanted in our nature to be all, without exception, enemies to virtue'. But, he adds, 'when the involuntary tear steals down at the scene of misery and distress; when indignation rises at disingenuous sentiments; when the blushes of modesty give the severest reproof to ribaldry and profaneness; shall we stigmatise these emotions?'[43] With its active verbs and vivid imagery, his description of the effect of drama stresses the symbiotic relationship between the stage, the act of spectatorship, and social virtue. Emotions stimulated by the act of spectatorship become not only indications of virtue within the breast of the spectator but virtues in and of themselves. In contrast to Jeremy Collier, who had argued at the turn of the century that virtuous women cannot 'Blush without disservice to their Modesty',[44] the eighteenth-century critic sees the modest woman's blushes as actively reproving immorality and thus reiterating the virtue of the blusher. Where Collier and other early eighteenth-century writers had seen a woman's blush as a signifier not of emotion but of improper knowledge, to later writers the blush signifies something very different: a discomfort born of sexual innocence.

Modesty had considerably fewer occasions to blush in the theatres of the mid to later eighteenth century, and concerns regarding sexuality, which had been so central to early commentary on the morality of the stage, are greatly muted. If later eighteenth-century discussions of the morality of the stage are less concerned with problems of sexuality than had been their predecessors, in part this is due to the general absence of bawdiness in contemporary drama and widespread repudiation of libertine literature. Proponents of the stage dismiss overtly sexual drama as a thing of the past, a testament to how much the codes of drama had changed since the beginning of the century. As if to prove their own virtue, eighteenth-century writers routinely castigate Restoration dramatists for their suspect morality. Even the ever popular Otway is chided for his consistent 'indecency'.[45] When plays from the Restoration were revived, they were almost invariably strictly edited, if not 'condemned to that oblivion they deserve', because of their sexual content.[46] *Theatrical Entertainments Consistent with Society, Morality, and Religion* associates deviant sexuality with the drama of the Restoration so strongly that it dominates the author's imagery as he exclaims 'how few of these productions are at this period exhibited to the public eye! and how cautiously are these few castrated, to obviate any bad effects'.[47] Use of the term 'castrate' in the this context is provocative: it not only suggests surgery to remove what is currently offensive but also implies that such surgery will prevent improper sexual behaviour in the future, those 'bad effects' the writer hints at. Such an attack on the explicit depiction of sexuality in the midst of a pamphlet that strongly supports the moral good of theatregoing provides a reminder of not simply the extent to which the codes of drama had changed but, perhaps more strikingly, the changed nature of the moral debate.

The Proper Subject of Drama

Elevating theatre's moral status had far-reaching ramifications. With sympathy accepted as the foundation of emotional response and through it virtue, critics were faced with developing new standards for judging literature. The ability to evoke a sympathetic response, rather than establish verisimilitude, which had been the foundation for earlier neoclassical theory, became the new theoretical standard for drama. Literary theory based on sympathetic response had a profound effect on the understanding of how drama should operate, what it should consist of, even how it should be written. At the most basic level, playwrights and critics rethink what – and who – drama should represent. As a result, once recognizable literary forms mutate and ultimately generic lines became blurred. The nature of the internal bond between spectators and the distress they witness becomes a central point in one of the most hotly debated issues in eighteenth-century dramatic theory, the controversy over the appropriate subject matter of tragedy. The success of George Lillo's *The London Merchant* in 1731 underscored the development of a new conception of tragedy, one which refused to portray the struggles of kings and the fates of empires and focused instead on characters more immediately familiar to an eighteenth-century theatre audience. One of a dwindling number of critics who prefer traditionally elevated tragic figures, William Guthrie sees this quality as a defect rather than a strength. While he admires Otway, he argues that in *Venice Preserv'd* 'the effects their [Pierre, Jaffeir and Belvidera] characters produce are owing to the poet's admirable application to the experience of mankind in common life, beyond which the distress of his fable does not rise; and in bringing the woes which the guilty suffered, home to the breast of the innocent'.[48] In Guthrie's judgement, *Venice Preserv'd* can never 'rise' to the heights of Shakespeare because of its emphasis on common life (even if that 'common-life' includes the Venetian Senate). The best tragedies, he contends, are those elevated by their elevated subject matter.[49]

More often, however, especially as the century progressed, critics rejected this rationale, arguing instead that without the identification encouraged by the representation of characters like ourselves, we cannot sympathize with the distress of the characters and thus the tragedy becomes ineffective. Writing about 'the present state of drama', an anonymous critic explained, 'all fellow-feeling has its source in self-feeling';[50] in order to create the bond of sympathy that makes drama function effectively, an identification between spectator and the character must be established. In *The Elements of Dramatic Criticism*, William Cook explains the importance of such 'fellow-feeling' to the success of a drama:

> The picture of a passion which we have never felt, or of a situation wherein we have never been, can never move us, in so lively a manner, as the descriptions of such passions and situations as either are, or have been formerly our own case; in the first place, the mind is but slightly touched with the picture of a passion, whose symptoms it is a stranger to; it is afraid even of being the dupe of an unfaithful imitation; now

> the mind has but an imperfect knowledge of passions which the heart never felt; all the information we can receive of others, being insufficient to give us a just and precise idea of the agitations of a heart over which they tyrannize.[51]

In his emphasis on the need for identification with the subjects of drama, Cook displays a marked similarity to Smith. The necessary connection between an external, observed 'picture of passion' and interior experience can be achieved only through subjective recognition. Reason is insufficient, for 'the mind has but an imperfect knowledge' of unfelt passions. A king's regret for his loss of empire does not move us in the same way that a father's grief for his child's unfeeling conduct would; the one is outside our realm of experience, while the other is something that any parent, whether high or low, may experience.

Although to a modern reader *The London Merchant* seemingly epitomizes the movement into a familiar or domestic realm, eighteenth-century critics more often turn to an earlier drama, Rowe's *Fair Penitent*, when considering the representation of 'common-life' in tragedy. A play whose upper-class characters do not represent a radical break with tradition as did Lillo's lower-class ones, *The Fair Penitent* is cited repeatedly for its movement into the domestic realm, a step many commentators find advantageous:

> Mr Row [*sic*], in his excellent tragedy, entitled, The Fair Penitent, has shewn, that the distresses of private life, are at least as well calculated for the scene, as the fate of kings and empires; nay, the former seem to have the advantage as they come more home to the bosoms of the spectators; who, as it is expressed in the Prologue to the above-mentioned piece,
>
> *Learn to pity woes so like their own.*
>
> Could we but divest ourselves of vulgar prejudices, and seriously attend to this maxim, the truth of which will be contested by few, *viz.* That all fellow-feeling has its source in self-feeling, we might even be induced to accept the boldness of a modern author who has ventured to introduce low-life into tragedy [i.e. George Lillo in *The London Merchant*].[52]

The author's stress on fellow-feeling necessarily having its source in self-feeling is the key to his theory of tragedy. While the 'fate of kings and empires' is not detrimental to a tragedy, neither is it a necessary ingredient, as Guthrie claims. Rather, it is the representation of scenes that pierce 'the bosoms of the spectators' which creates the power of a tragedy, a quality not restricted to emperors and empires. Only 'tyrant custom' requires that tragedy limit its subject.

Conversely, the insistence on inspiring fellow-feeling through self-feeling propels drama into a different realm, one with which the audience can identify. To do so, drama both emphasizes the affective as a means of provoking sympathy, but also, as the eighteenth century progresses, strives to depict the 'woes so like our own' celebrated in Rowe's play. Most often, playwrights, managers, and actors sought to achieve these results by evoking common familial incidents. The most popular new tragedies of the mid eighteenth century, such as Lillo's *London Merchant* and Home's *Douglas*, focus on domestic themes rather than imperial struggles. The affective centre of Home's *Douglas* is not the fate of Scotland but a mother's love for her son. The premium placed on sympathetic identification also explains the enduring success of the she-tragedies of the early eighteenth century, plays with intimate settings and intensely poignant scenes of female distress.[53]

With the 'fate of kings and empires' less compelling than the passions of husbands and wives, parents and children, older plays were frequently reinvented to take advantage of familial settings or incidents. Sometimes this simply meant a shift in a theatre's repertoire, as, for example, a surge of interest in *The Winter's Tale* after mid-century at the same time that more political plays, such as *Julius Caesar*, declined in popularity. (*Julius Caesar* was staged in London only twenty-three times between 1751 and 1800 after being among the most popular of Shakespeare's plays in the first half of the century, with 163 performances between 1701 and 1750.[54]) In other cases, playwrights and managers added domestic details to plays in which they were not previously present (Garrick was a master at this method of updating stock plays). Thus, as will be discussed further in Chapter 3, both King Lear and Timon of Athens become distressed fathers rather than frustrated kings or misanthropes. Shakespeare was not the only playwright to experience such alterations. Even a relatively contemporary play such as Dryden's *All for Love*, which had supplanted the more irregular *Antony and Cleopatra*, was quietly domesticated. The 1776 Drury Lane version of the play does not add new material but rather makes deep cuts to Dryden's tragedy, the effect of which is both to decrease the global scope of the events and also to render the central characters more appealing. In its altered form, Dryden's stylized representation of a king caught between the competing ties of love and honour is reshaped so that the play's focus lies clearly on the more intimate conflict between love and friendship. Cleopatra's character becomes more overtly modest as almost any reference to her sexuality is quietly deleted, as is the entire scene in which she and Octavia fight over Antony.

Perhaps the most obvious example of the ways in which the theory of sympathy affected eighteenth-century drama can be traced in the emergence of new forms of comedy. As sympathy became an increasingly popular response to theatre, providing in the process a means for measuring a spectator's own humanity, playwrights began to provide outlets for sympathy in their comedies as well as their tragedies. With their tales of woe prevented, these so-called 'sentimental comedies' recount the trials and tribulations of well-meaning characters and end with the triumph of virtue and the edification of vice, presenting the audience with examples of distress with which they could identify and resolutions at which they could rejoice. In a general discussion of morality and the arts, James Beattie provides insight into the reasons behind comedy's transformation from an often bawdy genre characterized by ridicule and satire to a 'softer' form in the which only notable differences from tragedy were occasional humorous scenes and a joyous conclusion:

> Nothing can give lasting delight to a moral being, but that which awakens sympathy and touches the heart ... Let it be observed further, that to awaken our sympathetic feelings, a lively conception of their object is necessary. This indeed is true of almost all our emotions; their keenness is in proportion to the vivacity of the perceptions that excite them.[55]

In order to achieve this morally satisfying 'lasting delight', comedy as well as tragedy had to provide occasions for sympathy. Older forms of comedy, most notably those from the Restoration, had been found indecent and unrefined to a more sensitive audience. To be redeemed as a literary form, comedy needed to remove the tarnish of Restoration wit, which had largely ignored the possibility of fellow-feeling, and take on some of the qualities that made tragedy the literary form most conducive to sympathy and its attendant virtues. Sentimental and humane comedies, with their chaste plots and benevolent emotions, sought to remedy these omissions. The result was a further blurring of traditional genre lines allowing comedy to be discussed in much the same terms as tragedy.

Although in general these new comedies satisfied theorists as well as audiences, some critics complained that this new development went too far in stretching the bounds of the genre. The debate over the proper subject matter of comedy had begun earlier in the century between Sir Richard Steele and John Dennis (Steele supported newer moral comedies, such as his own *Conscious Lovers*, while Dennis advocated for comedies of ridicule, such as George Etherege's *The Man of Mode; or Sir Fopling Flutter*).[56] The essay best known today on the subject is the often cited 'Essay on the Theatre; Or, A Comparison between Laughing and Sentimental Comedy' (1773), published anonymously in the *Westminster Magazine* but usually attributed to Goldsmith. In this essay, Goldsmith describes comedy as split into two mutually exclusive camps, one 'laughing' and near extinction and the other 'weeping'. He comments, 'It is now debated, whether the exhibition of human distress is likely to afford the mind more entertainment than that of human absurdity'.[57] As Robert D. Hume has observed, this was hardly an accurate picture of London theatre, but it did serve to further Goldsmith's personal ends; Hume suggests that the 'Essay' may even have been intended to serve as a puff for *She Stoops to Conquer* which was first performed a few months later.[58] While few shared Goldsmith's contention that laughter had deserted the English stage, some critics expressed disdain for the growth of sentimentalism, which they saw as formulaic and artificial. William Cook dedicates an entire chapter of his *Elements of Dramatic Criticism* to attacking sentimental comedy.[59] Much like Dennis, Cook argues for the moral education provided by ridicule and describes the popular fondness for sentimental drama as 'false taste'.[60] He attributes it to '*slavish effeminacy of manners*, and *universality of indolent dissipation*, unknown to former ages'.[61] People of fashion, unwilling to see themselves ridiculed, created sentimental comedy to cover up these defects, 'crying up a *theory* of morality as a kind of cover for the *breach* of it'.[62] Although supporting the increased virtue of the contemporary stage, others voice concern that the 'castration' of sexual matters may have been too extreme. After observing that as a result of Collier's 'chastisement' playwrights grew more guarded in their writing, the author of *The Playhouse Pocket-Companion* worries that 'it is rather now to be feared, that the stage is chastened into the other extreme of sentimental insipidity'.[63] In his eyes, 'castrating' plays may have led to emasculated drama.

Despite Goldsmith's 'Essay', and the fears of writers such as Cook, eighteenth-century audiences had not abandoned hilarity in favour of lugubrious, tear-jerking sentimental plays with only a happy ending to distinguish them from tragedy. It is important to remember, however, that critics and playwrights were united in agreeing that the comedy – and too frequently the tragedy – of the Restoration was immoral. Eighteenth-century critics and playwrights had no desire to return to the overtly sexual and often cynical drama of the Restoration. Even Goldsmith and Cook make no such argument. Instead, comments such as those cited above represent a relatively mild backlash against what was a currently popular form.

The Primacy of Pathos

The emphasis on the virtuous effect of watching distress and the intensifying effect which suffering virtue provides, even in comedy, underlines the continuing popularity of pathos in the drama of the eighteenth century. With the plays of a previous generation 'castrated' and made decent for the eighteenth-century stage, pathos becomes an even more dominant component of drama. If a desire to excite sympathy had the effect of causing playwrights to rethink the parameters of genre, it had an equally profound effect on how plots were constructed and, perhaps more suggestively, on the nature of the men and women who populate these plots.

In the literary theory of the later eighteenth century, traditional assumptions regarding form are ignored and at times inverted. Even the interest in poetic justice, which had been so much a part of the critical debate in the earlier part of the century, evaporates when the suffering of the innocent is portrayed as a means of exciting righteous indignation in the breast of the spectator. If distress, in and of itself, produces a potent effect, explains one writer 'how much greater must the effect be, if Virtue itself produces the distress? A misfortune becomes affecting in proportion to the virtue of him who falls into it ... innocence oppressed, or unsuspecting virtue betrayed, become more amiable by the hatred conceived for the oppressors or betrayers.'[64] Kames reaches a similar conclusion. In *The Elements of Criticism*, he devotes considerable attention to the form and subject of tragedy, and in the end rejects any narrow use of poetic justice. Moreover, he finds Aristotelian theory incomplete because it ignores the pathetic, which Kames considers an integral component of tragedy. For this reason, he imagines the 'happiest of all subjects for tragedy, if such a one could be invented, would be where a man of integrity falls into a great misfortune by doing an innocent action, but which by some singular means he conceives to be criminal'.[65] Such a scenario is both pathetic and conducive to sympathy. By contrast, he gives *Romeo and Juliet* as an example of the sort of play that leaves the audience 'discontented' as the tragedy 'is occasioned by Friar Laurence's coming to the monument a minute too late' so that chance causes the tragic action.[66] Chance is by its very nature not pathetic, nor can it generate sympathy. Natural causes rather than chance, even if they harm the good, must be the source of tragedy, therefore Desdemona's death at the hand of a jealous husband is natural and pathetic, even if undeserved.

Certainly not all critics agreed with Kames on the relative unimportance of poetic justice in the writing and viewing of tragedy. Famously, Samuel Johnson attacked Shakespeare's 'sacrifice of virtue to convenience' in the preface to his edition of Shakespeare's works, noting that Shakespeare 'carrie[d] his persons indifferently through right and wrong, and at the close dismisses them without further care, and leaves their examples to operate by chance'.[67] While like Kames he rejects the operations of chance as the conduit of tragedy, unlike Kames, he expresses concern that that outcome be just. As he claims, in his notes to *King Lear*, 'As all reasonable beings naturally love justice, I cannot easily be persuaded that the observation of justice makes a play worse; or, that if all other excellencies are equal, the audience will not always rise better pleased from the final triumph of persecuted virtue',[68] as in the case of Tate's adaptation of *King Lear*. But Johnson was the exception rather than the rule in his desire for formal justice, and he, like his contemporaries, praised pathos as a means to a dramatic end. In the notes to his edition of Shakespeare, he provides a fine example of a 'sympathetic' reader, unconsciously demonstrating what many of his contemporaries had suggested regarding the role of sympathy in the appreciation of drama, especially tragedy. His comments indicate not only his sensitivity as a critic but also the degree to which he favoured those plays which excited his sympathy. Regarding the death of Desdemona he writes: 'I am glad that I have finished the revisal of this dreadful scene. It is not to be endured', while by contrast *Julius Caesar* he finds 'somewhat cold and unaffecting'.[69]

Pathos's status as the most effective means of generating an emotional response had practical as well as theoretical consequences. Not surprisingly, those plays which successfully incorporated pathos tended to remain in the theatrical repertoire while "cold and unaffecting" plays such as *Julius Caesar* frequently did not. The primacy of pathos as a dramatic tool had a corresponding impact on the content of drama, even affecting the representation of gender, a topic to which I will return in later chapters. The introduction of pathos into male tragic subjects of necessity broke down some of the rigid gender lines distinguishing male and female characters in early eighteenth-century tragedy. In earlier tragedies, female characters suffered passively while male characters remained if not heroic, at least recognizably active. Figures such as Otway's Monimia and Belvidera, Southerne's Isabella, and Rowe's Jane Shore were the characters to whom Smith returned when articulating his ideas of our response to and identification with suffering. These were the plays that remained popular as the century progressed, and their dolorous heroines were joined by a series of equally pitiable male figures, most notably Lillo's George Barnwell and Edward Moore's weak-willed gambler Beverley in *The Gamester*, as well as in the increasingly poignant representations of figures from older plays such as Shakespeare's Lear.

* * *

> If when we observe a person humbled by adversity, weakened by sickness, borne down by oppression, stabbed by calumny, betrayed by his friends, or reduced to poverty, whose attitudes, motions, and gestures discover the concern or anxiety of his mind, we in imagination place ourselves in the same condition and endeavour to bring home to ourselves the most minute articles of distress which can possibly occur to him, the sufferer – then we, the spectators of his distress, are justly said to sympathise with him.[70]

Turner's description of sympathy in action provides an apt conclusion to a chapter that began with Pratt's more general vision of sympathy as the moral glue of the universe. In an age when the value of art was predicated on its ability to generate sympathy, aesthetics shifted its priorities away from formalist theories of drama common in discussions of drama in the Restoration and early eighteenth century, prompting new theories of how drama functioned. As a result, the form and content of drama itself shifted, metamorphosing into hybrid forms that elevated the sentiments of the common man at the same time as they domesticated the fall of kings and the fate of nations. The drama of the age sought to stimulate that state of mind which arose from being a 'spectator of distress', a state uniquely susceptible to moral edification and possible through the operation of sympathy. As the following chapters will explore, this interest in affective response promoted a common goal of establishing a sense of connection – of fellow-feeling – between the events on the stage and the audience in the theatre.

One graphic illustration of how closely linked sympathy, spectatorship, and the experience of theatre were in the popular imagination comes not from a philosopher nor from a literary critic but from the anonymous author of the novel *The Follies of St James's Street* (1789). In a chapter titled 'Effect of Sympathy', the author describes the events that occur when the virtuous heroine Emma and her gamester husband visit the theatre, not realizing that the play to be performed was Moore's *The Gamester*.

> The actors performed very well; and the heroine was even beyond herself! Nothing could be more affecting! Lord Watson felt it all! His Lady did not

> dare look at him: she heard him sigh! And once he whispered her not to be so much affected! The last act was almost too much! When Beverley had drunk the poison, and attempts to pray, Lord Watson, and another known gamester, called out, No prayers! No praying! The house was surprized! The whisper went round. 'They are gamesters!' was said aloud: everyone looked at the box. The beauteous weeping Emma hid her face: she was almost overcome. Mrs. Beverley, all that was great! all that was engaging! entered: What a scene! What a lesson to the world![71]

Although, aside from the title, the word itself is never used in the chapter, this episode provides a vivid example of the way in which theatre was believed to generate sympathy. The author's liberal use of exclamation marks signals the power of the emotions generated by the performance as the audience members, in particular Emma and her husband, identify with the distressed characters in Moore's tragedy. The performance spills beyond the stage as the entire audience recognizes the extent to which the gamesters in the audience identify with the gamester on stage. The vignette of the gamesters watching *The Gamester* and being overcome by the strength of their identification with the doomed titled character presents a fascinating vision of how sympathy was supposed to operate. The vividness of the gamesters' response is here presented in broadly moral terms as a 'lesson to the world', suggesting that virtuous actions, presumably repentance, should be the result of the gamesters' powerful emotional response – and the audience's response to the dual performance. However, as the novel continues, we see that the 'lesson' is never completed; Lord Watson returns to his dissolute ways as the anonymous author questions the efficacy of sympathy as a vehicle for morality. Cynically, the author suggests that while the theatrical experience is powerful enough to generate an involuntary response, this response is just as ephemeral as the performance that stimulated it. In this, it calls into question the moral system of sympathy described by Smith and endorsed by supporters of the theatre who argued for its ability to provoke lasting moral reform. This question forms the basis for the next chapter's exploration of the actual experience of theatregoing in the so-called Age of Sensibility.

CHAPTER 2

Dangerous Pleasures: Theatregoing in the Eighteenth Century

> The peculiar excellence of Mrs. Siddons is, that she makes the illusion perfect. From the first moment of her entrance on the stage to her exit she is ever the very character she professes to delineate. She never forgets herself for an instant, and her fine countenance expressing all the emotions of the soul, the spectator sits arrested to the scene. He becomes an agent in the play, and all his moral affections are aroused in the cause which she so forcibly represents. He rages, he melts in sympathy with the artist, and strives in vain to believe it a fable, so striking and irresistible is the force of her similitude!
>
> *Morning Chronicle*[1]

> FROM Mrs. Siddons's truly affecting representation of this character, I feel myself engaged in a work much too difficult for my limited powers. How can I delineate her perfections, when those very perfections, I sometimes thought, would have nearly deprived me of sensation?
>
> –A Lady of Distinction, *The Beauties of Mrs Siddons*[2]

The previous chapter presented views of how theatre audiences *should* react to the actions they saw represented on the stage, particularly to the performance of distress. In their hypothesizing on the mechanics of sympathy, Smith, Kames, and other Scottish Enlightenment figures articulated an idealized system of sympathetic response that depended upon the spectator's identification with the emotions he or she saw enacted. In a crucial secondary step, sympathetic response then moved the spectator to virtuous action, resulting in the establishment of a moral society; sympathetic response in these philosophical systems was thus a positive social good. The author of *The Follies of St James's Street*, on the other hand, while not ruling out the possibility that performance could generate virtuous emotion in the breast of the spectator, nonetheless depicted these 'effects of sympathy' as fleeting and ultimately ineffectual. In the end, however, the depictions of sympathy and its aftermath, as posited by philosophers and imagined by novelists, remain hypothetical. This chapter explores the actual experience of attending the theatre in the later eighteenth century. It charts spectators' responses to what they saw upon the stage and their emotions as they sat in the theatre and asks: in an age when 'sympathy' was conceptualized and broadly endorsed as a virtue, did audiences conform to these expectations? As postulated in the moral aesthetics of Smith and Kames, sympathy was morally directed; we sympathize as we should with those things that promote good. Accounts of attending the theatre in the 'age of sensibility', however, suggest that the reality was neither so easily mapped nor so unerringly virtuous; within the auditorium, sympathy could become an emotional connection with dark, even dangerous implications.

As with assessing performance itself, determining the nature and extent of audience response is difficult. When dealing with the history of audience response, we are limited to textual accounts of a past experience that can never be fully reconstituted. Even those who participated actively in the event frequently struggle to put their impressions into words. As the previous chapter demonstrates, the age was, however, fascinated with the entire concept of spectatorship and response, and while we cannot recreate the theatrical experience itself, audiences in the later eighteenth century were anxious to share what they saw and most importantly what they felt with their contemporaries. By the 1770s and 1780s, theatre reviews were a routine part of daily newspapers, and reviewers often dedicated as much space to discussing how audiences responded to what they saw as they did to the performance itself. Viewers wrote to friends about their experiences, and an avid readership consumed such personal accounts along with poems, parodies, and extensive commentaries describing performers and performances. Most of all, audiences felt it necessary to chronicle their feelings, to try to recreate in words what they experienced in the theatre.

Although not writing directly about the theatregoing experience, Adam Smith provided a generation of theatregoers with a vocabulary as they sought to articulate the relationship between spectatorship and emotional response. In these accounts, sympathy becomes the codeword for personal identification with the distresses of a character within a play, most often in tragedy but increasingly in comedy as well. The notion of 'melting' sympathy, mentioned approvingly in reviews, diverges from Hume's and Burke's understanding of the term and is best seen as an extrapolation from Smith's carefully delineated appraisal of the types of sympathetic identification and their potential applications. In this sense, references to sympathy represent an attempt to chronicle spectators' feelings, both good and bad, as they watched a play. As Helen Nicholson explains when writing about the theatrical experience, 'emotions are contagious, they act upon the body. Like other infections, emotions are both public and private; they temporarily inhabit the intimate spaces of your body but they also multiply, sometimes wantonly, from one person to another.'[3] In this world rife with shared feelings, spectators were almost as interested in the emotions of others as they were in their own, recording the reactions of those around them and describing, whenever possible, the collective response.

While the woman who played Mrs Beverley in the scene described in *The Follies of St James's Street* is never identified, it is likely that the actress envisioned as 'all that was great! all that was engaging!' was Sarah Siddons.[4] Mrs Beverley, the much put-upon wife of Moore's gamester, was one of her many popular roles, and she enjoyed great success in the role in the six years preceding the publication of the novel in 1789.[5] Siddons's powerful impact on her audiences was legendary, which makes her a useful illustration of the actual mechanics of audience response as it was experienced in the later eighteenth century. Much work has been done already exploring Siddons's life, her acting, and her position as a celebrity. Laura Engel, for example, begins her study of eighteenth-century actresses and celebrity with a chapter dedicated to Siddons, in which she explores the 'the lasting quality of a category of identity that Siddons invented: the modern female superstar'.[6] In this, Engel follows earlier work on Siddons and celebrity by scholars such as Cheryl Wanko, Robyn Asleson, Heather MacPherson, and David Román.[7]

Celebrity studies, however, is strongly focused upon the figure of the celebrity, upon her body and its image. In *It*, Joseph Roach demonstrates the importance of this paradigm; his chapter headings move from the exterior deeper and deeper into the physical being of the celebrity: 'accessories', 'clothes', 'hair', 'skin', 'flesh', 'bone'. This chapter, however, is not concerned with Siddons in herself but rather with the effect she had on her audiences. Embodiment is crucial here, but it is the embodiment not of the performer but of the theatregoers, those audience members who paid to see Siddons so that they could experience together the 'contagion' that Nicholson describes. This active desire to feel brought pain as well as pleasure, the 'infection' of response, to pursue Nicholson's metaphor, ran the risk of tipping the spectator over the line into physical and even moral danger. Often painstakingly recorded, these emotional and physiological responses demonstrate that, in the eyes of her contemporaries, Siddons's greatness lay not simply in her ability to create an accurate representation of a character but rather in her ability to animate her spectators. The reviewer cited at the beginning of this chapter notes that she displays, 'all the emotions of the soul', with the result that he is not a passive spectator but 'an agent in the play' with 'all his moral affections' aroused 'irresistibly'. She was in this sense not simply a performer who herself emoted upon the stage but the conduit for emotion in others, the force that drove her audiences into active participation rather than passive absorption. Because of the intensity and immediacy of response to her performances and the corresponding desire to record this experience, Siddons provides an ideal case study of audience response in the age of sensibility. The impact of her performances is especially notable in the early phase of Siddons's career, before she became established as the grand dame of the British theatre and while the astonishment she prompted was still fresh.

The general outline of Sarah Kemble Siddons's history is well known. She was born on 5 July 1755, the eldest child of Roger and Sarah Kemble. The Kembles were a famous theatrical family; Roger Kemble was an actor and theatre manager, and seven of Siddons's siblings also pursued theatrical careers. Of these, Sarah and her brother John Philip Kemble were the most successful, becoming the best-known and most revered actors of their day. While still in her teens, Sarah married another actor, Williams Siddons, and began acting in the provinces, in cities such as Cheltenham, Bath, and York. In 1775 David Garrick brought Siddons to Drury Lane Theatre in London, where she debuted, disastrously, as Portia in *The Merchant of Venice*. Critics dismissed her as 'very pretty but awkward' with 'vulgarity in her tones'.[8] Her contract at Drury Lane was not renewed, and she retreated to the provinces at the end of the season, waiting nearly seven years before chancing a return to London. Her second appearance on the London stage in 1782 was nothing like the first; her biographer James Boaden asserted that it was 'the most important season that the theatre has, perhaps, ever known'.[9] In contrast to the earlier disparaging remarks, reviews of her depiction of Isabella in Thomas Southerne's *The Fatal Marriage* (adapted by Garrick as *Isabella, or, the Fatal Marriage*) were glowing, even rapturous (the *Morning Chronicle*, for example, described her performance as 'irresistible' and noted that 'the Theatre resound[ed] with thunderous applause for more than a minute'). Her fame spread overnight as crowds flocked to see the new star; the receipts from her first appearance as Isabella on 10 October were a commendable £181 11s., but by her next appearance they had increased by more than £80, a tangible demonstration of the popularity of the new star.[10] Even if it was not perhaps the unprecedented event that Boaden describes in such hyperbolic terms, Siddons's 1782–1783 season was without question extraordinary. What distinguished the reaction to Siddons's performances at this time was the intensity of the emotions she generated in her audiences and the extent to which these audiences sought to chronicle their experiences. Although Siddons's brother John Philip Kemble was to become London's leading actor, accounts of his debut the following year do not come close to the overflowing enthusiasm displayed by Siddons's audiences.

Soon after her first London success, Siddons travelled to other major venues in Britain, such as Dublin and Edinburgh, once again overwhelming the crowds who thronged to see her act. By the time she appeared in Edinburgh in May 1784, news of her triumphs in London had generated wild enthusiasm well in advance of her actual appearance, and her reception in Edinburgh was, if anything, more extreme than in London. A group of gentlemen in Scotland raised money through subscription to bring the actress to Edinburgh, sparking a violent stampede of would-be spectators. According to a contemporary report,

> The gentlemen subscribers, who had been the occasion of her coming, thought themselves entitled to be secured in seats in the pit the evenings she performed. This, was thought very reasonable, and they were admitted a quarter of an hour before the doors opened. But the vast crouds that attended, eager for admission, creating much inconvenience and disturbance, a part of the pit was railed off for the subscribers, after the three first appearances of Mrs. Siddons. The anxiety to see this celebrated actress was so great, that crouds were often at the doors from eleven o'clock forenoon till five in the afternoon. This rage for seeing Mrs Siddons was so great that there were 2557 applications for 630 places.[11]

The struggle for tickets was referred to by one audience member as a 'SIDDONIAN war' in which the general public struggled with subscribers and those wealthy patrons who could bribe their way into the theatre. In a verse epistle to a friend, Miss Maria Belinda Bogle sardonically described the nightly struggle to get seats in the theatre as a literal battle:

> EACH evening the playhouse exhibits a mob,
> And the right of admission's turn'd into a job.
> By five the whole pit us'd to fill with subscribers,
> And those who had money enough to be bribers,
> But the public took fire, and began a loud jar,
> And I thought we'd have had a SIDDONIAN war.[12]

While the rage for tickets before the performance may have been intense, the actual audience response to Siddons's acting was still more impassioned. Spectators in London, Edinburgh, Dublin, and elsewhere described her performances as all-consuming, generating emotions that were irresistible in their force and intensity. These experiences were very real demonstrations of the sympathy that Smith, Kames and the moralists, philosophers and critics had written about in abstract terms. While we can never recapture the experience of watching Sarah Siddons on the stage and sharing the emotions felt by those in the theatre around us, we can search for the traces of this emotion in the words of those who were witnesses and who struggled themselves to explain what they had felt. In the words of the Lady of Distinction cited at the beginning of this chapter, the strength of the affect was beyond the scope of human powers of delineation, so strong it could almost blot out conscious sensation, an 'irresistible' and 'arresting' experience. Despite the sometimes overwhelming nature of such feelings, the very fact of experiencing them demonstrated not only the spectators' finely tuned sensibilities but, more importantly, their potential for good for themselves and for the world.

'Harrowing Up the Soul'

In her first appearance as Isabella, on 10 October 1782, Siddons electrified her audiences, prompting intense emotional responses unknown even in the days of David Garrick. Subsequent performances heightened the effect, and Isabella quickly became one of Siddons's signature roles. (So strongly was she associated with the role that in 1808 Thomas Gilliland wrote, 'when Mrs. Siddons dies, Isabella will be lost for ever to the stage'.[13]) Strikingly, while reviews and personal accounts recount details of her performance, they often focus less on the specifics of her interpretation (the actions, voice, or facial expressions) than on the behaviour of the audience. Attending a performance of *Isabella; or the Fatal Marriage* was not strictly about admiring fine acting; it represented an opportunity to participate in the communal experience of being in the auditorium and responding on a deeply personal and even physical level to the theatrical experience. With its ability to generate a visibly violent reaction in the audience, Siddons's Isabella represents an ideal example of the symbiotic relationship between spectator and performance. Responses to her performance were repeatedly chronicled both by spectators of Siddons's performance and by spectators of the spectators, providing some of the most vivid examples of the potency of the theatrical experience.

The role of Isabella had long been a vehicle for great actresses. Thomas Southerne's *The Fatal Marriage; Or, the Innocent Adultery* was originally staged in 1694 at Drury Lane with the renowned Elizabeth Barry as Isabella. As written, Southerne's play balanced a tragic main plot with a comic subplot (a technique he also used in another popular tragedy, *Oroonoko*; both plays are adaptations of novels by Aphra Behn). The clash of comedy and tragedy became increasingly distasteful to audiences and critics, and in 1757 Garrick completely abandoned the subplot, leaving the play focused entirely on the figure of Isabella and thus unrelentingly tragic.[14] As the play opens, Isabella is in deep mourning, grieving for her beloved husband Biron who she believes died in battle seven years earlier. Abandoned by Biron's family, Isabella and her young son live in poverty until, in desperation, Isabella finally agrees to marry her devoted suitor, Villeroy, who has loved her for many years. In reality, Biron is still alive, although his scheming brother Carlos has withheld this information from Isabella. Hoping to discredit her, Carlos urges Isabella to remarry. Inevitably, the day after the marriage is consummated, Biron returns home in disguise, seeking his wife. When Isabella recognizes this seeming 'stranger', the realization that she has betrayed her husband and committed bigamy drives her insane. The final two acts centre on Isabella's horror at her adultery, however innocent it may have been, her conflicted love for Biron, and her descent into madness during which she terrifies her son – played originally by Siddons's real-life son Henry – and nearly stabs Biron, drawing back only at the last moment. The play ultimately ends with her suicide.

Siddons's performance abounded in memorable moments: Isabella's embrace of Biron's ring; her maternal concern for her child; her near murder of Biron in her insanity and the horror with which she discovers the knife in her hand. Most famous of all was Siddons's representation of Isabella's response when she first recognizes Biron, at which point she realizes that she has committed bigamy, what the Lady of Distinction describes as 'a crime of a most shocking nature'.[15] As described by the Lady, this moment was truly arresting: 'her shriek, and immediate fall, on discovering Biron, as he threw off his disguise and exclaims "My Isabella!" was really astonishing – to describe their effect is impossible'.[16] The Lady's 'astonishment' at Siddons' rendition of this crucial moment arises not simply from her admiration of an example of fine acting; it is tied even more closely to the impact Siddons's performance had on the Lady and those around her. It is the powerful 'effect' or impression of the crucial moment that is so memorable and so impossible to express; words cannot convey the force of the memory, let alone the experience itself.

In writing of Siddons's Isabella, spectators like the Lady repeatedly stress the irresistible force of sympathy that bound the audience to the actor. Thomas Gilliland, for example, writes:

> When she is interrupted in her contemplation by the advice of Carlos, to give [her son], by accepting Villeroy's hand, 'a friend and father'; the violence and surprize with which she exclaims, 'a husband!' is so expressive of her horror at the idea, that every auditor instantly becomes pervaded with a correspondent sympathy.[17]

As with the Lady, Gilliland begins by describing the performance (Siddons's representation of Isabella's horror at the idea of a second marriage) but quickly moves on to recount the 'correspondent sympathy', the intense identification with Isabella's horror that 'instantly pervade[s]' the audience member, a seemingly inescapable and inevitable response. He reiterates this point, describing another celebrated incident, the moment when Isabella is on the brink of murdering her husband:

> Her start on approaching to stab Biron; her shock when going to take a last farewell of him, and the insanity which immediately follows, affects the spectator's mind with the most sympathetic horror. A thousand beauties are imparted to the eye and ear of her audience, which work upon the feelings with all their due effect.[18]

Gilliland's description of this moment exactly mirrors Smith's formulation of the mechanics of sympathy; the distress of another, here Isabella, creates a corresponding distress in the spectator. He was not alone in using these terms to express the personal impact of Siddons's performance. In its review of the opening night, the *Morning Chronicle* describes Siddons's control over the audience's emotions as established in the opening scenes of the play:

> In the very first scene there was something so affecting in her manner, – in fact, she wore her sorrow with so much persuasive sincerity, that she made the audience her advocates, and, it must be confessed, she never quitted the hold she had so early taken of their feelings, till she had created an universal and a melting sympathy all around.[19]

The reviewer first describes Siddons's performance as 'persuasive', so much so that it 'made' the audience her 'advocates', active participants in the play's affect rather than passive observers. By the end of his account, Siddons controls the audience's emotions, resulting in a more generalized sympathetic response the writer labels as both 'universal' and 'melting'.

And melt the audience did. After commenting on the 'universal and melting sympathy', the *Morning Chronicle* reported that 'there was scarcely a dry eye either male or female throughout the house'.[20] Two days later, after Siddons's second appearance as Isabella, the *Morning Chronicle* provides a more extensive account of the audience's emotional response, explaining that 'the audience were unanimous in their judgment, and pronounced her performance admirable, not only by loud and reiterated plaudits, but by that much more sure testimony, that their feelings were appealed to in a manner perfectly irresistible – an increasing torrent of tears'.[21] Applause is one form of expressing approval, but the 'irresistible' 'torrent of tears' provides a truer indication of both emotion and judgement. Words and applause are but voluntary; they cannot equal the sincerity of the tears that gush from the eyes of the spectators. Truth, the reviewer implies, lies in spontaneous physical demonstrations of feeling.

Tears were but one manifestation of the audience's response to Siddons's Isabella. Where torrents of tears appear to have been expected, accounts of more extravagant reactions to her performance abound as audience members are described as fainting and even falling into hysterical fits. As the Lady of Distinction notes, she herself felt that watching Siddons nearly 'deprived me of sensation'. With references to fainting and hysterics cited repeatedly in reviews of Siddons's Isabella, these incidents cannot be dismissed as nonsensical or even unusual; certainly they must have provided the readers of reviews and memoirs with vivid pictures of the events within the theatre as well as on the stage. Such spectacles are precisely noted, as in the *Public Advertiser* for 12 May 1784, which reports that '[Siddons's] exertions, among other great effects, so worked on one woman in the audience, that she was actually for some little time in a strong fit.'[22] Such violent – and highly visible – responses were indeed contagious, and the moment of Isabella's reunion with Biron became the focal point for such hysteria. At the moment where Siddons as Isabella looked upon her husband's face, shrieked, and fainted, audiences, in their sympathy for Isabella's distress, were known to scream along with Siddons and faint or worse at the moment when she swooned over Biron. (One commentator remarked that in Edinburgh the 'wailing and crying ... almost drowned Mrs. Siddons' voice'.[23]) The reproduction of the cry was clearly not a simple reaction to a horrific sight, as might be expected, for example, from viewing a corpse, but rather a profound identification with Siddons/Isabella and her intense emotional anguish. Not surprisingly, the universal scream was not noted during the first performance, but as the details of her performance became known, especially the famous shriek and subsequent collapse, they seem to have worked upon the minds of prospective audience members, leaving them primed for an appropriate emotional experience, much as Boswell prepared himself to weep over Garrick's King Lear.

By the time that Siddons played Isabella in Edinburgh in May 1784, audiences were prepared to respond to her performances with great enthusiasm as soon as she stepped upon the stage. One often-repeated anecdote describes George Gordon, Lord Byron's mother, in the throes of a memorable fit of hysteria. Byron's biographer Thomas Moore recounts that when attending a performance of *The Fatal Marriage*,

> A circumstance related, as having taken place before the marriage of this lady [Miss Gordon] not only shows the extreme quickness and vehemence of her feelings, but, if it be true that she had never at the time seen Captain Byron, is not a little striking. Being at the Edinburgh Theatre one night when the character of Isabella was performed by Mrs. Siddons, so affected was she by the powers of this great actress, that, towards the conclusion of the play, she fell into violent fits, and was carried out of the theatre, screaming loudly, 'Oh my Biron, my Biron.'[24]

In a footnote, Moore expands on this event, quoting Sir Walter Scott's more detailed account of the event. Scott prefaces his description of Miss Gordon's behaviour by providing a context that, in his eyes, helps explain the lady's conduct:

> It was during Mrs. Siddons's first or second visit to Edinburgh, when the music of that wonderful actress's voice, looks, manner, and person, produced the strongest effect which could possibly be exerted by a human being upon her fellow-creatures. Nothing of the kind that I ever witnessed approached it by a hundred degrees. The high state of excitation was aided by the difficulties of obtaining entrance, and the exhausting length of time that the audience were contented to wait until the piece commenced. When the curtain fell, a large proportion of the ladies were generally in hysterics.
>
> I remember Miss Gordon of Ghight, in particular, harrowing the house by the desperate and wild way in which she shrieked out Mrs. Siddons's exclamation, in the character of Isabella, 'Oh my Byron! Oh my Byron!' A well-known medical gentleman, the benevolent Dr. Alexander Wood, tendered his assistance; but the thick-pressed audience could not for a long time make way for the doctor to approach his patient, or the patient the physician. The remarkable circumstance was, that the lady had not then seen Captain Byron, who, like Sir Toby, made her conclude with 'Oh!' as she had begun with it.[25]

The lengthy wait (the report cited in *Edinburgh Fugitive Pieces* described it as being as much as six hours), combined with the extraordinary power of Siddons's acting, leads to this remarkable – and well documented – fit of hysteria. Even while he finishes with a sly reference to *Twelfth Night*, Scott takes care to validate his account by providing the name and qualifications of the doctor who attended to Miss Gordon just as he attempts to explain the reason for the seemingly fantastic nature of her response by citing the exact power of Siddons's affect. At this point, however, he runs out of superlatives: she 'produced the strongest effect which could possibly be exerted by a human being upon her fellow-creatures' and 'Nothing of the kind that I ever witnessed approached it by a hundred degrees.' In this sense, Miss Gordon becomes just a single example of human response to the stimulus of the theatrical experience.

With documented cases such as these, it is no wonder that critics such as W. R. Chetwood described the stage as more powerful than the pulpit ('Lessons for the Stage may be convey'd, in one respect, stronger than from the Pulpit . . . [because] the Eye is suppos'd to view the very Persons in the real Circumstances of History'[26]). These physiological responses to the powerful stimulus of performance bring to mind accounts of religious ecstasy in which worshippers were seized by the power of inspiration, infected, as it were, by the excitement of those around them. This secular transport validates not only the experience of the individual spectator but the emotions of the spectators throughout the theatre and, in the end, becomes the means by which art – that of the performer and even that of the playwright – can be judged.

Not everyone accepted such emotional displays at face value. Miss Bogle provides a distinctly more acerbic description of the hysteria in Scotland in which she suggests that these paroxysms of passion are ridiculous and even in some cases carefully choreographed. Like so many other accounts, her comic representation of Siddons's Isabella centres on the often-replicated shriek, which threatens to overwhelm all of Edinburgh:

> ISABELLA too rose all superior to sadness,
> And our hearts were well harrow'd with horror and madness.
> From all sides the house, hark the cry how it swells!
> While the boxes are torn with most heart piercing yells;
> The Misses all faint, it becomes them so vastly
> And their cheeks are so red that they never look ghastly
> Even Ladies advanced to their grand climacterics
> Are often led out in a fit of hysterics;

> The screams are wide-wafted East, West, South, and North,
> Loud Echo prolongs them on both sides the Forth.[27]

What begins as a 'cry' as uttered by Siddons quickly degenerates into less-exalted 'yells' and 'screams' when repeated by the female members of the audience. As with other observers, Miss Bogle concentrates on audience response rather than on the actual performance. Women rather than men are the object of her scrutiny as she insinuates that younger women 'faint' in a conscious attempt to appear to advantage, because 'it becomes them so vastly', while older women enjoy 'fit[s] of hysterics'. In this cynical depiction of audience behaviour, age as well as gender appear to dictate response.

Satirical representations of the 'harrowing' effect that Miss Bogle describes so vividly were not limited to verbal accounts of Siddons's acting. This cartoon from 1790[28] (Figure 2.1) shows Siddons practising the technique of 'Harrowing up the Soul'. With her hand outstretched for dramatic effect and her eyes half closed, she exclaims 'Oh – h – h – !' possibly practising the famously 'harrowing' cry Isabella gave upon recognizing Biron. The cartoon turns its focus on Siddons rather than the audience, suggesting that her carefully devised strategies were not necessarily designed with elevated purpose of embodying the essence of a character but rather with the distinctly earthbound goal of titillating her audiences with sensational thrills.

Excesses of emotion arising from the experience of watching Siddons in *Isabella* quickly became fodder for broadly humorous accounts of the theatre. A mock review of one of Siddons's appearances in Dublin as the 'all-tearful character of Isabella' solemnly relates the catastrophic impact of her performance. The details in the satire reveal how familiar the broader reading audience was with the spectacular effects of Siddons's performance. As the review notes,

> when she came to the scene of parting with her wedding ring, ah, what a sight was there! The very fiddlers in the orchestra blubbered like hungrey [*sic*] children for their bread and butter! and when the bell rung for music, between the acts, the tears run in such plentiful streams from the basoon [*sic*] player's eyes, that they choaked the finger-stops, and making a spout of the instrument, poured such a torrent on the first fiddler's book, that, not seeing the overture was in two sharps, the leader of the band actually played it in one flat: but the sobs and sighs of the groaning audience, and noise of corks from the smelling bottles, prevented the mistakes between flats and sharps being perceived.

In the serious manner of an actual news report, the parody proceeds to document casualties:

Figure 2.1 'How to Harrow up the Soul'. *Theatrical Portraiture No. 6*, in *Attic Miscellany, Or Characteristic Mirror of Men and Things*, vol. I (1791). Courtesy of the Lewis Walpole Library, Yale University.

> One hundred and nine ladies fainted, forty-six went into fits, ninety-five had strong hysterics. The world will scarce credit the assertion, when they are told, fourteen children, five old women, a one-handed sailor, and six common-council men, were actually drowned in the inundation of tears that flowed from the boxes and galleries to increase the briny flood in the pit. The water was three feet deep; and the people that were obliged to stand upon the benches, were, in that situation, up to their ancles in tears.[29]

The author clearly takes delight in exaggerating the tearful response to Isabella's grief, depicting a cacophony of discordant music and groaning spectators. He goes beyond recounting the familiar accounts of fainting and hysterics but imagines more gruesome outcomes: the mass drowning of men, women, children, and 'a one-handed sailor', overwhelmed like

Alice and the Mouse by a flood of tears. Unlike Miss Bogle, however, the author does not question the validity of the emotion (although he does suggest that such emotion could lead to unexpected dangers) but rather mocks the massive scale on which it seems to be produced. Although not drawn in conjunction with the newspaper parody, Thomas Rowlandson's cartoon 'Tragedy in London' cartoon (Figure 2.2) serves as a remarkably acute illustration of the phenomenon the parodic review explicated in such detail. Drawn as the second part of a paired caricature of theatregoing (the first is titled 'Comedy in the Country'), the cartoon depicts an audience awash with tears, from the gallery to the pit; men and women alike weep uncontrollably, and tears gush from the eyes of the bassoon player in the foreground.

While accounts such as Miss Bogle's depict women as the primary victims of hysteria, men were also prone to excesses of emotion. As the parody indicates, men as well as women participated in this overflow of emotion. In addition to depicting sobbing men in the orchestra pit as well as the auditorium, Rowlandson's cartoon prominently features a large gentleman in the lower left who has seemingly fainted and who requires the application of smelling salts. Men were also subject to fits of hysteria, as in the case of a 'Mr. Grabbe Robinson, a gentleman of the bar and a scholar well-known in the world of literature', who, during a performance of George Lillo's *Fatal Curiousity* in which Siddons as Agnes 'threw such an expression into her countenance as made the flesh of every spectator creep', fell into 'strong hysterics' to the point that he was nearly ejected from the theatre, although his hysteria took the form of wild laughter. He later declared that as the murder approached, 'his respiration grew difficult, and in a few seconds he lost all command of himself'.[30] Grabbe Robinson's account of his bout of hysteria stresses the involuntary and very physical nature of the phenomenon; he has problems breathing and loses control over his own body.

Such intensely personal descriptions of the emotional and even physiological reaction to Siddons's performances provide special insight into the experience within the theatre of feeling. One unusually detailed and thoughtful narrative occurs in the series of letters cited earlier written by an anonymous Lady of Distinction. The Lady's exploration of the Siddons effect is remarkable not simply for her precise descriptions of the specifics of Siddons's interpretation of Isabella and other roles but also for her careful delineation of her own response as a member of the audience and her analysis of this response. Her frank assessment of how she felt when experiencing Siddons's performance probes the nature of response at the

Figure 2.2 Thomas Rowlandson. *Comedy in the Country, Tragedy in London.* 29 May 1807. Hand-coloured engraving. Courtesy of the Lewis Walpole Library, Yale University.

same time that it incorporates aspects of moral aesthetics as she meditates on the ethics of spontaneous emotion. The scream so often described may well be an example of the vicariousness Joseph Roach describes as the desire to experience someone else's 'embodiment of [life]',[31] and certainly Miss Bogle suggests this in her references to the young ladies who faint while their elders luxuriate in fits of hysterics. What the Lady describes, however, is not merely a reflection of what is seen or experienced at a remove but something new, something dependent upon the theatrical event and yet distinct from it. It is created by performance but does not necessarily mirror it, although at times it may do so. In her comments on Isabella, the Lady attempts to evaluate the many layers of her feelings while watching Siddons. On the one hand, she does indeed sympathize with the figure Siddons represents, with the distresses of the 'poor exhausted Isabella', but she is troubled by the personal identification that accompanies this sympathy. Her explication of the famous shriek and swoon assesses both the performance and the disturbing nature of its impact on the audience:

> Her embrace with Biron's ring, in the fourth act, is full of agitating fears, and horrors acted with 'necromantic force' on the audience: her dread to behold him, and the fearful scrutiny with which she examines the features of the disguised Biron, with the horrid satisfaction visible in her countenance as she assures herself of life in his supposed death, was almost too interesting; – but her shriek, and immediate fall, on discovering Biron, as he threw of his disguise and exclaims 'My Isabella!' was really astonishing – to describe their effect is impossible, and perhaps – to feel it – undesirable.[32]

The passage stresses the involuntary nature of the audience's reaction: they are helpless against the 'necromantic force' of Siddons's acting, a force similar to that described by Scott. The scene is 'too interesting' (the Lady even feels the need to add an intensifier to 'astonishing' to convey the power of the scene). By the end of her account of the scene, the Lady describes the experience of sympathy with Siddons-as-Isabella as something that moves beyond painful (a term the Lady uses elsewhere to describe the affecting nature of the performance) to become actively objectionable. She struggles for words to explain the sensation but is left only with negatives. It is not the performance but the feeling it produces that is 'undesirable'.

As she writes, the Lady wrestles with the problem of the painful aesthetic experience. Her representation of what it felt like to be a spectator in the audience as Siddons embodied Isabella does not posit a kind of pleasant pain but rather a state of mental torment in which even the punishment of the villainous Carlos at the play's conclusion 'affords no compensation to minds already tortured by the subverted intellect and melancholy end of the poor exhausted Isabella'.[33] In all, the final act

> was painfully affecting: her reluctance to declare her misery, yet the dark hints she gives of it – in short, it is all so full of horror, that it is impossible for description to do justice to her inimitable acting. – Her start on approaching to stab Biron, – her shock when going to take a last farewell of him, – and the madness which immediately ensues; – 'twas impossible not to turn away, even from her. – I recollect a thousand beauties which struck me, but recollect them with a heart chilled with horror. – . . . – I must break off. – Upon the whole, as there is but one feeling excited in this play, and that of such an overbearing nature, and in the end annihilating all tender sensations, it unavoidably must have the same effect upon us.[34]

The emotion felt by this theatregoer, like so many others, cannot be controlled or even expressed. In the stops and starts that characterize the Lady's final comments on the play, the dashes and the ultimate 'I must break off', we see her struggle to convey the feeling generated by this final scene and the play as a whole. The spectator ultimately has no choice but to become part of the experience; as the reviewer cited at the beginning of this chapter explains, he 'becomes an agent in the play'. For the Lady, the feeling of horror excited by Siddons's embodiment of Isabella was so 'overbearing' and 'unavoidable' that it 'annihilated' any other sensation. The Lady's experience reveals the darker implications of sympathetic response, for while Siddons may have 'left an impression never to be effaced from the mind',[35] this indelible impression may be one of horror rather than delight. The experience may have been ephemeral; its legacy was not.

'Too Shocking for Human Nature to Support' – Emotion and Propriety

The emotional response generated by Siddons's Isabella was generally applauded as an indication of her genius, with the fainting and hysterical fits seen as simply one more indication of her power over an audience. However, as the Lady notes, such wholesale abandonment to emotion was not necessarily a universally positive experience. The Lady's questions regarding the problematic 'annihilation' of 'tender sensations' that resulted from viewing *The Fatal Marriage* were reiterated more emphatically two years after the original publication of her letters, upon the occasion of Siddons's appearance as the title character in Robert Dodsley's *Cleone.*

In Dodsley's tragedy, the title character, like Isabella, goes mad, but in her frenzy she kills her innocent child. Where Isabella pulls back in horror from her maddened impulse to stab her husband, Cleone does not. As the *Morning Chronicle* remarked the day after her first appearance on 22 November 1786, Siddons's interpretation of the character was brilliant: it possessed 'much strength of colouring, and by her superior skill awak[ed] the sincerest feelings of the brest'.[36] The problem with the production lay precisely in that representation of and subsequent excitation of 'sincerity'. Because theatregoers participated in this sincerity, they shared the truly disturbing experience of identifying with a crazed murderess. The impression was too intense, the emotions it produced too graphic. While *Cleone* had been revived several times since its successful debut in 1758, the feelings Siddons awakened were problematic; they were, in the eyes of the *Morning Chronicle*, 'too shocking to sensibility'. 'We freely own', the reviewer adds, 'we never wish to see her again in it'.[37] Likewise, the *London Chronicle*, while praising Siddons's performance, deplored its overall effect, attesting that 'the efforts that are made towards the conclusion, are destitute from interest and pathos, but on the contrary excite a horror from which sensibility must ever revolt'.[38] Brilliant acting, no matter how much admired on its own, cannot be divorced from the effect it produces. Siddons's Cleone pushed audience response too far, 'revolting' rather than delighting the sensibility of spectators. After 24 November, *Cleone* was removed from the repertoire and never staged again; Siddons had performed the role only twice.[39]

While no other role sparked a reaction as extreme or as immediate, the resistance to *Cleone* represents a vivid example of theatregoers questioning the ramifications of their response to Siddons's acting. Audiences had no doubt about what they felt (and what they were supposed to feel) when watching *Isabella*, but questions regarding the nature or appropriateness of sympathetic response lurked behind comments on other plays. Is it even appropriate for us to sympathize with the kind of suffering we see upon the stage? What moral and philosophical questions do these problems expose? Nicholas Rowe's *Jane Shore*, the third play to feature Siddons during her triumphant 1782–1783 season (the second, Arthur Murphy's *The Grecian Daughter*, is the subject of Chapter 3) became a nexus for considerations of properly directed audience response.

First staged in 1714, *Jane Shore* was the most popular of Rowe's three she-tragedies, remaining in the repertoire of both Drury Lane and Covent Garden for more than a century. The play centres on the historical figure of Jane Shore, the former mistress of Edward IV. Seduced by the charms and power of the king, Jane had abandoned her husband in order to live a life of luxury at court. The play begins after the death of Edward, as the conscience-stricken Jane seeks to live out her life in quiet repentance for her past sins. She addresses Edward's younger brother, Richard of Gloster, with this request, and he agrees, on the condition that she assist him in his plot to depose Edward's two young sons, who have been imprisoned in the tower, an act which would make him king. She refuses, and as punishment for her insubordination, he casts her out upon the streets of London with instructions that no one, upon pain of death, is to provide her food or shelter. The final act is devoted to Jane's tortuous wanderings, providing theatre-goers with a spectacle of misery unequalled on the eighteenth-century stage; the play dwells in loving detail on her suffering, the bloody footprints she leaves behind her, her famished pleading, and her final collapse.

Jane's physical suffering, like the mental anguish of Isabella, spurred powerful emotions in Siddons's audiences. As with her Isabella, spectators wept openly and 're-echo[ed] ev'ry sigh', and although there are fewer records of fainting fits or hysterics, anecdotes related to the play's final act are almost as common as those from *Isabella*. A famous although possibly apocryphal anecdote tells of a child who was so convinced of the reality of the performance that when Siddons moaned 'I have not tasted bread for three days', the little girl leaned out of a box and offered Siddons an orange to prevent the poor lady from starving.[40] Whether true or not, this story demonstrates that audiences found Siddons's representation of starvation both realistic and peculiarly poignant. Theatre afficionado and biographer Thomas Moore, who collected anecdotes regarding Siddons, noted an example of the common – and expected – reaction to the play's final scene:

> A gentleman whose taste and judgment are truly respectable, although he is so unjust to the world as not to publish his opinions, was observing to his friends that he considered Mrs. Siddons infinitely superior to any tragic actress he ever saw; But, really said the critic, there is, nevertheless, *something* wanting to constitute perfection. – At this moment Mrs. Siddons appeared in the scene where Jane Shore is supposed to be famishing, and at the same time expressing to her husband a sincere repentance for the errors of her past life. A particular sentence which she expressed in this scene had such an effect upon the critic, that he burst into tears. The gentleman to whom he addressed himself a few moments before, observing his situation, very calmly said – 'My Dear Friend, when you talk of this woman's acting again, be sure you do not introduce another – But.'[41]

An actor's genius, as both men seem to assume unquestioningly, does not lie in acting per se; rather, her 'perfection' can be judged by the emotional interplay between audience and performer. The man of supposed 'taste and judgment' finds Siddons lacking '*something*', although he seems unsure of exactly what is 'wanting' to 'constitute perfection'. He finds his answer in his own spontaneous burst of tears.

While unquestionably affecting, Siddons's performance of Jane Shore also spurred discussions of how audiences *should* respond to this representation of physical suffering and piteous death. The morality of audience response was the key issue in these debates. One anonymous poet writing, like the Lady of Distinction, about Siddons's most famous roles saw her representation of Jane Shore as the occasion for a specifically gendered moral rather than emotional response. Although the 'Preface' to *The Theatrical Portrait, a Poem* (1783) explains that spectators attend the theatre to learn to 'read Men',[42] in general the poem addresses how women should view themselves and reform their sins. This is especially true of the poet's comments on Jane Shore, where Siddons becomes a vehicle for female moral edification. His graphic illustration of the fruits of sin is indicative of the strain of criticism that saw the play as especially appropriate for female members of the audience because it served as a horrifying spectacle of the miserable consequences of sexual transgressions. Referring to the scenes leading up to Jane's piteous death, the poet addresses female sinners – specifically adulteresses – and warns them:

> If we look round and view the House all o'er
> Shall we not find, at least one modern Shore?
> Does not fair SIDDONS many a Heart expose
> And sting some guilty Mind with bleeding Woes?
> Ye faithless Fair that stain the Marriage Bed
> Like wretched Shore from virtuous Husbands fled!
> Avoid these Scenes with most industrious Care,
> Least sudden Horror, seize you with Despair.
> SIDDONS strikes Home, will wound each tender Part
> Awake your conscience, terrify your Heart;
> Inflict a Dagger in your guilty Breast,
> Poison your Joys, deprive your Soul of Rest:
> Haunt you all Day in ev'ry Place and Hour,
> Prey on your Vitals, ev'ry Hope devour.
> Make you with Grief your hapless State deplore
> Curse the bright Day, and wish you were no more![43]

The poet moves from scanning the theatre audience to speculating about the women in the audience whose behaviour has replicated that of Jane Shore. They will recognize themselves in the figure they see upon the stage and suffer 'bloody woes' even more grotesque than those endured by Jane.

In a virtual cavalcade of bodily tortures, the poet predicts that the vision of Siddons-as-Jane will 'wound each tender part', 'inflict a dagger', 'poison', 'haunt', and 'prey upon your vitals'.

In his exegesis of Siddons's Jane, the poet posits a concept of identification very different from that articulated by Smith, one predicated more on theories of satire or comedy in which readers/audiences see themselves in a mirror and use this recognition as the basis for moral or social reformation. His interpretation of Siddons's performance is narrowly focused on its exemplary potential: women, even virtuous ones, will learn from the gruesome example before them and avoid the sexual crimes that Jane committed. In this narrow vision of audience response, male sinners, adulterers or otherwise, were presumably not expected to respond in this way and in fact are not addressed as subject to the lessons of *Jane Shore*.[44] This is not to say that no woman ever responded in the manner he described, however actual cases of women redeemed by the vision of Jane's suffering seem to be non-existent.

In reality, women did not respond with the 'sudden Horror' the poet predicted, nor were their joys poisoned or their nights haunted. They reacted, in fact, much as their male contemporaries did, with sighs and tears. In this sense they do identify with Jane's distress, but the effect of this identification, unlike that posited by the anonymous poet, results in sympathy, a bond of humanity rather than a self-referential reflection. As with the poet and with the man who burst into tears while watching the 'famishing' Jane, most spectators focus their attention on the play's final act when considering their response and the response of those around them. It is this scene that proves Siddons's genius in the tearful eyes of the sceptic as well as in the judgmental fantasy of the poet. Clearly, Siddons made concrete Jane's exquisitely physical rather than mental suffering; illustrations of her as Jane Shore, such as Sir Thomas Lawrence's portrait of Siddons in the role, emphasize the qualities that so moved her audiences: the bare feet, the pallor, the shroud-like gown, the loosened hair, all indicative of physical distress.

Nonetheless, this final act troubled some spectators, most notably the Lady of Distinction. As she did with Siddons's performance of Isabella, the Lady probes the nature of her response as well as the broader question of the propriety of responding as we do to the spectacle of Jane Shore and her ordeal. She finds Siddons's performance in the first four acts 'affecting beyond description' and even 'charmingly pathetic',[45] however for this playgoer, while the spectacle of Siddons in the final act generates deep 'compassion', it also prompts her to contemplate the ethical implications of reacting so strongly to Siddons's performance. The very realism that so moved the little girl with the orange in itself constitutes a moral problem. To the Lady's mind, Siddons 'ceases to excite pleasure' in the role of Jane Shore because her ability to represent grievous physical suffering was so true to life that 'the idea of deception is lost to the mind'.

> Through the remainder of the part, her representation is so near real life, that, under that persuasion, when she appeared tottering under the weight of an apparently emaciated frame, I absolutely thought her the creature perishing through want, 'fainting from loss of food'; – shocked at the sight, I could not avoid turning from the suffering object . . . Her soliloquy was painfully affecting; but, on discovering Alicia's door, the severe sharp hunger expressed in her looks, the ravenous flame which seemed to dart from her sunk eyes, the universal weakness which prevailed through her whole frame, the trepidation with which she knocks at the door, and the fear and terror least she should be observed craving a relief from false friendship, altogether rendered an object too shocking for human nature to support.[46]

Her words emphasize the reality of Siddons's embodiment of Jane, with her 'apparently emaciated frame' and 'sunk eyes'. As she observes, enjoying the skilful enactment of a fellow human's death throes is a disquieting concept, 'too shocking for human nature to support'. The Lady reasons that we would not take pleasure in this final scene if it were as real as Siddons made it seem, and she finds herself obliged to turn away from the spectacle because she is unable to distinguish between the reality and the fictive representation.

Contemplating the ethics of emotional response, she sees an additional, more significant, problem in the graphic physicality of the staged suffering:

> I was disgusted at the idea, that an event affecting our mortal frame only, should be capable of producing greater misery than the most poignant anguish of the mind. – We wish to have something exalted in the distress to interest us, and there is nothing of that kind in the famishing Shore, whose sufferings have no immediate reference to any but herself; yet, with hearts chilled with horror, we still anxiously wish to follow through her misery.[47]

Because the final act of *Jane Shore* is composed almost entirely of an extended display of Jane's bodily pain, we are asked to sympathize with something which affects her 'mortal frame'; she does not suffer mentally but by contrast feels confident in the morality of her rejection of Richard Gloster and his evil schemes. Is the gush of emotion we feel as we watch a 'creature perishing through want, "fainting from loss of food"' really appropriate? The Lady argues that it is not.

In her comments on *Jane Shore*, she echoes Adam Smith's discussion of the proper objects of sympathy in his *Theory of Moral Sentiments* but applies his more general notions to the specifics of performance. In his discussion of the 'propriety' or appropriateness of sympathetic response, Smith considers the sources of sympathy, those events that prompt sympathetic response from the spectator. Like the Lady, Smith states that our sympathy for another's physical pain, while understandable, is nonetheless limited; we may wince when a man is struck, but we do not actually feel his pain – what we do sympathize with is how he endures his pain. He goes on to point to plays that he finds flawed because of their emphasis on the purely physical suffering of their protagonists: Sophocles' *Philoctetes* and Euripides' *Hippolytus*. When the plays succeed, he notes, 'it is not the pain which interests us, but some other circumstances . . . What a tragedy would that be of which the distress consisted in a colic! Yet no pain is more exquisite.'[48] We cannot sympathize with bodily pain because it is individual: as Smith says of 'appetites of the body'; we feel disgust for them because 'we cannot enter into them'.[49] As a result, Smith, like the Lady, denigrates dramas that depend on the hero's physical pain to arouse compassion and states with some scorn, 'these attempts to excite compassion by the representation of bodily pain, may be regarded as among the greatest breaches of decorum of which the Greek theatre has set the example'.[50]

Smith's comments on drama and spectatorship operate in the realm of theory, as discussed in the previous chapter. Where he considers the moral and aesthetic appropriateness of a character's suffering as the object of sympathy, the Lady turns these ideas back towards the audience. Like Smith, she sees Jane's *physical* sufferings as an inadequate, even improper, catalyst for audience sympathy because those sufferings refer only to Jane and her physical condition. Despite the painfully overwhelming nature of her own response to Isabella's mental torment, the Lady finds such distress more elevated and elevating. Audiences should not identify with Jane as they did with Isabella's mental and emotional sufferings as the sight is gruesome, and the scene should nauseate rather than please us. Nonetheless, as she observes, 'we still anxiously wish to follow her through her misery'. Dror Wahrman cites the passage as evidence of changing understanding of identity; he argues that the Lady is 'disgusted' because she feels that such verisimilitude obliterates the sense of Sarah Siddons as individual. 'Every actor – *pace* Garrick', Wahrman explains, 'is constrained by his own inescapable individual identity.'[51] This argument, however, overlooks the Lady's real source of distress, namely the problematic fact that she cannot control her personal feelings in accordance with her personal beliefs. As with Siddons's representation of Isabella, it is not the actress's identity that is the issue but rather the response that she generates. What is proper in theory does not necessarily translate into reality because emotional response cannot be neatly governed by moral or philosophical guidelines.

This paradox, that while we should recognize that an emphasis on bodily pain is a 'breach of decorum' and remain unmoved, we instead 'anxiously' follow Jane through her misery, demonstrates one of the greatest discontinuities between the theory and practice of sympathy, theatrical response as it should be experienced and the actuality of audience experience. Systems of thought break down in the here and now of performance and the emotions it generates. What the popular accounts of theatregoing in the later eighteenth century indicate, however, is that an audience's emotional response does not adhere to a system and cannot be neatly controlled. The Lady knows she should not in good conscience be deeply moved by the plight of the dying Jane Shore, but against her will she is. The anonymous reviewer's reaction to Siddons's representation of Cleone presents a more disturbing possibility, that against our wills we can sympathize with someone and something we find monstrous, in essence identifying with something so horrible that it shocks sensibility. The fact that the production was halted and the play never again staged in London during the eighteenth century suggests that his concern was experienced by others as well. Appropriate or inappropriate, sympathy cannot be directed; it can occur even when we know that the feeling ought not to be endorsed, a reality that runs counter to the tenants of moral philosophy.

Not everyone was as scrupulous as the Lady in their concern for the source of their sympathy. For many theatregoers, the emotional response was in itself a pleasure; they went to the theatre to feel, and they wanted to feel to excess. For them, the ethical issues she raises are irrelevant. Rather, they take pleasure in the emotion they experience, the synthetic emotion generated by Siddons's performance. It is clear from accounts of Siddons' performances in the 1780s that audiences delighted in their responses to Siddons. If anything, after seeing Siddons as Isabella, some viewers found her subsequent performances a little tame; they missed the thrill Isabella produced, the emotional excitement that was the catalyst for the shrieks, swoons, and hysteria. Miss Bogle, for example, even though she mocks those whose intense feelings lead to shrieks, swoons, or hysterical fits, *wants* to feel something out of the ordinary, something profound. In her poetical account of Siddons's performances in Edinburgh, she criticizes the actress's interpretation of both Mrs Beverley and Jane Shore as dull, even enervating in their affect:

> In the terrible trials of BEVERLEY'S wife,
> She rose not above the dull level of life,
> She was greatly too simple to strike very deep,
> And I thought more than once to have fallen asleep.
> Her sorrows in SHORE, were so soft and so still,
> That my heart lay as snug as a thief in a mill:
> I never as yet have been much overcome,
> With distress that's so simple, with grief that's so dumb.[52]

The problem with these characters is that in them Siddons represents 'the dull level of life', and the result is that this audience member is has not been '[struck] very deep', thus her heart lies 'snug'. She wants Siddons's performance to 'strike' her heart, to be 'overcome' by her emotional response. Miss Bogle goes on to express her preference for the 'tumble' that characterized Mary Ann Yates's performance as Mandane in Arthur Murphy's *Orphan of China* (1759) and as well as the 'storm' of Siddons's performance of Zara from William Congreve's *The Mourning Bride* (1697) and the 'harrowing' that her Isabella produced.

Given this desire to feel, the question arises regarding the extent to which these expressions of feeling, the tears, the fainting fits, and the hysteria, can be considered truly involuntary. Cynical observers raised this point, suggesting that the very public display of feeling was a fashionable affectation. Miss Bogle, for example, refers to the misses who faint because 'it becomes them so vastly', implying that they are doing no more than performing for their own audience. Some cartoonists and illustrators went one step further, representing audiences using sham displays of emotion for their own private ends; in one case while playgoers around her weep, a young lady pretends to faint so that she can surreptitiously pass a note to her lover. Yet even those who questioned the sincerity of these demonstrations in one sentence validate them in the next. At the same time that Miss Bogle denigrates other women in the audience for their overt demonstration of feeling, she herself embraces the sensation of losing control over her emotions. The author of *The Follies of St James's Street* cites hysterical fits and floods of tears as examples of fashionable excess yet also portrays her heroine being sincerely overwhelmed by emotion while watching Siddons in the role of Mrs Beverley. This duality is perhaps best expressed by a reviewer in the *Public Advertiser* for 12 May 1784 who describes a woman who 'was actually for some little time in a strong fit' and then comments 'If this had happened among certain Circles in the Boxes, we should, as we did last year, have supposed it a *Voluntary*. But under the circumstances of last Night, there is every reason to believe it *in* voluntary – *real*.'[53] The reviewer suggests, as did Miss Bogle, that in very visible circles, here the Boxes, displays of emotion were carefully calibrated and potentially fraudulent. However, in this case he dismisses that possibility and identifies it unhesitatingly as *in*voluntary and 'real'.

The line between voluntary and involuntary response is blurred, and determining exactly where it falls is in the end is perhaps irrelevant. As Nicholson comments, 'the theatre is a very good place to spread emotions, as actors are intent on them passing on and audiences expect to be infected'.[54] For Siddons's audiences, the thrill of the theatrical experience existed precisely in this experience of infection, in the individual's experience of being swept along on a tide of emotion, and this effect was enhanced by being part of an audience that watched other spectators perform their own experience of sympathy. Thus, the performer and the audience create a symbiotic connection between the desire to feel, the communal situation, and the social validation of demonstrations of feeling. As spectators such as the Lady of Distinction and the audiences horrified by *Cleone* demonstrate, 'affect may not always inspire happiness',[55] but it was 'catching' nonetheless, and to remain emotionless would have been a worse commentary on themselves and on the performer than even the most painful sensations. As Scott proclaimed, Siddons 'produced the strongest effect which could possibly be exerted by a human being upon her fellow-creatures'; for her audiences her greatness lay in that irresistible emotive power.

* * *

If the theatres of the later eighteenth century were awash with feeling, to what end was all this emotion directed – if any? While Miss Bogle and others of her ilk seem most strongly interested in feeling itself, in the experience of being overwrought, overwhelmed, or harrowed, the Lady desires something more elevated, 'something exalted in the distress to interest us', what Smith might consider the form of sympathy which takes its 'origin from the imagination'.[56] If as audience members we are indeed made agents or participants in the drama that we watch, as the quotation that opened this chapter suggests, what is the ultimate goal of this participatory experience? Or were audiences simply luxuriating in their emotions with onanistic pleasure (an experience that, as Roach demonstrates, was literally the case with Samuel Pepys).[57] This problem is articulated directly by the narrator of *The Follies of St James's Street*, who, speaking not of the events of the novel but of life in general, comments on the hypocrisy of the society woman who gossips happily over the sorrows of others and then 'in the evening, goes into hysterics at Mrs. Beverley, which she knows to be all fiction'.[58] The narrator asks:

> What avails the powers of an admirable actress in awakening the passions, if our sensibility is only shewn to the world, and put on with our best looks, to grace the side-box? What avails, if it mend not the heart, and teach us to feel for real, not fictitious woe? The fair one who weeps for a Calista, acts, perhaps, the very part herself. She who blames a Beverley – is, herself, a gamester. Who admires Cordelia, wounds her parent: and while she approves conjugal and maternal duties, wrongs her husband and neglects her children. Is this an age of sensibility, as it is called?[59]

Like the author of *The Theatrical Portrait* who saw audience members as potential Jane Shores, she points to ways in which the audience may mirror the figures they watch upon the stage, but where the poet uses Siddons's acting to convey an admonitory message to the female members of the audience, this author seeks a broader, more fundamental application for the emotions stirred by the 'admirable actress' (presumably Siddons). The passions aroused by performance, she asserts, should not be an end in themselves. Not only must sensibility be more than superficial, 'only shewn to the world', but it should inculcate personal virtue, what the heroine had hoped would be the result of her husband's identification with the gamester Beverley.

Exploring the same problem of the moral end of emotion, one reviewer sees a more positive view of the workings of sensibility, finding a direct connection between emotion, even the painful emotion experienced when watching Siddons's Isabella, and personal and communal good:

> Mrs. Siddons, in this Part of Isabella ... produced last Night the same sublime and soothing Effects we have always experienced in Isabella. We add the Epithet soothing, because we think with the many – and the Repetition of this Play, frequently beyond every other Drama, shews we think with the many, and that we think right – that the Emotions excited by this Representation, though in the very deepest Degree, are yet not only not repulsive, but in the strongest Manner attracting also. Mimic Sorrows, for us at least, cannot be too profuse and penetrating – The deeper the sweeter! We are soothed and gratified with something like the moral Approbations of Sympathy – the Feelings soften, and as they soften, never fail also to refine![60]

This author finds virtue in the very strength of the emotion he and, importantly, his fellow audience members, feel in the theatre. Such feeling is not simply self directed, nor does it happen in a vacuum, as the author of *Follies* fears. Rather, the reviewer insists that it is the collective experience, demonstrated by the demand for this play, 'frequently beyond every other drama', that verifies the truth of the emotions felt. As he explains, 'we think with the many, and that we think right'; the 'rightness' of the emotion lies in communal nature. By means of the 'Approbations of Sympathy' shared by the audience, emotion becomes moral and reformative. Pausing in his description of Siddons's first season to discuss the impact of her performance in general terms, Siddons's biographer James Boaden expands upon this idea, finding emotion the essential purpose of theatre: 'the whole mystery [of theatre] is in the emotions it raises in us, and the kindred emotions which the wonderful principle of association is sure to awaken. And as when the benevolent emotions are excited, the heart swells and the hand is liberal ... We owe it to the bounty of Providence that we sympathise only with actions that promote the happiness of the species.'[61] Guided by the hand of Providence, audience response is divinely ordained.

Powerful response to the stimulus of performance is, of course, not unique to the eighteenth century. What does distinguish this 'age of sensibility', as the author of *The Follies of St James's Street* labels it, is the intense interest in this response, in articulating what was felt and monitoring the extent and purpose of this feeling. Emotion was the rage, so to speak, and delineating its appearance was an important part of the culture, along with an almost obsessive desire to document how one felt and how one's neighbours felt, thus demonstrating one's immersion in emotion.

The anonymous author's identification of the later eighteenth century as 'an age of sensibility' was shared not only with other spectators but with the playwrights of the later eighteenth century, and the next three chapters explore a series of plays written specifically to appeal to and in some cases to manipulate the emotions of the theatre audience. The first, 'Roman Fathers and Grecian Daughters', explores the ways in which playwrights harnessed the emotions generated by the father–daughter bond, a trope that had particular resonance in the second half of the eighteenth century, and directed them towards specific political and national ends. The final two chapters explore the appeal of affective comedy, beginning with a collection of plays that use sentimental representations of Britain's colonial relations as a means of establishing its troubling identity as an imperial power. The book closes with a study of Richard Cumberland's *The Jew*, a play directed entirely towards the goal of arousing emotion in its audience and through this emotion achieving a specific social end. By focusing on the workings of emotion on the stage and in the auditorium, I seek to explore not simply the plays and their authors but more generally the nature of audience response, and in the process to understand how affective drama operated within the theatre and within the broader culture of Britain and its world.

CHAPTER 3

Roman Fathers and Grecian Daughters: Tragedy and the Nation

> Nothing can be more deeply interesting than the beautiful scene, in the second act, between the father and the daughter.
>
> *London Magazine: Or, Gentleman's Monthly Intelligencer*[1]

Early in the eighteenth century, Richard Steele rhapsodized over the beauties of the filial love between a daughter and her father: 'Certain it is, that there is no Kind of Affection so pure and angelic as that of a Father to a Daughter. He beholds her both with, and without regard to her Sex. In Love to our Wives there is Desire, to our Sons, there is ambition; but in that to our Daughters, there is something which there are no Words to express.'o[2] In Steele's essay, he cites examples of female virtue, singling out a good daughter, aptly named Fidelia, to lead the 'heroines' he cites. Despite his panegyric to fatherly love, Steele dedicates his essay to portraying the faithful daughter's self-sacrificing love for her father. Fidelia puts her father before herself, giving up gay society, suitors, and marriage for his sake; her greatest joy is tending to her father's humblest needs. As Steele ecstatically notes, 'How have I been charmed to see one of the most beauteous Women the Age has produced on her Knees helping on an old Man's Slipper. Her filial Regard to him is what she makes her Diversion, her Business, and her Glory.'[3]

Perhaps words could not express a father's affections, but they could portray the endlessly fascinating sight of the adoring daughter at her father's feet, rejecting her own pleasure to serve him. This idealized view of the loving daughter was one of the most powerful motifs of the mid to later eighteenth century, appearing repeatedly in literature and art. In fiction, the depiction of the father–daughter bond is commonplace (Ruth Perry cites more than a dozen examples ranging from sentimental reunions to the 'dangerous intimacies' of the Gothic novel). Frances Burney's Evelina, for example, spends much of *Evelina* in search of her father; in Elizabeth Inchbald's *A Simple Story*, Miss Milner marries her fatherlike guardian, while her daughter Matilda in turn devotes herself to the stern father she alternately fears and desires. The special bond between father and daughter even shaped the later eighteenth century's most popular conduct book, Dr John Gregory's *A Father's Legacy to His Daughters* (1774), a series of letters written by a 'tender father' on his deathbed to his daughters.

The frequency with which father–daughter ties appear and the intensity with which they are represented has not passed unnoticed. Perry, for example, comments that 'the representation of this consanguineal relationship seemed to pull at the heartstrings of the eighteenth-century English public like no other: sentimental treatment of the father–daughter connection could be counted on to move audiences.'[4] Margaret Doody sees the fascination with the father–daughter connection as almost pathological, writing that 'close relations between father and daughter were insisted on as never before, even to the point of where we can question the emotional health of a culture whose literature gave rise to such elaborate representations of those feelings as we find in England in the eighteenth century'.[5] The words of fictional characters may gush with emotion, but as Doody and Perry along with Caroline Gonda and Elizabeth Kowaleski-Wallace agree, complications lie beneath the sentimental language that sheaths depictions of fathers and daughters, especially in the private world of the eighteenth-century novel.[6]

Examinations of father-daughter relationships in literature have been largely confined to the fiction of the mid-to later eighteenth century, with particular attention devoted to novels such as Richardson's *Clarissa*, Inchbald's *A Simple Story*, and the works of Frances Burney and Maria Edgeworth. Critical works from the 1980s and early 1990s, such as those by Doody, Kowaleski-Wallace, and Lynda Zwinger have tended to read the novels in psychoanalytic terms, dissecting the behaviour of both the characters and of their creators.[7] More recently, scholars such as Gonda and Perry have applied eighteenth-century sociological and legal developments to the novels and writers they discuss. Gonda, for example, places her discussion firmly within the social and legal culture, noting that 'the family is both a microcosm of the wider society, and – if properly regulated – the best assurance of that society's continuing order'.[8] The most wide-ranging of these studies, Perry's *Novel Relations: The Transformation of Kinship in English Literature and Culture, 1748–1818*, includes father–daughter relationships within a larger network of family ties, reading them in terms of ongoing changes in social structures.

With their concern over the psychological and social nature of the father's authority over the daughter, these approaches provide useful insights into the interior world of eighteenth-century fiction; however, they are less effective when applied to the overtly public world of eighteenth-century theatre. On the stage, familial relationships take on broadly political implications, a trend which is especially notable in the serious drama of the second half of the century. These later plays are especially distinctive in their depictions of a childlike father sustained by the strength of his devoted daughter, an idealized relationship that takes on special force in the serious drama of the last decades of the century. Increasingly, the tie between father and daughter becomes the play's emotional centre, constituting a spectacle that drew audiences into the theatres and reliably moved them to tears. Like the daughter lauded by Steele, these daughters reject lovers and husbands to support their father, creating a stage picture that grew in potency as fathers became weaker and daughters stronger. In these plays, romantic love pales in comparison to filial devotion, that 'first law' of nature, a dynamic that recalls Adam Smith's argument that family ties are easier to sympathize with than is romantic love. As he notes, romantic passion is individual while that between parent and child is social.[9] In the public world of eighteenth-century theatre, these relationships become broadly symbolic; in contrast to the private world of Steele's idealized daughter, whose 'Life is designed wholly domestick', and to the daughters that populate so much of the fiction of the period, the actions of their counterparts on the stage take on national importance.

Rereading Daughters: The Case of *King Lear*

Obviously, the representation of intense bonds between fathers and daughters is not unique to the drama of the later eighteenth century. Perhaps the most memorable father–daughter relationships in the drama of the Restoration and the eighteenth century occur early on, in Otway's *Venice Preserv'd* (1682) and Rowe's *The Fair Penitent* (1703). Each play is fraught with familial tension as the daughter rejects her father: in *Venice Preserv'd*, to marry and cleave to her husband, and in *The Fair Penitent* to argue harshly against her father's choice of a husband. By mid-century the nature and purpose of the father–daughter relationship had changed. No longer was it a site of conflict; rather, in these plays the characters reject conflict as the daughters acquiesce to their fathers' wills at almost every juncture. In the very public family dynamic played out upon the stage, the father–daughter relation becomes the ideal stabilizing force, uniting generations, protecting honour, and ultimately restoring kingdoms.

Even works from the previous generation were envisioned in this new light. While much Restoration tragedy focuses on the depiction of marital ties, or the frequently fraught relations of fathers and sons, plays such as Thomas Otway's *Venice Preserv'd* or Nicholas Rowe's *Fair Penitent* interweave portrayals of paternal and daughterly love into their stories of marriages shattered and friendships betrayed. Significantly, however, by the last half of the eighteenth century, critics such as William Hawkins reconstruct earlier plays such as *The Fair Penitent* not as tragedies of sexual sin and betrayal but rather as portrayals of parental failure. Refuting earlier commentaries on the play, Hawkins writes: 'The subject of this play [*The Fair Penitent*] is an excellent moral; it shews in an eminent degree, the dangerous consequence of parents forcing their children into marriage against their own inclinations; and paints nature in a very conspicuous manner.'[10] In contrast to critics in the early eighteenth century, who had labelled Calista a whore, Hawkins claims that she is rather to be pitied and that Sciolto, her father, is 'in the wrong, when he knows she loves Lothario, to force her into marriage with another man'.[11] He concludes his analysis of the play by reconceiving the play as a warning to fathers, claiming at the end that 'as for Sciolto the father, [he] claims scarce any compassion; as he may partly thank himself for all the sorrow and shame he has brought on his old age'.[12]

Nowhere are these rereadings more vivid than in the interpretation and performance of Shakespeare,[13] most notably *King Lear*, a play that could be said to be the *Ur* representation of the father–daughter bond on the eighteenth-century stage. Notably, the power of Lear's pathos was attributed to his position not as fallen king but almost universally to his position as wronged father. Francis Gentleman's 'Introduction' to *King Lear* in *Bell's Shakespeare*, as well as his notes throughout the play, frames the play entirely within the context of father–child relations. While no one, he states, wants to think that 'such a trespass on human nature could exist as filial ingratitude', we know that it does exist; the greatness of Shakespeare's play lies in its ability to expose this vice 'in its proper odious colours and fatal tendency'.[14] Likewise, Arthur Murphy attacks the notion that Lear's madness has its source in the King's fall from power. Instead, Murphy stresses that the play's emotional impact is embodied in Lear's feelings towards his children rather than towards his crown, arguing that Lear is 'driven by the ingratitude of his two eldest daughters to an extreme of madness, which produces the finest tragic distress ever seen on any stage'.[15]

Frances Brooke echoes these sentiments, noting approvingly of Spranger Barry's portrayal of Lear that 'I think it a great mark of judgment in Mr. *Barry*, that he has thrown so strong and affecting a cast of tenderness into the character: he never loses sight of the Father.'[16] In his Jubilee *Ode* (1769), Garrick himself describes the emotional experience Lear provokes in terms of the audience's ability to identify with the spectacle of Lear's distress, distress which he identifies as specifically linked to Lear's position as father:

> Tho' conscious that the vision only seems,
> The woe-struck mind finds no relief:
> Ingratitude would drop the tear,
> Cold-blooded age takes fire,
> To see the thankless children of old Lear,
> Spurn at their king and sire!
> With *his* our reason too grows wild![17]

Whereas the loss of a crown would be a passion most theatregoers could not identify as they would never experience it themselves, 'thankless children' were an all-too-common experience; Garrick not only emphasizes this aspect of Lear but cites it as the source for the audience's sympathetic identification with Lear, an identification so strong that (Garrick claims) we too are in danger of going mad.

Concrete traces of this interpretation of Lear exist within editions of Garrick's *Lear*. Although his version of *Lear* was not published until 1773, when it appeared as part of John Bell's popular edition of Shakespeare, by the 1750s Garrick had begun to replace large segments of Nahum Tate's adaptation with long-unstaged passages from Shakespeare, in particular curtailing Tate's interpolated romance between Edgar and Cordelia and shifting focus instead onto Lear. It is probable that by 1756 Garrick was staging the combination of Tate and Shakespeare that would play at Drury Lane until John Philip Kemble staged his own version in 1795.[18] Garrick's version brought Lear into even greater relief, and one effect of augmenting Lear's role was the corresponding growth of Cordelia's character *as a daughter*, specifically a daughter who tends to her father in his time of need, when he, not she, is in need of protection. On the most fundamental level, Garrick trimmed away large segments of Tate's representation of the secondary plot, de-emphasizing the figures of Edgar, Edmund, and Gloucester and keeping just enough of the Edgar–Cordelia romance to enable Tate's now infamous happy ending. This shift in emphasis can be seen as early as the play's opening scene, as Garrick breaks from Tate to open not with Edmund's soliloquy but with Shakespeare's scene of two gentlemen discussing Lear and his daughters. The depiction of virtuous love represented through the figures of Edgar and Cordelia is likewise truncated, directing attention instead to Lear and his daughters. One such rejection of Tate occurs as Lear divides his kingdom. In Tate, Cordelia explains her seemingly heartless answer to her father as a means of avoiding an unwanted marriage; Garrick removes this explanation and with it Cordelia's romantic motivation for avoiding marriage. He replaces the lines with Shakespeare's, refocusing the scene on the interaction between father and child. (In fact, in Garrick's version, the first suggestion of a love story does not appear until II.iv, and Cordelia does not even mention Edgar until midway through the third act, when – in a scene drawn from Tate – he saves her from Edmund's attempted rape.)

Perhaps most interesting are the specific elements of Tate that Garrick did include. While much of Tate's augmentation of the secondary plot vanishes, the interpolations that remain are almost invariably scenes involving Cordelia, most often those in which she expresses her concern for her father and her desire to succour him in his weakness. Just as Garrick omitted Cordelia's reference to Edgar in the first act, thus shifting the focus back to Lear, he retains speeches from Tate demonstrating Cordelia's concern for her father. In one such example, Cordelia expresses her desire to sacrifice herself for her father:

> With my torn robe to wrap his hoary head,
> With my torn hair to bind his hands and feet,
> Then, with a shower of tears,
> To wash his clay-smeared cheeks, and die beside him.[19]

Similar examples occur in IV.i, and in V.i, when Garrick replaces a Shakespearean scene between Kent and a gentleman with a speech from Tate in which Cordelia bemoans her father's injuries, wishing she could take up arms for his sake. Certainly Shakespeare's *Lear* explores the topic of filial piety and uses the lack of it as the catalyst for the tragedy, but Garrick's adaptation makes such piety the source of pathos, and from this pathos flows our sympathy.

The influence of *King Lear* was widespread, shaping even the most unlikely subjects; Richard Cumberland's adaptation of *Timon of Athens* (1772) presents an especially unexpected example. While Cumberland looks back to Thomas Shadwell's earlier adaptation of *Timon* and, like Shadwell, adds female characters to Shakespeare's predominately male tragedy,[20] the major figure he adds is not a mistress, as in Shadwell's play, but a daughter, and a daughter whose highest goal in life is to tend to her abandoned and despairing father.[21] Much like Lear, this Timon goes mad in the final acts and wanders in the wilderness, regaining his sanity only after the kind ministrations of his devoted daughter, Evanthe.

> Give me your pardon; I have suffer'd much,
> And much I fear sorrow has shook my wits;
> But in the bitterest moments of affliction,
> I have remember'd still to bless my child.[22]

This reunion represents the emotional climax of the play, and this father can drift into death sighing, 'all is well, for thou art in my sight'.[23] Although never revived, Cumberland's play was reasonably successful, with eleven performances in the 1771–1772 season. While the presence of Evanthe may have been designed to construct Timon as a more congenial man, Thomas Davies damned the play specifically because of its portrayal of an incompetent and wastrel father, complaining 'what generous and noble minded man, as Shakespeare has drawn his Timon, would be guilty of such baseness, as to wrong his child, by treating his visitors with the wealth that should be reserved for her portion?'[24] Like Hawkins's comments on *The Fair Penitent*, Davies's indignant response demonstrates the extent to which audiences assessed the quality of the father–daughter bonds represented on the stage and the ways in which they could be applied to a modern context.

Roman Daughters and the Cause of Liberty

Midway between the strained familial bonds of the early eighteenth century and the heroic daughters of its final decades, British drama of the 1750s turned to the ideal of Rome as source for dramatic inspiration. The years between 1750 and 1756 present a fascinating nexus of plays depicting the father–daughter bond as emblematic of a specifically national enterprise, each couched within the framework of Roman history. Here I differ with Brett D. Wilson's reading of later eighteenth-century drama as increasingly masculinized after the ascension of George III, a development he sees as leading to 'the precipitous decline of the female patriot as catalyst of commonwealth',[25] largely because George III appropriated the role of father of his country. Rather, I suggest, the identification of George III as father of his country accentuated the potency of the depiction of father–daughter pairings, and this relationship becomes the catalyst for patriotic feelings on the stage and in the audience. In a movement away from the intensely personal dramas of Otway and Rowe, and from the novels of mid-century, these plays envision filial piety in the public arena, with daughters who define themselves jointly as Romans and daughters, and who, through their deaths, promote the liberty of their fatherland.

The most enduringly popular of the plays from the 1750s, William Whitehead's *The Roman Father* (1750),[26] is based in part on Pierre Corneille's *Horace* (1640), and, like Corneille's play, dramatizes Livy's account of the battle between the Horatii and the Curiatii (*History of Rome*, I.23–26); the story tells of two groups of three brothers who engage in combat to decide the fate of their country. In doing so, they place patriotism above personal ties; they are friends off the battlefield, and one of the Curiatii is betrothed to the sister of the Horatii. In Corneille's hands, the play explores the conflict between public honour and private feelings; its main character, Horace, resolutely puts aside his personal ties, even killing his sister Camille when she bitterly attacks him for killing her lover. Whitehead made several key changes to the storyline that heightened both the play's distress and its potential for sympathetic response, noting that 'the difference of his plan, and characters, would not admit of a strict adherence [to Corneille's play], and often required a total deviation'.[27] In contrast to Corneille, Whitehead deliberately enhances the emotions of his characters, explaining in the 'Advertisement' to the play that it was his endeavour to show a variety of distress, especially in his title character.[28] The play's major departure from its source lies in its focus on the father Horatius and his sorrows and in its depiction of his daughter Horatia, here linked directly to her father by name. Unlike Corneille's Camille, who cannot see beyond her love for one of the Curiatii, Whitehead's character struggles to reconcile her grief for her betrothed and her love for her country, a patriotism so strong it is described as a 'Religion'. Unable to live with her two greatest passions in conflict, she knowingly provokes her brother to kill her, determined to die by the hand of Rome's greatest hero. Patriotism is upheld, but only at the cost of the daughter's suffering.

A second group of Roman tragedies soon followed. Perhaps hoping to trade upon the popularity of Whitehead's play, each used as its source another famous Roman tale, in this case that of Virginius and Virginia. The story would have been familiar to eighteenth-century audiences; taken again from Livy's *History of Rome* (III.44–51), it was reprinted almost word for word in histories and collections of moral tales throughout the century. It chronicles the downfall of the decemvir Appius, who developed an ungovernable passion for Virginia, the daughter of Virginius, a Roman general. When Appius's attempts to woo Virginia were unsuccessful, he collaborated with a fellow patrician to have her falsely proclaimed a slave so that he could possess her. Her father, hearing of the plot, rushed to try and save her. He could not prevail upon the lictors of Rome to stop the proceedings, and, in order to keep his daughter chaste and thus a true daughter of Rome, Virginius plunged a knife into her breast, an act that ultimately resulted in Appius's downfall.

This story had a long history in literature, appearing in *Roman de la Rose* and *The Canterbury Tales*, as well as providing the plot for John Webster's final play.[29] But the tale held special resonance for eighteenth-century audiences, with the threat to Virginia's personal liberty emblematic of the fate of Rome and its citizens – and by extension Britain itself. Between 1709 and 1782, the topic generated four plays (one unstaged) and an opera.[30] Remarkably, three of the plays appeared within a two-year period in the mid 1750s: Samuel Crisp's *Virginia* (first staged in February 1754), John Moncreiff's *Appius* (first staged in February 1755), and Frances Brooke's unstaged *Virginia* (pub. 1756). In contrast to John Dennis's earlier *Appius and Virginia* (1709), all three plays centre around the relationship between Virginia and Virginius and its tragic yet triumphant conclusion. Where Dennis used his final act to showcase hand-to-hand combat between Virginia's suitor Icilius and Appius, emblematic of the struggle of liberty against tyranny,[31] in these plays the focus is not only on the father and daughter but on a daughter who defines herself jointly as 'a Roman Maid, and Daughter to Virginius',[32] and who, through her death, represents the cause of liberty.

Despite the story's general appeal, no eighteenth-century version achieved lasting success. In his commentary on Crisp's *Virginia* in *Biographia Dramatica* (1782), David Erskine Baker remarks more generally of the story that it is 'truly dramatic, and formed as it were to be the subject of a tragedy'.[33] He continues on to deplore the fact that, despite such potential, it had never been effectively dramatized:

> How much is it to be lamented, that the immortal Shakespeare, who had in so many instances made history his own; or that the pathetic Rowe, whose merit in scenes of domestic distress, and the conduct of historical incidents, and who has even hinted at this very story in his *Fair Penitent*; had not undertaken the task; and given us, by that means, as frequent occasion of sympathising with the distress of a *Virginia*, as we have at present of weeping for a *Juliet* or a *Desdemona*, a *Jane Shore* or a *Calista*.[34]

While Crisp, Moncrieff, and Brooke certainly lack the talent of Shakespeare and Rowe, Baker does not consider the possibility that the problem with Virginia is not in the writing but in the story itself. When confronted with death, Virginia feels no distress – how could she when to do so would suggest that the cause of liberty results in innocent suffering? These plays thus represent an interesting problem – the draw of sympathy versus the use of a Roman tale as patriotic fable. This is likely one reason why *The Roman Father* had a longer life upon the stage; Horatius's and Horatia's distress is graphically represented, but this distress is not linked with the cause of Roman triumph. Unlike Whitehead's Horatia, the eighteenth century's Virginia is never torn between duty and love. In her eyes, her father is a metonym for Rome; loving him is no different from loving her country.

Despite the absence of affecting distress, these depictions of Virginia and her willingness to give up all for her father were very much of their time. With hostilities against the French ongoing in the American colonies and the Seven Years War looming in Europe, the plays provide a reassuring representation of Roman/British liberty triumphant against the threat of tyranny, tyranny most often coded as foreign and in particular as French. With filial piety and patriotism aligned, romantic love operates in opposition to nationalism, and thus, unlike so many novels written just a few decades later, love must be rejected in favour of the stronger and more 'natural' bond between father and daughter. In these plays, the father sacrifices the willing daughter for the greater good. By contrast, it is the male lover who succumbs to passion and who is denigrated as a lesser patriot because of it.

Crisp's *Virginia* was the most memorable of the three mid-century plays, with a moderate run of eleven days in 1754. (Baker notes that it was acted 'with some success and indeed not undeservedly'.[35]) Although to Crisp's annoyance it was never revived,[36] it was reprinted three times, once in Dublin and twice in the last decades of the century, and was even anthologized in *Bell's British Theatre* (volume eighteen, published in 1777), unlike any other version of the Virginia and Virginius story. While not as undramatic as *The Monthly Review*'s attack on the play as 'uninteresting' and unaffecting would suggest,[37] Crisp's fusing of patriotic and family bonds is rarely subtle. Thus, when Virginia is confronted by her lover who asks her to defy her father's wishes, she reacts with scorn:

> Away ICILIUS!
> It seems, thou know'st me not – Hast thou forgot,
> I am VIRGINIUS' daughter? – Would'st thou cancel
> The bond of my obedience? Learn to render
> Thy passion worthier of thyself and me!
> Learn to respect my duty, and my glory;
> For tho' I love, yet still I am a Roman!

To which Icilius replies:

> Farewell to all my hopes! – VIRGINIA's heart,
> Which once I fondly thought my own, it seems
> Is Roman all! And in the blaze of glory,
> Love's weaker flame is lost! (61)

Virginia defines herself specifically in relation to her father: 'it seems, thou know'st me not . . . I am VIRGINIUS's daughter' – this fact of identity not only determines her behaviour but also establishes her as a Roman. In order to demonstrate her love for Rome, then, she must obey her father's wishes and such an act is in itself both glorious and patriotic. In contrast to Whitehead's Horatia, whose heart is torn between her lover and her country – and whose relationship with her father is therefore fraught – Virginia suffers no such conflict. As Icilius himself observes, her love for him is a 'weaker flame'. If her heart is 'Roman all', then loving her father is the same as loving her country.

Crisp repeats this conflation of father and fatherland throughout the play as Virginia reiterates her faith in her father, tying this faith to her national identity. Thus, even as Virginius cringes from the idea of killing his beloved daughter, she reassures him that

> – whatever be
> The purpose of your soul (it must be noble,
> Since 'tis my father's) oh, unfold it all!
> I will not shrink, but meet it as becomes
> A Roman Maid, and Daughter to VIRGINIUS!" (60)

When her father reveals his purpose to her at the last as she is about to be dragged into slavery, Virginia states 'my soul feels, and owns the deed is noble, / And worthy of my father!' (70). Stabbing her, Virginius exclaims 'thus / The only way I can, I set thee free!' (71). By setting Virginia 'free' – and displaying the 'hot knife, smoking with blood' – Virginius figuratively is able to 'reach the tyrant's heart' by inciting rebellion (74). The play ends with Virginia and Rome freed from tyranny, as Virginius proclaims the triumph of 'fair Liberty'.

It is hard not to read Crisp's play in terms of his own personal history, given the tragedy's idealization of the father and self-abnegating daughter that he would later enact with Frances Burney. Margaret Doody, one of the few scholars to consider Crisp's *Virginia*, turns to it in her discussion of Burney and her relationship with the two 'Daddys' in her life. For Doody, the play represents the type of father–daughter bond that obsessed the later eighteenth century in which 'the father is intense and tender, even when exerting authority in licensed destruction', a dynamic which, she suggests was played out in the Burney household.[38] While the dynamic might have a personal resonance for Crisp later in life, at the time the play was written, Frances was not even two years old and thus unlikely to have influenced Crisp's choice of topic. Rather, the 'intense and tender' relationship that Doody describes is clearly drawn in political terms specific to its era, enacting a national drama rather than a private bond.

One year later, Covent Garden presented its own version of the story, John Moncreiff's *Appius. A Tragedy*, again with relative success, running for eight nights in February and early March. As its title indicates, Moncreiff's play focuses firmly on the evils of tyranny, and, even more so than Crisp's *Virginia*, frames itself within an expressly national context. The Prologue encourages the audience to link the fate of Rome to that of Britain through an interesting brand of national sympathy:

> Each Hardship, ev'ry Obstacle surpast,
> *Virginius* comes upon the Stage at last;
> That Father comes, whose dire, whose mournful Deed
> *Rome* from the bloody Yoke of *Appius* freed.
> For this his Name was to his Country dear –
> What drew the *Roman*, claims the *British* Tear. (Reverse italics)

This call for sympathy focuses upon Virginius rather than Virginia, upon the father who must cast the blow rather than upon the daughter who welcomes it. It is the father who struggles, not the daughter, and a British audience can sympathize with Virginius because his action represents the cause of liberty; the heartsick father stabs his daughter in order to protect her freedom and in the process prompts the downfall of the figure who had condemned her, and by extension the Roman state, to slavery. By contrast, the daughter has the easier task, at least according to the play's political logic. Her love for her father is patriotic as well as filial so that accepting his blow fulfils both her desire for her father's love as well as her need for personal and political freedom. Given this approach, it is no surprise that Baker complains that Moncreiff's play (and Crisp's as well) provide no 'occasion of sympathising with the distress of a *Virginia*'.

Even the Epilogue, which is largely comic, ends by reiterating the connection between Roman and English virtue as demonstrated through the play's events – and sets it as well within a contemporary context:

> This must be *Roman, English*, or Romance: –
> Such Virtue would not be believ'd in *France*. (Reverse italics)

Moncreiff included his own 'Occasional Epilogue' when *Appius* was published; more explicitly topical than the original, it links the greatness of the British empire to its status as a parliamentary monarchy, unlike Rome which fell into vice and anarchy without a monarch. This strident patriotism becomes problematic as Moncreiff struggles to reconcile the play's equation of Roman and British love of liberty with his attack on 'the Frail Form' of a republic and his reification of the English monarch's 'godlike' power.[39] As Moncreiff's somewhat muddled bombast suggests, the story of Virginia was inescapably political.

The third dramatization of the tale, Frances Brooke's *Virginia* (1756), was never staged. (It is likely that Brooke's annoyance over this experience provided the foundation for the depiction of fledgling playwright Maria in *The Excursion*, Brooke's 1777 novel with its satirical look at Garrick and the theatre business.) Brooke's play adheres to strict Senecan ideals of tragedy, with all the substantive action occurring offstage so that the stabbing of Virginia is never seen, and even her cry of pain is announced rather than heard; only in the play's final moments does she enter, dying. Yet it, like Crisp's and Moncreiff's versions, links Virginia's fate with the cause of liberty. When Virginia's plight is made public, 'All Romans' cry as one 'Liberty! Virginia!';[40] 'Is not Virginia's Cause, the Cause of Rome,/ of Liberty, and Virtue?' exclaims one loyal general.[41] Brooke's version is perhaps most notable in that it diverges from other historical and dramatic representations in showing Virginia herself producing the dagger – in the historical account Virginius seizes a knife from a butcher shop while in Crisp's tragedy Virginius pulls his own weapon. Bidding farewell to her lover, she gives her father the fatal dagger, demonstrating an element of personal agency absent in all other versions. While such a moment of agency is both fleeting and self-destructive, it hints at the active and even forceful daughters to follow in the later decades of the century – figures who were to provide the occasion for sympathy in a way that no Virginia ever could.

'Wonder-Working Virtue'

If *King Lear* was the prototype for later eighteenth-century representations of fathers and daughters, the subject found its most intense representation in Arthur Murphy's *The Grecian Daughter*, a play immensely popular with eighteenth-century audiences but largely overlooked today.[42] *The Grecian Daughter* first appeared in February 1772 at Drury Lane to 'great applause'; it featured Anne Barry as the title character, while her husband played the role of her father, as he had in *King Lear* and *Timon of Athens*. Barry's performance as a dutiful daughter would have been familiar to her audience – she debuted Murphy's character in the same season that she appeared as both Cordelia and Evanthe. Murphy's version of the motif, however, was a success, unlike Cumberland's grafting of daughterly devotion onto a strikingly unsentimental play, and Barry was widely acclaimed for her strong, emotional performance as Euphrasia. The play was staged more than a hundred times over the next thirty years, at one point sparking a theatrical battle between Drury Lane and Covent Garden with Mrs Barry (now Mrs Crawford), performing at Covent Garden while Sarah Siddons, the rising star of the London stage, appeared at Drury Lane.[43] The theatrical contest between the two actresses was much anticipated by London audiences; Daniel Malthus, for example, wrote to his son, the young Thomas Robert Malthus, expressing the general anticipation: 'the contention is to be in The Grecian Daughter I hear; but you shall know more of this matter'.[44] Although Crawford was praised for her 'affecting' qualities, it was Siddons, with her display of noble heroism, who eventually won this particular war. Euphrasia, the titular Grecian daughter, would become one of her most popular roles.[45]

Unlike the Roman daughters of the 1750s, *The Grecian Daughter* survived as a powerful dramatic event for more than seventy years. A part in any major actress's repertoire, Euphrasia was performed routinely not only by Siddons but also, forty-five years later, by her niece Fanny Kemble as well.[46] In 1834, Siddons's biographer Thomas Campbell notes that 'since its first appearance, sixty-three years ago, there has not been a great tragic actress who has not felt the part of *Euphrasia* worthy of her ambition'.[47] One measure of its widespread popularity is the extent to which it was established in literary and popular culture as, for example, in actress-author

Mary Robinson's novel *The Natural Daughter* (1799), where one of the two heroines makes her stage debut in the role of the Grecian Daughter, taking the town by storm and being heralded (at least temporarily) as a second Siddons.[48]

The Grecian Daughter, with this long history of popularity, presents an intriguing demonstration of the unique power of performance. While applauded for its propriety of expression, it was rarely praised for its fine verse or dramatic construction. In fact, as several critics noted, acts three and four flagged noticeably and the language was in places decidedly turgid. As Elizabeth Inchbald commented nearly forty years after its premiere, the play's reception was decidedly 'peculiar', 'ha[ving] been so rapturously applauded on the stage, and so severely criticised in the closet'.[49] Campbell described the play as 'a tolerable tragedy in all but the words',[50] noting that its virtues were best seen in performance, when it achieved what Inchbald had described as 'charms more theatrical' than better written dramas. *The Grecian Daughter*, with its distinct 'peculiarity' and easily recognizable literary flaws, exemplifies the radical distinction between event and artefact that constitutes theatrical experience. The continued success enjoyed by Murphy's play can be traced to the response generated by two central incidents, those moments when the title character performs thrilling acts of filial piety. The effect of watching these scenes prompted applause – applause that was not possible when the play was simply read.

Murphy bases his play on a story popular in both popular culture and high art. Taken from a passage in Valerius Maximus's *Memorable Deeds and Sayings* (*Factorum et dictorum memorabilium novem libri*, c. 30), the tale involves a parent thrown into prison and a good daughter, who rescues him. Unable to bring her starving father food or drink, the daughter saves him from certain death by feeding him with her own milk. The ruler who had imprisoned the father is so moved by this act of 'charity' that he frees him, and thus the daughter once again saves her parent. While Valerius Maximus actually cites two stories, the first portraying the good daughter saving her mother, it was the second, in which the daughter, Pero, nurses her father, Cymon, that endured.[51] Often referred to simply as 'Roman Charity', the story of Cymon and Pero inspired dozens of paintings and sculptures, including works by Rubens, Cerrini, and Murillo and, in the eighteenth century, Jean-Baptiste Greuze *c.* 1767 and Johan Zoffany *c.* 1769. So recognizable was it as the occasion for popular art that Vermeer even includes a representation of Cymon and Pero in the background of the genteel drawing room that forms the setting for 'The Music Lesson'.

Figure 3.1 Johan Zoffany. *Roman Charity*, *c.* 1769. Oil on canvas, 76.3 x 63.5 cm. National Gallery of Victoria, Melbourne, Felton Bequest, 1932 (4614–3).

The elements of these images are universal and combine the eroticism of the grown man suckling at the woman's exposed breast with the religious overtones of the madonna-like daughter, all set against the forbidding backdrop of a prison cell (see Figure 3.1).[52] This specific account of a feeble father and his dutiful daughter had a long history in print as well, appearing in the form of a frequently reprinted (and even anthologized) broadside ballad.[53] Once again, the illustration depicts the daughter furtively nursing her father, although in this example the guards are clearly visible, emphasizing the daughter's dedication by making visible the risk she takes.

In Murphy's hands, the story becomes more elaborate. The nursing incident remains the centre of the play (both literally and figuratively), but it is complemented by an extension of the heroic daughter's role. In this version, although in no other representation, the daughter, Euphrasia, not only saves her father, Evander, from starvation, but with her own hand destroys the tyrant who has imprisoned her father and usurped his throne. In marked contrast to the Roman plays of the previous generation in which daughters willingly put their lives into their fathers' hands, *The Grecian Daughter* depicts a woman who takes complete responsibility for her father's life and, in the process, for the future of her country.

As Elizabeth Inchbald wryly notes, 'the men's characters have been all sacrificed by the author to the valour of the woman – he has made his female do the deed of a man, and his best man perform the act of a child'. (She adds subsequently that although Evander is the main male role, no actor likes to take on the part because the character is so infirm and so secondary.)[54]

A distilled representation of filial piety, Murphy's play consists of little beyond Euphrasia's search for her father and her two attempts to save him against all odds; the rest of the play is in essence merely filler, a quality noted by contemporary commentary on the play. A review of the play in *The London Magazine: Or, Gentleman's Monthly Intelligencer* observes that

> It is impossible to avoid remarking a very essential fault in the general management of the piece. That is, that the *interest* does not keep pace with the progress of the *action*. Nothing can be more deeply interesting than the beautiful scene, in the second act, between the father and the daughter; and the catastrophe, in the fifth, affords one of the finest theatrical situations that has ever been exhibited. But between these two, through the whole third and fourth acts, we find nothing to excite anxious emotion, hardly anything even to fix attention.[55]

Even with this lack of action, *The Grecian Daughter* clearly did satisfy the need for the experience of 'anxious emotion' on the part of the audience, an experience that was strong enough to generate the phenomenal stage success of what could be said to be a mediocre play.

The theme of daughterly devotion is introduced as soon as Euphrasia appears on the stage. Although described in conventionally feminine terms as possessing a 'gentle nature' that will 'rave with impotence of sorrow'[56] at news of her father's fate, in reality her character is heroic rather than timid. In contrast to Shakespeare's Cordelia, who scolds her sisters for their (supposed) willingness to set their father above their husbands, Murphy emphasizes his heroine's willingness to let her father 'be all'[57] as Euphrasia rejects her marital bond in deference to those higher ties to her father:

> The Gods can witness how I lov'd my Phocion.
> And yet I went not with him. Could I do it?
> Could I desert my father? Could I leave
> The venerable man, who gave me being,
> A victim here in Syracuse, nor stay
> To watch his fate, to visit his affliction,
> To cheer his prison-hours, and with the tear
> Of filial virtue bid ev'n bondage smile? (7)

Tearing her unweaned child from her breast, she demonstrates that even maternal love comes second to what Murphy, following Valerius Maximus, described as 'the *first* law of nature' (my emphasis).

The 'beautiful scene in the second act' cited by the *London Magazine* incorporates the act of 'Roman charity' taken from Valerius and familiar to eighteenth-century audiences (as the *Monthly Review* commented, 'everyone knows the famous and affecting Story of the *Roman Charity*, immortalized by pen and pencil').[58] Notably, Murphy's theatrical rendition of this well-known scene contains virtually no action; the central 'event' takes place in narration and in the familiar image this narrative creates in the mind of the audience. As depicted in the play, Euphrasia arrives at the remote location where her father has been imprisoned, and there is no need for Murphy to provide a physical representation of the scene that follows once Evander and Euphrasia retreat into a cave at the back of the stage. The audience, familiar with the story and with the widespread popular images of the act itself, needs only a verbal description to recreate the image when the guard Philotas exits to warn Euphrasia of approaching danger. Returning from the cave with 'sudden haste' and 'pale disorder'd look', Philotas exclaims:

> O! I can hold no more; at such a sight
> Ev'n the hard heart of tyranny would melt
> To infant softness. Arcas, go, behold
> The pious fraud of charity and love;
> Behold that unexampled goodness; see
> Th' expedient sharp necessity has taught her;
> Thy heart will burn, will melt, will yearn to view
> A child like her. (24–25)

Even without the benefit of physical representation, the audience can, as Philotas's words indicate, participate in the emotional response appropriate to the scene; their hearts can melt – and even the obdurate heart of the tyrant could not be immune.

The intensity of Philotas's emotion and the vividness of his description allow his two audiences, both Arcas and the larger audience in the theatre's auditorium, to, in Adam Smith's words, 'render as perfect as possible, that imaginary change of situation upon which [this] sympathy is founded' (21). When Arcas questions Philotas about the nature of this 'pious fraud', Philotas explains the source of his response, and this favourite tale of filial piety is told once again, first as a general outline and next with the specific brush strokes that allow the audience to visualize the act they cannot see so that, as the *Monthly Review* explains, 'the heart would so feelingly improve the exquisite tenderness of the scene'.[59]

> Wonder-working virtue!
> The father foster'd at his daughter's breast! –
> O! Filial piety! – The milk design'd
> For her own offspring, on the parent's lip
> Allays the parching fever.
>
> [. . .]
>
> on the bare earth
> Evander lies; and as his languid pow'rs
> Imbibe with eager thirst the kind refreshment,
> And his looks speak unutterable thanks,
> Euphrasia views him with the tend'rest glance,
> Ev'n as a mother doating on her child,
> And, ever and anon, amidst the smiles
> Of pure delight, of exquisite sensation,
> A silent tear steals down; the tear of virtue,
> That sweetens grief to rapture.
> All her laws
> Inverted quite, great Nature triumphs still. (25)

The scene presents a seeming paradox: the father becomes the child, the daughter the parent, giving to her father that most intimate form of aid. The 'natural' law of patriarchy in which the father rules, protects, controls, would seem indeed to be inverted here, yet 'Nature' still triumphs because filial piety is observed.

Overwhelmed by the sight, the guards themselves dissolve in tears, as Arcas exclaims: 'The tale unmans my soul' (25), and, unmanned as they are, this spectacle, which they have recreated for the theatre audience, propels them to assist Euphrasia and save her father. While the 'unmanning' of men may seem yet another inversion of 'nature's laws', it is the proper response as it leads to the restoration of the proper political order; moved by the scene he has witnessed, Philotas declares, 'Thou are my king, and now no more my pris'ner' (26). Notably, it is not simply the act of saving Evander that is crucial here but the effect that witnessing such an act has upon others. Murphy thus dramatizes concepts advanced by Scottish Enlightenment figures such as Smith and Kames. The guards' behaviour illustrates Kames's argument that the sight of virtue moves others to virtuous action while also demonstrating Smith's conviction that sympathy such as that exhibited by Philotas and Arcas results in a properly structured moral society. By narrating the crucial scene rather than providing a physical representation, Murphy skilfully shifts the emphasis onto the experience of the spectator rather than the central figures (whose physical interaction cannot be fully realized on stage). Through the words and response of these mediating figures, we are instructed on how we, as a properly sympathetic audience, should respond, and like Philotas, our 'sympathizing hearts' should 'feel the touch of soft Humanity', a feeling that is its own reward (72). The erotic overtones inherent in the artistic renditions of the act fade while the political implications of filial piety become more prominent, and the event becomes public rather than intimate. The daughter who saves her father saves her state.

The image Murphy evoked was as popular on stage as it was in the visual arts, with Murphy lauded for the emotive nature of his dramatization. Large segments of the scene were quoted verbatim in *The Critical Review, The Gentleman's Magazine*, and *The Theatrical Review; or, New Companion to the Play-House*; writers described it as 'deeply interesting', 'beautiful', or, even more hyperbolically, as one of the most affecting incidents in recorded history. Inchbald notes that dramatizing the incident of Roman charity required considerable restraint:

> Perhaps, of all the incidents recorded in history, that filial piety, on which the fable of this play is founded, may be classed among the most affecting – yet it was one of the most hazardous for a dramatist to adopt; for nothing less than complete skill could have given to this singular occurrence effective force, joined to becoming delicacy. In this arduous effect Mr. Murphy has evinced the most exact judgment, and the nicest execution.[60]

Inchbald's comments outline succinctly the dangers and the rewards of staging the famous tale, both rooted in the inherently public nature of theatre. Because of the act's intimacy, it must be represented discretely (with 'becoming delicacy'), yet it must at the same time be rendered publicly recognizable in order to have sufficient emotional impact, what Inchbald describes as 'effective force'. The creation of this experience is the challenge that Murphy overcomes so successfully in a work that *reads* as mediocre. The fact that Inchbald and so many others before her found the scene so profoundly affecting demonstrates the power of performance in the generation of emotional response.

The Imperial Daughter

The Grecian Daughter's climax, the moment the *London Magazine* had described as 'one of the finest theatrical situations that has ever been exhibited', provided a very different sort of emotional impact. In the play's final scenes, the good daughter acts not simply as her father's personal saviour but as the saviour of her fatherland. The 'unexciting' third and fourth acts (to use the *London Magazine*'s terminology) set up the final catastrophe: Euphrasia hides her father in the tomb of her mother; finding them, the tyrant Dionysius threatens to kill Evander if Euphrasia does not send a message halting the Greek attack.[61] Appropriately, this second physical threat to Evander prompts an even grander, more public, triumph. Inchbald glosses this 'last, and greatest incident of all' as an imperial triumph, one that 'fills every mind with enthusiasm in the cause of virtue and justice – in the cause of empire made free by the overthrow of its tyrant'.[62]

Before the usurper Dionysius can execute Evander, Euphrasia herself seizes a dagger in her father's defence, exclaiming:

EUPHRASIA Now one glorious effort! *(Aside.)*
DIONYSIUS Let me dispatch; thou traitor, thus my arm –
EUPHRASIA A daughter's arm, fell monster, strikes the blow.
Yes, first she strikes; an injur'd daughter's arm
Send thee devoted to th' infernal gods. *(Stabs him.)*
DIONYSIUS Detested fiend! – Thus by a woman's hand! – *(He falls.)*
EUPHRASIA Yes, tyrant, yes; in a dear father's cause
A woman's vengeance tow'rs above her sex.
DIONYSIUS May curses blast thy arm! May Aetna's fires
Convulse the land; to its foundation shake
The groaning isle! May civil discord bear
Her flaming brand through all the realms of Greece;
And the whole race expire in pangs like mine! *(Dies)* (70–71)

As the wording of Dionysius's speech makes clear, Euphrasia's act is more than the private affair of a daughter protecting her father; rather, it constitutes a specifically political act: namely the overthrow of a ruler. Tellingly he curses not Euphrasia (as, for example, Lear curses Regan and Goneril) but rather all of Sicily, calling for natural disasters, civil war, and ultimate extermination. Euphrasia's response partakes of the same rhetoric:

> Behold, all Sicily behold! – The point
> Glows with the tyrant's blood. Ye slaves, *(to the guards)* look there;
> Kneel to your rightful king; the blow for freedom
> Gives you the rights of men! – And, oh! My father,
> My ever honour'd sire, it gives thee life.
> *Evander.* My child; my daughter; sav'd again by thee! (71)

He embraces her, trumpets sound, and the troops arrive, making clear the fact that Euphrasia needs no outside aid; her heroic act is the culmination of a struggle for the safety of her father and the freedom of her country. Much as Virginius used his bloody dagger to incite rebellion, Euphrasia uses hers, 'glow[ing] with the tyrant's blood', to signal a nation's liberation.

Here, however, the father remains passive while his daughter slays the despot in contrast to *Virginia*, where the sacrifice of the daughter serves the dual purpose of saving her country and preserving her virginity. In fact, if this daughter *had* remained a virgin, her father and her country would have been lost – a point the broadside ballad emphasizes in its closing lines. (Despite having disapproved of the daughter's marriage, the father recognizes that without it she could not have saved his life: 'Her Father ever after that / loved her as his Life: / And bless'd the Day when she was made / a Vituous [*sic*] Loving WIFE'.)

In *The Grecian Daughter*, as in the Roman plays of the mid eighteenth century, the body of the daughter determines the fate of the country; in the earlier examples, the daughter's body is the site of the struggle between the usurper and the father cum patriot; the father penetrates the daughter with his phallic dagger to prevent the tyrant from penetrating the daughter. Through her death, the daughter is saved from rape and Rome from tyranny. In Murphy's play, it is the maternal body of the daughter that resurrects her father, the emblem of his kingdom, and her martial arm that destroys the tyrant who threatens them both. The political implications of the maternal daughter are spelled out in the play's closing moments. As in the final scene of Tate's *King Lear*, where Lear, newly restored to his kingdom, bestows it upon Cordelia and Edgar, Evander entrusts his country to his daughter's rule, asking her to parent the land as she has parented him. Calling down a blessing from the gods, he prays

> that she may prove,
> If e'er distress like mine invade the land,
> A parent to her people; stretch the ray
> Of filial piety to times unborn,
> That men may hear her unexampled virtue
> And learn to emulate THE GRECIAN DAUGHTER! (72)

As in the second act, Murphy explicitly links filial piety to proper governance by stressing that it is not women who must imitate Euphrasia, but men. This is the stirring moral that reviewers of the play commended and a reminder that in the case of the Grecian Daughter, filial piety is a patriotic rather than a domestic act.[63]

This vision of parenting on a national scope was peculiarly appealing in the later eighteenth century. Murphy's Postscript to *The Grecian Daughter* provides clues to this attraction. After explaining the source of his play, he discusses the original story recounted by Valerius Maximus in which the good daughter rescues her mother from prison, quoting the passage at length and adding:

> 'This incident might, at the first view, be thought repugnant to the order of nature, if TO LOVE OUR PARENTS were not the FIRST LAW stampt by the hand of Nature on the human heart.' Thus far VALERIUS MAXIMUS. He goes on in the same place, and tells a Greek tale, in which the heroine performs the same act of piety to a father in the decline of life. For the purposes of the drama, the latter story has been preferred. (n.p.)

The obvious question arises, how does changing the sex of the parent, the only difference between the two stories, make one plot line more inherently 'dramatic' than the other? Clearly, given the longevity of the play, its popularity, and its highly visible role in later eighteenth-century popular culture, Murphy was correct in his assessment of dramatic merit; the daughter nurturing the father clearly enhanced the play's affective qualities, making it more advantageous for dramatic representation. Significantly, had Murphy chosen to dramatize the mother–daughter bond, his play would, of necessity, have become a domestic drama, limited to the private world of home and family. With the father, the play becomes public and ultimately imperial. Herein lies one source of its popularity *as theatre*. This dynamic of civic rather than individual feeling presents an interesting contrast to the many paintings of so-called 'Roman Charity'. As painted, the scene is invariably intimate (as seen in Figure 3.1); set within the confines of a prison cell, these renditions focus on the physical union between father and daughter. By contrast, *The Grecian Daughter* is overtly public even in its representation of private family relationships. The father is a king, and his misery signals the downfall of both a man and a kingdom.

Murphy enhances this grand effect by historicizing the play's setting in order to give it added gravitas. As he explains in the Postscript, 'the Author has taken the liberty to place it in the reign of DIONYSIUS the Younger, at the point of time when TIMOLEON laid siege to SYRACUSE. The general effect, it was thought, would be better produced, if the whole had an air of real history' (n.p.). Murphy's choice is not based on aesthetic principles but rather from his desire to provoke the strongest possible response from his audience. In the midst of an attack on indecorously humorous epilogues, *The Grecian Daughter*'s epilogue spells out the significance attendant on the play's sweeping action:

> A Father rais'd from Death, a Nation sav'd.
> A Tyrant's crimes by Female Spirit brav'd,
> That Tyrant stabb'd, and by her nerveless arm,
> While Virtue's Spell surrounding Guards could charm!
> Can she, this sacred tumult in her breast,
> Turn Father, Freedom, Virtue, all to Jest? (6–7)

Father, freedom, and virtue are intrinsically linked through Euphrasia's heroism; laughter is inappropriate after the exalted emotions such actions should have prompted.

The success of Murphy's decision to reject domestic in favour of imperial drama can be seen in responses to the play's final scene, that moment Inchbald designates the 'last, and greatest incident of all', when Euphrasia 'fills every mind with enthusiasm in the cause of virtue and justice – in the cause of empire made free by the overthrow of its tyrant'.[64] For audiences in this expansionist era, this figure of Euphrasia represents the daughter as a heroic ideal – woman as both nurturer and protector – an ideal image of British imperialism. Where the 'beautiful' scene in the second act is performative in the imagination of the audience rather than on the stage, the final scene 'fills the mind with enthusiasm' through its vivid action, captured most impressively in the vision of Euphrasia striking down the usurper,[65] here represented with Sarah Siddons in the title role (Figure 3.2). At this moment, the daughter is the force of justice and virtue; she is the defender of the greater realm and all that it stands for. The triumph of Euphrasia endorses the viability of such a realm while the rhetoric of 'liberty' versus tyranny that permeates the play's final act links it none too subtly to England and its own growing empire.

Heroic Loveliness

It was this vision of Euphrasia as parent to her country as well as to her father that Sarah Siddons embodied so successfully. While today we tend to remember Siddons in terms of her many Shakespearean roles, perhaps especially for her rendition of Lady Macbeth, her contemporaries included Euphrasia among her most memorable roles. She played the Grecian Daughter as early as 1777 in York and in Bath 1780, two years before her triumphant return to London. After opening at Drury

Figure 3.2 *Sarah Siddons as Euphrasia.* Hand-tinted engraving by Caroline Watson, from a painting by Robert Edge Pine. 1784. Courtesy of the Lewis Walpole Library, Yale University.

Lane as Isabella, she turned next to Euphrasia, again to rapturous applause. While Siddons clearly depicted the pain Euphrasia feels at the plight of her father, the dominant tone of her performance was grandeur not pathos, and this impression dominates descriptions of her performance. James Boaden, for example, stresses the awe-inspiring qualities Siddons brought to the role, noting that the 'settled sorrow' she had displayed as Isabella 'had given way to a mental and personal elasticity obviously capable of efforts "above heroic". Hope seemed to brighten her crest and duty to nerve her arm.'[66] The role was a perfect showpiece for her acting abilities, certainly more so than lighter Shakespearean roles such as Juliet (a play Boaden disliked intensely). In Boaden's words,

> The person of Mrs. Siddons rather courted the regal attire, and her beauty became more vivid from the decorations of her rank. The commanding height and powerful action of her figure, though always feminine, seemed to tower beyond her sex. Till this night [her first appearance in *The Grecian Daughter*] we had not heard the full extent, nor much of the quality of her voice ... The audience trembled

> when, in a voice that never broke nor faltered in its climax, she thus to earth and heaven denounced the tyrant.[67]

Siddons emphasized the heroic qualities of Murphy's character, with her regal bearing and garb. Seeming to 'tower beyond her sex', she becomes an almost androgynous figure, especially, one would imagine, when compared with the feeble and hardly regal Evander. Boaden hastens to assure his readers that despite this grandeur she is nonetheless feminine, even when her righteous fury caused her audience to 'tremble'.

Another description of Siddons' first appearance in *The Grecian Daughter* echoes Boaden's account but provides a more colourful account of the performance and its impact:

> On October 30, she acted *Euphrasia* in the 'Grecian Daughter' with equal success. In this part she was a perfectly different being from *Isabella*. The heart-broken woman had given way to the Queen. Her commanding figure suited regal roles. She wore a diadem better than most sovereigns, and her tall person, enshrouded in classical garments, seemed to tower beyond her sex and yet was not masculine. So great was her passion in uttering the lines, when she denounces the tyrant in the play –
>
> 'Shall he not tremble when a daughter comes,
> Wild with her grief, and terrible with wrongs,
> The MAN OF BLOOD shall HEAR me! – Yes, my voice,
> Shall mount aloft upon the whirlwind's wing.'
>
> that the audience actually rose in consternation at the sight of her fearful wrath, and several persons fled from the theatre in fright, as if they had beheld a pythones [*sic*] or evil sybil.[68]

The author cites the same passage as does Boaden but increases the affect in terms evocative of the potent response to Siddons's Isabella; this audience does not merely 'tremble' but actually rises 'in consternation' and physically recoils from Siddons's regal wrath, prompting the author to compare her to a 'pythones' or sybil. Here not only does Siddons 'tower beyond her sex', but she represents a more clearly androgynous being: she is 'beyond' female and yet not masculine. Ironically, given its depiction of Roman charity, with its entirely female act of breastfeeding, *The Grecian Daughter* became the perfect vehicle for Siddons's imperial and seemingly ungendered genius.

Siddons's contemporaries repeatedly describe Euphrasia as peculiarly appropriate for Siddons's histrionic abilities, applying terms such as majestic, regal, and heroic. Like Boaden and the anonymous reviewer, Siddons's biographer Thomas Campbell stresses the commanding power of

Siddons's performance, explaining that it 'allowed her to assume a royal loftiness still more imposing (at least to the many), and a look of majesty which she alone could assume . . . she was a picture to every eye, and she spoke passion to every heart'.[69] The enthusiasm for Siddons's Euphrasia seems to have been both universal and extravagant. Hester Thrale Piozzi famously described Siddons as one of the two 'noblest specimens of the human race I ever saw'.[70] As Euphrasia, Piozzi claimed, Siddons represented the ideal human, who, 'looking like radiant Truth led by the hand of withered Time, seemed alone fit to be sent into some distant planet, for the purpose of shewing to its inhabitants what a race of exalted creatures God had been pleased to give this earth as a possession'.[71] Here Piozzi extrapolates from the events of *The Grecian Daughter* to their larger implications as the good daughter becomes 'radiant Truth' and her enfeebled father 'withered Time'. More profoundly, as Euphrasia, Siddons stands *alone* as the most exalted example of God's creation.

This vision of Siddons lived for decades in the minds of her admirers. Campbell recalls the longevity of the image, 'I have seen the oldest countenances of her contemporaries lighten up with pleasure in trying to do justice to their recollections of her *Euphrasia*. They spoke of the semi-diadem upon her brow, and of the veil that flowed so gracefully on her shoulders; but they always concluded by owning that words could not express '*her heroic loveliness*'.[72] These qualities are more clearly evident in the engraving of Pine's painting (Figure 3.2): we see the diadem and veil so fondly remembered by Siddons's admirers, as well as the heroic pose with bloody dagger held on high. Dionysius lies crumpled on the floor, the crown he had stolen from Evander symbolically fallen from his head. Bathed in light, Siddons dominates the scene.

So closely was Siddons associated with this role, that she was frequently depicted in her Euphrasia garb, in particular her regal diadem and veil. In her aptly titled essay 'She was Tragedy Personified': Crafting the Siddons Legend in Art and Life', Robyn Asleson observes:

> The unusual number of paintings and prints representing Siddons as Euphrasia suggests that artists shared the actress's enthusiasm for the role. Indeed, pictorially speaking, her 1782–83 London season was devoted to eliding Siddons with this righteously vengeful, dagger-wielding Greek heroine.[73]

Some of the earliest portraits of Siddons represent her in the role; William Hamilton's large portrait of her as Euphrasia was painted while she was still acting in Bath and exhibited at the Royal Academy in 1780, two years before her triumphant return to London. Sir Thomas Lawrence also painted Siddons in the role, and in 1785 Wedgewood produced a cameo plaque of her as Euphrasia. *The Biographical Dictionary of Actors* lists seventeen different representations of Siddons in *The Grecian Daughter*, second in number only to portraits of her as Lady Macbeth.

The trademark diadem and veil seen in Watson's engraving and all other representations of her in the guise of Euphrasia became a metonymy for Siddons the tragedienne. Joseph Roach describes Siddons, like Thomas Betterton before her, as a 'role icon', 'a part that certain exceptional performers play on and off stage, no matter what other parts they enact from night to night'. Siddons's career-long role, he argues, was that of 'the tragedy queen'.[74] Applying Roach's observation more directly, I would argue that the tragedy queen that Siddons enacted so successfully during the 1780s was specifically that of the Grecian Daughter. This association goes beyond the simple ubiquity of representations of Siddons as Murphy's heroic figure. In 1783, a year before Sir Joshua Reynolds painted Siddons in his iconic rendition of The Tragic Muse, Siddons had been portrayed as the tragic muse by Thomas Cook. In Cook's engraving Siddons wears a costume virtually identical to her garb as Euphrasia in Hamilton's 1780 portrait, complete with the memorable diadem and veil. A year later, James Gillray used the same iconography in 'Melpomene' (Figure 3.3), a satiric cartoon attacking Siddons for allegedly refusing to participate in another actor's benefit night. Here, Siddons, once again attired in diadem and veil, drops her avenging dagger to grasp the money bags above her head.[75] While other actresses were depicted as the tragic muse, only Siddons was characterized by such distinctive accoutrements.[76]

The potency of Murphy's heroic daughter may have seemed mysterious by the mid nineteenth century, but Euphrasia's triumph was especially important in the 1780s, a time, Daniel O'Quinn argues, that was dominated by concern over the loss of the American colonies.[77] This sense of national trauma provides a broader context for *The Grecian Daughter*'s enduring popularity, especially with the imperial Siddons in the title role. Jay Fliegelman has demonstrated the prevalent overlay of family iconography onto the politics and literature of eighteenth-century America, with the colonies representing themselves (and being represented) specifically as *sons* in an increasingly dysfunctional family.[78] These prodigal sons reject their parental authority, challenging and ultimately defeating their 'father' George III, who had himself deliberately adopted the sobriquet 'father' to his empire. It is within this broader cultural and political context that we need to consider the heroic daughter whose heart belongs unswervingly to

Figure 3.3 James Gillray. *Melpomene*. 6 December 1784. Hand-tinted etching. Courtesy of the Lewis Walpole Library, Yale University.

her father and whose every action is devoted to his care. Unlike the son who can rise up against the father and into whose relationship is built an inherent power struggle and risk of usurpation, the daughters of the later eighteenth century dedicate their lives to supporting their fathers. If the prodigal and ultimately rebellious son of the American colonies stands at one extreme, the maternal daughter stands at the other – at once the ideal subject and protector of her realm. Daughter to her king and parent of her country, she invokes the famed female emblem of the British Isles: Britannia.

Links between Murphy's play and this emblem of Britishness appeared early on, as seen in this cartoon entitled 'The Mother and the Child' (Figure 3.4). Published in the *London Magazine* in January 1773, the cartoon appeared shortly after a fall season during which *The Grecian Daughter* was revived several times, the most recent on 10 December, just a few weeks before the magazine's publication. Attached to a 'Fragment of a Speech' attacking George III's spending, the cartoon depicts Britannia in the posture of Euphrasia, nursing the King, the self-styled 'Father of his Country'. This Britannia is sorrowful and exhausted, her face drawn and

Figure 3.4 *The Mother and the Child.* Anonymous cartoon from *The London Magazine: Or, Gentleman's Monthly Intelligencer*, v. 42 (January 1773). HD P 270.1. Widener Library, Harvard University.

her breasts seemingly sucked dry, much like the money bag depicted above her head. Meanwhile, King George demands 'more Supplies'.[79] The cartoon's attack on a spendthrift king takes on added force through its visual connection to the popular play and its 'deeply interesting' act of charity.

Perhaps most remarkable is the overlay of Britannia and Euphrasia in the very person of Sarah Siddons. Five years after she first performed in *The Grecian Daughter*, Siddons took on another role, that of Britannia herself. In 1788, George III had suffered a prolonged period of illness (his famous 'madness'), but in spring of 1789 his reason returned, and a celebration of this blessed event was held in the King's Theatre on 21 April. A central component of the celebration was Robert Merry's *Ode on the Restoration of his Majesty*, recited by no less than Sarah Siddons herself, heroically attired as Britannia, complete with helmet and spear.

Like Euphrasia rejoicing in the recovery of her king and the return of liberty to her land, this Britannia declaims at one point, 'Fate gives th' inspiring word – 'Tis GEORGE and LIBERTY!'[80] After completing her recitation, Siddons sat, and, as observers noted, assumed the pose held by Britannia on the penny coin. The memorable 'heroic loveliness' and majesty so praised by the admirers of her Euphrasia clearly suited this role (even if her nineteenth-century biographers cringed at the idea), so much so that Siddons even chose to recite the *Ode* a second time at a benefit performance later that year.[81]

* * *

As the daughters I have discussed and the plays in which they appear demonstrate, staging filial piety presents a radically different dynamic from the more intimate pictures of family relations familiar from the novels of the later eighteenth century where the ties are personal and the rejections or reconciliations social. These plays do not lack touching demonstrations of filial and parental love, as the second act of *The Grecian Daughter* demonstrates. But such scenes do not constitute the climax of the dramas. In this way, these differ from novels such as Burney's *Evelina*, in which the interchange between father and daughter represents the emotional high point of the novel and, as Ruth Perry notes, provides a necessary prelude to marriage and its convenient narrative and social closure. Instead, these plays conclude almost inevitably on a triumphantly patriotic note, declaring the triumph of Rome, of Greece, of Liberty, and, in the end, of Britain.

If, in the iconography of the American colonies, George III represents the misuse of parental power, abuse that will ultimately lead to filial rebellion, in England the iconography of the dutiful daughter represents a necessary antidote, a picture of filial piety as the embodiment of a loyal country and its people; as the *Ode* spoken by Britannia exclaims of George III, 'Long may he rule a willing land'. On the stage, in the public realm in which these fathers and daughters dwell, it is not simply that a daughter like Euphrasia supports the patriarchy; in her parental role she literally *is* the patriarchy, and the apotheosis of the good daughter is complete. Thus, at the end of *The Grecian Daughter*, the daughter takes on the role of the father as Evander entrusts his country to his daughter's rule, asking her to parent the land as she has parented him so that 'she may prove, / If e'er distress like mine invade the land, / A parent to her people' (72). In this reassuring vision of filial loyalty, Murphy can turn back to *King Lear* and invert Lear's parental lament ('How sharper than a serpent's tooth it is / To have a thankless child!' [I.iv.88–89]). His father/king can exclaim

> The life I gave her –
> Oh! she has us'd it for the noblest ends!
> To fill each duty; make her father feel
> The purest joy, the heart-dissolving bliss
> To have a grateful child. (71)

In the end, the play does provide 'heart-dissolving bliss' for the audience as well as for the father. It is here that *The Grecian Daughter* succeeds where Crisp's and Moncreiff's Virginia plays could not – in its ability to evoke an emotional response. Here, the spectacle of the daughter fulfilling her noble duty 'fills every mind with enthusiasm in the cause of virtue and justice'. Just as the guards are moved to moral action by the sight of virtue, so should the audience engage in patriotic fervour through their participation in the theatrical event. Overthrowing tyranny and supporting freedom, Euphrasia is more than the ideal daughter; she is the ideal Briton.

CHAPTER 4

Performing the West Indies: Comedy, Feeling, and British Identity

> In this nation, we have certainly more characters than are seen in any other, owing perhaps to two causes, our liberty and the uncertainty of our climate.
>
> –Horace Walpole, 'Thoughts on Comedy'[1]

> There never have been any statute-laws for comedy; there never can be any; it is only referable to the unwritten law of the heart, and that is nature.
>
> –Richard Cumberland, *Memoirs*[2]

Where a serious drama such as *The Grecian Daughter* could stir the passions with the apotheosis of Sarah Siddons's Euphrasia into Britannia, comedy of the same era operated on a more modest scale. Comedy no less than tragedy appealed directly to the emotions, what Cumberland calls 'the unwritten law of the heart', in its desire to improve its audience; moralists who supported the theatre did not distinguish between genres in this respect. Like tragedy, comedy depended on an audience's sympathetic response for its success, but the figures that prompted this outburst of fellow-feeling were radically different, denizens of everyday life, and later eighteenth-century comedy depended for its affect on the audience's ability to recognize and connect with its portrayal of contemporary life.[3] As a result, although writers and their characters may have adopted what Lisa A. Freeman refers to as 'a rhetorical position of sincerity',[4] the practice of comedy in the later eighteenth century was not that of tragedy, despite the claims of disgruntled writers such as Goldsmith and Cook. The last two chapters of this study explore the ways in which the so-called sentimental comedies of the later eighteenth century established a sympathetic connection with their audiences – and to what ends.

A great afficionado of comedy, Horace Walpole argued that the source of comedy's appeal lay in its humour (not necessarily its laughter) and especially in its ability to gauge the moment. When comparing comedy and tragedy, Walpole described comedy as the greatest and most difficult province of drama: 'Not only equal genius is required, but a comedy demands a more uncommon assemblage of qualities – knowledge of the world, wit, good sense, &c.; and these qualities superadded to those requisite for tragical composition.'[5] A tragedy can escape, it would seem, without wit or good sense (certainly critics attacked *The Grecian Daughter* for its lack of both qualities), but comedy cannot. Its greatness – and difficulty – lies in its need to represent 'mankind in its present state of civilized society'.[6] Lord Kames had argued more generally for the importance of presentness and immediacy in drama, but Walpole explicitly links this quality to comedy, emphasizing that comedy's difference from tragedy arises from the necessity it presents of representing not the timeless but the immediate, what he termed '*the view of writing to the present taste*'. In this Walpole recognized that comedy, more than tragedy, lives in the minute. Its characters are those of eighteenth-century England; they are the contemporaries of the audience, and the plays in which they appear engage with contemporary events, fashions, and mores. Because comedy represents the quotidian rather than the ideal, the audience is looking at itself, at the world around it, and, perhaps most important, at its vision of itself. Such immediacy requires comedy to do more than simply mirror contemporary manners; it must provide a view inward. Comedy's goal, then, is to reflect how its audience of English men and women wanted to view themselves and the world around them. This ideal identification was the means by which they could sympathize with the characters and action they saw upon the stage. It is the core source of comedy's affective presence.

As a writer of comedy rather than a critic, Richard Cumberland described his approach to comedy more abstractly, as 'design'd as an attempt upon [his audience's] heart, and as such proceeds with little deviation from mine'.[7] More than thirty-five years later, he reiterated this sentiment in the passage from his *Memoirs* quoted at the beginning of this chapter, emphasizing comedy's freedom from formal strictures because 'it is only referable to the unwritten law of the heart'. The affect of comedy depends on this idealized internal communion between feeling hearts; later eighteenth-century comedies, the plays Walpole valued so greatly, were expressly designed to promote this 'undeviating' connection between playwright and audience, a connection that can only work, it would seem, when the feeling hearts share certain natural affinities. If tragedy can bypass the need to portray a specific 'knowledge of the world' because of its employment of timeless character types and settings, comedy must establish a bond within a more transient and ephemeral present.[8]

The immediacy of the theatrical experience was crucial. It changed with the times as new audiences demanded new ideals.

In the two plays examined in this chapter, the communion of hearts that Cumberland described as his dramatic goal provides a means of coordinating the values audiences associated with 'Englishness'. These two popular comedies, Richard Cumberland's *The West Indian* (1771) and George Colman's *Inkle and Yarico* (1787), explore a specific aspect of England's eighteenth-century 'present', Britain's fascination and even obsession with its role as an imperial power. These plays, written sixteen years apart by British authors for a British audience, display England's vision of itself in this imperial present. As part of this imagined reality, each play displays the disenfranchised and exotic characters who, along with their connections to colonialism, mercantilism, and slavery, arouse the audience's emotions, providing a conduit for each author's goal of effecting moral reform in an imperial world that is at once an expression of British goals of commerce and at odds with the oft-exalted British ideal of liberty.

Liberty, Climate, and the Practice of Comedy

Civilized, feeling Britons took their comedy very seriously. Lord Kames, for example, sees comedy as a matter of national security, warning that 'odious' writers such as the Restoration comic playwrights 'spread infection through their native country'.[9] Many writers follow Kames in attaching national importance to the practice of a specific, recognizably English, mode of comedy. Thus, when comparing English and French comedy, Hugh Blair writes:

> From the English Theatre, we are naturally led to expect a greater variety of original characters in Comedy, and bolder strokes of wit and humour, than are to be found on any other Modern Stage. Humour is, in a great measure, the peculiar province of the English nation. The nature of such a free Government as ours; and that unrestrained liberty which our manners allow to every man, of living entirely after his own taste, afford full scope to the display of singularity of character, and to the indulgence of humour in all its forms.[10]

In Blair's eyes, the link between politics and literature is direct and unproblematic; 'unrestrained liberty', that quality most frequently associated with the British nation, produces bold and original drama (despite the restrictions posed by the Licensing Act). By contrast, the 'influence of a despotic court' in France, combined with 'established subordination of ranks' and an overly decorous culture precludes truly comic drama because the lack of freedom results in a uniformity that stifles comedy.

Although perhaps not something Blair would have admitted, comedy's depiction of contemporary society provides a reflection of how the English staged themselves. Unlike the physical, often fantastical, performance of farce or pantomime, eighteenth-century comedy featured figures and foibles that the audience could recognize. In this way, English comedy does indeed represent and create a type of national character. Blair's comments provide an example of this self-creation; it is not simply that the English character and political system provide the breeding ground for originality, but that these qualities can be determined through an examination of the nation's comedies. 'Boldness', 'originality', and 'singularity of character' must be the product of an English pen, 'uniformity' of the slavish French. Thus comedy can be seen as indicative of the society that produced it: its theatre, its government, and its national character.

Cumberland's comments on his own approach to comedy provide a useful gloss on the ideal of a national genre. Writing shortly after the immense success of *The West Indian*, a play whose popularity spawned both praise for the elevated state of English comedy and dismal warnings regarding the denigration of English taste, Cumberland provided his own apocalyptic view of the future of English drama. Angered by the hostile response to his play's success, he argues such hostility threatens to stifle all drama:

> [I]t will drive men from a necessary confidence in their own powers, and it will be thought convenient to get out of the torrent's way, by mooring under the lee of some great name, either French or Italian, and sitting down contented with the humble, but less exposed, task of translation. Should this take place, a cold elaborate stile will prevail in our drama, clearly opposite to the national character, and not at all at union with the taste of our writers themselves. Correctness will become our chief object in view.[11]

Cumberland fears that the venom of his detractors will curtail the practice of comedy so that potential playwrights will be driven away from even contemplating the stage, with dire consequences. England will not lose the ability to laugh but rather its 'national character', bringing it closer to the 'cold, elaborate stile' that defines other cultures. As 'correctness' becomes the goal, Englishness is lost. Walpole shared this concern, writing in somewhat less cataclysmic terms that 'while the liberty of our government exists, there will be more originality in our manners than in those of other nations, though an inundation of politeness has softened our features as well as weakened our constitution'.[12]

The assumption that a comedy's form and content demonstrate national identity and, conversely, that the nature and content of comedy are nationally determined, links the plays examined here with the tragedies with which they shared the stage. If tragedy's broadly symbolic action provided the scope for explicit articulations of nationalist ideology, then comedy's reliance on the contemporary world allowed a more narrowly focused vision not simply of English society but, more crucially, of English self-representation. Daniel O'Quinn has described the drama of the later decades of the eighteenth century as engaged in a process of 'autoethnicity', dependent on 'the relationship between the performance of character on stage, the enactment of character in the boxes and the pit, and the ensuing analysis of character in the newspapers'.[13] Where O'Quinn's exploration of autoethnicity focuses on the complex interrelationship between news media and theatrical experience, I take my consideration of the comedies of the later eighteenth century in a somewhat different direction, examining their creation of an identity less dependent on actual world events and more tied to the need to represent an ideal British empire. In this sense, theatre does not so much reflect and interact with world events as mediate between the audience's desired vision of itself and a sometimes uncomfortable reality. As Blair et al. indicate, British audiences saw comedy as reflecting not only general genius, but, more important, a distillation of English character. Theatrical performance thus becomes a means of affirming national virtue.

In an age increasingly uncomfortable with its image as a mercantile, imperial nation, staging these virtues takes on increased urgency. These tensions are most vividly embodied in the plays' male characters, the figures who participate actively in the commerce that makes possible Britain's imperial might. Making these mercantile men sympathetic becomes of paramount importance; to do so requires that they demonstrate a true heart of gold, valuing moral rather monetary worth. Expanding upon Edward Said's comment that 'the rhetoric of power all too easily produces an illusion of benevolence when deployed in an imperial setting',[14] I have chosen to examine plays that deploy an aura of benevolence *within* the home of the imperial power as well as beyond it. Playwrights such as Cumberland and Colman depend upon benevolence as a means of negotiating the tensions England faced in its own self-image. These creations of identity embody what Said describes as the imperial nation's need to believe itself right, to believe itself different from the flawed empires that came before it. In *The West Indian*, England's 'need to be right', to truly be that land of liberty and freedom that Blair describes, leads to the performance of benevolence as a means of creating and performing a British identity mediated through figures such as the title character. In Colman's *Inkle and Yarico*, benevolence prevails, however uneasily, despite the collision of idealized British freedom and the ugly fact of slavery.

Merchants and Planters – Cumberland's *The West Indian*

Omnipresent in eighteenth-century culture, the tension between Britain's cherished 'liberty' and its necessary dependence on trade is vividly expressed in England's most famous patriotic poem, 'Rule Britannia' (1740). With its reification of a Britain that both 'rules the waves' and which itself will never be enslaved, 'Rule Britannia' presents perhaps the most vivid expression of the slippage between the rhetoric and reality of England's self-styled noble independence. At the same time that it touts the power of a land that 'shalt flourish great and free, / The dread and envy of them all' (ll. 9–10),[15] Thomson's poem directly links this picture of international power with another aspect of England's self-identification: its reputation as a nation of shopkeepers. By the later eighteenth century, England relied upon its well-established West Indian empire, and, as Thomson makes clear, the connection between might and mercantilism is essential.

> To thee belongs the rural reign
> Thy cities shall with commerce shine;
> And thine shall be the subject main
> And every shore it circles thine. (ll.22–25)

'Commerce' – a term that reverberates within the literature of the eighteenth century – 'shines' within England while its empire circles the globe, rendering the oceans and all the lands they touch its subject; all are connected as parts of an economic enterprise just as they are bound together within a single sentence of Thomson's poem.

The connection between liberty and commerce is implicitly expressed through the juxtaposition of this exaltation of British empire with a paean to English freedom. In the climax of the poem, Thomson, like the critics who would follow him, ties artistic endeavours inextricably to national identity, specifically the native liberty that prevents Britons (although not others) from succumbing to slavery.

> The Muses, still with freedom found,
> Shall to thy happy coast repair;
> Blessed isle! with matchless beauty crowned,
> And manly hearts to guard the fair.
> Rule, Britannia, rule the waves;
> Britons never will be slaves. (ll.27–32)

'Freedom' defines England, defines England's comedy, and it defines those 'manly hearts' that guard the fair, rule the waves, and polish commerce. As the final stanza of Thomson's poem suggests, Britain is dependent upon 'manly hearts' not simply to guard the fair but also to burnish its position as a commercial power, which in turn allows it to rule the waves, in a natural and unending cycle.

For Richard Cumberland, as for Thomson, a properly manly heart protects both Britain's mercantile success and its freedom. *The West Indian*, Cumberland's first significant success, enacts this vision of masculinity in an age of commerce, famously employing sentiment to underline the worth of its central male figures. The link between the trade that had long been a part of England's identity and the source of the wealth that made that trade possible is expressed directly in the play's prologue. Referring to Jamaica, and by extension to England's holdings in the West Indies, Cumberland writes: 'For sure that country has no feeble claim, / Which swells your commerce and supports your fame.' In its title character, *The West Indian* presents a figure who both swells commerce and supports fame, a figure, whose sensibility is closely identified with an entire colonial community, for good or bad. Expecting the worse, a group of West Indian planters came to the opening performance determined to, in Cumberland's words, 'chastise the author'.[16] Moments after the prologue began, the planters created so much noise that the speaker had to start again, quieting only when a reference to the West Indian's 'noble mind' convinced them of the play's pro-colonial agenda.

Despite the opening night fracas, *The West Indian* was immediately successful, running for more than twenty nights and quickly becoming part of the theatrical repertoire from London to America, and from there to the West Indies, where it was staged regularly by travelling companies.[17] The plot involves a young and fabulously rich Jamaican planter, the aptly named Belcour, who comes to London and encounters a variety of misadventures that are ultimately resolved because of his innate benevolence and generosity. In Belcour, Cumberland provides a figure who not only reassures his audience that the European inhabitants of the West Indies are indeed 'good hearted' but with whose goodness the audience can identify. As he had stated in the 'Advertisement' to *The Fashionable Lover*, Cumberland designed his comedies as a direct attempt upon the heart of his audience. But the cold world of fashionable London does not provide him with sufficient opportunities for emotional connection, and, in order to accomplish his goal of communion with his audience, he has had to 'betake [himself] to the out-skirts of the empire; the center is too equal and refined for such purposes'.[18] *The West Indian* allowed Cumberland to yoke emotional response to the representation of England's far-flung empire. In their native land, paradoxically, the English can emotionally connect only through the exotic person of Belcour, a figure at once both known and unknown. They can identify with him precisely because he is not of their world.

This link between the West Indian stranger and the English audience is addressed most explicitly when Belcour makes his first appearance on the stage in act I, scene v. David Garrick, manager of Drury Lane, demanded numerous drafts of the scene in order to ensure that Belcour's entrance made the greatest possible impact on the audience.[19] In a letter to Garrick (2 July 1770), Cumberland assures Garrick that he 'entirely adopt[ed] your Observation on the first scene and have already executed it in a manner that I hope embraces your Ideas'.[20] In his *Memoirs*, Cumberland provided more details of the changes Garrick requested:

> At his suggestion I added the preparatory scene in the house of Stockwell, before the arrival of Belcour, where his baggage is brought in, and the domestics of the Merchant are setting things in readiness for his coming ... [Garrick said] 'I want something more to be announced of your West Indian before you bring him on the stage to give eclat to his entrance, and rouse the curiosity of the audience; that they may say – Aye, here he comes with all his colours flying.'[21]

The care that Cumberland and Garrick devoted to the opening scenes paid off; not only was the play as a whole successful, but the scene introducing Belcour was cited repeatedly in novels and periodicals. *The Monthly Review*, for example, quoted at length Belcour's opening conversation with Stockwell describing it as crucial to understanding the character and the play.[22] The scene was even reprinted wholesale in elocution manuals such as *The Speaker*, a collection of select recitation passages chosen specifically to 'improve' the young through the performance of recognizably national virtue. As the 'Dedication' to *The Speaker* explains, these passages are part of 'an extensive plan' of instruction that has produced 'respectable characters' 'who are now filling up their stations in society with reputation to themselves and advantage to the Public'.[23] Through the experience of memorizing and performing appropriate passages, young men will become useful and respectable characters, a goal William Enfield, anthologist and author of the Dedication, articulates by turning to the words of Anna Letitia Barbauld. These students will both 'adorn the state, and that defend', by upholding the larger British empire; in the end, they will 'fix [their country's] laws, her spirit to sustain, / And light up glory thro' her wide domain.'[24]

Why was this scene in particular so widely seen as a means to inculcate proper national pride? On the most basic level, it introduces the play's title character and establishes his good nature. More important, the scene establishes Belcour's participation in an imagined community shared with the theatre audience as well as the young men who later would declaim the passage in preparation for their roles as model citizens. Belcour aligns himself with his audience as he describes his first experiences on English soil: 'Accustomed to a land of slaves and out of patience with the whole tribe of custom-house extortioners, boatmen, tidewaiters, and water-bailiffs that beset me on all sides worse than a swarm of mosquitos', he admits that he 'brushed them aside' too roughly and that a 'furious scuffle' ensued.[25] Despite the beating he endures, he explains that he likes his assailants the better for it precisely because he can claim kinship with them and by extension all other Britons: 'Was I only a visitor, I might, perhaps, wish them a little more tractable; but as a fellow subject and a sharer in their freedom, I applaud their spirit though I feel the effect of it in every bone in my skin' (8). The reference to the 'land of slaves' becomes not a colonial descriptor but rather a means of differentiating a generalized foreign servility from the innate freedom of the British national character.

Freedom is not the only English virtue introduced in the scene. Shortly after Belcour's praise of his fellow subjects, the English merchant Stockwell, later discovered to be Belcour's long-lost father, employs the language of empire to lecture Belcour on the proper use of wealth. Money must be used wisely, he instructs, treated 'not as a vassal, over whom you have a wanton and despotic power, but as a subject which you are bound to govern with a temperate and restrained authority' (8). Stockwell's words indicate Cumberland's concern with the broader social and political implications of personal benevolence. Pledging to use his wealth as a 'commission' not a 'right', Belcour proceeds to follow Stockwell's advice, using his riches to help those in need, in contrast to Lady Rusport, the other wealthy character in the play, who uses her ill-gotten gains as a means of intimidation. Through her character, Cumberland literalizes Stockwell's dictum comparing the rightful use of material wealth to a properly regulated monarchy. The daughter of a puritan appropriately named Oliver Roundhead, Lady Rusport usurps her father's fortune from its rightful heirs much as her father's namesake Oliver Cromwell did with the English throne.

These two figures, the warm-hearted and generous Creole and his antithesis the tight-fisted puritan, provide the framework for the play's commentary on the moral use of capital. Cumberland's neat plot establishes Captain Dudley, Lady Rusport's impoverished brother-in-law, as the object by which other characters demonstrate their ability to govern wealth properly. While a relatively minor character in himself, he becomes the means by which other characters are judged: the essential worth of a character can be judged by his or her ability to sympathize with his distress and to express this sympathy in monetary terms. Lady Rusport's sister married Captain Dudley against her father's wishes, and the father cast the couple off, seemingly leaving all his money to Lady Rusport rather than to the Captain and his children, Charles and Louisa. Now an elderly soldier, too poor to support himself, Dudley seeks to buy a commission and rejoin his regiment on a mission to Africa. In a display of 'despotic power' that dooms her later in the play, Lady Rusport repeatedly rejects solicitations from Dudley and his son Charles for a loan of 200 pounds, arguing that if he deserved the money, it would have been left to him in her father's will.

By contrast, from his first appearance on the stage, Belcour's character is defined by his ability to identify with and respond to the distress of others, and he deploys his fortune according to this innate experience of fellow-feeling. As he explains at the beginning of the play, 'I am the offspring of distress, and every child of sorrow is my brother. While I have hands to hold, therefore, I will hold them open to mankind' (8). His adventures and misadventures in and around London illustrate the 'warmth' of his character, both good and bad. Belcour's unruly passions are demonstrated chiefly through his fervent pursuit of Louisa Dudley, whom he mistakenly believes is a kept woman and whose favours he attempts to buy with another woman's jewels. But fellow-feeling has an even stronger hold on him than lust, and upon hearing of Captain Dudley's hardships, he instantly resolves to help him.

> I've lost the girl, it seems; that's clear. She was the first object of my pursuit; but the case of this poor officer touches me; and, after all, there may be as much true delight in rescuing a fellow creature from distress as there would be in plunging one into it. (27)

Demonstrating that his hands are indeed open, he promptly gives Dudley the money that no one in London would even lend. Where his rude advances on Louisa are the result of the money-hungry scheming of her landlords who convince him of the foreignness of English familial and sexual relationships, his generosity towards Captain Dudley is the honest response of a warm heart that needs no translation.

It was this effusion of generosity that prompted Goldsmith's denunciation of sentimental comedy the following year. Goldsmith's essay pointedly describes characters like Belcour as being unrealistically virtuous figures 'lavish enough of their tin money on the stage'.[26] In suggesting that the performance of generosity in the theatre is meaningless because the money as well as the gesture are make believe, Goldsmith trivializes Cumberland's argument about the necessary link between capital and benevolence and ignores the role of empathy – between characters on the stage and between characters and audience – in establishing and maintaining this connection. The fact that Belcour casts his tin money around freely is not an indication that the theatrical act of generosity is meaningless but rather that it should inspire audience members to follow his example. By recognizing and applauding Belcour's virtues, audience members engage in the process of sympathetic identification that Kames and that Smith had described as a necessary step to the practice of virtue.

Belcour's origins are central to *The West Indian*'s depiction of both empire and empathy, and he is repeatedly defined by his colonial background, in terms of both wealth and 'heat'. The play begins with a parade of his West Indian signifiers: black servants, 'two green monkies, a pair of grey parrots, a Jamaica sow and pigs, and a mangrove dog' as well as the rumour that he has 'rum and sugar enough belonging to him to make all the water in the Thames into punch' (4–5). His actions throughout the play reinforce this vision of abundance, as Cumberland portrays an economy of colonial material and moral resources. In this way Charles Dudley can equate Belcour's origins with his generosity, describing him as 'a young West Indian, rich, and with a warmth of heart peculiar to his climate' (57). By contrast, the frigid English climate, that 'equal and refined' centre Cumberland deplored, inhibits sympathetic responses. As Charlotte Rusport exclaims, the climate does not nourish moral values such as empathy: 'O blessed be the torrid zone forever whose rapid vegetation quickens nature into such benignity! These latitudes are made for politics and philosophy; friendship has no root in this soil' (58), a sentiment expressed earlier by Belcour when he discovers that no one in London will come to Captain Dudley's aid ('why, then, your town is a damned good-for-nothing town, and I wish I had never come into it' (26)).

This easy association of wealth, benevolence, and empire, of warmth of heart and warmth of climate, creates an illusion of unproblematic colonial relations in which England's colonies enrich the empire not simply through wealth of resources, as indicated in the list of signifiers with which the play begins, but more crucially through the colonies' ability to complement English identity. The warmth that promotes the growth of sugar cane also promotes the growth of a liberality England needs as much as it needs West Indian material goods, providing a much-needed infusion of generosity along with the more obvious infusion of wealth. Philosophy and politics, those traits that Charlotte isolates as peculiarly English, are limited and even sound suspiciously like the cold and slavish qualities Cumberland fears may overtake comedy if sentiment is eliminated from the stage. In this sense, colonialism enhances British morality – at least on English soil.

Nonetheless, Cumberland reminds his audience that this colonial beneficence is an asset and not superior to native British culture. Belcour, after all, has unrestrained passions, a concern voiced in several reviews of the play,[27] and must learn to moderate his warmth in keeping with his new habitat. Even at the end of the play, he is still 'hot as the soil, the clime which gave him birth' (Prologue) and in need of self-governance, as Stockwell reminds Louisa:

> You will not be over strict, madam, in weighing Mr. Belcour's conduct to the minutest scruple. His manners, passions, and opinions are not as yet assimilated to this climate. He comes amongst you a new character, an inhabitant of a new world; and both our hospitality as well as pity recommend him to our indulgence. (90)

The cold climate Charlotte had decried is here transformed into a temperate world in which manners and money are prudently governed, and the warm-hearted stranger becomes an object of pity as well as a welcome guest. The West Indian has already begun the process of acculturation; his marriage to Louisa, an emblem of virtuous English womanhood, will become the vehicle for Belcour's ultimate assimilation. Belcour's passions may be 'hot', like the Caribbean climate of his birth, but by 'governing' his fortune temperately, he epitomizes the link between British financial and moral rectitude, a rectitude that is a far cry from the 'wanton and despotic' power wielded by other imperial nations. In the end, the West Indian is British, after all.

A Secondary Hero – Benevolence and Property

In *The West Indian*'s second plot, Cumberland once again turns to the 'out-skirts of empire', featuring another colonial citizen, albeit one from a very different sort of colony: the Irish soldier and would-be fortunate hunter, Major O'Flaherty. While seemingly little more than a stage Irishman at first, he plays a key role in the play's plot and in its depiction of an untroubled liaison between property and benevolence, and he would ultimately become the play's most popular figure. Cumberland's prologue explicitly designates O'Flaherty as the play's second 'hero' and locates his heroism, like Belcour's, in the goodness of his heart.

> Another hero your excuse implores,
> Sent by your sister kingdom to your shores,
> Doomed by religion's too severe command
> To fight for bread against his native land.
> A brave, unthinking, animated rogue,
> With here and there a touch upon the brogue;
> Laugh, but despise him not, for on his lip
> His errors lie; his heart can never trip.

Cumberland's words here indirectly establish Ireland as an English colony. Originally separate ('Sister Kingdom'), Ireland quickly becomes subsumed into the British empire, as two lines later O'Flaherty is described as fighting 'against his native land', a land that we know must be England, judging by the catalogue of foreign wars (and scars) he provides later in the play.[28]

Even though his native climate is far from 'torrid', O'Flaherty, like Belcour, responds emotionally to the plight of others. In this, his 'unthinking' response stands opposed to the cold philosophy that Charlotte cites as characteristic of the English. Crucially, O'Flaherty's character is validated by his moral response to monetary gain. A Roman Catholic Irishman, he has been barred from fighting for England,[29] and thus he has spent his life as a mercenary fighting against it; having fallen upon hard times in his old age, O'Flaherty enters the play on the brink of cajoling Lady Rusport into matrimony. Despite his seemingly acquisitive history, he shares Belcour's innate warmth of heart, and his immediate impulse when confronted with distress or inequity is to open his hands. Like Belcour, his generosity towards Captain Dudley provides the means of calibrating his benevolence. Although he does not try to hide his desire for Lady Rusport's money, he reacts with horror when he discovers that she has rejected her impoverished brother-in-law's request for a loan of 200 pounds. Describing her as nothing more than a hyena, he pledges 'to share the little modicum that thirty years hard service has left me. I wish it was more for his sake' (40).

In rejecting Lady Rusport's person and fortune, O'Flaherty impacts others more profoundly than does Belcour, for he discovers the fraud that Lady Rusport has perpetrated and exposes the will that leaves Charles Dudley the beneficiary, thus stripping Lady Rusport of her money. In the process he not only benefits others but also dashes his own hopes of gain. He couches his loss as a positive good for himself as well as others, exclaiming 'I'm glad you've trounced the old cat, for on my conscience I believe I must otherwise have married her myself to have let you in for a share of her fortune' (95). O'Flaherty's actions represent an important piece of *The West Indian*'s exploration of the morally correct use of capital, in this case the landed wealth that constitutes England proper – the literal centre of the British empire. While Belcour would have funded Captain Dudley's expedition to Africa, a colonial venture that never occurs, O'Flaherty benefits him more materially by reasserting the proper lines of inheritance. Under his guidance, property, like the monarchy, is passed through the appropriate male heirs, bypassing in the process the 'unrestrained authority' represented by Lady Rusport and her regicidal forebears.

Like the Irish Major and the Creole planter, the English merchant Stockwell is distinguished by his proper use of and attitude towards money. This triumvirate of men manipulate its proper use, whether through the generous dispensing of funds, the moral realignment of the lines of inheritance, or, in Stockwell's case, through the articulation of proper monetary philosophy. Belcour's mentor and long-lost father, Stockwell operates as the play's narrator:[30] his moderate voice begins the play and provides its underlying message of proper monetary practice in the imperial state ('to use it, not to waste it . . . treat it . . . as a subject, which you are bound to govern with a temperate and restrained authority' (8)). By owning Belcour as his son at the play's end, Stockwell indicates that Belcour has upheld this principle, one that Stockwell's words suggest is crucial to the governance of British subjects far and wide.[31]

The play's other characters serve as a backdrop to Cumberland's representation of benevolence. In contrast to Belcour, O'Flaherty and Stockwell, Charles Dudley, Charlotte Rusport's self-sacrificing lover, does little; despite his military office (Ensign), his role is as an heir, not as a soldier. This martial man, like his father, is relegated to the sidelines and ultimately resigns his commission.[32] Likewise, the play's female characters play a largely secondary role, in keeping with *The West Indian*'s exploration of money and masculinity.[33] They are not crucial to the play's affect, nor do they participate actively in the economic interplay of the male characters around them. They constitute objects of exchange, both literal and figurative. If Charles's role is to be the passive recipient of money at the play's conclusion, Charlotte and Louisa operate as objects of exchange: Charlotte's material wealth, represented symbolically in the form of her jewels, which circulate throughout the play; and Louisa's moral worth, awarded to Belcour in order to prompt his assimilation into English culture.

The easy connection of colonial wealth and virtue was ubiquitous in the early 1770s. Not only did London audiences make *The West Indian* the most successful new play of the season, but the image of the rich, unpolished but well-meaning planter permeated contemporary culture. In her novel *The Rambles of Mr Frankly*, published the year following the premiere of *The West Indian*, Elizabeth Bonhote draws from Belcour in her description of a West Indian planter. Much like Belcour, this West Indian is unaccustomed to English freedom, but his generous heart excuses his bad behaviour:

> A West Indian! – He seems to forget he has left a land of slaves. He never was in England before – That is an excuse for him. He knows not that the poor of England are as free as he is. – He is not, however, deaf to the cries of distress and his disposition is as noble as his fortune. He struck a poor wretch for standing in his way – but when he found it was to supplicate his pity, he gave him five guineas. – The man is a Christian, and charity will guide him to Heaven.[34]

As in *The West Indian*, the existence of slavery elsewhere in the British empire is not the problem; rather, it is the West Indian's assumption that the native English are not 'as free as he'. After all, as Thomson had assured his readers, 'Britons never, never will be slaves.'

While this untroubled view of the West Indian and his land of slaves would change over the ensuing decades, in 1771 England could view itself as partaking in a mutually enriching colonial enterprise, where the more uncomfortable realities of imperialism such as slavery could be forgotten, especially in a London theatre. The world Cumberland constructs in this play is that of a happy mercantile family in which England, the temperate father, oversees a series of English colonies grateful for their father's guidance and, in return, munificent to their father's land. The warmth of feeling expressed by these characters and through them transmitted to the audience becomes a means of washing away the stain of slavery and oppression. Through the figure of Belcour, benevolence becomes a rationalization for colonialism; England depends on its colonies, near and far, not only for its material riches, but for its moral riches as well, a justification for the development, maintenance, and expansion of its empire.

Inkle and Yarico

The optimism inherent in Cumberland's delineation of the benevolent representative of empire had eroded by 1787 when Colman's *Inkle and Yarico* first appeared at the Little Theatre in the Haymarket. In the intervening years, Britain had lost the American colonies, thereby complicating its relationship with its West Indian colonies. Describing the American Revolution as 'the pivotal event' in the history of British attitudes towards slavery, Christopher Leslie Brown notes that while the war itself did not cause the British abolitionist movement, it did direct attention to 'the moral character of colonial institutions and imperial practices'.[35] For many in England, this new focus required a reassessment not only of the colonies but of England's comfortable vision of itself:

> Those who thought about imperial questions long had assumed that Britain did not rule overseas at all, that the colonies were composed of peaceful, settler communities, with colonists who enjoyed the rights of freeborn Englishmen and who possessed a preeminent commitment to trade rather than dominion. The results of the Seven Years war had begun to challenge this self-image, and the outcome of the Revolution revealed the many ways that the interests associated with imperial rule could conflict with the preservation of established rights and liberties. Among a broader public, during the American war, there arose, too, a desire for Britain to rule in a way consistent with the nation's self-ascribed reputation for a commitment to freedom.[36]

The English, in other words, needed to find ways to reconcile the myth of the liberty-loving Briton with the knowledge that being an empire whose colonies depended on slave labour necessarily 'conflict[ed] with the preservation of established rights and liberties'.

Simply representing the West Indies became more problematic as the abolitionist movement gained momentum. Josiah Wedgewood began the manufacture of his popular cameos depicting a kneeling slave encircled with the phrase 'Am I not a Man and a Brother?' in 1787, and the popularity of this image indicates the emotion that images of slavery could incite. Slavery had become, in common parlance, the 'blush' on Britain's cheek,[37] the conflict between England's self-declared love of liberty and its embrace of commerce. By the time *Inkle and Yarico* was staged, English audiences were disturbed not simply by the idea of the horrors of slavery, both abstract and concrete, but by the implications the practice of slavery had on Britain's vision of itself. The commercial network powered by West Indian sugar plantations could no longer be glossed over as Belcour does when he first appears upon the stage. By the time Colman composed his comic opera, being '*accustomed* to a land of slaves' (my emphasis) damns rather than excuses the speaker.

As Lawrence Price (1937) and Frank Felsenstein (1999) have documented,[38] the basic plot of Colman's comic opera was well known to British audiences. Earlier versions of the story focus on two figures: Inkle, a mercantile trader shipwrecked on a Caribbean island, and Yarico, his Indian mistress, who loves him and saves him from harm. Presented with the opportunity, he sells her, rejoicing that he can pocket still more money because she is pregnant with his child. In *Spectator* no. 11, the most frequently cited source, Richard Steele uses the tale as an example of male perfidy, setting it in opposition to the well-known story of the Ephesian matron.[39] Colman recreates this story of love and avarice as a comic opera, including additional characters and subplots interlaced with songs and dances – and bringing the whole to a rather unlikely happy ending. His representation includes two characters who parallel Inkle and Yarico, Inkle's servant Trudge, and Yarico's darker companion Wowski. In Colman's 'opera', Inkle had been accompanying his fiancée Narcissa, the daughter of the governor of Barbados, when he and Trudge were left behind on Yarico's island; by reaching Barbados, he has the opportunity to marry an heiress. The two couples are rescued, and the second and third acts take place in Barbados, where, as in Steele's tale, Inkle does attempt to sell Yarico, but in this case to Sir Christopher Curry, Narcissa's father and the Governor of the island. Confronted with his mercenary and unEnglish behaviour, Inkle repents and gathers the faithful Yarico to his bosom.

In contrast to *The West Indian*, female characters in *Inkle and Yarico* play an important role in both the play's plot and its affect. The pathos of Yarico, memorably portrayed by Mrs Stephen Kemble, and the comic simplicity of her companion Wowski throw into relief the behaviour of the play's male characters, who, unlike Yarico and Wowski, are all white and English. Kemble won universal praise for her performance as a figure who 'ravishe[ed] each heart',[40] and she was remembered years later by many spectators, including Robert Burns, who wrote an impromptu poem after seeing her perform.[41] While the role of Wowski was less directly associated with a specific actress, the character's comic scenes with Trudge and more overt sexuality made it immediately recognizable over the following decades: in January 1788, cartoonist James Gillray attached the name Wouski to a caricature of Prince William Henry in the arms of a black woman; twenty-five years later, Wowski, like Cumberland's O'Flaherty, was used to promote the lottery.

Colman infused his play with a generic abolitionism that contributed to its widespread popularity, and the harsh outlines of Steele's *Spectator* fable were further softened by Samuel Arnold's music and by sentiment that aimed to move but not to shock, an effect achieved most poignantly through the gentle pathos of Mrs Kemble's Yarico, and through the opera's somewhat improbable happy ending. As a result, *Inkle and Yarico*, like *The West Indian*, was immediately and enormously successful, earning a place in the theatre repertoire at the Haymarket and subsequently at the patent theatres for years to come. Richardson Wright notes that it was even performed in Jamaica shortly after its enormously successful premiere in London, although it seemingly played to sparse houses.[42] Other translations and variations proliferated; a French pantomime (*L'Heroine Americaine, au Inkle and Zarika*) appeared in 1808, the same year that saw the play translated into Hungarian. Later it was even included in the Garland edition of *American* ballad operas (my emphasis).[43] While largely ignored for the first half of the twentieth century, it was successfully revived twice in the 1990s, first by the Show of Strength theatre company in Bristol, England, and seven years later at the Holder's Season in Barbados.[44]

Despite the play's overwhelming success, its text was notoriously unstable. As Felsenstein notes, the script was in flux through the very last days of rehearsal, including changes made to the nature of the play's conclusion. According to John Bannister's biographer, the actor first suggested Inkle's repentance when Colman was stymied for a way to end to end his comedy: '"But after all," said Colman, "what are we to do with Inkle?" "Oh!" said Bannister, "let him repent"; and so it was settled.'[45] The play premiered on 5 August 1787, but by the second night the text had already modulated in response to reviews of the original performance, and the *Morning Chronicle* for 7 August 1787 notes with approval that 'Mr. Colman has attended our hint of yesterday, and weeded the dialogue of Trudge, by taking away the transposed epithets.' (As the Larpent manuscript indicates, Trudge originally boasted that his job required him to 'powder parchments, pounce hair, ink shoes and black paper'; by the time the play was published, the offending phrase had been changed to connect the verbs with their appropriate nouns: 'pounce parchment, powder hair, black shoes, and ink paper'.) Still more changes were made in the ensuing days, and editions of the play published shortly after specify 'as performed at the Theatre-Royal in the Hay-Market on Saturday, August 11th, 1787' and include inverted commas indicating the segments of the play omitted in that performance and thereafter. By the time Elizabeth Inchbald included *Inkle and Yarico* in *The British Theatre* (1808), the omissions and alterations were silently included.

Recognizing the fluid nature of *Inkle and Yarico*'s text is crucial to understanding the implications of our own approaches to Colman's play. As Williams reminds us, art (and one might say especially theatre) 'is never in the past tense. It is always a formative process within a specific present.'[46] With a text that underwent so many transformations and a theatrical event that remained popular for more than fifty years, the 'present' represented on the stage and experienced by the audience was not static. As comments such as that in the *Morning Chronicle* indicate, the play text often changed due to audience reaction while this new version, when performed, was itself the source of fresh audience response. More than almost any other play of its era, *Inkle and Yarico* provides a glimpse into this process of change.

The modern editions of Colman's play themselves reflect the implications of its changing script. The Cambridge edition of Colman's play edited by Barry Sutcliffe, for example, makes use of the complete, unexpurgated text, reconciling the manuscript held in the Larpent Collection of the Huntington Library with the published editions.[47] Frank Felsenstein, on the other hand, uses the edition published in Inchbald's *British Theatre* in his widely used casebook, *English Trader, Indian Maid*, arguing that Inchbald's edition was the one most widely known to audiences in the play's nineteenth-century afterlife. Both sources, while valid, provide only a snapshot of Colman's comic opera: in one the play as it was (presumably) staged on its opening night but not six days later; in the other the way in which the play had come to be staged twenty years later. The changes between these two versions of the single play are substantial and can shape the nature of any discussion of it. In the original version of the play, for example, the roles of Narcissa and Captain Campley, the gallant sailor who won her heart during her voyage to Barbados, are almost as prominent as those of the interracial couples. A week later, both roles had been significantly trimmed; the 'new' Narcissa is less proactive in achieving her desires and more representative of proper English womanhood, while Campley's role is shortened in keeping with hers. One result of these omissions is to focus more attention on the figures of Inkle and Yarico, Wowski and Trudge, the characters who represent the play's popular combination of pathos and comedy.[48]

There have been several excellent examinations of the women in Colman's play and of the implications of the story of Inkle and Yarico in its many variations.[49] My interest here is in examining how Colman and those who staged his play dealt with the difficult problem of representing

Englishmen in a colonial economy dependent on slavery. Where Yarico and Wowski are a source of fascination and concern due to their racial difference, Inkle, Trudge, and Sir Christopher Curry constitute a different sort of challenge precisely because they are not different. It is not the female characters in *Inkle and Yarico* who are dangerous but the male figures, figures who are closely aligned to audiences not simply by their masculinity but by their very Englishness. This connection between the Englishmen on the stage and the English men and women in the audience reveals the tension between the British self-identification as a nation of liberty and its simultaneous recognition that it does not, in reality, support this ideal. The history of these plays on the eighteenth-century stage reveals the depth of this discomfort.

The Trouble with Inkle

In 1795, a self-proclaimed 'Description of the Opera' commented that *Inkle and Yarico* follows the story in *The Spectator* 'in every Circumstance, except Inkle's selling Yarico for a Slave; wisely judging, we may suppose, that would be a dangerous Circumstance, to represent before an English Audience'.[50] The anonymous author here sums up the crux of the problem: English audiences cannot tolerate watching one of their own selling human flesh. To do so lays bare the inherent flaws in England's self-creation as the bastion of liberty. In particular, Inkle presented audiences and Colman himself with the greatest difficulty; as one spectator of a later performance noted, 'Nothing can be made of INKLE, and I think it condescension in Mr. Woods to appear in the character.'[51] Colman's attempt to render the character more palatable by having him abase himself and renounce interest resulted in an awkwardly achieved happy ending. Nonetheless, for English audiences Inkle's willingness to sell Yarico represented empire at its most disturbing, with its commercial connections to the purchase and sale of sympathetic and recognizably human figures made visible through the physical immediacy of performance. Both acquisitive and repentant, the figure of Inkle embodies those internal relations, 'at once interlocking and in tension', that constitute a 'structure of feeling'.[52] These tensions can be clearly seen in responses to Colman's opera, such as this commentary from *The Unsespected* [sic] *Observer* No. 57 (1792), in which the 'conflict of passions' described by the writer translates itself into his own prose:

> The piece is fraught with the most noble sentiments; and the conflict of passions between love and interest in the breast of Incle [*sic*], well depicted. – Some excuse, to be sure, is to be made for him; he is brought up in the sordid

> idea, that gold alone will confer happiness; he has attended close to calculations, and finds the loss of time and interest he has undergone in his intercourse with Yarico: yet, with all the excuses we can make for him, the mind recoils at his idea of selling her; especially after those heart-piercing and plaintive supplications she has before been making on her knees to him, not to desert her.[53]

Mrs Kemble's representation of these 'plaintive supplications' intensified the work's affective power and made the figure of Inkle even more discomfiting to an 'English Audience'. In contrast to Belcour, with his universal generosity, the dramatization of Inkle represents the anxiety that, rather than a nation characterized by benevolence, Britain might actually be a nation of Inkles: mercenary, ungrateful, and sordid, a nation whose dedication to commerce has corrupted its moral fibre. The author of *The Unsespected Observer* expresses this concern explicitly, writing 'Let us hope such a wretch as Inkle (as represented [in *The Spectator*]) never existed: – Young Colman has merited the credit of his countrymen, in making that charming opera he has penned on the subject, end so happily.'[54] 'Credit', in this author's mind, involves not the financial interest that had driven the Inkle of Steele's essay but a stake in the larger endeavour of maintaining the credit of a nation's character, preserving it from at least the appearance of amoral mercantilism.

Despite his native English origins, Inkle proved to be more difficult to assimilate than Belcour, and even the earliest editions of the play indicate words and passages that had already been carefully excised in performance. Through these omissions Inkle's character is consistently softened: his curses are omitted, and he does not address Trudge as a 'cowardly scoundrel'[55] or refer to the ship's crew as 'treacherous villains' (16). More interesting, however, are the systematic alterations made to his behaviour regarding Yarico. In the second act, Inkle encounters a planter who councils him to consider his own interest and sell Yarico. After conversing with the planter in the original version he muses:

> Let me reflect a little. This honest planter councils well. Part with her – what is there in it which cannot easily be justified? Justified! – Pshaw – My interest, honour, engagements to Narcissa, all demand it . . . And shall I now, at once, kick down the character, which I have rais'd so warily? – Part with her, – sell her, – The thought once struck me in our cabin, as she lay sleeping by me; but, in her slumbers, she past her arm around me, murmur'd a blessing on my name, and broke my meditations. (40–41)

As altered, the passage presents an Inkle who is more torn and less calculating:

> Let me reflect a little. Part with her – Justified! – My interest, honour, engagements to Narcissa, all demand it . . . And shall I now, at once, kick down the character, which I have rais'd so warily? – Part with her, – The thought once struck me in our cabin, as she lay sleeping by me; but, in her slumbers, she past her arm around me, murmur'd a blessing on my name, and broke my meditations. (40–41)

Without the reference to the 'honest planter's' councils and especially with the small but crucial phrase 'sell her' omitted, this Inkle's concern lies more squarely on personal separation rather than the squalid act of enslavement. Inkle has considered parting with Yarico while in their island idyll rather than contemplate even then the possibility of selling the woman he supposedly loved.

In the final act, Inkle's disparaging remarks about women in general and Yarico in particular are carefully trimmed or omitted altogether. In one striking example, Inkle's meditation regarding how to manage women like horses is radically shortened. The speech which in the original production appeared:

> I must be blunt with Yarico. I wish this marriage were more distant, that I might break it by degrees: She'd take my purpose better, were it less suddenly deliver'd. Women's weak minds bear grief as colts do burdens: Load them with their full weight at once, and they sink under it; but, every day, add little imperceptibly, to little, 'tis wonderful how much they carry. (60)

Becomes the more innocuous

> I wish this marriage were more distant, that I might break it by degrees: She'd take my purpose better, were it less suddenly deliver'd. (60)

Here, as earlier, the Inkle who, in his original incarnation, calculates how he can turn everything to his advantage is mitigated to a figure who demonstrates some degree of 'humane' concern, suggesting a movement away from the mercenary figure seen in the play's opening scene who calculates 'how much [natives] would fetch at the West India markets' (10). In yet another instance, the remoulded Inkle no longer dismisses Yarico's pleas not to leave her, as 'This is mere trifling – the trifling of an unenlighten'd Indian' (67); rather, he moves immediately to his own entreaty. The effect of these omissions is the representation of a softer, more emotional Inkle, one who exhibits at least some degree of growth. So popular – or necessary – were these changes that by the second decade of the nineteenth century almost all editions of the play included them.[56]

Performances at Covent Garden in October 1788 further enhanced the softening effect by adding new songs written specifically for Inkle. In the original production, Inkle had significantly fewer songs than Yarico and ultimately remained silent as the other characters performed the rousing finale in praise of love. The added songs are notable for their stress on sentiment and feeling; they give Inkle, at Covent Garden played by the actor John Henry Johnstone, the opportunity to emphasize the depth of his feelings for Yarico. In one air, for example, Inkle contrasts his earlier life, 'long in frozen maxims arm'd', with his current happiness 'Dissolv'd in tenderness, when warm'd / With Gratitude and Yarico.' Inkle's rehabilitation was accentuated by providing him with a verse in praise of love and Yarico in the newly expanded finale:

Love's convert here behold;
Banish'd now by thirst of gold,
Blest in these arms to fold
My gentle Yarico.
Hence all care, doubt and fear,
Love and joy each heart shall cheer,
Happy night, pure delight
Shall make our bosoms glow.[57]

The *Public Advertiser*, which published the songs along with a review the following day, noted approvingly that 'Johnston's [*sic*] Inkle evinced a very proper degree of feeling and chaste animation'.[58] The *Advertiser*'s emphasis on emotion highlights the central problem facing the audience: sentiment and pathos – embodied in Yarico – collide with England's cold-hearted participation in the slave trade, personified all too graphically in Inkle. As the alterations to Inkle's character in performance indicate, the solution to this dilemma is through an increased emphasis on 'feeling'. If our problematic hero feels and feels with increasing warmth, then his crime is less heinous and his redemption more demonstratively sincere. In this manner, Inkle's revised capacity for a 'proper degree of feeling' becomes an attempt to downplay the ugly act that is the central event of the opera. Yet the project of reclaiming Inkle can only go so far. No matter how emotional Inkle may be, no matter how torn he is at the prospect of parting from Yarico, he still tries to *sell* her, not abandon her. The problem with Inkle, then, is that he is a slave trader. He is an Englishman who does something unEnglish, something Sir Christopher, himself a slave owner, describes as 'shame[ful] [in] men, who so fully feel the blessings of liberty' (63).

Ultimately, the sentimentalization of Inkle's character represents an attempt to make less visible the connection between England and slavery. Making Inkle less monstrous, to use Daniel O'Quinn's term,[59] makes the audience itself less monstrous. If, as Said explains, an imperial nation has a 'need to be right'[60] in its vision of itself, then the changes to the character of Inkle, represent steps taken to reassure Britain of its essential 'rightness'. In this project, appropriate 'feeling', both on the stage and in the audience, becomes a means to this end, ameliorating a most unpleasant problem.

The Generosity of an English Breast

Colman's addition of two new characters, Inkle's factotum Trudge and Sir Christopher Curry, the Governor of Barbados, proved more palatable to contemporary audiences. Trudge was particularly appealing to contemporary audiences because of his humour and especially because of his rejection of the mercantile principles that drive his employer. A convenient foil to Inkle, he is rescued and succoured by a 'dusky' maiden who also accompanies him to Barbados. But unlike his master, he cannot assess her worth in material terms. When a planter tries to bid on Wowski (warning Trudge not to try any tricks to 'raise your price'), Trudge responds incredulously:

PLANTER Is she for our sale of slaves? Our black fair?
TRUDGE A black fair, ha! ha! ha! You hold it on a brown green, I suppose.
PLANTER She's your slave, I take it?
TRUDGE Yes; and I'm her humble servant, I take it.
PLANTER Aye, aye, natural enough at sea. – But at how much do you value her?
TRUDGE Just as much as she has saved me – My own life.
PLANTER Pshaw! You mean to sell her?
TRUDGE [*Staring*] Zounds! What a devil of a fellow! Sell Wows! – my poor, dear, dingy, wife! (37)

The language of capital means nothing to Trudge; he replaces it with terms of mutuality. His exclamation that he should be 'hang'd like a dog' (71) if he tried to sell 'dear, dingy wife' prompted widespread praise, and his freedom from avarice provided a reassuring contrast to the spectre of an Inkle-ized England. As *The Unsespected Observer* notes happily, 'Trudge, with all the native gratitude and generosity of an English breast, unshackled by those golden calculations of interest, weds his Wowski of his own accord.'[61]

Trudge's demonstration of the 'generosity of an English breast', along with the role's comic potential, made it popular with actors as well as audiences. Despite his success as Inkle, Bannister was impatient to exchange it for the more congenial Trudge. As his biographer John Adolphus explains, the death of John Edwin in 1790 'made a vacancy in Trudge', thus allowing Bannister to take over the role, which he did almost immediately.[62] The part was one of his most popular, remembered fondly by audiences even after his death. Adolphus describes the performance as both comic and heart-warming:

> His quaking timidity in danger, his boastful display of courage which he had never possessed, his rueful recollections of the gay delights, not unmixed with supercilious affronts, in Threadneedle Street, afforded true and delicious amusement; while his sturdy resolution not to play the part of a villain, by whatever example it might be graced, stamped on every heart the true impression of his genuine powers.[63]

Adolphus's emphasis on Bannister's impression on every heart reveals the essence of Trudge's appeal: his ability to incite feeling in his audience. Where Yarico's pathos moved audiences to tears, Trudge's refusal to play the villain prompted audiences to applaud him and implicitly themselves. The repeated emphasis on the 'Englishness' of Trudge's virtues demonstrates the depths of a British audience's desire to identify with him. Cockney or otherwise, Trudge's representation of the imperial Englishman is palatable in a way that Inkle could never be. It is perhaps for this reason that fewer changes were made to Trudge's part than to any other male character.[64]

Despite their differences in class, Trudge's 'generous', 'uncalculating' English nature aligns him with Cumberland's Belcour, an alignment made possible by the earlier play's London setting. In Colman's Barbados, not only is an assumption of general benevolence difficult, but the inescapable fact of slavery permeates the play; the lives of the planters, the merchants, and the entire upper class are dependent upon it. Where Colman can offset Inkle's calculations with Trudge's good heart, there is no easy solution to the problem of representing sympathetic colonial figures – who just happen to own slaves. Sir Christopher Curry is the literal embodiment of this problem. As Governor of Barbados, Sir Christopher is the official representative of British authority in *Inkle and Yarico*. He is at once the designated mouthpiece for English values of liberty and the representation of a system that contradicts them. To complicate matters, as originally written Sir Christopher was broadly drawn, a figure of humours characterized by his inability to rein in his passions. With England's colonial representative precariously in control of himself, the play suggested at best incompetence and at worst England's potential lack of control over its own empire; not surprisingly, his character was redrawn within days of the first performance.

While Sir Christopher's worst eccentricities quickly vanished, the tensions related to his official position were less easily solved, as can be seen in the following exchange with Inkle. Inkle has just offered to sell Yarico to the Governor (the quotation marks or 'inverted commas' indicate lines omitted in performance):

SIR CHRISTOPHER Look ye, young man; I love to be plain: I shall treat her a good deal better than you wou'd, I fancy; for though I witness this custom [the selling of slaves] every day, I can't help thinking the only excuse for buying our fellow creatures, is to rescue 'em from the hands of those who are unfeeling enough to bring 'em to market.

INKLE 'Somewhat too blunt, Sir; I am no common trafficker, dependent upon rich planters.' Fair words, old gentleman; an Englishman won't put up an affront.

SIR CHRISTOPHER An Englishman! More shame for you; 'Let Englishmen blush at such practices.' Men, who so fully feel the blessings of liberty, are doubly cruel in depriving the helpless of their freedom.

'INKLE Confusion!'

'SIR CHRISTOPHER Tis not my place to say so much; but I can't help speaking my mind.' (63)

On the surface, this exchange seems familiar, including the by now standard claim that only the English truly value the 'blessings of liberty'. Yet the changes made in performance are telling. The reference to Sir Christopher's bluntness is removed, along with his statement that he 'can't help' speaking his mind, a statement that reduces the idea of English liberty to a personal opinion rather than a national characteristic. More interesting yet is the excision of Sir Christopher's reference to the 'blush of shame' that any Englishman participating in the slave trade should feel. Such a comment, often used by abolitionists to describe England's involvement in the slave trade, may have seemed too radical coming from the lips of the Governor of one of England's profitable slave-holding colonies.

Sir Christopher's stirring words are not problematic when the Englishman being rebuked is Inkle. But the blush of shame is less easily eradicated when Colman cannot avoid the fact that the speaker participates in the practice he abhors, or, to express the problem more generally, that the England that defines itself in terms of its own value for liberty is a willing participant in the ongoing enslavement of others. This paradox underlies Sir Christopher's peculiar justification for buying 'our fellow creatures': namely that even though the purchase of slaves enables the institution of slavery, it saves them from the brute who is so insensitive as to 'bring them to market'. Participating in an abhorrent custom can thus be recast as benevolence, at least in the case of the Governor of a colony. Even more telling, Sir Christopher's stirring words on an Englishman's respect for the liberty of others comes immediately after he himself has expressed interest in buying Yarico, provided she is 'delicate' rather than African in appearance. Moments before the exchange quoted above, Inkle approaches Sir Christopher:

INKLE – I have a female, whom I wish to part with.

SIR CHRISTOPHER Very likely; it's a common case, now-a-days, with many a man.

INKLE If you could satisfy me you would use her mildly, and treat her with more kindness than is usual; for I can tell you she's of no common stamp – perhaps we might agree.

SIR CHRISTOPHER Oho! a slave! Faith, now I think on't, my daughter may want an attendant or two extraordinary; and as you say she's a delicate girl, above the common run, and none of your thick-lipped, flat-nosed, squabby, dumpling dowdies, I don't much care if –

INKLE And for her treatment – (62–63)

Curiously, it is Inkle's request at this point in the conversation that Sir Christopher treat Yarico gently, rather than any reference to a sale, that prompts Sir Christopher's defence of liberty and attack on the general principle of selling 'our fellow creatures'. But Sir Christopher's almost scientific delineation of two different classes of 'females': 'delicate girls' and 'your thick-lipped, flat-nosed, squabby, dumpling dowdies' makes even these 'noble sentiments' problematic. When he sees Yarico he exclaims 'Ods my life, as comely a wench as ever I saw!' (66), an exclamation that places Yarico in the company of the 'fellow creatures' whose freedom he had defended so vigorously rather than the almost subhuman 'thick-lipped, flat-nosed, squabby' females he had rejected. Racial appearance is key to this Englishman's assessment of humanity, as it is only after he sees Yarico that he can see her as potentially equivalent to his own daughter.

The exchange between Sir Christopher and Inkle exposes the tensions inherent in England's carefully cultivated national identity. Like Trudge's defence of his bond to Wowski, Sir Christopher's zealous defence of British liberty was cited extensively (the *Monthly Review*, for example, quoted nearly the entire final scene[65]) while critics praised his 'blunt, honest, manly sentiments'.[66] Yet, perhaps inevitably, the praise for these sentiments itself replicates this underlying tension. Having lauded Trudge's native English generosity, *The Unsespected Observer* turns to Sir Christopher:

> Sir Christopher Curry, the Governor of Barbados, is a feeling, honest, good man; the scene that passes between him and Inkle is an excellent one, – where they are unknown to each other, and where Sir Christopher disinterestedly offers to take Yarico under his protection, being struck by the native beauty of her figure, and shocked at the inhumanity of Inkle.[67]

The reference to Sir Christopher's 'disinterested' response to Yarico is certainly relevant in a commentary attacking a character – Inkle – who is governed by concerns of interest. Yet, in reality, just how 'disinterested' is Sir Christopher? After all, despite his pledge to Yarico that 'you shan't want a friend to protect you, I warrant you' (69), the fact remains that he was at one point willing to consider buying her. Unlike Inkle, who must engage in a process of abasement and repentance, no matter how awkward and unlikely such a reformation may seem, the Governor's participation in the same market is glossed over by both the playwright and his audience, an evasiveness necessary to the myth of national virtue the play struggles to promote.

The friction between these two very different roles suggests what Williams terms a moment of 'latency', when the time 'of conscious comparison has not yet come',[68] yet where it is becoming more and more difficult for England to elide its rhetoric with its reality, its need to be in the right morally with its actual practice. *Inkle and Yarico* exemplifies this growing stress. On the one hand, English audiences could weep for Yarico and join with Sir Christopher in his rebuke of Inkle. Even this response, however, demonstrates an underlying sense of unease, for, in contrast to *The West Indian*, with its genial picture of a general benevolence that united British subjects in the colonies and at home, *Inkle and Yarico* represents the British colonial enterprise as inherently fractured. In it, the 'Other' whom the audience must reject does not represent some marginalized country or race but an Englishman, born and bred – and bred badly at that. The play asks audiences to reject the mercantile upbringing that produced an Inkle, but in the process it also asks them to reject an established aspect of British identity, that commerce that allows British citizens to 'flourish great and free'. In the end, *Inkle and Yarico* portrays an empire trying to solve a moral problem of its own making as, despite the rhetoric of Sir Christopher and the repentance of Inkle, the play cannot quite eradicate the 'blush of shame' induced by England's participation in a practice that 'depriv[es] the helpless of their freedom'.

Benevolent Planters and Grateful Slaves

A very different solution to the problem of England's participation in the slave trade appeared in another Haymarket production, Thomas Bellamy's one-act interlude, *The Benevolent Planters*.[69] The play was staged only twice, first on 5 August 1789, for Mrs Kemble's benefit, and second on 10 August 1789, on the occasion of the premiere of *The Comet*, another dramatic piece by Bellamy. In addition to its connection to Mrs Kemble (the manuscript of the play sent to the Lord Chamberlain includes a note from Colman identifying the play as 'designed for representation Wednesday next for the benefit of Mrs. Kemble'[70]), the first performance featured a prologue delivered by J. P. Kemble 'in the Character of an African Sailor', lamenting the lot of the speaker who was snatched into slavery but who looks with gratitude towards that 'hallow'd band' that seeks to 'stop the woes of slavery'. The prologue was advertised along with the play as 'An Address to the Humane Society, on the Abolition of the Slave Trade'. In its call for brotherhood among all races, the prologue aligns itself with the rhetoric of the abolitionist movement; however, its sentiments are startlingly incongruous when linked to the content of the play that followed it, in which a group of planters justify an Englishman's moral right to own slaves. Notably, while Bellamy's interlude was not reviewed in any of the major London newspapers, the prologue was published independently several times, suggesting the general popularity of its sentiments.[71]

Bellamy's play depended for its effect on the popularity of Mrs Kemble's depiction of Yarico. Advertised as for the benefit of Mrs Kemble, the play included a female lead who, much like Yarico, is a woman of colour, here explicitly African, characterized by her pathos and separated from her true love. The play has little action: the first scene presents the three benevolent planters of the title talking about the importance of treating slaves with humanity and concludes with the story of two slaves, Selima, played by Mrs Kemble, and Oran, played by Kemble, who were betrothed in Africa when they were overtaken by war and separated, Oran to be burnt alive and Selima carried off by the conquering chief. Just then European slavers burst upon the scene and 'rescued' many of the vanquished, among them Selima and Oran. The second scene depicts Selima with her owner and is distinguished only by a mournful song sung by Mrs Kemble, similar to those sung by Yarico in Colman's play. The final scene depicts the annual day of sport sponsored by the planters, who sit at a distance on 'decorated chairs'[72] and watch their slaves dances and engage in archery where the winner of each bout is freed and given the bride of his choice. At this point, Oran and Selima are reunited and fall upon their knees in front of their masters. In the final lines, Oran declaims:

> O my masters! For such, though free, suffer me still to call you; for my restored partner and myself bend to such exalted worth; while for ourselves, and for our surrounding brethren, we declare, that you have proved yourselves *The Benevolent Planters*, and that under subjection like yours,
> SLAVERY IS BUT A NAME.[73]

The play concludes with an ode to mercy, sung to the tune of 'Rule Britannia'.

Bellamy's piece presents a sanitized vision of slavery that seeks to avoid the tensions that surface in *Inkle and Yarico* by ignoring the uncomfortable notion that slavery may be immoral. In contrast to Colman's Sir Christopher, who sternly reproves the English Inkle, lecturing 'men, who so fully feel the blessings of liberty, are doubly cruel in depriving the helpless of their freedom', Bellamy justifies the slave trade as a kind of necessary paternalism. Unlike the morally deformed Inkle and the concurrently slave-owning and slavery-detesting Sir Christopher, the Englishmen depicted in *The Benevolent Planters* are meant to be seen as models of moral rectitude. Representatives of European colonial philosophy, they explain in the play's long first scene that slavery is essential for the true happiness of Africans, for without the mitigating influence of the English, they would remain no more than a savage tribe. Slavery refines them by teaching them religion and obedience, and only after learning these vital lessons are they ready for the responsibilities of freedom. In this world, Selima's suffering is caused by her savage countrymen, not, like Yarico, by European betrayal and the threat of slavery.

Despite Bellamy's efforts to render slavery benign by stating that it is nothing but a name when properly administered, the topic and its depiction were evidently problematic, as can be seen by the actual history of the script. Like *Inkle and Yarico, The Benevolent Planters*'s text was unstable, although in the case of Bellamy's play, the problems arose on the official level. The play as printed and performed differs significantly from the manuscript submitted to the Lord Chamberlain's office, beginning with the play's title, which was originally listed as *The Benevolent Planters; or, Slavery but a Name*. In the Larpent manuscript, the subtitle has been struck out, and other omissions can be seen when comparing the manuscript to the published text. One of the largest and most telling of these omissions occurs in the opening scene as the Jamaican planters Steady and Goodwin speak to the Englishman Heartfree and agree upon the rationale for slavery, properly administered: The Larpent manuscript includes a lengthy explanation,

HEARTFREE Humanity Sirs, confers dignity upon authority. The grateful africans [*sic*] have hearts like ours. The degrading lash is but seldom needful to subdue them to reasonable obedience, – and may those who dare claim a right beyond that, feel, and severely feel, the sting of mistreatment.

STEADY I respect your sentiments, and subscribe to your opinion. And punishment, in justice to the worthy, ought to be inflicted on the worthless. Turn to your own great city [London], placed in the heart of boasted refinement, and view the unhappy multitudes among your white men, who with their forfeit lives attone [*sic*] for iniquities unknown among those over whom it has been argued we have no right to rule. Yet by the enforcement of industry, producing health, and order curbing licentiousness, we prevent the commission of enormities replete with ruin. The violated laws of your own land [England] sacrifice, yearly, their rebel hundreds. The continual wars on the shores of the uninformed African, are alike terrible and destructive. Reason and Humanity therefore unite to justify their mild subjection, till the errors of uncultivated nature can be done away; – a work not quickly to be effected. And till then, it is certainly far better to take them from among the cruel of their own country, than by a weak attention to false reasoning, suffer them to perish by tortures inflicted by their barbarous victors.

HEARTFREE The subject we are upon, is realized by a poor fellow in my possession. His story is briefly this ...

In this uncensored passage, Bellamy not only argues for the necessity of slavery as a means to save Africans from themselves but also stresses the need to 'subdue them to reasonable obedience', by means of the 'degrading lash' if necessary, until enlightened Europeans possessed of 'Reason and Humanity' can, by means of the 'mild subjection' of slavery, smooth away the 'errors of [their] uncultivated nature'. Abolition, it is implied, is no more than 'a weak attention to false reasoning' that is in actuality crueller than slavery itself. Oran's story, with its account of 'barbarous victors' subjecting their victims to rape and torture thus directly supports Steady's argument.

The passage also provides a more unusual justification for slavery, claiming that African slaves in the West Indies are better off than the poor in the slums of London. This strikes at the heart of English rhetoric about the essential freedom of the British subject as made, for example, by Belcour upon his arrival in London when he contrasts even low-born English subjects with a 'nation of slaves' (he is, as he says, 'a fellow subject and a sharer in their freedom') or by Sir Christopher who, in the passage so admired by the audiences of *Inkle and Yarico*, declares that Englishmen 'fully feel the blessings of liberty'. By contrast, Bellamy states that London's poor commit 'iniquities unknown among those over whom it has been argued we have no right to rule' and even suggests that the 'enforcement of industry' – slavery – would cure these 'enormities' and prevent rebellion. In justifying the slavery of Africans by reason of their barbaric nature, Reason and Humanity suggest that by the same logic civilized nations should enslave their own people to save them from themselves. England, the nation that so carefully defined itself as the great bastion of liberty, that 'Blessed Isle' whose citizens 'never will be slaves', finds itself in need of the very thing it supposedly detests.

This direct challenge to the British self-image did not make it past the Examiner. As performed and published the passage reads:

HEARTFREE Generous man! Humanity confers dignity upon authority. The grateful Africans have hearts as large as ours, and shame on the degrading lash, when it can be spared – Reasonable obedience is what we expect, and let those who look for more, feel and severely feel the sting of disappointment.
STEADY Will your poor fellow attend the festival?[74]

The overt justification for enslaving Africans, as well as the uncomfortable suggestion that England's poor are in their own way slaves, has been excised, while the reference to the use of the 'degrading lash' here is described as an evil employed only by slave owners less enlightened than the three friends, who expect no more than 'reasonable' obedience. The story of Oran and Selima follows as presented in the manuscript, but, in contrast to the original version, it does not serve as an illustration of the necessity for Reason and Humanity to rescue Africans from the 'tortures inflicted by the[] barbarous victors' of their own country. Rather, the history of the two lovers represents a simple story of pathos to be solved by the elevated humanity of the three benevolent planters. Seemingly, the explicit endorsement of slavery posited in the manuscript could not be accepted as officially sanctioned.

While the Examiner's office may have expunged Bellamy's uncomfortably direct articulation of the benefits of slavery to Englishmen as well as Africans, the tensions latent within the manuscript become glaringly obvious when we consider how *The Benevolent Planters* would have appeared in performance.

Sandwiched between productions of *Inkle and Yarico* and starring Mrs Kemble in a role designed to evoke the pathos of her Yarico (the mournful Selima is even pictured on the title page of the published play),[75] the clash between England's need to be right morally and its rhetoric of liberty, already under stress in *Inkle and Yarico*, would have been unmistakable. These fault lines would have appeared as soon as the production began, as it must have been disconcerting at the least to have a prologue spoken on behalf of an abolitionist organization whose goal was to 'stop the widespread woes of slavery', where the 'savages' are identified as white not black (Prologue) followed by a play which defends slavery as a kindly act. More jarring yet, the prologue would have been delivered by Kemble, in the guise of a victimized African – the same actor who would soon after perform the role of a slave proclaiming that slavery, that condition the prologue declared was a state of 'constant toil', was nothing more than a name. As the African Sailor, Kemble describes his history:

> To Afric's torrid clime, where every day
> The sun oppresses with his scorching ray,
> My birth I owe; and there for many a year,
> I tasted pleasure free from every care.
> There 'twas my happy fortune long to prove
> The fond endearments of parental love.
> 'Twas there my Adela, my favourite maid,
> Return'd my passion, love with love repaid.[76]

But this idyll was disrupted by white savages, not black, as in Bellamy's play:

> But ah! This happiness was not to last,
> Clouds now the brightness of my fate o'ercast;
> For the white savage fierce upon me sprung,
> Wrath in his eye, and fury on his tongue,
> And dragg'd me to a loathsome vessel near,
> Dragged me from every thing I held most dear,
> And plung'd me in the horrors of despair.[77]

The opening scene in which a group of slave owners discuss slavery as a comfortably mild form of subjection must have been unnerving immediately following an emotional speech by an actor describing slave owners as tyrants and oppressors.[78]

The play's final scene in which the slaves perform sports for their masters and Oran and Selima are reunited encapsulates Bellamy's general thesis as the planters demonstrate their humane principles in action while the reunion of Oran and Selima provides a *frisson* of sentimental emotion, happiness made possible through European participation in the slave trade. Where Yarico's plight revealed the schism between the British ideal of liberty and the fact of slavery in *Inkle and Yarico, The Benevolent Planters* seeks to resurrect the vision of colonial benevolence embodied by Belcour in *The West Indian.*[79] In performance, this nostalgic vision becomes unsustainable. Where Belcour could represent benevolent colonialism in London, far from the 'land of slaves' he left behind, *The Benevolent Planters*, like *Inkle and Yarico*, is set in the West Indies, providing a physical representation of those aspects of colonialism conveniently out of sight in *The West Indian*. Unlike *Inkle and Yarico*, which had avoided the physical depictions of slaves, in particular those bought and sold by Britons, Bellamy's play depends upon the presence of slaves for its moral and emotional effect; the final scene uses the display of slaves playing games for their masters' entertainment to demonstrate that slavery can be a happy state. By embodying slavery, Bellamy's play forced its audience to witness the reality of British engagement in a commercial practice increasingly seen as distasteful if not immoral. Here actors in blackface perform for the white planters, who represent both the audience within the play and the white, British, audience in the theatre auditorium, demonstrating that while the Planters may be benevolent, they do not see the slaves as 'children of one gracious Parent' (Prologue). As the pageant makes visible, liberty belongs inherently to white British colonists and is bestowed by them upon other races. Bellamy's slaves are not men and brothers but rather objects of the commerce that made it possible for Britain to 'rule the waves', gave Belcour his vast wealth, and allowed Sir Christopher to first converse with Inkle about buying slaves. Within this context, the greatest irony of Bellamy's play comes at its conclusion, when, using the well-known melody of 'Rule Britannia', the slaves praise mercy:

> In honour of this happy day,
> Let Afric's sable sons rejoice;
> To mercy we devote the lay,
> To heaven-born mercy raise the voice.
> Long may she reign, and call each heart her own,
> And nations guard her sacred throne.
>
> Fair child of heaven, our rites approve,
> With smiles attend the votive song,
> Inspire with universal love,
> For joy and peace to thee belong.
> Long may'st thou reign, and call each heart thy own,
> While nations guard thy sacred throne.[80]

The comfortable picture of British virtue supposedly evoked through the play's performance of benevolent colonialism is undercut by the impossibility of divorcing the familiar melody from its equally familiar words. Where Britons can sing of never being slaves, 'Afric's sable sons' can only hope to be objects of mercy as, despite Bellamy's attempt to render slavery palatable, *The Benevolent Planters* succeeds only in exposing the conflicts inherent in Britain's vision of itself, its ideals, and its imperial reality.

CHAPTER 5

The Moral Muse: Comedy and Social Engineering

> I hope I shall not give offence by adding a postscript, to say that if you could persuade one of the gentlemen or ladies, who write plays (with all of whom I conclude you have great interest) to give us poor Jews a kind of lift in a new comedy, I am bold to promise we should not prove ungrateful on a third night. A.A.
>
> –Richard Cumberland, *The Observer*[1]

> In seeing, and in commenting on the Play, the Critick is lost in the man. We are happy to have a Drama of this tendency – and we feel for the credit and advantage of our country, that it was received with the warmest applause.
>
> *St James's Chronicle*[2]

In October 1788, *Inkle and Yarico* appeared for the first time at Covent Garden Theatre, featuring new songs and a new cast. On the day of its second performance, Drury Lane staged *The West Indian*, with John Bannister, the original Inkle, in the leading role of Belcour. This intersection of the two plays that served as the focus of the previous chapter represents more than a simple act of marketing by a rival theatre. The juxtaposition of the two plays, both linked to England's commercial heritage and both overtly dependent on arousing emotion in the hearts and eyes of their audiences, represents a critical juncture in English comedy and especially in the nature of the emotion it sought to generate. While Drury Lane undoubtedly sought to compete with Covent Garden's revival of Colman's popular representation of the West Indies with its own evocation of Britain's colonial ties, *The West Indian* was a play that had become outdated, both in subject matter and in the more intangible property of audience response.[3] Daniel O'Quinn aptly describes this revival as a 'nostalgic rehearsal of a past moment in the political and representational history of the circum-Atlantic';[4] the world depicted in Cumberland's play no longer existed. Equally important, the play itself represented a theatrical mode that had become stale and increasingly irrelevant. In essence, what we see in these competing performances is the rise of a distinctive type of social comedy existing alongside the slow decline of an earlier form, epitomized most famously by *The West Indian.*

At the moment when *Inkle and Yarico* gained its hold on the public imagination, *The West Indian* was losing popularity and was increasingly seen as dated. It had held the stage for much of the 1770s and early 1780s, but by the 1790s it was seldom staged, appearing only seven times in the last decade of the century. This fall from favour of a once popular play, and, I would argue, a once popular form of drama, runs counter to the common perceptions perpetuated by the history of English drama popularized in the twentieth and twenty-first centuries. *The West Indian* is the sentimental comedy most commonly anthologized today, and the assumption lingers that it remains the prototype of a form that characterized comedy in the last decades of the eighteenth century. However, while the play still held a place in the theatrical repertoire, by the early nineteenth century, *The West Indian* and the form of drama it represented were perceived as outmoded, the product of a bygone age. In her 'Remarks' on *The West Indian*, written in 1808, Elizabeth Inchbald sums up this common view:

> A good play, like a female beauty, may go out of fashion before it becomes old. Men may still admire, till admiration is exhausted, and forsake both the one and the other, for that novelty, which has less intrinsic worth.
>
> This is exactly the case with The West Indian. Its attraction has been so powerful, that the custom of seeing it has weakened its force. Still its value is acknowledged. Every one commends it as a most excellent comedy; but it is no longer for the advantage of the theatre to perform it often.[5]

Inchbald's comments indicate that what we today think of as the prototypical sentimental comedy was, in reality, seen as antiquated within twenty-five years of its premiere. While respected as a well-made play, it no longer has 'force' on stage, and it is 'no longer for the advantage of the theatre to perform it often' because this once popular play has lost its power over audiences (and thus its profitability).

As Inchbald's comments suggest, the celebration of English virtues Cumberland sought to generate by turning to the 'out-skirts of empire' had worn thin, and by the early nineteenth century, the play was better known as a vehicle for the actor playing Major O'Flaherty than for the benevolence practised by Belcour. The play, in a sense, became ossified; it was perceived as well made and amusing but no longer vibrant. Prompt books and editions of *The West Indian* reveal a text that rarely changed.

Belcour's occasional swearing, colourful language used to suggest his Creole background, disappeared, but these minor changes began to be made to play texts and prompt books not long after the play premiered. Extensive revisions were made to the character of Charlotte Rusport; in productions after 1780, Charlotte's pursuit of Charles Dudley vanishes, leaving a smaller but more decorous role. With the diminution of Charlotte into a proper lady who is not the active agent in her own romantic life, the play loses its most vibrant woman, leaving *The West Indian* almost devoid of substantive female roles. (Referring to the play as staged in the early nineteenth century, Inchbald comments disparagingly that 'Mr. Cumberland has not always the talent to make his female characters prominent.'[6]) *Inkle and Yarico*, by contrast, outlived the century and remained relevant to audiences well into the nineteenth century. The myth-making that *Inkle and Yarico* promoted, of a liberty-loving empire where the sordid details of colonialism are negated by feeling, remained potent, as British audiences congratulated themselves on their own noble sentiments. The marks of the play's continuing relevance are legible in editions and prompt books of Colman's comic opera. As discussed in the previous chapter, the play text of *Inkle and Yarico* was pliable, undergoing changes from the first days of its performance throughout the height of its popularity in the eighteenth and nineteenth centuries. Prompt books reveal a series of changes that allowed the play to change with the times, softening Inkle's character and removing references to England's participation in the slave trade (a prompt book circa 1819, for example, completely eliminates all depictions of planters[7]). A second series of changes occurred regarding Narcissa and through her Captain Campley. Much of Narcissa's banter with Campley is cut in the early decades of the nineteenth century, perhaps most notably her arguments in favour of eloping; these excisions serve two important purposes: one, they allow Narcissa to remain a proper lady; and two, they move Yarico even more to the centre of the action, thus intensifying the emotional impact of the play at a time when England's involvement with slavery was a topic of widespread debate.[8]

These intertwined components of sensibility and social applicability provide a key as to why *The West Indian* lost its appeal at the same time that *Inkle and Yarico* remained fresh. The problem with *The West Indian* was not its frank emotionality and fine sentiments but the unfocused nature of the emotion that it generated. By the 1790s, this affect was too tame to appeal to theatre audiences. Instead, audiences celebrated plays that had a palpable design upon them, that sought to arouse emotion and through it promote a specific, virtuous response. They wished, as the epigraph to this chapter affirms, to 'lose the Critick in the Man', to feel that emotion has a higher purpose and to embrace this emotion for its pretensions to virtue. *Inkle and Yarico* yoked the tears generated by Yarico's pathos to a generalized abolitionist sentiment much applauded in discussions of the play.

This newer form of directed sensibility can be seen in a second play by Cumberland, written more than twenty-years after *The West Indian*. Often overlooked today, *The Jew* (1794) was not only popular well into the nineteenth century but also universally praised and rapturously applauded for its stated goal of making the stage a moral school in order to rid Britain of prejudice, thus creating a more ethical society. With *Inkle and Yarico*, the project is in part sincere and in part happenstance as Colman caught the wave of a popular movement. But with Cumberland's *Jew*, the goal was not only sincere but deliberately plotted from ideas Cumberland had formed years before. In each case, however, the means to the end of social reform is the generation of emotion in the audience. *The Jew* represents one man's attempt to control the essential paradox of theatre, the emotional power generated by the physical immediacy of the performance with the ephemeral nature of that performance. In his comedy, Cumberland sought to harness the communal power of the theatrical experience and make it concrete. What he proposed was a three-part process in which performance became the means of generating widespread emotion which, in turn, would be translated into lasting social change. In this sense, the performance of a play such as *The Jew* becomes an exercise in engineering a more perfect society, one in which moral goals are achieved by means of emotional appeal. *The Jew* presents a different twist on Joseph Roach's concept of 'vicariousness' cited earlier in this book. Here, rather than seeing audiences seeking to 'experience experience (by vicariously living through someone else's embodiment of it)',[9] we see that the experience that playgoers sought was not that of the embodiment of life but rather of their own virtue. Cumberland sought to take this desire to experience an experience and make it lasting and effective, creating through this process a moral nation.

In the context of the theatre, emotion is contagious, and this contagion was a necessary component of any successful sentimental play, a component that was even more integral when the audience was directed to feel with a purpose. As Helen Nicholson explains, 'the political efficacy, morality, and sensibility of theatre are predicated, one way or another, on the affective qualities of emotion, how they are caught and their effect on the actors and audience's minds and bodies'.[10] Without this affective response, sentiment has no meaning and its theatrical expression fails. Cumberland's play succeeded admirably in arousing profound feeling, and the reception of *The Jew* demonstrates that the intensity of this collective experience was enhanced by a secondary response, a sense of self-congratulation on the virtue of feeling in this particular manner. In this sense, the author's overt scripting of emotional response is endorsed by his audience. We congratulate ourselves on our virtuous response and extend this congratulation to those around us. The fact of this shared response extends outwards, demonstrating the superiority of the nation that experiences it, as that national identification reflects back to the individual spectator, in a seemingly endless cycle. These mutually reinforcing emotions make the illusion of social amelioration possible.

The Moral Muse

The problem that Cumberland chose to attack by means of what he termed his 'simple lesson of the heart' was the widespread anti-Semitism that pervaded England.[11] In the Prologue to *The Jew*, the 'Comic Muse' clearly articulates his goal and locates it within a national context. As the Muse gazes with delight upon his home with all her natural beauties:

> 'Here, here,' he cries, 'on ALBIONS's fostering brest,
> 'The Arts are shelter'd, and the Muses rest,
> 'Here I will build my stage, by moral rule
> 'And scenic measure here erect my school;
> 'A school for prejudice: – Oh! That my stroke
> 'Cou'd strip that creeper from the British Oak!
> 'Twin'd round his generous shaft, the tangled weed
> 'Sheds on the undergrowth it's baneful seed. (Prologue)

After the convention praise of England as the home of the Arts, Cumberland boldly states his didactic aim; the British character, figured as the stately 'British Oak', has been defiled by its prejudice, here represented as a 'weed', a 'baneful' but largely superficial blemish that can be remedied by careful gardening. This goal can only be accomplished through proper education, and for Cumberland, the stage is a school of morality, the playwright the schoolmaster, and the audience members the students. The stakes are high; the Muse / teacher 'bids us strike the daring blow, / That lays his fame or this defiler low.'

Over the course of his long career as a playwright, Cumberland had made a practice of using the stage to strip the creeper of ethnic prejudice from the British oak. The figure of O'Flaherty in *The West Indian*, for example, while encumbered with the familiar trappings of Irish bulls, was nonetheless good-hearted and key to the play's happy resolution. Cumberland's next play, *The Fashionable Lover* (1772), included a Scottish servant, Colin MacLeod, who was characterized by a kind heart and strong sense of honour along with his thick accent.[12] This is not to say that Cumberland consistently rejected ethnic stereotyping; *The Fashionable Lover* also features a comic Welshman and an unscrupulous Jewish broker and money lender,[13] and it was not until years later that Cumberland turned to recuperating the image of the Jew. Yet in neither of these earlier works could the attempt to redress bias be said to be the play's driving force, as it was to be in *The Jew*. It was in this work that he developed his methodology for using the emotions generated by performance as a tool to school the audience.

Despite his use of the stereotypical stage Jew in *The Fashionable Lover*, Cumberland did have a long-standing interest in the (mis)treatment of the Jews in eighteenth-century England. Evidence of this concern can be traced in Cumberland's essays in *The Observer*, published nearly a decade before writing *The Jew*. These essays return repeatedly to the subject of anti-Semitism and approach the topic from a number of different angles. In them, Cumberland discusses theology and concludes that Judaism, while not fully enlightened, is still better than Catholicism (he was particularly horrified by the treatment of Jews in Spain, and references to the *auto de fe* appear repeatedly in his writings). Most striking, however, are a series of essays portraying the experiences of Abraham Abrahams, an elderly Jew. As Cumberland was to note years later in his *Memoirs*, he first conceived of the figure of the persecuted but benevolent Jew in these essays. His purpose was explicitly moral: 'I take credit to myself for the character of Abraham Abrahams; I wrote it on principle thinking it high time something should be done for a persecuted race: I seconded my appeal to the charity of mankind by the character of Sheva, which I copied from this of Abrahams.'[14]

Abraham Abrahams makes his first appearance in *Observer* #64, as the author of a letter begging Cumberland's assistance with an appropriately theatrical problem. His wife would like to attend a play, but he is afraid to take her because of the often violent response he has received simply for daring to enter the theatre:

> You must know, Sir, I am a Jew, and probably have that national cast of countenance, which a people so separate and unmixt may well be supposed to have: The consequence of this is, that I no sooner enter a playhouse I no sooner enter a playhouse, than I find all eyes turned upon me . . . I no sooner put my head into an obscure corner of the gallery, than some fellow or other roars out to his comrades – *Smoke the Jew! – Smoke the cunning little Isaac! – Throw him over*, says another, *and over the smoutch! – Out with Shylock*, cries a third, *out with the pound of man's flesh*.[15]

Finally, he leaves the theatre, 'amongst hootings and hissings, with a shower of rotten apples and chewed oranges vollied at my head, when all the offence I have given is an humble offer to be a peaceable spectator, jointly with them, of the same common amusement'.[16] This mob behaviour is more than physically violent; it blackens England's general reputation for tolerance and liberality of mind. Abrahams avoids taking his wife to the theatre not simply because he does not want her to be attacked and humiliated but because he does not want to disillusion her about the nature of the nation she has adopted as her home.

Abrahams' account of his experience in the playhouse highlights the potent role that the stage plays in creating and reinforcing the stereotypes that fuel anti-Semitic prejudice. Once he enters the auditorium, Abrahams becomes the spectacle rather than the spectator; his attempt to participate in a communal experience instead reinforces his status as 'other'. He is despised all the more for daring to join with other Britons in a 'common amusement' rather than remaining 'separate and unmixt'. The affront is twofold for, as Abrahams' words make evident, not only is the theatre a space which fosters acts of prejudice but the stage itself perpetuates this bias by giving those stereotypes tangible form. Because they perpetuate ridiculous and even inhuman visions of the Jew, playwrights are complicit in the acts of physical violence; the two specific insults thrown at Abrahams have their origins in drama. The first, the 'cunning little Isaac', appeared in Richard Brinsley Sheridan's popular comic opera *The Duenna* (1775). Isaac Mendoza is distinguished not only by his desire for riches but by his passion for 'tricks of cunning' although, as one character notes dismissively, 'the fool predominates so much over the knave, that I am told he is generally the dupe of his own art'.[17] Despite his pride in his own cunning, Isaac ends up the butt of the joke when his schemes to elope with the wealthy daughter of Don Jerome result instead in his marrying her old duenna instead.

Even more damaging is the most famous stage Jew of them all, Shakespeare's Shylock, with his 'pound of man's flesh'. The picture of

Shylock the theatregoers described in Cumberland's essay envisioned was mostly likely derived from Charles Macklin's conception of the role. Until Macklin revived Shakespeare's play in 1741, Shylock had appeared as a largely secondary, often clownish character, in George Glanville, Lord Lansdown's *The Jew of Venice* (1701), an adaptation of *The Merchant of Venice*. Despite the altered title, Lansdown's play reduces the role of Shylock in order to focus on the courtship of Bassanio and Portia. By contrast, in a move that 'every stage history then and now records as a theatrical watershed',[18] Macklin made Shylock the play's driving force. Stripping the character of its red wig and exaggerated nose, he created a figure of almost pure malice. Macklin's biographer James Kirkman describes the impact of Macklin's first appearance as Shylock:

> Upon the entrance of *Antonio*, the Jew makes the audience acquainted with his motives of antipathy against the Merchant. *Mr. Macklin* had no sooner delivered this speech, than the audience suddenly burst out into a thunder of applause, and in proportion as he afterwards proceeded to exhibit and mark the malevolence, the villainy, and the diabolical atrocity of the character, so in proportion did the admiring and delighted audience testify their approbation of the Actor's astonishing merit, by still louder and louder plaudits and acclamations.[19]

In Kirkman's description, the delight of the audience increases 'in proportion' to Macklin's representation of the 'diabolical atrocity' of Shylock's character; the more malicious, the more evil, the greater their 'approbation' and the greater their desire for his ultimate humiliation. If not exactly 'the Jew that Shakespeare drew',[20] Macklin's Shylock became the image most commonly associated with Judaism in the theatre and in the world beyond it. As a result, Abrahams points specifically to this final figure as the source of virulent anti-Semitic prejudice, saying 'I verily believe the odious character of Shylock has brought little less persecution upon us poor scattered sons of Abraham, than the Inquisition itself.'[21]

Observing with concern that 'your great writers of plays take delight in hanging us out to public ridicule and contempt on all occasions',[22] Abrahams adds a postscript to his letter:

> I hope that I shall not give offence by adding a postscript, to say that if you could persuade one of the gentlemen or ladies, who write plays (with all of whom I conclude you have great interest) to give us poor Jews a kind lift in a new comedy, I am bold to promise that we should not prove ungrateful on a third night. A.A.[23]

Just as drama acts to promote prejudice, it can, Abrahams suggests, help remedy the problem by providing a new kind of stage Jew. Abrahams himself represents a counterexample to the Shylocks and the Isaacs that populate the stage. He is generous and, as his postscript indicates, grateful for the kindness of others – in contrast to the recipients of his generosity who accept his largesse and yet handle him roughly when given the chance. Despite his virtues, he is unable to changes the attitudes of the British citizens around him who cannot look beyond the 'national cast of character' Abrahams shares with the stage Jew to see the true worth that lies beneath, what Cumberland in his prologue to *The Jew* will later describe as 'rich ores [that] lie buried under piles of snow'.

After modestly declining any influence he might have over his fellow writers, Cumberland contemplates the problem of anti-Semitism that Abrahams describes.

> I am persuaded that my countrymen are much too generous and good natured to sport with the feelings of a fellow-creature, if they were once fairly convinced that a Jew is their fellow-creature, and really has fellow-feelings with their own: Satisfy them in this point, and their humanity will do the rest.[24]

Prejudice is in this sense a form of ignorance; the theatre audiences that Abrahams describes cannot (or will not) see the common humanity that binds them together. Despite their willingness to evoke Shylock, they are not willing to consider the words that Cumberland goes on to quote: 'Hath not a Jew eyes?' (*Merchant of Venice*, III.i.58). But Cumberland's comments go beyond Shylock's; where Shakespeare's character stresses the physical commonality that binds Jews and Christians ('hands, organs, dimensions, senses, affections, passions'), Cumberland focuses his argument on sympathy. The Jew not only is a fellow *creature*, he has fellow-feelings, those shared emotions central to the moral philosophy of Smith, Kames, and other Scottish Enlightenment figures. The innately humane British people can be taught to recognize this fact, with theatrical performance the means to this end. When, eight years later, Cumberland does respond to Abrahams' request, his play seeks to satisfy the audience that Jews – or at least one Jew – are human and have human feelings. In other words, the object of fellow-feeling has to be made tangible, just as the despicable stage Jews were made tangible. Ultimately, Cumberland did more than simply write a play with a well-meaning Jew – he set out to write a play with a deliberate social agenda. In this new form of comedy, the playwright does not create characters who are simply benevolent on a general level; he creates characters whose words and actions are carefully designed to motivate the members of the audience to change their behaviour in the theatre and on a daily basis. In *The Elements of Criticism*, Kames describes the experience of 'virtuous emotions' such as those generated by *The Jew* as 'an exercise of virtue', explaining that 'every exercise of virtue, internal and external, leads to habit; for a disposition or propensity of the mind, like a limb of the body, becomes stronger through exercise'.[25] Attending the theatre and watching this new form of comedy should constitute a sort of moral calisthenics that leads ultimately to habit, and, on a more communal level, to positive social change.

Cumberland reintroduces Abraham Abrahams later in *The Observer*, in a series of essays that provide an example of a Jew who has fellow-feelings with his Christian compatriots. These essays, nos. 119 through 122, also provide a sketch of the characters and plot that will become the basis for Cumberland's comedy eight years later. The essays are highly theatrical both in their staging of events and in location; the climax of the tale occurs at one of the Theatres Royal and the symbiotic relationship between play and audience leads to this drama's happy ending. The episode begins as Abrahams comes in person to the narrator's lodgings, where he recounts a recent experience to the narrator, a curate, and the narrator's young friend Ned Drowsy, a well-meaning but indolent young man. He is described as a 'little swarthy old man with short grey hair and whimsically dressed; having on a dark brown coat with a tarnished gold edging, black figured velvet waistcoat and breeches of scarlet cloth with long gold knee-bands, dangling down a pair of black silk stockings, which cloathed two legs not exactly cast in the mould of the Belvedere Apollo'.[26] Abrahams greets his audience almost apologetically. He has a story to relate, and he hopes that the narrator can help him assist two worthy but helpless women. As Abrahams explains, he was recently approached by a desperate young woman begging for help. She and her dying mother are being evicted because they owe their landlord money. 'Can there be such human monsters', Abrahams exclaims upon hearing of the man who would thrust a dying woman into the streets because she could not pay a small debt A man rather than a human monster, Abrahams resolves to help the women. He hurries to the ailing woman's bedside, and, where the landlord sees the Jew, the daughter sees the Christian:

> I have found a fellow-creature, said my conductress, whose pity will redeem us from the clutches of one, who has none; be comforted, my dear mother, for this gentleman has some Christian charity in his heart. I don't know

> what charity may be in his heart, cried the fellow, but he has so little of the Christian in his countenance, that I'll bet ten to one he is a Jew. Be that as it may, said I, a Jew may have feeling, and therefore say what these poor women are indebted to you, and I will pay down the money.[27]

As with the audiences in the theatre that judge Abrahams only by his appearance, the landlord dismisses the Jew's feelings as well as his money. The daughter, on the other hand, can only describe Abrahams' generosity in Christian terms. (Jewish charity seems to both characters to be almost a contradiction in terms.)

Abrahams' story is remarkable not only in its depiction of his benevolent heart and generous actions but also in its effect on its audience. The curate (who functions to represent Christian hypocrisy) pontificates on virtue, but he cannot see beyond the surface to the ore beneath; he can do no more than regard Abrahams with 'complacency' and promise to include him in his prayers along with 'all Jews, Turks, infidels and heretics'. By contrast, Ned is deeply moved by Abrahams' account. As the old Jew speaks, this previously indolent youth jumps from his chair in agitation, shakes the Jew's hand, and praises his benevolence. The episode has a profound effect upon Ned as the next morning the narrator finds Ned up early: 'I dare say you will wonder, said he, what could provoke my laziness to quit my pillow thus early, but I am resolved to shakes off a slothful habit, which till our discourse last night I never considered as criminal.' Here is the crucial aspect of the Jew's story – the effect it has upon its auditors. Ned Drowsy is drowsy no more; hearing virtuous action performed has moved him to action as well. His sympathy of the previous night has resulted in reformation – the ideal goal of moral philosophers such as Smith and Kames.

In *Observer* #121, Cumberland takes his narrative into the theatre, focusing in particular on the potential for reform made possible by the interaction between performance and audience. The narrator, Ned Drowsy, Mrs Abrahams, and the Constantia – the young woman old Abrahams had protected – go to the theatre to see *The Clandestine Marriage*, an appropriate choice as Constantia's poverty is the result of her mother's clandestine marriage. As did the father in the Garrick-Colman play, Constantia's grandfather cast off his daughter after her unsanctioned marriage. Since that time, he has refused to see his daughter or granddaughter and has thrown Abrahams out of his house simply because he was a Jew. As the party watches the play, an elderly man enters the box. He is, of course, the hard-hearted grandfather. The scene presents a fascinating example of the later eighteenth century's understanding of the dynamic between spectator and performance, with the audience as a spectacle in itself. The two young people are caught up in the performance and in its immediate applicability to their own lives. The old man, on the contrary, focuses intently on the young people beside him; for him the play is incidental to the words and actions of his granddaughter. Our narrator, however, is able to watch both spectacles, the one on the stage and the other in the theatre box, and to interpret both. He recognizes not only the reason for the old man's interest in Constantia but also the way in which both 'plays' cause him to relent.

The turning point in Cumberland's meta-drama occurs during the final moments of the play. In the Garrick-Colman comedy, the play centres around the confusion and distress that attend two appealing young lovers who have married in secret. When all is revealed in the final act and the aggrieved father casts off his daughter, the warm-hearted Lord Ogleby offers to receive the couple into his own home. At this speech,

> The whole theatre gave a loud applause, and Constantia, whilst the tear of sensibility and gratitude started in her eye, taking advantage of the general noise to address herself to Ned without being overheard, remarked to him – That this was an effusion of generosity she could not scruple to applaud, since she had an example in her eye, which convinced her it was in nature. – Pardon me, replied Ned, I find nothing in the sentiment to call for my applause; every man would act as *Lord Ogleby* does, but there is only one father living, who would play the part of that brute *Sterling*, and I wish old Goodison was here at my elbow to see the copy of his own hateful features.[28]

Constantia, of course, refers to Abrahams, and her 'tear of sensibility and gratitude' is prompted by his generosity rather than by events on the stage. Expanding Constantia's remark, Ned argues generally for the inherent good nature of all men, in much the same manner that Cumberland claims that the humanity of the English audience would erase prejudice if given a chance. In the end, Goodison relents, much as Sterling does in *The Clandestine Marriage*, proving the truth of Ned's (and Cumberland's) view of the goodwill of the English.

This final instalment in the story of Abraham Abrahams, while less specific to Cumberland's project of recuperating the representation of the Jew, is nonetheless predicated upon bias. Abrahams cannot effect the final reconciliation precisely because he is a Jew – his attempts are thwarted by the prejudices of the stubborn grandfather. The final step in the process of reconciliation depends upon establishing a bond of sympathy between grandfather and granddaughter. The power of theatrical performance can do what Abrahams cannot and excite emotion within the breast of 'old

Goodison'. In his next appeal to 'the charity of mankind', Cumberland would turn directly to theatre, staging the story of Abrahams in an attempt to excite the tear of sensibility in the English people as a whole.

Staging the Jew

> If to your candour we appeal this night
> For a poor client, for a luckless Wight,
> Whom Bard ne'er favour'd, whose sad fate has been
> Never to share in one applauding scene,
> In Souls like your's there should be found a place
> For every Victim of unjust disgrace.
>
> Prologue, *The Jew*

In 1794, Cumberland finally put forth the project he had sketched out in his *Observer* essays of the 1780s. His approach to the problem of prejudice he had identified years earlier was to create the anti-Shylock, a Jewish figure who gives rather than takes and asks nothing in return for the generosity he bestows on others. As he noted in his *Memoirs*, his title character, Sheva, was derived largely from the sketch of Abraham Abrahams; he is a modest man who assists those in need, even if they insult him. Here, however, Cumberland uses stage conventions to denote Sheva's ethnicity, much as he did with O'Flaherty in *The West Indian* and Colin MacLeod in *The Fashionable Lover*. In contrast to Abrahams, whose distinctive Jewishness was indicated most noticeably by his behaviour (he greets the narrator with 'all those civil assiduities, which some people are constrained to practice, who must first turn prejudice out of company, before they can sit down in it'), Sheva specifically looks and sounds the part. He is dressed in what the theatre understands as 'Jewish' clothing (the edition of the play in *Cumberland's British Theatre* describes Sheva's costume as: 'gray gaberdine and tunic – gray stockings – shoes and brass buckles – cravat – Jew's hat'), and he has the distinctive 'gray hair and beard' that sets him apart from the clean-shaven Christians in the play.[29] As written, he speaks with a stereotypical Jewish accent that audiences would recognize more from their experiences in the theatre than from their actual conversations with Jews.

In discussing the phenomenon of Christian characters who 'cross dress' as Jews, Michael Ragussis notes, '[through these characters] the theater revealed that the stage Jew was simply the sum of his costume and props – his beard, his hat, his dialect – and thereby exposed the culture's theatrical construction of Jewish identity'.[30] Certainly these qualities, as mentioned above, are characteristic of Sheva. In addition, unlike Abrahams, Sheva is presented as a miser, a man who starves himself and his two servants in order to save money. When he attends the theatre, Abrahams is confronted with stage Jews who are overdrawn figures of otherness and Sheva would seemingly be one of this number; his miserliness is comic (his servants bemoan the fact that they have to share a single egg for dinner), and his accent is equally exaggerated as he exclaims 'goot lack, goot lack!' and worries repeatedly about his 'monies'. Why then, if Cumberland meant to gain his audience's sympathy for 'a poor client, a luckless Wight / Whom Bard ne'er favour'd, whose sad fate has been / Never to share in one applauding scene' does he present his audience with one more example of the figure that has perpetuated negative biases against Jews? Significantly, Sheva must be seen to be Jewish in order for the play's argument to work. The conventions of the stereotype allow Cumberland to establish a visual and aural difference so that the audience recognizes Sheva's Jewishness. Paradoxically, Sheva must be rendered superficially different in order to be identified in the end as fundamentally the same, recognition that can then promote applause and acceptance.

Cumberland quickly represents conventional anti-Semitic prejudices and establishes Sheva's character as the antidote to these biased stereotypes. The play opens with two young men, Frederic Bertram and Charles Radcliffe, both despondent about their finances and their futures. Frederic's father, the merchant Sir Stephen Bertram, has dismissed Charles from his counting house and cast off Frederic because of his marriage to Charles's sister, a marriage kept secret even from Charles. As they bemoan their fates, Sheva enters. Even in the midst of his self-pity, Frederic finds the idea of Jew-baiting good entertainment, describing Sheva as 'the merest muckworm in the city of London' (4). He adds, distracted from his own miseries, 'how the old Hebrew casts about for prodigals to snap at! I'll throw him out a bait for sport' (4). While Charles, who has saved Sheva from a mob in the past, urges Frederic to refrain, his words are qualified; Sheva's 'infirmities' afford no sport, and he should not be taunted because 'the *thing* is courteous' (5, emphasis added). In the space of a few lines of dialogue, these two likeable gentlemen articulate what many of their coarser, crueller, compatriots act out on a daily basis: the Jew is lesser being, a 'thing', a 'muckworm', at best an object of sport to the Christians around him.

As surrogates for the English men and women in the audience, Frederic and Charles share both the common prejudices against Jews and the humanity that Cumberland believes can operate to strip away bias. In particular, they harbour the popular assumption that Jews are misers, love money, and take delight in obtaining it through usury. Ironically, it is Charles Radcliffe, the character who has sympathized most strongly with Sheva's plight, who expresses this conventional vision of the Jew as the worst kind of miser. Spurned by his employer, he turns to Sheva, saying 'And thou has hoarded wealth, till thou art sick with gold, even to plethora: thy bags run over with the spoils of usury, thy veins are glutted with the blood of prodigals and gamesters' (12). Money is the crucial factor in this equation, as exposed in an early exchange between Frederic and Sheva. When Frederic comments that 'all the world knows you roll in riches' (6), Sheva responds by commenting on the prejudice he and his fellow Jews have experienced in the past and continue to experience:

> The world knows no great deal of me . . . I live sparingly, and labour hard, therefore I am called a miser. – I cannot help it – an uncharitable dog – I must endure it – a bloodsucker, an extortioner, a Shylock – hard names, Mr. Frederic; but what can a poor Jew say in return, if a Christian chooses to abuse him? (6)

Frederic's retort, 'Say nothing, but spend your money like a Christian' (6), concisely sums up the perceived connection between money and religion: Jews take money; Christians spend it. A man's faith can be determined by his monetary habits.

Although Sheva verbally rejects the view of the Jew as pitiless usurer ('I am not made', he says, 'of gold extorted from the prodigal: I am no shark to prey upon mankind'), words are insufficient (12). No one can conceive of Sheva outside of the stereotype until his actions prove otherwise. Christians, as Sheva notes, identify all Jews as Shylocks, their veins, in Charles Radcliffe's lurid terms, 'glutted with the blood of prodigals'. Sheva reverses this cannibalistic vision; where Shylock sought figuratively to feed off the flesh of a Christian, Sheva, like the Christian image of the pelican, takes from himself to feed others:

> Bowels, you shall pinch for this: I'll not eat flesh this fortnight: I'll suck the air for nourishment: I'll feed upon the steam of an alderman's kitchen, as I put my nose down his area. – Well, well! but soft, a word, friend Sheva! Art thou not rich? Monstrous rich, abominably rich? And yet thou livest on a crust – Be it so! Thou dost stint thine appetites, to pamper thine affections; thou dost make thyself to live in poverty, that the poor may live in plenty. Well, well! So long as thou art a miser only to thine own cost, thou mayest hug thyself in this poor habit, and set the world's contempt at nought. (11)

These words, which Sheva speaks to himself and to the audience after deciding to give Frederic 300 pounds, set up the argument of the Cumberland's play. The 'world's contempt' has been represented and Sheva's benevolence set in place as the means by which the prejudices will be revealed to be false.

The Jew pivots on the contrast between Sheva and Frederic's father, the ostensibly Christian merchant Sir Stephan Bertram, who notably refuses all requests to spend his money like a Christian. In Sir Stephen's counting house, emotions have no place, and value is based entirely on monetary rather than moral worth. He has rejected his son solely because he refused to marry an heiress, choosing love and virtue over cold cash. Sheva, realizing that for Sir Stephen all women are interchangeable except in their cash value, provides Eliza, Frederic's wife, with a fortune. This clash of moral feeling is encapsulated in a scene in which Sheva demonstrates his virtue concretely in the form of Eliza's dowry while Sir Stephen falls back on unthinking bias. When Sir Stephen sneers, 'You! You to talk of charity!' Sheva responds, 'I do not talk of it: I feel it' (40) as Cumberland emphasizes his Jew's fellow-feeling with the poor and oppressed around him. He drives home this point when Sir Stephen accuses Sheva of usury, sneering 'What claim have you to generosity, humanity, or any manly virtue? Which of your money-making tribe ever had a sense of pity?' (41), Sheva, by contrast, calls the logic of stereotyping into question:

> And what has Sheva done to be called villain? – I am a Jew, what then? Is that a reason none of my tribe should have a sense of pity? You have not great deal of pity yourself, but I do know many noble British merchants that abound in pity, therefore I do not abuse your tribe. (42)

Sheva's pithy reply suggests not only that a Jew possesses feeling but that, disturbingly, the English merchant, depicted as the standard bearer for British authority in popular earlier plays such as Sir Richard Steele's *The Conscious Lovers* (1722), George Lillo's *The London Merchant* (1731), and *The West Indian*, may actually be morally bankrupt.

No longer is the pedagogical project of sentiment mediated through the figure of the virtuous merchant; we are a long way from the kindly Stockwell, with his admonition about the need to govern wealth with temperance. Instead, what Cumberland gives us is not only a rejection of Shylock but a complete reversal of *The Merchant of Venice*. Here it is the merchant not the Jew who is motivated by greed and the Jew who gives of himself to the young and needy. Sheva, like Antonio, promotes the marriage of a young and penniless friend, while it is Sir Stephen who figuratively wants his 'pound of flesh' in the material form of a woman with a ten-thousand pound dowry. This critique of the merchant, absent from much of English drama in the eighteenth century, did not pass unnoticed.[31] The author of the 'Remarks' prefacing *The Jew* in *Cumberland's British Theatre* exclaims approvingly:

> Mark the effect of prosperity upon the haughty merchant! The noble lady, for whom he could find no title but a base one, when he thought her poor, suddenly becomes an angel, when, by some unexpected windfall, ten thousand pounds are thrown into her lap! How mean are his apologies and contrition to Sheva, the bearer of the happy news?! How contemptible his fulsome civility to the high-spirited Charles Radcliffe (his discharged clerk!) when he congratulates him on his sister's good fortune and his own! His pride is doomed to perpetual prostration and reproof, from the fine humanity and superior bearing of the Jew.[32]

'Haughty', 'mean', 'contemptible', the merchant fails specifically because of his 'prosperity'; commercial success results in moral ruin. The praise for Sheva's willingness to mortify his flesh so that he can give away his wealth rather than govern it represents a radical re-visioning of the principles on which the British empire had been built.

By the end of the play, having given away his fortune to the Radcliffe family among others, thus enabling marriage and relieving genteel poverty, Sheva is hailed as the 'universal philanthropist', the 'widows' friend, the orphan's father, the poor man's protector' (73). In the play's final lines, he rejects material possessions while reaffirming the primacy of feeling, as he has throughout the play: 'I do not bury it [wealth] in a synagogue, or any other pile; I do not waste it upon vanity, or public works; I leave it to a charitable heir, and build my hospital in the human heart' (75). Charles Radcliffe uses similar terms as he delivers the play's moral charge:

> You [Sheva] must face the world and transfer the blush from your own cheeks to theirs, whom prejudice had taught to scorn you. For your single sake, we must reform our hearts, and inspire them with candour towards your whole nation. (73)

With their echo of the Prologue's appeal to the 'candour of the audience', Charles's words challenge the audience, along with Frederic and ultimately Sir Stephan, to 'reform its heart', as the result of watching Cumberland's play and see not just Sheva but his 'whole nation' as fellow creatures. Cumberland believes that the recognition of these ties of 'fellow feeling' along with the general humanity that motivates the English people cannot help but change first the perception of and then the treatment of the Jewish people. In this way, the theatrical experience, that common enjoyment that Abrahams had so longed for, becomes the conduit for social change.

The conclusion of *The Jew* exposes Cumberland's approach to the problem of *staging* the sympathetic Jew. As Elizabeth Inchbald notes in her remarks on the play, in contrast to most plays of the era, Sheva carries the entire play and 'those persons introduced exclusive of the Jew are insignificant or merely foils to him'.[33] Given the play's explicit purpose, as stated in the prologue, of ridding the British oak of the creeping vine of prejudice, the plot line of the play could be said to consist of actions this central figure takes that will allow the audience to see (quoting again from the prologue) that 'Virtue's strong root in every soil will grow / rich ores lie buried under piles of snow.' How does Cumberland's character accomplish this feat? By 'spending his money like a Christian', Cumberland's characters repeatedly articulate virtue as Christian, as seen in this exchange between Charles and Sheva:

CHARLES Thou hast affections, feelings, charities –
SHEVA I am a man, sir, call me how you please.
CHARLES I'll call you Christian, then, and this proud merchant Jew.
SHEVA I shall not thank you for that compliment. (II)

Although Cumberland has Sheva stress his status as a man of feeling rather than as a faux Christian, his audience did not necessarily recognize this distinction. As *The Lady's Magazine* notes approvingly, 'the author has made the Jew act like a *Christian* in opposition to Shakespeare's Jew'.[34]

The nature of this approbation exposes the limitations of Cumberland's pedagogical project. Strip away Sheva's recognizably 'Jewish' garb, his stock miserliness and stage accent, and he becomes the emblem of Christian charity, sacrificing himself in order to succour the poor and the oppressed. The Jew can find favour and acceptance among Christians by becoming more Christian than they are, a move that Ragussis describes as 'covert conversion'.[35] Cumberland's audience, it would seem, has to be able to sympathize with Sheva as a fellow-Christian, however closeted, rather than simply as a fellow creature. Such covert conversion is an unavoidable component of Cumberland's undertaking. Whether consciously or unconsciously, he realizes that he must provide a recognizable framework for his demonstration of virtue. His audience can distinguish Sheva's virtue because it is packaged in a form that they understand as virtuous. The 'fellow-feelings' that they recognize are not general expressions of common humanity, as Cumberland had argued in *The Observer*; but those of a specifically British Protestantism. (Catholics, after all, were the villains who nearly murdered Sheva in the Inquisition; in this sense celebrating Sheva's goodness represents a repudiation of Catholic absolutism.) As responses to the play will demonstrate, applauding Sheva and his virtues becomes a means of applauding oneself and the virtues of one's nation.

The Benevolence of the Audience

The Jew was by all accounts a stunning success. Remarkably, despite the potentially controversial subject matter, response to the play was overwhelmingly positive (aside from occasional references to the play's 'slender plot'[36]) as critics lavished praise on Sheva for the nobility of his character and for his elevated sentiments. *The Jew* went on to become one of Cumberland's most popular plays and almost undoubtedly his most long lived, being staged well into the nineteenth century. The play's influence quickly spread beyond England, with performances in Boston, New York, Philadelphia in 1794, and Charleston, South Carolina in 1795. It remained a viable part of the theatrical repertoire in England and American until the last decades of the nineteenth century and was subsequently revived in London in 1917, and adapted by playwright Robert Armin in 2000.[37] Translations of the play appeared almost immediately in German (1795), followed by versions in Russian (1875), Hebrew (1878), Czech (1880), and Yiddish (1882), and as well as a French adaptation in 1811.[38] By 1803 the play and its characters had become so firmly established in the public imagination that the *Charleston Courier* could comment 'OF a Play so well known as the JEW, . . . it would be superfluous to enter into a detailed account, since every one to whom such an account would be acceptable, or on whom it would worth the while of Criticism to bestow it, must long since have been sufficiently acquainted with its plan and its merits.'[39]

Praise for the play takes a variety of forms, usually circling back to the noble sentiments embedded in the play and in its moral. While critics commended John Bannister for his portrayal of Sheva, references to individual actors seem secondary to the emotional effect of the play as a whole, in contrast to a play such as *The Grecian Daughter*, where the actress and her performance rather than the play became the focal point. Critics express universal praise for the nobility of the general enterprise and for its 'benevolent and sublime moral',[40] applauding Cumberland and his 'amiable nature' almost more than they do the play itself. The praise takes on a distinctly personal tone, as Cumberland is personally singled out repeatedly for his general humanity; his noble motivation in writing the play is crucial here, both in terms of the comments on the play and even more so, as we shall later, in the audience's vision of itself watching the play. Overall, *The Jew* was cited by British writers as an exquisite example of English dramatic art, with one critic concluding that 'On the whole, we congratulate Mr. Cumberland on producing the best modern Comedy, since the days of the School for Scandal, on the Stage', a compliment Sheridan certainly would not have appreciated.[41] Audiences delighted in the directness of the play's emotional appeal; in an echo of Cumberland's own words from the 'Advertisement' to *The Fashionable Lover*, the sentiments 'flow naturally from the heart', originating with the 'amiable' Cumberland and, through the medium of the play, with its 'sublime moral', transforming its audience. In one typical response to the play, the reviewer gives a general overview of the plot, then provides an assessment of the play's admirable affect:

> The above, which is but a very rude outline of the fable, can convey no idea of the merit and beauties of a drama in which human nature is represented in the most amiable colours, and in which the most forcible appeals are momentarily made to the heart. Tears are involuntarily forced in many places, by the finest touches of philanthropy; while the mind is very artfully relieved by occasional scenes of humour from the [illegible] of Jabel [*sic*].[42]

The virtues of the play are its 'amiable' depiction of human nature, and the 'forcible' quality of its emotional appeal. The reviewer and his fellow audience members relish the very power of the emotions that they experience, as indicated by the physicality of the author's description. Even the reference to the humour provided by Sheva's servant Jabal is couched in terms of its ability to enhance the overall impact of the play. Laugher provides a pause that then allows tears to be forced once more.

The stress on the appeal to the heart – and on the spectators' delight in responding to these appeals – culminates in the audience's pleasure in being a part of Cumberland's goal of social improvement. Even before the play begins, the audience is brought into the project as the prologue appeals to the playgoer's 'candour' 'for a poor client, for a luckless Wight'. Through its benevolence in applauding the play, the audience becomes the benefactor and the Jew the 'poor' client, despite the actual events of the play in which Sheva is 'the poor man's protector' and the 'universal philanthropist'. They become the active party and the Jew the object of their generosity, a generosity displayed through an appreciation of the play. By simply sympathizing with Sheva, spectators are able to demonstrate their moral worth as noble 'souls such as [theirs]' will automatically have a place 'for every Victim of unjust disgrace'. Thus, the amiable nature associated with Cumberland is quickly transferred to the audience itself, as seen in the *Morning Chronicle*'s review of the play, which dwells approving on the virtue of the author and audience alike: 'The generous idea of rescuing a people from the wretched prejudices under which they labour, is worth the pen of a philosophical writer, and the success which the play obtained does honour to the feelings and the justice of the House.'[43] By applauding the play, thus guaranteeing its (financial) success, theatergoers indicate first that they have feelings and, more specifically, a sense of justice.

Years later, when writing his *Memoirs*, Cumberland similarly connected theatrical success and virtue, just as he had in *Observer* #64, where he argued that the general good nature of the English audience would solve the problems of prejudice. He notes that

> The benevolence of the audience assisted me in rescuing a forlorn and persecuted character, which till then had only been brought upon the stage for the unmanly purpose of being made a spectacle of contempt, and a butt for ridicule: In the success of this comedy I felt of course a greater gratification, than I had ever felt upon a like occasion.[44]

As in the reviews of the play, there is a distinctly self-congratulatory quality to Cumberland's words. The emphasis shifts from the persecuted Jew to Cumberland's personal experience as he describes his own 'greater gratification' on the success of the play.[45] His gratification matches that of the spectators so that ultimately *The Jew* is not about the Jew but about the 'benevolent audience' that Cumberland theorizes.

Interwoven with critics' enthusiasm for the play (and their appreciation for their own enthusiasm) is a strong sense of what this personal response means on national terms. If being moved by the figure of Sheva demonstrates individual generosity of character,[46] a theatre of individuals commonly sharing the same emotions represents a more general disposition of virtue. Following the cue of the Prologue, with its reference to the British oak, most critics equate popular success with national virtue. As *The St James Chronicle* exclaims, 'In seeing, and in commenting on the Play, the Critick is lost in the man. We are happy to have a Drama of this tendency – and we feel for the credit and advantage of our country, that it was received with the warmest applause.'[47] Criticism gives way to personal feeling, which is in turn swept up in national pride: England is a righteous country because it can applaud virtue (even if it has done nothing other than applaud). Two years later, a writer known only as 'Carlos' describes the play's overall moral impact as a natural process which allowed 'the confined stream of benevolence to overflow; and, by overflowing, to fertilize the human mind'. Extrapolating from what he sees as the fruition of this development, he basks in national pride: 'For my own part, I am proud, I feel my bosom glow with the most pleasing sensations, when I reflect, that I am in a country where the mist of prejudice is daily passing away; and where Jews are treated with fellow-feeling and humanity.'[48] Carlos's words are notable more for their emphasis on personal satisfaction than for their claim of improved conditions for England's Jewish population. The author takes an almost sensual pleasure in his patriotic reflections; just the thought of England makes his bosom 'glow' with 'the most pleasing sensations'. In the same way that critics such as Hugh Blair saw eighteenth-century comedy as an indication of British moral superiority, 'Carlos' finds national merit in audience response.

Across the ocean, American audiences responded warmly to *The Jew*, and Cumberland's moral goals found if anything a more engaged audience in the new United States. The drama of sensibility was popular, described approvingly by Boston's *Federal Orrery* as a mixture of the best parts of comedy and tragedy, 'Its scenes possess the *humor* of the one, and the *pathos* of the other. Like TRAGEDY, it ameliorates the heart, by touching the tenderest passions; but, like COMEDY, it chills not the soul, by the horrors of bloodshed.'[49] Foreshadowing the common use of sentiment for political ends in the nineteenth-century American novel, critics praised Cumberland's use of this mixed form, in particular his attempt to use drama to effect social good, 'for, to retrieve from public odium and derision, those national characters, which have been rendered ignoble or ridiculous, by the licentious ribaldry of stage-representation, is the glorious task, to which has been devoted the whole literary life of the immortal CUMBERLAND'. Mere writers of comedy who do not attempt to 'ameliorate the heart' cannot achieve this loft goal, and the reviewer draws a comparison with Sheridan that finds the comic writer lacking. He notes scathingly that Sheridan has attacked Cumberland under the 'unjust' title of Sir Fretful Plagiary, 'but the author of the "*School for scandal*" [*sic*] was little aware, that his sentimental rival was endued with species of *originality*, of which HE was not even a *pilferer* – the philanthropy of the *heart*'.[50] Even more so than Walpole, who had elevated feeling above mere laughter in comedy, this reviewer proposes a literary standard based entirely on feeling; Cumberland is superior to Sheridan because his works display more heart.

This praise for 'the immortal Cumberland' is coded with its own nationalist agenda, as writers suggest that his works can be more truly appreciated by the open minds and warm hearts of the American public, a people who had rejected the shackles of British tyranny. Mixed with the accolades for Cumberland and his play, American reviewers pointedly comment on English prejudices, contrasting them with America's more generous attitudes. One such review in Philadelphia's *Aurora General Advertiser* remarks that 'in England, where the prejudice against that unfortunate people [the Jews] is strong, the comedy met with considerable success, but in the hearts of an American audience unfettered by prejudice, the sentiments it holds out found a soil perfectly congenial, and the piece was received with distinguished applause.'[51] As with 'Carlos', the author uses a natural metaphor to express his national pride, implicitly claiming that his 'land' more perfectly nurtures the enlightenment ideals of liberty and tolerance.[52] In showing their appreciation for Cumberland's broader moral agenda, spectators on both sides of the Atlantic celebrate their appreciation of their own moral worth and that of their nation. Largely absent from these paeans to noble emotion are references to the status of contemporary Jews; what takes precedence is the commemoration of a secondary performance, as audiences watch each other watching, applauding *that* performance as much as they applaud the play upon the stage. They are, in the end, actors in their own drama of national sentiment.

Shylock and Sheva

Not surprisingly, the appearance of *The Jew* spurred comparisons between Cumberland's 'benevolent Hebrew' and other literary Jews, most notably Shakespeare's Shylock. Because *The Merchant of Venice* was one of the most frequently staged Shakespearean plays of the later eighteenth century,[53] Shylock had an embodied reality firmly fixed in the age's cultural consciousness. Almost every review of *The Jew* acknowledges Cumberland's goal of countering Shylock, trying at the same time to balance their praise of Cumberland's social project with their admiration for Shakespeare's characterization of the frequently malicious Jew, a characterization enhanced by Macklin's interpretation of the role as a figure of almost unbearable malignity. Taking delight in the machinations and downfall of Shylock seems to have represented an almost guilty pleasure to these later eighteenth-century writers, one that must be explained by finding ways to absolve Shakespeare of intentional bias and at the same time validate the popularity of a character credited with promoting animosity against all Jews – in Abraham Abrahams' words bringing 'little less persecution upon us poor scattered sons of Abraham, that the Inquisition itself'.[54]

Even before he wrote *The Jew*, Cumberland had considered the problem of such a strongly prejudicial character coming from the pen of the immortal Shakespeare. In Abraham Abrahams' first appearance in *Observer* #64, he asks whether 'this blood-thirsty villain really existed in nature' and 'whether we must of necessity own this Shylock'.[55] In the following essay, Cumberland goes on to consider the problem of Shylock, concluding that the Jew of Venice is not 'the proper offspring of Shakespeare'.[56] Instead, he attributes the creation of the unpleasant aspects of the character to Thomas Nashe's *The Unfortunate Traveler*, in which the unfortunate Jack Wilton is nearly 'anatomize[d]' by a Jew named Zadock. While his argument is not particularly convincing (he quotes a long passage between Zadock and a fellow Jew Zackary that is notable more for its gruesome depictions of Jewish villainy than for any similarity with *The Merchant of Venice*),[57] it does demonstrate the strength of Cumberland's desire to absolve Shakespeare of deliberate ethnic bias. He wants desperately to believe that Shakespeare had no inherent dislike of the Jews; prejudice could not be part of his native genius. Rather than accepting the possibility that genius and bias can coexist, Cumberland argues that in Shylock Shakespeare simply recognized a potentially interesting character and gave it life, not realizing the damage it could do to an entire people.

When debating the merits of Sheva and Shylock together as characters, other writers are less anxious to distance Shakespeare from the active creation of Shylock but instead focus on finding touches of 'nature' in Shylock and using these to gloss his actions. Unlike Macklin's biographer James Kirkman, these critics do not see Shylock as 'drawn, what we think man never was, all shade, not a gleam of light',[58] but rather as a man pushed beyond endurance – unlikeable, yes, but not unnatural. Where Kirkman stresses that Macklin's *acting* was believable ('[Macklin] was at once malevolent and then infuriate, and then malevolent again: the transitions were strictly natural'[59]), the critics look to Shakespeare's character, seeking explanations for his cunning and apparent cruelty. Their explanations, much like those of critics today, tend to centre on the odium to which Shylock has been subjected by the Christians around him. As *the St James's Chronicle* explains, Shakespeare's Jew is true to nature, 'but it is to *Nature in Desperation:* for we find men in despair from ill usage become savage, whatever be their profession or religion'.[60] Presenting this explanation for

Shylock's behaviour, some writers such as 'Carlos' find Shakespeare's character truer to nature than Cumberland's – Sheva is simply too generous under similar circumstances.

Describing Cumberland's character as 'perfectly natural, and truly dramatic', the author of a letter to the *Morning Chronicle* responds to such charges with an argument that reveals how closely Shylock and Sheva were linked in the popular imagination.

> It has been said by some writers on the subject, that Shylock is too much overcharged with rigid and unrelenting malice, and that Sheba [*sic*] is equally faulty in the other extreme. Is the writer aware, that he has thus inadvertently pleaded Shakespeare's authority in full justification for Sheba's generosity? The fact is, they are both designed most evidently as instances of bad and good characters, and each of them is perfectly in nature. – Hence Sheba pursues his object upon a broad consistent principle, while Shylock, substituting cunning for wisdom, so far from over-reaching the merchant, is entrapped himself, and becomes as much the object of general scorn, as Sheba does of universal applause.[61]

As with the critic from the *St James's Chronicle*, this writer 'plead[s] Shakespeare's authority' to justify the characterization of Sheva. If Shylock is natural, then Sheva, of necessity must be as well. From his first appearance of the stage, Sheva could not be discussed without reference to Shylock, and, increasingly, it seems that the same was true of Shylock. As long as *The Jew* remained a play 'so well known' that it needed no introduction, as claimed by the *Charleston Courier*, Shakespeare's character was also envisioned in the context of his opposite. In the eighteenth-century mind, the two characters are conjoined. Conceived of as a means to counter prejudices spawned by characters such as Shylock, Sheva becomes inseparable from his antithesis.

Managers played to such associations, sometimes staging *The Merchant of Venice* and *The Jew* in close succession, as in September and October of 1796, when Covent Garden staged both plays at the same time that Drury Lane mounted its own production of *The Jew*.[62] Less successfully, John Bannister attempted to extend his success in Jewish roles from Sheva to Shylock by appearing in *The Jew* at the Haymarket on 25 July 1795, and in *The Merchant of Venice* nine days later. The experiment was an unmitigated failure, and a later attempt to resurrect the role received strongly negative reviews.[63] To his contemporaries, Bannister's inability to represent Shylock's cunning nature indicated an inherently generous heart. By contrast, his biographer argues that his performance as Sheva employed the best qualities of the actor and the man:

> Never was the confidence of an author more amply repaid, or his hopes more abundantly gratified, or even exceeded. In every passage the feelings of the audience were at his entire command. They tranquilly approved, they laughed, they wept, they yielded to every emotion which the actor sought to impart; and their applause, like their sensibility and their delight, was unbounded. Bannister never was greater or more successful.[64]

As with Kirkman's description of Macklin's Shylock, Adolphus's praise of Bannister is grounded in the actor's power over his audience, as 'they *yielded* to every emotion which the actor sought to impart' (my emphasis). This ability to seize control and manipulate emotion is the source of the actor's greatness – and the audience's delight. By publicly demonstrating their sensibility, they validate their moral worth as well the actor's talent.

Even anti-Semitic prejudices could be traced to audience sensibility, in a move that absolved both Britons and their beloved national Bard from blame. As the author of the letter to the *Morning Chronicle* observes, Shakespeare's 'masterly pencil' made Shylock almost too vivid, so that 'our great Bard, without having in his idea so cruel a purpose, has unfortunately handed down the character of a Jew to posterity, with a degree of prejudice too strong for the reason of most men to resist, and under an impression of odium and detestation almost insurmountable'.[65] The power of the theatre, so frequently remarked upon in moral aesthetics, inadvertently becomes a tool for ill will rather than virtue as audiences are merely weak rather than vicious. They are simply too easily affected to 'resist' the power of Shakespeare's genius. The fault thus is not prejudice at all, but the less culpable qualities of strong sensibility and weak reason. If the frailty of human reason allows men to succumb to the power of Shakespeare's Jew, then Cumberland's 'exalted soul' provides them with a means to combat their weakness. Although he could not paint nature as could Shakespeare, 'he has done more', explains 'Carlos'; 'he has kindled into a flame the latent sparks of philanthropy, roused the dormant feelings of humanity, and taught the confined stream of benevolence to overflow; and, by overflowing, to fertilize the human mind'.[66] In its own way, Cumberland's drama proves almost as irresistible as Shakespeare's, 'kindling', 'rousing', and ultimately fertilizing its audience's good nature.

A very different point of contact can be seen in another later eighteenth-century drama espousing religious tolerance. Gotthold Ephraim Lessing's drama *Nathan the Wise*, like *The Jew*, sought to battle bias through the representation of a virtuous Jew. Written in 1779 but never staged during Lessing's lifetime, *Nathan the Wise* (*Nathan der Weise*) was largely unknown in England until the nineteenth century.[67] While the two plays share a similar motivation, to offset narrow-minded prejudice through the creation of a noble character who stands in opposition to Shylock, they differ radically in form and in the methods they employ in pursuit of their goal. Set in medieval Jerusalem, Lessing's philosophical drama argues for the equal righteousness of all faiths, using the figure of the wise Jew Nathan to propound Lessing's message of toleration. In addition to the title character, the play also features a young Templar and a thoughtful Muslim sultan; Nathan displays his wisdom when asked to name the best religion: he answers with a parable in which the three religions are compared to the three rings a father gives to his three sons; one may be the authentic ring and the others replicas – or all three could be replicas. As Nathan explains, all three religions share the same principles. Rather than quarrelling (or worse) over which religion is the true or authentic faith, men should strive to follow their common first principles and love God and their fellow men. Set in the distant past, Lessing's drama is not intended to be realistic; his goal is to promote the values expressed in Nathan's parable without the distractions of contemporary characters or expectations.

By contrast, Cumberland deliberately chose a contemporary and recognizable setting for his educational project. As the anonymous author of a letter to the *Morning Chronicle* explains, Cumberland chose to 'effect[] his object, through the medium of a Drama, that best mirror of the manners of the time'. By having his play mirror 'manners of the time', Cumberland can force his audience to recognize parallels between their lives and those of the characters on stage. There are no parables in *The Jew*; the connections between dramatic fiction and reality are obvious as Cumberland's characters converse in contemporary idioms, inhabit contemporary London, and wear contemporary fashions. Religious tolerance is effected not through reason, as occurs with Lessing's parable, but instead by means of an immediate emotional connection that 'ameliorates the heart'. If Lessing's Middle Eastern setting provides the distance necessary for reflection, the immediacy of modern London, while uncomfortable and potentially controversial, seeks to eliminate distance by means of identification and fellow-feeling. Ironically, while Cumberland's play had the more direct impact, Lessing's drama had the longer cultural life. Specifically designed to effect change through the presentness of performance, *The Jew*'s potency eventually eroded as the social context changed, and a play designed for theatrical impact could not sustain its popular success when read in solitude. With Lessing's work, it is the play rather than the performance which is the crucial entity. Existing in the realm of ideas, *Nathan* became a symbol, while *The Jew*, by contrast, was an experience, existing in the realm of feeling and dependent for its efficacy on immediacy and the contagion of communal emotion. For Cumberland and his sentimental agenda, symbolic meaning was not sufficient.

Future Shevas

The Jew did not, of course, rid Britain of prejudice or dissipate the legacy of anti-Semitism in England and abroad. However, it did represent enough of a threat to certain established biases that William Cobbett, for example, attacked Cumberland and his play several times, at one point labelling Sheva a 'monstrous caricature'.[68] Nineteenth-century English productions trimmed the play, consistently omitting some of Sheva's most direct condemnations of English bias, such as his remarks to Frederick Bertram that 'when your playwriters want a butt or a buffoon, or a knave to be made sport of, out comes a Jew to be baited and buffeted through five long acts for the amusement of all good Christians – Cruel sport, merciless amusement!' Excised in performance, these passages also disappeared from many editions of the play.[69]

While Cumberland complained in his *Memoirs* that he received no thanks from British Jews for his efforts on their behalf, he and his play became increasingly popular with Jewish communities in England and America during the nineteenth and twentieth centuries. On the centenary of Cumberland's death in 1911, Louis Zangwill presented the 'Richard Cumberland Centenary Memorial Paper' before the Jewish Historical Society of England and subsequently published it.[70] In the United States, an abridged version of *The Jew* was revived for private performance in 1919, and the text of this adaptation published along with a study of Cumberland by Rabbi Louis I. Newman as *Richard Cumberland: Critic and Friend of the Jews*.[71] Newman laments the 'seeming indifference' of an earlier age and concludes his essay emotionally, rejoicing that he 'is able to pay honor and tribute in America to the British pioneer of pro-Jewish liberalism. For high on the scroll, the Recording Angel can write down Richard Cumberland as a true friend of the Jewish people.'[72]

Cumberland's work was presented to a broader audience on 8 May 1917, exactly 123 years after the play's premiere, when *The Jew* was revived in London, at the Strand Theatre. Adapted and produced by Gertrude and M. J. Landa, the play was staged for one performance only, with an appropriately charitable purpose: to aid Jewish war victims. In his book *The Jew in Drama*, Landa praises Cumberland as a 'champion' of the Jews and describes *The Jew* as the only work of Cumberland remembered one hundred years after his death.

> On May 8, 1917, I had the satisfaction of producing it at a matinee on behalf of a war charity at the Strand Theatre, London. Mrs. Landa and I condensed the play into three; we eliminated the super-sentimental speeches and one minor character, Mrs. Goodison. The play proved itself rather too simple for modern tastes, but it showed that the character of Sheva is worthy of a first-class actor and that for Jews the piece must always retain a deep interest. Sheva was excellently portrayed by Mr. S. Teitelbaum, a Yiddish actor, who had only once before played in English.[73]

Landa's account suggests that the production was more of a historical curiosity than a dramatic success, with the 'super-sentimentality' of the play a liability rather than a prompt for emotion. He echoes Inchbald's observation that Sheva is the play's one significant character and thus worthy of a 'first-class' actor, especially one of Jewish ancestry. In this revival, it is significant to the actors and the audience that Sheva is decidedly *not* half a Christian.

While Cumberland's play could not dislodge the Shylocks and cunning little Isaacs from the stage, it is through the history of performance that the legacy of *The Jew* lives today, traceable through the career of a boy watching from the wings at Drury Lane Theatre during the years of *The Jew*'s greatest success. That boy was Edmund Kean, who, according to his biographer, relieved 'the tedium of his existence by imitating Jack Bannister [the original Sheva] and other famous players'.[74] The trace of this childhood experience can be found in Kean's interpretation of a more famous role when, in 1814, twenty years after the premiere of Cumberland's play, Kean made a stunning appearance at Drury Lane in *The Merchant of Venice*. His performance presented a radically different interpretation of Shylock, one which humanized Shakespeare's Jew and elicited not horror but sympathy, as did the more humble Jew Kean had imitated twenty years before.[75] This revisioning of the most famous of all stage Jews, an interpretation that remains current today, represents Sheva's greatest legacy.

Afterword

> The whole mystery [of theatre] is in the emotions it raises in us, and the kindred emotions which the wonderful principle of association is sure to awaken.
>
> –James Boaden, *Memoirs of Mrs Siddons*[1]

In the end, Cumberland's larger project was thwarted by the very elements that made his play and so many other sentimental plays successful: the profound emotional impact of the play in performance. The emotions experienced by his audiences, while powerful, were, like the performance itself, ephemeral, and the sense of virtue experienced by spectators dissipated after they left the theatre. The feelings experienced by eighteenth-century audiences demanded a distinct cultural context, and when that context slipped away, the impact of the drama, its *raison d'être*, was lost as well. It is not that prejudice against Jews has vanished but rather that the method of calling attention to this prejudice has become distasteful; as Landa notes, by the early twentieth century, *The Jew* was 'too simple' and 'super-sentimental' for modern taste. Thus the play becomes a historical entity rather than a lived experience, even to an audience sympathetic to the lesson the play teaches. *The Grecian Daughter*, along with its predecessors *The Roman Father* and *Virginia*, has likewise slipped into the past, while *The West Indian* has become an object of study rather than a stage presence. Only *Inkle and Yarico* has appeared on the stage in recent years. Our context has changed and with it our response to these plays and to others. In a post-Holocaust world, anti-Semitism no longer bears the face of Macklin's Shylock; English nationalism no longer takes the imperial form that animated *The Grecian Daughter* and *The West Indian*. Slavery, both past and present, still haunts us, and thus the reminder embodied in Yarico's stage presence has the power to move us still.

The sentimental dramas of the later eighteenth century are not brilliant literary works by our standards; their plots and language seem lacklustre and even insipid. Instead, authors strove to evoke emotion, their works designed to move an audience that believed that the capability to feel was proof of benevolent humanity. The play, as a document, was secondary; it existed as a vehicle for actors, who were themselves the conduit through which emotions were aroused in the audience. Without this symbiotic relationship, without the fellow-feeling that welcomed Sheva or the rapturous applause that elevated *The Grecian Daughter*, we are left with nothing but words, with plays that are in some cases embarrassingly 'simple' and others not even 'tolerable'. These plays found their meaning when performed in front of spectators who shared moral values, spectators primed to feel and to believe that their emotions, even when painful, had the potential for good.

With its association of fellow-feeling and moral worth, the theatre of the later eighteenth century manifests social forces now foreign to our twentieth-first century theatregoing experience. On the most basic level, the theatres we attend and the way in which we attend them have changed radically over the past 200 years. David Mendelsohn describes the experience of attending the theatre today as 'private, personal, anonymous, invisible'. When entering a theatre, 'we assume a kind of willed anonymity, exchanging the familiar world of lights and activity and noise for an uncanny, hushed darkness'.[2] He contrasts this anonymous invisibility with the physically and thematically public theatre to be encountered in the amphitheatres of fifth century BCE Greece. The enclosed and illuminated spaces of theatres in later eighteenth-century London intensified the public and communal nature of theatregoing, making it possible for audiences to be spectators of events in the audience as well as on the stage. Chief among these events was the demonstration of proper feeling. At a time when feeling was perceived as evidence of humanity and moral potential, providing visible evidence that one felt appropriately was a moral imperative, and attending the theatre provided an opportunity to feel *and* to display these emotions externally.

In this sense, the theatre constituted a panopticon in which spectators were able to witness and judge each others' response. It is important to remember that for Jeremy Bentham, the panopticon was not simply a model for a prison but a physical vision of morality writ large, a kind of moral architecture. It was a place where 'morals [are] reformed, health preserved, industry invigorated, instruction diffused, public burthens lightened, economy seated as it were upon a rock',[3] ideals achieved by watching others. In the theatre, spectators thrilled to these moral opportunities, revelling in the possibility that the *frisson* of the theatrical experience was virtue writ large. The regulation so approved by Bentham can be seen at work in the case of Mr Grabbe Robinson, whose seemingly inappropriate behaviour – laughter at a tragedy – was socially sanctioned when it was discovered to be hysteria and thus the expression of proper feeling rather than insensitivity. For us, the theatre no longer constitutes a site for the display and regulation of proper emotion. While our society still expects us to respond publicly with proper emotion, such displays arise from different stimuli and within different settings; the cord between theatre and the expression of moral response has been severed. We may even feel a whiff of nostalgia for an age in which theatre was so all-consuming and so venerated, so very much the expression of a country's moral worth.

Even though these plays are not lost gems to be revived and revered, they are products of a specific time and place, and as such a record of lived experience, a nexus of social ideals, practical realities and the emotions generated by these experiences. Playwrights and audiences in the eighteenth century understood this intersection of thought and feeling or, in Raymond Williams's phrase, 'thought as felt and feeling as thought'.[4] Emotion had a moral imperative; man was the sympathizing animal, and this fellow-feeling was the first step on the road to personal as well as national virtue, for a nation made up of properly sympathetic subjects was in itself inherently good. Thus the desire to feel and the ability to represent these feelings confirmed personal worth, and, on a larger scale, provided the foundation for a moral society and at the same time demonstrated that such a society did exist. In this way, the focus on feeling reveals core social values, the qualities that audiences on both sides of the Atlantic extolled as representative of their own national virtue. For British audiences, this idealized society was one in which benevolence guided commerce and where empire, even one dependent on slavery, could be defined by liberty. That this identity did not exist was in many ways irrelevant; the playhouse was a place of desires rather than realities.

In the gap between the powerful response these works generated in the past and the lack of such a response in our present, we can recognize the contingent nature of theatre, its dependence on the collective experience shared by actors and audiences. This synergy differentiates it from other forms of art; its power resides in the synthesis of performance and response, event and experience. To eighteenth-century writers, human response became the way to understand theatre, just as theatre became a way to understand the workings of the individual soul and the formation of society. Thus, they considered theatre's affect in the here and now, recognizing that the present, the passing moment, is what makes theatre unique, more powerful than the static work of art, than philosophy, than the pulpit itself. In no time since the eighteenth century has emotion been so venerated or has theatre held such an elevated position in the popular imagination. If the drama of the later eighteenth century resists formal exegesis, if its power has dissipated, its existence bears witness to the way in which emotion shapes our understanding of both text and performance. They are inseparable parts of a whole, now as in the past, and as long as theatre exists, so too will the response that defines it.

Notes

Introduction

1. Charles Dibdin, *A Complete History of the Stage*, 5 vols. (London, 1800), V: 61. In an uncanny echo of Dibdin, John Limon writes, 'the audience cannot err, it cannot feign'. *Stand-up Comedy in Theory, or, Abjection in America* (Durham, NC: Duke University Press, 2000), 13.
2. W. R. Chetwood, *A General History of the Stage, from its Origin in Greece down to the present Time. With Memoirs of most of the principal Performers that have appeared on the English and Irish Stage for these last Fifty Years* (1749), 28.
3. James Boswell, *London Journal, 1762–1763*, ed. Frederick Pottle (New York: McGraw-Hill, 1950), 257.
4. Brett D. Wilson, *A Race of Female Patriots: Women and the Public Spirit on the British Stage, 1688–1745* (Lewisburg: Bucknell University Press, 2011), ix.
5. For a detailed exploration of shifting forms of antitheatricality, see Lisa A. Freeman, *Antitheatricality and the Body Politic* (Philadelphia: University of Pennsylvania Press, 2017).
6. *St James's Chronicle or the British Evening Post* (10 May 1794).
7. Robin Bernstein, 'Toward the Integration of Theatre History and Affect Studies: Shame and the Rude Mechs's *The Method Gun*', *Theatre Journal* 64, no. 2 (May 2012): 218.
8. See, for example, *Culture and Society, 1780–1950* (London: Chatto and Windus, 1958); *The Long Revolution* (London: Chatto and Windus, 1961); and *The City and the Country* (Oxford: Oxford University Press, 1973).
9. Sean Matthews, 'Change and Theory in Raymond Williams's Structures of Feeling', *Pretexts: Literary and Cultural Studies* 10, no. 2 (2001): 179–194. Williams's term, although widely used, is rarely defined, and, as Matthews notes, although Williams used the phrase throughout his career, it has 'provoked bemusement, vexation, and even censure' (179).
10. Raymond Williams, *Marxism and Literature* (Oxford: Oxford University Press, 1977), 132.
11. Ibid.
12. Ibid., 130.

13. Ibid., 133.
14. Ibid., 132.
15. Ibid., 129.
16. Kames discusses what he termed 'ideal presence' in *The Elements of Criticism* (1762):

> In contradistinction to real presence, ideal presence may properly be termed *a waking dream*; because, like a dream, it vanisheth the moment we reflect upon our present situation: real presence, on the contrary, vouched by eye-sight, commands our belief, not only during the direct perception, but in reflecting afterward on the object. To distinguish ideal presence from reflective remembrance, I give the following illustration: when I think of an event as past, without forming an image, it is barely reflecting or remember that I was an eye-witness: but when I recall the event so distinctly as to form a complete image of it, I perceive it as passing in my presence, and this perception is an action of intuition, into which reflection enter not, more than into an act of sight.
>
> Tho' ideal presence is thus distinguished from real presence on the one side, and from reflective remembrance on the other, it is however variable without any precise limits; rising sometimes toward the former, and often sinking toward the latter.

Henry Home, Lord Kames, *The Elements of Criticism*, 2 vols., ed. Peter Jones (Indianapolis: Liberty Fund, 2005), I: 68. Kames revised *The Elements of Criticism* several times in his lifetime; this edition is based on the 1785 edition. Unless otherwise noted, all references to *Elements of Criticism* refer to this edition.

17. Herbert Blau, *Take Up the Bodies: Theater at the Vanishing Point* (Champaign: University of Illinois Press, 1982), 83.
18. Joseph Roach, *It* (Ann Arbor: University of Michigan Press, 2007), 28. Roach addresses the topic of vicariousness in an earlier article, 'Vicarious: Theater and the Rise of Synthetic Experience', in *Theorizing Practice: Redefining Theatre History*, ed. W. B. Worthen and Peter Holland (New York: Palgrave, 2005), 15–30.
19. Emile Durkheim, *The Elementary Forms of Religious Life*, trans. Joseph Ward Swain (London: George Allen and Unwin, Ltd, 1915), 215.
20. James Boaden, *Memoirs of Mrs Siddons. Interspersed with Anecdotes of Authors and Actors*, 2 vols. (London: Henry Colburn, 1827), I: 314.
21. Joseph Roach, *The Player's Passion: Studies in the Science of Acting* (Newark: University of Delaware Press, 1985), 31–32. See especially chapter 2 ('Nature Still, But Nature Mechanized', 58–92) for a discussion of the impact of Le Brun and for the eighteenth-century's use of theories of the passions in acting and the arts.
22. As discussed in *Entretiens sur le Fil naturel* (1757).
23. Arthur Sherbo, *English Sentimental Drama* (East Lansing: Michigan State University Press, 1957), vii, 123. Despite his distaste for his subject matter, Sherbo clearly articulates some of the complications that emerge when approaching so-called sentimental drama. He notes the instability of the word 'sentimental' and rigorously deconstructs earlier critics such as Ernest Bernbaum's

and Joseph Krutch's use of the term, effectively demonstrating how broadly and sometimes inaccurately some of their standards can be applied. (He points to overly general criteria such as 'moral purpose', 'good or perfectible human beings as characters', 'artificiality', and 'appeal to the emotions'.) He substitutes his own set of identifying 'considerations' that he sees as essential components of sentimental drama: the prolonged treatment of overly familiar characters and situations; the 'eschewal' of humour and the bawdy; and an overly determined goal. Even so, he admits that non-sentimental plays may possess all of these considerations and yet not truly qualify as a sentimental drama, the same difficulty he found in earlier studies. In a chapter titled 'Other Criteria', he turns to aesthetics as the ultimate solution, explaining: 'Sentimental drama is almost always sophisticated and deliberately calculated; simplicity and sincerity seldom have a place in it. Following logically upon the preceding statement comes the very important consideration that plays of obvious artistic distinction and integrity cannot be called sentimental drama. The very essence of sentimental drama is to be found in its artificiality, its improbability, and its illogicality' (123).

24. Lynn Festa, *Sentimental Figures of Empire in Eighteenth-Century Britain and France* (Baltimore: Johns Hopkins University Press, 2006), 14.
25. Drawing from Laura Brown as well as Ian Watt and other proponents of the eighteenth-century novel, David Marshall even states inaccurately that 'in the course of the eighteenth century the public would increasingly abandon the playhouse and reconstitute itself around the individual acts of reading; historically, spectators would give way to readers'. *The Figure of Theater: Shaftsbury, Defoe, Adam Smith, and George Eliot* (New York: Columbia University Press, 1986), 10.
26. Laura Brown, *English Dramatic Form, 1660–1760: an Essay in Generic History* (New Haven: Yale University Press, 1981), 180.
27. Frank H. Ellis encounters these problems in *Sentimental Comedy: Theory and Practice* (Cambridge: Cambridge University Press, 1991), when he endeavours to devise a blueprint for the form and subject matter of sentimental comedy. See especially 'Theory' (3–22) where Ellis provides a chart of objects of pity, explaining that '[sentimentality] is a spectrum of attitudes reaching from pity for a non-existing object at one extreme to pity for all humanity at the other' (4–5). Earlier studies of sentimental drama such as Arthur Sherbo's *English Sentimental Drama* are less schematic and ultimately more successful.
28. Robert D. Hume, 'The Multifarious Forms of Eighteenth-Century Comedy', in *The Rakish Stage: Studies in English Drama, 1660–1800* (Carbonsdale and Edwardsville: Southern Illinois University Press, 1983), 214–244. Aparna Gollapudi, *Moral Reform in Comedy and Culture, 1696-1747* (Farnham: Ashgate, 2011).
29. Wilson, *A Race of Female Patriots*, viii.
30. See, for example, foundational works by Gillian Russell (*Theatres of War: Performance, Politics and Society 1793–1815* [1995]) and Lisa A. Freeman in

Character's Theater: Gender and Identity on the Eighteen-Century English Stage (Philadelphia: University of Pennsylvania Press, 2002) which broke from more traditional formalist approaches, with Russell examining the social and political operation of theatre at the end of the eighteenth century and Freeman focusing on the performance of character and the ways in which the staging of identity reflected cultural values. Recent notable studies have explored gender and ethnic issues, such as works by Felicity Nussbaum (*Rival Queens: Actresses, Performance, and the Eighteenth-Century British Theater*, Philadelphia: University of Pennsylvania Press, 2010) and Michael Raggusis (*Theatrical Nation: Jews and Other Outlandish Englishmen in Georgian Britain*, Philadelphia: University of Pennsylvania, 2010). Daniel O'Quinn connects theatrical performance to political issues involving colonialism and the British empire (*Staging Governance: Theatrical Imperialism in London, 1770–1800*, Baltimore: Johns Hopkins' University Press, 2005; *Entertaining Crisis in the Atlantic Imperium 1770–1790*, Baltimore: Johns Hopkins' University Press, 2011). Other scholarly works, while less directly centred on theatre in the eighteenth century, promote an understanding of the operation of theatre and drama by introducing a variety of cultural phenomena that inflect performance. See, for example, Misty Anderson's examination of the performance of Methodism in *Imagining Methodism in Eighteenth-Century Britain* (Baltimore: Johns Hopkins University Press, 2012) as well as a forthcoming work by Kathleen Wilson that expands the study of theatre beyond England and into the broader British empire (*Strolling Players of Empire: Theatre, Culture and Modernity in the British Provinces*, Cambridge: Cambridge University Press). Useful discussions of the figure of the actor in culture also appear in recent work in celebrity studies, see especially Heather McPherson, *Art and Celebrity in the Age of Reynolds and Siddons* (University Park: Penn State University Press, 2017), as well as works by Cheryl Wanko (*Roles of Authority: Thespian Biography and Celebrity in Eighteenth-Century England*, Lubbock: Texas Tech University Press, 2003) and Laura Engel (*Fashioning Celebrity: Eighteenth-Century British Actresses and Strategies for Image Making*, Columbus: Ohio State University Press, 2011).

My own work is greatly indebted to these and other scholars whose expertise has expanded our understanding of the workings of theatre in Britain and its colonies.

31. George Colman the Younger, *Inkle and Yarico* (London, 1787), 63.
32. Richard Brinsley Sheridan, *School for Scandal*, in *The Dramatic Works of Richard Brinsley Sheridan*, ed. Cecil Price, 2 vols. (London: Oxford University Press, 1973), I.1.99–109.
33. Ibid., 4.3.419–423.
34. Festa, *Sentimental Figures of Empire*, 3.
35. Samuel Johnson, *Dictionary*, 2 vols. (London, 1755), II, n.p., 'sense', fourth definition.

36. Through all the mental powers thy soft control.
Study through thee by lively taste refin'd
The quick perception know, and flowing thought;
Through thee warm Fancy dares a bolder flight,
And graver Wisdom, by thy quick'ning aid,
Smiles with superior grace. Benevolence
Borrows her kindliest glow of thee. From thee
Friendship her sweetness takes; and Love, thy child,
Without thee dies. Is not thine the power,
That lifts Religion to the heaven of heavens,
And bears her dauntless, mid the angelic throngs,
E'en to the throne of Truth?

[Samuel Johnson], 'Sensibility'. *A Poem. Written in the Year 1773* ([London], n.d.), 34.

37. Janet Todd, *Sensibility: An Introduction* (London: Methuen, 1986), 4.

38. History will record, that on the morning of the 6th of October 1789, the king and queen of France, after a day of confusion, alarm, dismay and slaughter, lay down, under the pledge security of public faith, to indulge nature in a few hours of respite, and troubled melancholy repose. From this sleep the queen was first startled by the voice of the centinel at her door, who cried out to save herself by flight – that was the last proof of fidelity he could give – that they were upon him, and he was dead. Instantly he was cut down. A band of cruel ruffians and assassins, reeking with his blood, rushed into the chamber of the queen, and pierced with a hundred strokes of bayonets and poniards the bed, from whence this persecuted woman had but just time to fly almost naked, and through ways unknown to the murderers had escaped to seek refuge in at the feet of a king and husband, not secure of his own life for a moment.

This king, to say no more of him, and this queen, and their infant children (who once would been the pride and hope of a great generous people) were then forced to abandon the sanctuary of the most splendid palace in the world, which they left swimming in blood, polluted by massacre, and strew with scattered limbs and mutilated carcases.

Edmund Burke, *Reflections on the Revolution in France*, in *The Writings and Speeches of Edmund Burke*, ed. L. G. Mitchell and William B. Todd, 9 vols. (Oxford: Clarendon Press, 1989), VIII: 121–122.

39. Chris Jones, *Radical Sensibility: Literature and Ideas in the 1790s* (New York: Routledge, 1993), 3. Jones describes sensibility as 'apparently an appeal to unconditional natural feelings, it was also a social construction which translated prevailing power-based relationships into loyalties upheld by "natural" feelings' (7).

40. Mary Wollstonecraft, *A Vindication of the Rights of Woman*, in *The Works of Mary Wollstonecraft*, ed. Janet Todd and Marilyn Butler, 8 vols. (New York: New York University Press, 1989), V: 130.

41. Burke, *Reflections on the Revolution in France*, VIII: 57. 'I flatter myself that I love a manly, moral, regulated liberty as well as any gentleman of that society [France], be he who he may.' He goes on to qualify this statement by emphasizing that 'circumstances' determine the true virtue of freedom. Liberty in the abstract may be a good, but in practice it is dependent upon context, as Burke uses the example of the need to restrain madmen and criminals as cases where freedom is counterproductive or even an evil (VIII: 57–59).

42. This is not to say that riots did not occur within theatres in London and elsewhere during the later eighteenth century. David Garrick's attempt to charge full price for tickets purchased after the third act of plays (in a break with the convention of allowing spectators to buy tickets for half-price later in the performance) precipitated riots at Drury Lane in 1763. For details on this riot, see Heather McPherson, 'Theater Riots and Cultural Politics in Eighteenth-Century London', *The Eighteenth Century: Theory and Interpretation* 43, no. 3 (2002): 236–252. In 1784 in Edinburgh, riots broke out caused by a combination of a shortage of tickets for Sarah Siddons's performances and an overabundance of alcohol. In these cases, however, the riots have little to do with the content of the dramas performed or the emotions provoked specifically by the sensibility of the characters or the audience.
43. Williams, *Marxism and Literature*, 135.
44. Ibid., 133.

1 Divine Sympathy: Theatre, Connection, and Virtue

1. Samuel Jackson Pratt, *Sympathy; Or, a Sketch of the Social Passion. A Poem written at the Villa of a Friend, in his Absence* (London, 1781), 15.
2. David Hume, *Enquiry concerning the Principles of Morals*, ed. Tom L. Beauchamp (Oxford: Clarendon Press, 1998), 39.
3. Andrew Wilson, MD, *Medical Researches: Being an ENQUIRY into the NATURE and ORIGIN of HYSTERICS in the FEMALE CONSTITUTION, and into the Distinction between that Disease and HYPOCHONDRIAC or Nervous Disorders* (London, 1776), 38.
4. 'Benevolence to the afflicted is *Pity* or *Compassion*. When to this is joined a fellow-feeling of their distress, arising either from similar experience, or from natural humanity and *tenderness* of heart, it is called *Sympathy* and If these dispose us to favour or relieve them, without hopes of a return, or even to think and judge favourably with respect to them, it has the name of *Charity*.' John Bethum, *A Short View of the Human Faculties and Passions. With Remarks and Directions respecting their Nature, Improvement, and Government*, 2nd edn. (Edinburgh, 1770), 35.
5. James Beattie, *Essays on Poetry and Music, as they affect the Mind. On Laughter, and Ludicrous Composition. On the Utility of Classical Learning* (Edinburgh, 1776), 194–195.
6. Daniel Turner, 'On Sympathy', in *The Breathings of Genius. Being a Collection of Poems; to which are added, Essays, Moral and Philosophical*, by Elizabeth Gilding (London, 1786), 98.
7. For example, 'I am proud of having united in sentiment with Adam Smith in this argument of the Social Passion, some years before I had ever met with his Theory.' Samuel Jackson Pratt, *Sympathy, and Other Poems. Including Landscapes in Verse, and Cottage-Pictures. Revised, Corrected, and Enlarged* (London, 1807), 70. Likewise, Daniel Turner praises Smith in his own paean to sympathy ('On Sympathy', 95).

8. Edward Henry Iliff, *A Tear of Sympathy!!! Or, Striking Objects of Travel, Antient, and Modern! In Italy, Prussia, Spain, Russia, &c. With Reflections Critical, Moral, and Biographical* (London, 1796).
9. *The Redresser, Or, Weekly Strictures of Simon Sympathy, Esq.* No. 1, Saturday, 25 July 1778. The goal of the periodical is to bring the wrongs of the oppressed to the public eye and by moving public sympathy to right these wrongs.
10. 'We partake of [others'] uneasiness by *sympathy*; and as every thing, which gives uneasiness in human actions, upon the general survey, is call'd Vice, and whatever produces satisfaction, in the same manner, is denominated Virtue; this is the reason why the sense of moral good and evil follows upon justice and injustice . . . *a* sympathy *with public interest is the source of the* moral approbation, *which attends that virtue.*' David Hume, *A Treatise of Human Nature*, ed. L. A. Selby-Bigge (Oxford: Clarendon Press, 1888, repr. 1967), 499.
11. Hume, *Enquiry concerning the Principles of Morals*, 9.
12. Quoted by D. D. Raphael and A. L. MacFie, 'Introduction' to Adam Smith, *The Theory of Moral Sentiments*, ed. Raphael and MacFie (Oxford: Oxford University Press, 1979), 3. All further references to Smith's *Theory* will be to this edition.
13. Smith, *The Theory of Moral Sentiments*, 10.
14. Ibid.
15. *The Theory of Moral Sentiments* opens with a reference to spectatorship and its moral implications: 'How selfish soever man may be supposed, there are evidently some principles in his nature, which interest him in the fortunes of others, and render their happiness necessary to him, though he derives nothing from it except the pleasure of seeing it' (9).
16. Ibid., 21.
17. Ibid., 25.
18. Turner, 'On Sympathy', 93.
19. Henry Home, Lord Kames, *The Elements of Criticism*, ed. Peter Jones, 2 vols. (Indianapolis: Liberty Fund, 2005), I: 48. This edition is based on the 1785 edition. Unless otherwise noted, all references to *The Elements of Criticism* refer to this edition.
20. Ibid., I: 68. Like Smith and Kames, David Hume discusses moral principles in terms of sight and spectatorship as a means of explaining how sympathy initiates moral sentiments. As he explains, the sight of virtue and harmony naturally gives pleasure, just as the sight of violence and injury incites indignation: 'In general, it is certain, that, wherever we go, whatever we reflect on or converse about, everything still presents us with the view of human happiness or misery, and excites in our breast a sympathetic movement of pleasure or uneasiness. In our serious occupations, in our careless amusements, this principle still exerts its active energy.' Hume, *Enquiry concerning the Principles of Morals*, 39.
21. Pratt, *Sympathy; Or, a Sketch of the Social Passion*, 30.

22. Ibid., 31.
23. Kames, *The Elements of Criticism*, I: 51.
24. 'It is by [Sympathy] that we enter into the concerns of others; that we are moved as they are moved, and are never suffered to be indifferent spectators of almost any thing which men can do or suffer. For sympathy must be considered as a sort of substitution, by which we are put into the place of another man, and affected in many respects as he is affected; so that this passion may either partake of the nature of those which regard self-preservation, and turning upon pain may be a source of the sublime; or it may turn upon ideas of pleasure.' Edmund Burke, *A Philosophical Enquiry into the Origin of our Ideas of the Sublime and Beautiful*, ed. J. T. Boulton (London: Routledge and Kegan Paul, 1958), 44. Unlike Johnson, who would later argue in his 'Preface to Shakespeare' that we can enjoy tragedy only because we know that it is a fiction, for 'if we thought murders and treasons real, they would please no more' (in *Johnson on Shakespeare*, ed. Arthur Sherbo, New Haven: Yale University Press, 1968), Burke claims we actually take pleasure in the suffering of others: 'I am convinced we have a degree of delight, and that no small one, in the real misfortunes and pains of others' (45).
25. Beattie, *On Poetry and Music*, 194.
26. The other three are 'the Machinery of Sympathy', 'Sociable Sympathy', and 'Complete Sympathy'. Jonathan Lamb, *The Evolution of Sympathy in the Long Eighteenth Century* (London: Pickering and Chatto, 2009).
27. Lamb, *Evolution of Sympathy*, 64.
28. David Marshall, *The Surprising Effects of Sympathy: Marivaus, Diderot, Rousseau, and Mary Shelley* (Chicago: University of Chicago Press, 1988), 2.
29. Ibid.
30. David Marshall, *The Figure of Theater: Shaftsbury, Defoe, Adam Smith, and George Eliot* (New York: Columbia University Press, 1986), 168. Marshall points to Jonas Barish as one of the very few critics who have noticed the 'theatrical construction' of *The Theory of Moral Sentiments*. Jonas Barish, *The Antitheatrical Prejudice* (Berkeley: University of California Press, 1981), 244.
31. Smith, *The Theory of Moral Sentiments*, 43.
32. Hume, *Enquiry concerning the Principles of Morals*, 39.
33. Henry Home, Lord Kames, *The Elements of Criticism. In Three Volumes* (Edinburgh, 1762), I: 115. This statement appears in Kames's discussion of fables and history and the times in which they fail to excite sympathy. He revises this statement in the 1785 edition to read, 'if the reflection that a story is a pure fiction presents our sympathy, so will equally the reflection that the persons described are no long existing'. *The Elements of Criticism*, ed. Jones, I: 71.
34. Beattie, *On Poetry and Music*, 277. Similar comments appear in other writings on sympathy. Turner comments that 'since just and lively representations of

distress, which for the most part we meet with in tragedies, and frequently in pictures, rouse to a very great degree our social affections, and warmly interest us in the fortunes of those whose condition they are intended to describe or represent. The more natural these descriptions or representations are, the deeper they affect us' (94). He goes on to point to Garrick's Hamlet as a particularly effective example.

35. Kames, *The Elements of Criticism*, I: 71.
36. Ibid., II: 651.
37. Ibid., II: 654.
38. W. R. Chetwood, *A General History of the Stage, From its Origin in Greece down to the present Time. With Memoirs of most of the principal Performers that have appeared on the English and Irish Stage for these last Fifty Years* (1749), 28.
39. [Henry Flitcroft], *Theatrical Entertainments Consistent with Society, Morality, and Religion, in a Letter to the Author of 'The Stage the High road to Hell.' Shewing that Writer's Arguments to be fallacious, his Principles enthusiastic, and his Authorities (particularly from the Ancients) misconstrued and perverted* (London, 1768), 7.
40. Lisa A. Freeman, 'The Cultural Politics of Antitheatricality: The Case of John Home's *Douglas*', *The Eighteenth Century: Theory and Interpretation* 43, no. 3 (Fall 2002): 210–235.
41. 'All these instances of immorality have made the Gallican church stigmatize plays and players in a very extraordinary manner. The host is never carried by the opera-house; and all the actors or actresses of the French companies are denied access to the sacrament, and buried in a dunghill, if they die without renouncing the stage.' *The Stage the High Road to Hell: Being an Essay on the Pernicious Nature of Theatrical Entertainments; shewing them to be at once inconsistent with Religion, and subversive of Morality. With Strictures on the vicious and dissolute Characters of the most eminent Performers of both Sexes. The whole enforced and supported by the best Authorities, both Antient and Modern* (London, [1767]), 33.
42. [Adam Gibb], *The Players Scourge: Or a Detection of the ranting prophanity and regnant impiety of stage plays, and their wicked encouragers and frequenters; and especially against the nine prophane Pagan Priests, falsely called ministers of the gospel, who countenanced the thrice cursed tragedy called* Douglas (Edinburgh, n.d.), 2.
43. [Flitcroft], *Theatrical Entertainments Consistent with Society, Morality, and Religion*, iii.
44. Jeremy Collier, *A Short View of the Immorality and Profaneness of the English Stage: Together with the Sense of the Antiquity upon this Argument* (London, 1698), 8.
45. Even Flitcroft refers to the 'lasciviousness' of Dryden, Otway, and Rowe, *Theatrical Entertainments Consistent with Society, Morality, and Religion*, v.
46. Ibid., 3. Flitcroft admits that 'indecency and profaneness . . . overflowed our theatres in the days of Charles II', but he reminds the reader that most of these

'exceptionable pieces' have been 'banished from the world' (3) In his eyes, anyone who attempts to bring attention to them, even if to use them as examples of the evils of theatrical entertainments, is as corrupt as the 'wretches who penned them' (iv).

47. Ibid., iv.
48. William Guthrie, *An Essay upon English Tragedy. With Remarks upon the Abbe de* Blanc's Observations *on the English Stage* (London, [1757]), 22.
49. Smith himself argues that kings are the best subjects for tragedy, not because of the dignity of their position, but because the spectator imagines that they are happier than ordinary citizens and thus their fall excites more emotion. Despite this rather convoluted claim, Smith's examples of effective tragedy are taken from the she-tragedies of a previous generation (*The Theory of Moral Sentiments*, 52).
50. *An Essay upon the Present State of the Theatre in France, England and Italy, with Reflections upon Dramatic Poetry in General, And the Characters of the Principal Authors and Performers of these Nations. A work absolutely necessary to be read by every Lover of Theatrical Exhibitions* (London, 1760), 4.
51. William Cook, *The Elements of Dramatic Criticism. Containing an Analysis of The Stage under the following Heads, Tragedy, Tragi-comedy, Comedy; Pantomime and Farce* (London, 1775), 43.
52. *Essay upon the Present State of the Theatre*, 3–4.
53. Ibid., 3.
54. All figures taken from Charles Beecher Hogan, *Shakespeare in the Theatre, 1701–1800*, 2 vols. (Oxford: Clarendon Press, 1957).
55. Beattie, *On Poetry and Music*, 277.
56. Richard Steele wrote in favour of the new mode of comedy in his periodical, *The Theatre* (1720), while Dennis countered with pamphlets in support of Restoration comedy, specifically Etherege's *Man of Mode* (*A Defence of Sir* Fopling Flutter, *A Comedy Written by Sir George Etheridge. In which Defence is shewn, That Sir* Fopling, *that merry Knight, was rightly compos'd by the Knight his Father, to answer the Ends of Comedy; and that he has been barbarously and scurrilously attack'd by the Knight his Brother, in the 65th* Spectator. *By which it appears, That the latter Knight knows nothing of the Nature of Comedy* (London, 1722). Dennis later attacked Steele's play even more directly in *Remarks on a Play, call'd* The Conscious Lovers, *A Comedy* (London, 1723). Both essays appear in *The Critical Works of John Dennis*, ed. Edward Niles Hooker, 2 vols. (Baltimore: Johns Hopkins University Press, 1939), II: 241–250 and 251–274, respectively.
57. Oliver Goldsmith, 'Essay on the Theatre', in *The Collected Works of Oliver Goldsmith*, ed. Arthur Friedman, 5 vols. (Oxford: Clarendon Press, 1966), III: 210.
58. Robert D. Hume, 'Goldsmith and Sheridan and the Supposed Revolution of "Laughing" against "Sentimental" Comedy', in *The Rakish Stage: Studies in English* Drama, *1660–1800* (Carbonsdale and Edwardsville: Southern Illinois University Press, 1983), 314.

59. Cook, *Elements of Dramatic Criticism*, 141–150.
60. Ibid., 142.
61. Ibid.
62. Ibid.
63. *The Playhouse Pocket-Companion, or Theatrical Vade-Mecum* (London, 1779), 38.
64. *Essay upon the Present State of the Theatre*, 68–69.
65. Kames, *The Elements of Criticism*, II: 653.
66. Ibid., II: 655.
67. Johnson, *Preface to Shakespeare*, 71.
68. Johnson, 'Notes' to *King Lear, Johnson on Shakespeare*, 704.
69. Johnson, 'Notes' to *Othello*, 'Notes' to *Julius Caesar, Johnson on Shakespeare*, 1045, 836.
70. Turner, 'On Sympathy', 93.
71. *The Follies of St James's Street*, 2 vols. (London, 1789), I: 91–92.

2 Dangerous Pleasures: Theatregoing in the Eighteenth Century

1. *Morning Chronicle* (31 October 1797).
2. *The Beauties* of *Mrs Siddons: Or, a Review of Her Performance of the characters of Belvidera, Zara, Isabella, Margaret of Anjou, Jane Shore, – and Lady Randolph; in Letters from a Lady of Distinction, to her Friend in the Country* (London, 1786), 22.
3. Helen Nicholson, 'Emotion', *Contemporary Theatre Review* 23, no. 1 (2013): 20–22.
4. Siddons is later mentioned explicitly in terms of her performance as Mrs Beverley. *The Follies of St James's Street*, 2 vols. (London, 1789), II: 128.
5. Siddons first performed the role in London in November 1783, after which it became a standard part of her repertoire.
6. Laura Engel, *Fashioning Celebrity: Eighteenth-Century British Actresses and Strategies for Image Making* (Columbus: Ohio State University Press, 2011), 26.
7. Cheryl Wanko, *Roles of Authority: Thespian Biography and Celebrity in Eighteenth-Century England* (Lubbock: Texas Tech University Press,2003); Robyn Asleson, ed., *The Notorious Muse: The Actress in British Art and Culture* (New Haven: Yale University Press, 2003); Shearer West, 'Siddons, Celebrity, and Regality', in *Theatre and Celebrity in Britain, 1660–2000*, ed. Mary Luckhurst and Jane Moody (New York: Palgrave Macmillan, 2005), 191–213. Heather McPherson has written extensively about portraits of Siddons as well as representations of her image and roles in popular culture. See especially 'Searching for Sarah Siddons: Portraiture and the History of Fame', *Eighteenth-Century Studies* 33, no. 2 (1999): 281–287, 'Picturing Tragedy: Sarah Siddons as the Tragic Muse Revisited', *Eighteenth-Century Studies* 33, no. 3 (2000): 401–430, and 'Tragic Pallor and Siddons', *Eighteenth-Century Studies* 48, no. 4 (Summer 2015): 479–502. See also David Román's work on celebrity and the afterlife of Siddons, *Performance in America:*

Contemporary US Culture and the Performing Arts (Durham, NC: Duke University Press, 2005), 140–158.

8. *Middlesex Journal and Evening Advertiser* (30 December 1775).
9. James Boaden, *Memoirs of Mrs Siddons. Interspersed with Anecdotes of Authors and Actors*, 2 vols. (London: Henry Colburn, 1827), I: 277.
10. The receipts for Siddons's second appearance on 12 October were £264 9s. Receipts remained high: £247 4s. 6d. (15 October); £253 13s. 6d (18 October). All figures taken from *The London Stage*.
11. This account was originally published in the *Edinburgh Courant* and subsequently reprinted in *Edinburgh Fugitive Pieces* (Edinburgh, 1791), 171–172.
12. Maria Belinda Bogle, 'Epistle from Miss Maria Belinda B-gle, at Edinburgh, to her friend, Miss Lavinia L-tch, at Glasgow'. Also reprinted in *Edinburgh Fugitive Pieces*, 172–175, Bogle's poem is cited as having been published in the *Edinburgh Courant* and dated 7 June 1785. Although the poem is attributed to a Miss Maria Belinda B—gle, rhymes within the poem (B–gle/ogle) suggest that her name was Bogle, and thus I have used that name when referring to her work.
13. Thomas Gilliland, *The Dramatic Mirror: containing The History of the Stage, from the Earliest Period to the Present Time; including a Biographical and Critical Account of All the Dramatic Writers, from 1660; and also of the most Distinguished Performers, from the days of Shakspeare to 1807: and a History of the Country Theatres, in England, Ireland, and Scotland. Embellished with Seventeen Elegant Engravings*, 2 vols. (London: C. Chapple, 1808), II: 975–976.
14. Garrick had staged Southerne's play with the comic scenes in 1751 but did not revive it again until 1757, when he staged it without the comic subplot under the title *Isabella: or, The Fatal Marriage*, with Susannah Cibber in the title role.
15. *The Beauties of Mrs Siddons*, 21.
16. Ibid., 27.
17. Gilliland, *The Dramatic Mirror*, II: 974.
18. Ibid., II: 975–976.
19. *Morning Chronicle and London Advertiser* (11 October 1782).
20. Ibid. The *London Chronicle* uses the same language in its review of this first performance, reporting 'that there was scarce a dry eye in the whole house' (11 October 1782).
21. *Morning Chronicle* (14 October 1782).
22. *Public Advertiser* (12 May 1784). Thomas Campbell transcribes a similar incident cited in a review (no source or date given):

> Mrs. Siddons performance of Isabella at D.L.T. [Drury Lane Theatre] had such an affect upon the audience, that most of the fair circle shone in tears. At the conclusion of the last act, a lady in the boxes, who had for time endeavoured to suppress her grief, was thrown into convulsions and continued in that miserable state for a considerable time after the curtain dropt.

Manuscript notebook on Sarah Siddons, Huntington Library shelfmark: HM 33780.

23. *Remarks on Mrs Siddons, in some of her Principal Characters* (Edinburgh, 1784), 19.
24. Thomas Moore, *Letters and Journals of Lord Byron: With Notices of His Life*, 2 vols. (London: John Murray, 1830), I: 5. This comment is taken from Moore's personal copy, Huntington Library shelfmark: 263213. The marriage occurred in 1785, so it is likely that the anecdote refers to events the previous year.
25. Ibid., I: 614. In the footnote, Moore provides more material from Scott:

> A few passages at the these beginning of recollections have been omitted, as containing particulars relative to Lord Byron's mother, which have already been mentioned in the early part of this work. Among these, however, there is one anecdote, the repetition of which will be easily pardoned, on account of the infinitely greater interest and authenticity imparted to its details from coming from such an eye-witness as Sir Walter Scott: – 'I remember,' he says, 'Having seen Lord Byron's mother before she was married, and a certain coincidence rendered the circumstance rather remarkable. It was during Mrs. Siddons's first or second visit to Edinburgh, when the music of that wonderful actress's voice, looks, manner, and person, produced the strongest effect which could possibly be exerted by a human being upon her fellow-creatures. Nothing of the kind that I ever witnessed approached it by a hundred degrees. The high state of excitation was aided by the difficulties of obtaining entrance, and exhausting length of time that the audience were content to waited until the piece commenced. When the curtain fell, a large proportion of the ladies were generally in hysterics.

26. W. R. Chetwood, *A General History of the Stage, From its Origin in Greece down to the present Time. With Memoirs of most of the principal Performers that have appeared on the English and Irish Stage for these last Fifty Years* (London, 1749), 28.
27. Bogle, 'Epistle', 174.
28. 'Theatrical Portraiture No. 6', in *Attic Miscellany; or, Characteristic Mirror of Men and Things*, vol. I (London: Bentley & Co., 1789).
29. *Edwin's Pills to Purge Melancholy: Containing all the Songs Sung by Mr Edwin, of Covent Garden Theatre, Since his First Appearance in London; And Many Duets Mr Edwin has a Part in. With a Humourous Account of Mrs. Siddons's First Reception in Dublin. And a Portrait of Mr Edwin Finely Executed. The Second Edition, with Considerable Additions* (London, 1788), v–viii. The 'humourous account' leads off the volume, taking precedence over Edwin's songs, and a footnote claims that this account was originally published in Dublin shortly after Siddons first appeared there in 1784 (this claim is probably facetious).
30. This account appears in an undated and unidentified newspaper clipping in the Harvard Theatre Collection's clipping file for Sarah Siddons.
31. Joseph Roach, *It* (Ann Arbor: University of Michigan Press, 2007), 29.
32. *The Beauties of Mrs Siddons*, 27.
33. Ibid., 21.
34. Ibid., 29.

35. Ibid., 23.
36. *Morning Chronicle* (23 November 1786).
37. Ibid.
38. *London Chronicle* (23 November 1786). Another review cites horror rather than sorrow.
39. 22 and 24 November at Drury Lane.
40. This anecdote is cited by Barbara Marinacci in *Leading Ladies: A Gallery of Famous Actresses* (New York: Dodd, Mead and Company, 1961), 62. Marinacci does not provide a source for the story.
41. *Morning Post and Daily Advertiser* (12 November 1782).
42. *The Theatrical Portrait, a Poem, on the Celebrated Mrs. Siddons in the Characters of Calista, Jane Shore, Belvidera, and Isabella* (London, 1783), viii.
43. Ibid., 6.
44. Even the 'virtuous FAIR' (7) are supposed to see in Siddons's Jane Shore a powerful moral lesson teaching them to 'shun the gay Paths which lead to guilty Love'. The discussion of *Jane Shore* ends with an attack on 'gay LOTHARIOS' (9); however, the poet's comments have nothing to do with Siddons's representation of Jane Shore and instead refer back to Calista (who was discussed in the opening pages of the poem).
45. *The Beauties of Mrs Siddons*, 47.
46. Ibid., 47–49.
47. Ibid., 48.
48. Adam Smith, *The Theory of Moral Sentiments*, ed. D. D. Raphael and A. L. Macfie (Oxford: Oxford University Press, 1979), 30. *Philoctetes*, for example, focuses on the suffering endured by the title character because of an injured foot. In *Hippolytus*, the emphasis rests on the title character's physical suffering after having been dragged behind his chariot.
49. Ibid., 28.
50. Ibid., 30.
51. Dror Wahrman, *The Making of the Modern Self: Identity and Culture in Eighteenth-Century England* (New Haven: Yale University Press, 2004), 270–271.
52. Bogle, 'Epistle', 13–14.
53. *Public Advertiser* (12 May 1784).
54. Nicholson, 'Emotion', 20.
55. Ibid., 22.
56. Smith, *The Theory of Moral Sentiments*, 29.
57. Roach, *It*, especially 70–76.
58. At this point the author refers directly to Siddons and her performance of Mrs Beverley. *Follies*, II: 128.
59. *Follies*, II: 128–129.
60. *Public Advertiser* (11 April 1783).

61. Boaden, *Memoirs of Mrs Siddons*, I: 327–328. Boaden goes on to quote Kames, identified only as an unnamed 'profound philosopher', on the ways in which the 'frequent reiteration' of 'sympathetic emotion' leads to a more general social virtue (I: 329).

3 Roman Fathers and Grecian Daughters: Tragedy and the Nation

1. *The London Magazine: Or, Gentleman's Monthly Intelligencer* (March 1772): 106.
2. *Spectator* 449 (5 August 1712).
3. Ibid.
4. Ruth Perry, *Novel Relations: The Transformation of Kinship in English Literature and Culture, 1748–1818* (Cambridge: Cambridge University Press, 2004), 78.
5. Margaret Doody, *Frances Burney: The Life in the Works* (New Brunswick: Rutgers University Press, 1988), 24. She later states that 'the late Georgian period seems addicted to the pleasures of the father–daughter relationship' (184).
6. Caroline Gonda, *Reading Daughters' Fictions, 1709–1834: Novels and Society from Manley to Edgeworth* (Cambridge: Cambridge University Press, 1996); Elizabeth Kowaleski-Wallace, *Their Fathers' Daughters: Hannah More, Maria Edgeworth, and Patriarchal Complicity* (Oxford: Oxford University Press, 1991).
7. Lynda Zwinger, *Daughters, Fathers, and the Novel: The Sentimental Romance of Heterosexuality* (Madison: University of Wisconsin Press, 1991).
8. Gonda, *Reading Daughters' Fictions*, xv.
9. Smith argues that because love is a 'passion derived from the imagination' it is innately 'ridiculous': 'Our imagination not having run in the same channel with that of the lover, we cannot enter into the eagerness of his emotions . . . the passion appears to every body, but the man who feels it, entirely disproportioned to the value of the object; and love, though it is pardoned in a certain age because we know it is natural, is always laughed at because we cannot enter into it.' By contrast, in his discussion of the social passions, Smith uses the contented family as his example of affection that generates sympathy in the breast of the 'indifferent spectator'. *Theory of Moral Sentiments*, ed. D. D. Raphael and A. L. Macfie (Oxford: Oxford University Press, 1979), 31, 39.
10. William Hawkins, *Miscellanies in prose and verse. Containing candid and impartial observations on the principal performers belonging to the two Theatres-Royal; from January 1773, to May 1775. Likewise strictures on two favourite tragedies, viz. The ORPHAN and The FAIR PENITENT. Being part of an epistolary Correspondence on those Subjects with a young Lady. With Many other agreeable and interesting Articles, such as Pastoral Songs, Epitaphs, &c. &c.* (London, 1775), 81–82.
11. Ibid., 82–83.

12. Ibid., 86.
13. As I have discussed elsewhere, revisionings of Shakespeare's plays as father–daughter parables appeared throughout the mid to later eighteenth century. See Marsden, 'Daddy's Girls: Shakespearean Daughters and Eighteenth-Century Ideology', *Shakespeare Survey* 51 (1998): 17–26.
14. Francis Gentleman, 'Introduction' to *King Lear* in *Bell's Edition of Shakespeare's Plays, as they are now performed at the Theatre Royal in London. Regulated from the Prompt Books of each House by Permission; with Notes Critical and Illustrative; by the Authors of the Dramatic Censor*, 9 vols. (London, 1773), II: 3.
15. Arthur Murphy, *Gray's-Inn Journal* (12 January 1754).
16. Frances Brooke, *The Old Maid*, no. 18 (13 March 1756), 146.
17. David Garrick, *An Ode upon Dedicating a Building and Erecting a Statue, to Shakespeare, at Stratford Upon Avon* (London, 1769).
18. For details on the probable dates of Garrick's revision of Tate's *Lear*, see *The Plays of David Garrick*, ed. Harry William Pedicord and Fredrick Louis Bergmann, 7 vols. (Carbondale: Southern Illinois University Press, 1981), III: 446–450, and George Winchester Stone, Jr., 'Garrick's Production of *King Lear*: A Study in the Temper of the Eighteenth-Century Mind', *Studies in Philology* 45, no. 1 (1948): 89–102. Dates and casts for specific performances can be found in Charles Beecher Hogan, *Shakespeare in the Theatre, 1701–1800*, 2 vols. (Oxford: Clarendon Press, 1957).
19. David Garrick, *King Lear*, in *The Plays of David Garrick*, ed. Pedicord and Bergmann, III: 347 (3.2.45–47).
20. Thomas Shadwell, *Timon of Athens; Or, the Man-Hater* (London, 1678). Like most Restoration adaptors of Shakespeare, Shadwell creates new roles for female characters, giving Timon two mistresses. While one deserts him, the other, Evandra, remains faithful and dies with him in the wilderness. Cumberland's choice of the name 'Evanthe' for his faithful daughter indicates his familiarity with Shadwell's play.
21. For a more detailed discussion of Cumberland's *Timon*, see Marsden, 'Shakespeare and Sympathy', in *Shakespeare and the Eighteenth Century*, ed. Peter Sabor and Paul Yachnin (London: Ashgate, 2008), 29–41, and 'Daddy's Girls'.
22. Richard Cumberland, *Timon of Athens* (London, 1771), 57–58.
23. Ibid., 58.
24. Thomas Davies, *The Memoirs of David Garrick, Esq. Interspersed with Characters and Anecdotes of his Theatrical Contemporaries. The Whole Forming a History of the Stage, which Includes a Period of Thirty-Six Years*, 2 vols. (London, 1780), II: 269.
25. Brett D. Wilson, *A Race of Female Patriots: Women and Public Spirit on the British Stage, 1688–1745* (Lewisburg: Bucknell University Press, 2012), 204.

26. After a successful opening run, the play was revived regularly over the course of the next five decades.
27. William Whitehead, 'Advertisement' to the *The Roman Father*, in *Plays and Poems of William Whitehead*, 2 vols. (London, 1774), I: n.p.
28. Ibid.
29. Webster's *Appius and Virginia* was published in 1654, 1655, and 1659. After the Restoration, Thomas Betterton adapted and staged Webster's play; an edition of the play was published in 1679 with the title *Appius and Virginia. Acted at the Dukes Theater under the name The Roman Virgin; or, the Unjust Judge: A Tragedy* and attributed to Webster. Despite the fact that Charles Gildon's *Life of Betterton* (1710) states that Betterton's adaptation was never published, it seems likely that the 1679 version is his adaptation of Webster's play.
30. John Dennis's tragedy *Appius and Virginia* (1709) ran for four nights in February 1709 and was never revived. The story reappeared later in the century, in 1786, this time in the form of an opera by Italian composer Angelo Tarchi. Because the events were deemed 'too ferocious and tragical for an Opera', the opera ends with Virginius, Virginia, and Icilius leaving for the lictors' judgement, before Virginius's fatal stroke. In Emilia Galotti (1772), Gotthold Ephraim Lessing followed the general plot line of the father stabbing the daughter to maintain her honour. Frequently described as a bourgeois tragedy, Lessing's play updates the story and uses it as a means of attacking the aristocracy rather than as a vehicle for nationalist glorification.
31. In *Appius and Virginia*, Dennis stresses the cause of liberty, but unlike later productions, he downplays the relationship between father and daughter, and even the death itself. Virginia dies in the fourth act, and the play's climax becomes a struggle word between Appius – the representative of tyrannical force – and Lucius Icilius – the representative of liberty. *Appius and Virginia* is perhaps most memorable in its association with the famous anecdote of Dennis and the stolen thunder.
32. Samuel Crisp, *Virginia* (London, 1754), 60. All further references to this play are from this text and will be made parenthetically.
33. David Erskine Baker, *Biographica Dramatica, Or, a Companion to the Playhouse. A new Edition: Carefully corrected, greatly enlarged, and continued from 1764 to 1782*, 2 vols. (London, 1782), II: 391.
34. Ibid.
35. Ibid., II: 390.
36. A revival in April 1755 was advertised but never occurred.
37. 'There appears great want of invention, and little knowledge of the stage, in this author; the scenes are so uncemented, and so uninteresting, that, for four acts, we are hardly ever awakened to any feelings that employ our minds.' *The Monthly Review* 10 (1754): 226.
38. Doody makes a similar observation: the play 'presents some odd attitudes to filial–parental relationships which Crisp may have unconsciously carried into the psuedo-father–daughter connection with Frances' (*Frances Burney*, 71).

39. Moncreiff's epilogue concludes with a paean to George II who never 'the widow-making sword' draws 'except for Freedom and in *Europe*'s Cause'. This fulsome praise of George II is somewhat out of keeping with the play's Dedication to the dowager Princess of Wales, the King's daughter-in-law and widow of Prince Frederick, who was not on good terms with the King.
40. Frances Brooke, *Virginia a Tragedy, with Odes, Pastorals and Translations* (London, 1756), 15.
41. Ibid., 17.
42. Howard Hunter Dunbar provides an excellent overview of *The Grecian Daughter* and its reception in chapter 11 ('Scarce a Dry Eye in the House') of *The Dramatic Career of Arthur Murphy* (New York: Modern Language Association of American, 1946), 209–223. Catherine Burroughs gives the only recent in-depth examination of the play. See Catherine Burroughs, '"The Father Foster'd at His Daughter's Breast": Fanny Kemble and *The Grecian Daughter,' Nineteenth-Century Contexts* 28, no. 4 (December 2006): 335–345.
43. Barry had originally starred in the role at Drury Lane, garnering particular praise for her rendition of pathos. On 30 October 1783, Siddons first played Euphrasia at Drury Lane, and the following November both actresses appeared in the role, Siddons at Drury Lane and Barry (now Crawford) at Covent Garden.
44. Thomas Robert Malthus, *T. R. Malthus: The Unpublished Papers in the Collection of Kanto Gakuen University*, ed. John Pullen and Trevor Hughes Perry, 2 vols. (Cambridge: Cambridge University Press, 2011), I: 14.
45. *The Gazetteer* (30 November 1784).
46. In the 'Memoir of Fanny Kemble', written by S. D. L. and published with the sixth edition of Kemble's play *Francis the First*, the author describes Kemble's success in the role of Euphrasia in 1829, during her first season at Covent Garden. *Francis the First: A Tragedy in Five Acts. With Other Poetical Pieces by Frances Ann Kemble. In which is Included an Original Memoir and a Full length Portrait* (New York: Peabody & Co., 1833). The 'full-length portrait' touted in the title portrays Kemble in the role of Euphrasia.
47. Thomas Campbell, *The Life of Mrs Siddons*, 2 vols. (London: Effingham Wilson, 1834), I: 166. Quoting the *Morning Post*'s description of *The Grecian Daughter* as '*an abortion of Melpomene*', Campbell counters: 'This was rather hard language; for there must be some merit in a drama that can be made the medium of popular acting' (I: 166).
48. Mary Robinson, *The Natural Daughter*, 2 vols. (London, 1799). See volume I, chapter 26.
49. Elizabeth Inchbald, 'Remarks' to *The Grecian Daughter*, in *The British Theatre; Or, a Collection of Plays, Which Are Acted at the Theatres Royal, Drury Lane, Covent Garden, and Haymarket*, 25 vols. (London: Longman, Hurst, Rees Orme, 1808), XV: 3. Even while she references the artistic

weakness of the play, Inchbald acquits audiences of bad taste, commenting: 'This play had, on its first appearance, the most brilliant success, and still holds a place in the list of dramas performed during every season. There is a splendour of decoration, a glow of military action, events of such deep interest, and, above all, a moral of such excellent tendency which concludes the performances, that its attraction can readily be accounted for, without the slighted imputation on the judgment of the public' (3).

50. Campbell, *The Life of Mrs. Siddons*, 168. He adds that while Shakespeare's plays would continue to be read even if never staged, 'if poor Murphy, as a tragedian, were to be banished from the stage to the library, it may be said, in the fullest sense of the phrase, that he would be laid on the shelf. And yet Murphy might affirm with truth, that in playing his heroine, Mrs. Siddons herself increased her reputation.'
51. Book V, 4.7.ext.1. 'Idem praedicatum de pietate Perus existimetur, quae patrem suum Mycona consi<mi>li fortuna adfectum parique custodiae traditum iam ultimae senectutis uelut infantem pectori suo admotum aluit. haerent ac stupent hominum oculi, cum huius facti pictam imaginem uident, casusque antiqui condicionem praesentis spectaculi admiratione renouant, in illis mutis membrorum liniamentis uiua ac spirantia corpora intueri credentes. quod necesse est animo quoque euenire, aliquanto efficaciore pictura litterarum uetera pro recentibus admonito recordari' (text taken from www.thelatinlibrary.com/valmax5.html).
52. Representations of the dutiful daughter and her ailing mother, on the other hand, are much less common, particularly in 'high art'.
53. *A Worthy Example of a Virtuous Wife, Who Fed her Father with her own MILK, he being Commanded by the Emperor to be Starved to Death, but afterwards Pardoned* (London, [1760]). In the ballad, the daughter has married against her father's wishes, but despite his harsh treatment of her, she still feeds him 'a Twelvemonth and a Day'. Discovering her virtuous behaviour, the Emperor pardons the father.
54. Inchbald, 'Remarks' to *The Grecian Daughter*, 5.
55. *The London Magazine: Or, the Gentleman's Monthly Intelligencer* (March 1772): 106. The author praises Mrs Barry (Euphrasia) and Mr Barry (Evander) in their roles, but adds, 'the other characters are scarcely deserving of particular notice' (106).
56. Arthur Murphy, *The Grecian Daughter: A Tragedy. As it is acted at the Theatre-Royal in Drury-Lane* (London, 1772), 5. All further references will be taken from this edition and noted parenthetically in the text.
57. 'Why have my sisters husbands, if they say / They love you all?' (*King Lear*, I.i. 99–100).
58. *Monthly Review* 46 (March 1772): 259.
59. Ibid.
60. Inchbald, 'Remarks' to *The Grecian Daughter*, 3.
61. I have greatly simplified the plot here.

62. Inchbald, 'Remarks' to *The Grecian Daughter*, 4.
63. In this, the representation of the maternal breast is strikingly different from the movement in the later eighteenth century that saw the breast as maternal rather than sexual, although in both cases the property of a man. See Ruth Perry, 'Colonizing the Breast: Sexuality and Maternity in Eighteenth-Century England', *Journal of the History of Sexuality* 2, no. 2 (1991): 204–234. The *Grecian Daughter* does not so much de-sexualize the breast so much as de-sex the daughter.
64. Inchbald, 'Remarks' to *The Grecian Daughter*, 4.
65. The original painting on which the engraving is based has been lost, however an earlier drawing by Pine does exist. See Robyn Asleson, '"She was Tragedy Personified": Crafting the Siddons Legend in Art and Life', in *A Passion for Performance: Sarah Siddons and Her Portraitists*, ed. Robyn Asleson (Los Angeles: J. Paul Getty Museum, 1999), 60–63.
66. James Boaden, *Memoirs of Mrs Siddons. Interspersed with Anecdotes of Authors and Actors*, 2 vols. (London: Henry Colburn, 1827), I: 312.
67. Ibid.
68. From the Harvard Theatre Collection clippings file for Sarah Siddons. I have not been able to locate the source or date of this item.
69. 'The part of *Isabella* had developed her strength as well as her tenderness; but *Euphrasia* allowed her to assume a royal loftiness still more imposing (at least to the many), and a look of majesty which she alone could assume. When she rushed on the stage addressing the Grecian patriots, "War on, ye heroes!" she was a picture to every eye, and she spoke passion to every heart.' Campbell, *The Life of Mrs Siddons*, I: 168–169.
70. The other was the Earl of Errol at the coronation of George III. Hester Thrale Piozzi, *British Synonymy; or, an Attempt at Regulating the Choice of Words in Familiar Conversation*, 2 vols. (London, 1794), I: 43.
71. Ibid.
72. Campbell, *The Life of Mrs Siddons*, I: 169.
73. Asleson, 'She was Tragedy Personified', 59.
74. Joseph Roach, *It* (Ann Arbor: University of Michigan Press, 2007), 39–40.
75. See Heather McPherson's examination of portraits of Sarah Siddons for a more detailed reading of the cartoon. 'Picturing Tragedy: Mrs Siddons as the Tragic Muse Revisited', *Eighteenth-Century Studies* 33, no. 3 (Spring 2000): 401–430.
76. Mary Ann Yates, Siddons's original rival in the role of Euphrasia, was also depicted as the tragic muse, but in each example Yates is crowned with laurel leaves rather than the more regal diadem.
77. Daniel O'Quinn, *Entertaining Crisis in the Atlantic Imperium, 1770–1790* (Baltimore: Johns Hopkins University Press, 2011).
78. Jay Fliegelman, *Prodigals and Pilgrims: The American Revolution against Patriarchal Authority, 1750–1800* (Cambridge: Cambridge University Press, 1982).

79. *London Magazine*, January 1773. The 'Fragment of a Speech' appears on page 33 and the cartoon on the facing page.
80. Robert Merry, 'Ode on the Restoration of his Majesty, Recited by Mrs. Siddons', in *An Asylum for Fugitive Pieces, in Prose and Verse not in any Other Collection: with Several Pieces never before Published* (London, 1789), III: 258.
81. Boaden is especially dismissive of the poem and tableau describing Siddons as 'idly condescend[ing] to be dressed as Britannia' (II: 220). He grudgingly admits that Siddons's use of the ode for her benefit night was appropriate, although he links his distaste with the ode to his dislike of *Romeo and Juliet*: 'with the policy which the best taste is pardonable for exercising as to a benefit night, Mrs. Siddons repeated this ode on the 11th of May at Drury Lane Theatre, after acting Juliet, which, I think, never became one of her current parts. The passion of "Romeo and Juliet" is entirely without dignity: it springs up like the mushroom in a night, and its flavour is earthy'. *Memoirs of Mrs Siddons* (II: 221–222).

4 Performing the West Indies: Comedy, Feeling, and British Identity

1. Horace Walpole, 'Thoughts on Comedy', in *The Works of Horatio Walpole, Earl of Oxford*, 5 vols. (London: G.G. and J. Robinson and J. Edwards, 1798), II: 319.
2. Richard Cumberland, *The Memoirs of Richard Cumberland*, ed. Richard J. Dircks, 2 vols. (New York: AMS, 2002), I: 171–172.
3. While Daniel O'Quinn argues for the allegorical nature of some eighteenth-century comedies, such as Sheridan's *The Duenna*, he admits that such plays were seen in their own time as going against the true nature of comedy. *Entertaining Crisis in the Atlantic* Imperium, *1770–1790* (Baltimore: Johns Hopkins University Press, 2011), 130–133.
4. Lisa A. Freeman, *Character's Theater: Gender and Identity on the Eighteenth-Century Stage* (Philadelphia: University of Pennsylvania Press, 2002), 193.
5. Walpole, 'Tragedy and Comedy', *Walpoliana*, 2 vols. (London, [1799]), I: 43. In 'Thoughts on Tragedy: In Three Letters to Robert Jephson', Walpole writes, 'As I hold a good comedy the chef-oeuvre of human genius, I wish, I say, you would try comedy'. *Works of Horatio Walpole*, II: 306.
6. Ibid., II: 320.
7. Richard Cumberland, 'Advertisement' to *The Fashionable Lover* (1772), i.
8. Once again, Walpole was prescient in his recognition of this inherent difficulty facing the comic playwright, admitting comic writers must to some extent put aside their desire for 'durable fame' because 'even high comedy must risk a little of its immortality by consulting the ruling taste. And thence a comedy always loses some of its beauties, the transient – and some of its intelligibility.' 'Dramatic Composition', *Walpoliana*, 42.

9. Henry Home, Lord Kames, *The Elements of Criticism. The Third Edition*, 2 vols. (Edinburgh, 1765), II: 479. This comment, which occurs at the end of a chapter on architecture in the third edition, is somewhat revised in wording although not in meaning and moved to the chapter on emotions and passions in the sixth edition of *Elements*.
10. Hugh Blair, *Lectures on Rhetoric and Belles Lettres*, ed. Harold F. Harding, 2 vols. (Carbondale: Southern Illinois University Press, 1965), II: 541–542.
11. Cumberland, 'Advertisement', vii-viii. Cumberland obviously felt strongly about this topic; he reprinted parts of this paragraph thirty-five years later in his *Memoirs*, I: 197.
12. Walpole, 'Thoughts on Comedy', II: 319.
13. Daniel O'Quinn, *Staging Governance: Theatrical Imperialism in London, 1770–1800* (Baltimore: Johns Hopkins University Press, 2005), 11.
14. Edward Said, *Culture and Imperialism* (New York: Knopf, 1993), xvii.
15. James Thomson, 'Rule Britannia', in*The Complete Poetical Works of James Thomson*, ed. with notes by J. Logie Robertson (Oxford: Oxford University Press, 1908), 422–423.
16. Cumberland, *Memoirs*, I: 167.
17. Although extant records are incomplete, Richardson Wright notes numerous performances in Jamaica. See *Revels in Jamaica, 1683–1838: Plays and Players of a Century, Tumblers and Conjurors, Musical Refugees and Solitary Showmen, Dinners, Balls and Cockfights, Darky Mummers and Other Memories of High Times and Merry Hearts* (New York: Dodd, Mead, 1937).
18. Cumberland, 'Advertisement', i.
19. Cumberland's *Memoirs* provide details of the revisions Garrick requested (I: 165–166). Cumberland was also concerned with heightening the impact of this scene. In a letter to Garrick he asks, 'I could very much wish, that if this Comedy comes out next Season at your Theatre, it might steal quietly and silently into the world ... I don't know whether you will think me ridiculous in wishing to conceal the Title of *The West Indian* but I think it robs it of its novelty in some degree by announcing it under that Character.' *The Letters of Richard Cumberland*, ed. Richard J. Dircks (New York: AMS Press, 1988), 65.
20. Ibid., 64.
21. *Memoirs*, I: 165. While in his *Memoirs* Cumberland claims that these were the only significant changes he made to the play, his letters to Garrick indicate otherwise, including references to a scene depicting the caning of Fulmer, the lawyer, and one with a constable that were omitted and replaced with other scenes at Garrick's recommendation. See *Letters*, 2 July 1770, 64.
22. *Monthly Review* 40 (February 1771): 142–150.
23. William Enfield, 'Dedication' to *The Speaker: Or, Miscellaneous Pieces, selected from the Best English Writers, and disposed under proper heads, with a view to facilitate the Improvement of Youth in Reading and Speaking. To which is Prefixed an Essay on Elocution* (London, 1774), iii–iv.

24. Anna Letitia Barbauld, from 'The Invitation to Miss B*****', in *Poems* (London, 1773), 21.
25. Richard Cumberland, *The West Indian: A Comedy. As it is Performed at the Theatre Royal at Drury-Lane* (London, 1771), 8. All further references to this play will be made parenthetically.
26. This passage in full reads: 'In these plays almost all the characters are good, and exceedingly generous; they are lavish enough of their tin money on the stage, and though they want humor, have abundance of sentiment and feeling. If they happen to have faults or foibles, the spectator is taught not only to pardon, but to applaud them, in consideration of the goodness of their hearts; so that folly, instead of being ridiculed, is commended, and the comedy aims at touching our passions, without the power of being truly pathetic'. *The Collected Works of Oliver Goldsmith*, ed. Arthur Friedman, 5 vols. (Oxford: Clarendon Press, 1966), III: 210.
27. *Monthly Review* 40 (February 1771), for example, complains that 'in the character of the West Indian, the Author has furnished an apology for vice . . . he makes high spirits, strong feelings, and warm passions, a kind of dispensation for debauchery' (144).
28. 'In the war before last [the War of Austrian Succession] I served in the Irish Brigade, d'ye see? There after bringing off the French monarch, I left his service with a British bullet in my body and this ribband in my button-hole. Last war [the Seven Years War] I followed the fortunes of the German eagle, in the corps of grenadiers; there I had my belly-full of fighting and a plentiful scarcity of everything else. After six and twenty engagements, great and small, I went off this gash on my skull and a kiss of the empress queen's sweet hand (heaven bless it) for my pains. Since the peace, my dear, I took a little turn with the Confederates in Poland – but such another set of madcaps! – By the Lord Harry, I never knew what it was they were scuffling about' (31).
29. Penal laws dating back to 1607 prohibited Irish Catholics from serving in the military.
30. Early nineteenth-century prompt books of *The West Indian* repeatedly cut out large segments of Stockwell's expository interludes.
31. In her excellent discussion of *The West Indian*, Freeman notes the importance of paternity in *The West Indian*'s representation of feeling, observing that 'by substituting a familial for a political relation, the play allows sentiment to do the work of ideology: paternity supplies the rationale for benevolent paternalism.' *Character's Theater*, 232.
32. O'Quinn argues persuasively for the importance of the martial man in England's construction of its autoethnicity, but in *The West Indian* the English military figures are both passive. The only active and effective military figure is McFlaherty, whose Irish rather than English ethnicity is stressed throughout the play.
33. In her 'Remarks' on the version of the play printed in *The British Theatre*, Elizabeth Inchbald comments:

> Mr Cumberland has not always the talent to make his female characters prominent. Elegance in Charlotte Rusport, and beauty in Louisa Dudley, are the only qualities which the actresses, who represent those parts, require; and these gifts were perfectly in the possession of the original performers – Mrs Abington and Mrs Baddeley.

Despite Inchbald's rather caustic assessment, Charlotte was one of Frances Abington's popular roles. However, after Abington left the stage, the role was edited repeatedly, invariably to eliminate the character's trespasses against proper feminine decorum. 'Remarks' on *The West Indian*, in *The British Theatre; Or, a Collection of Plays, Which Are Acted at the Theatres Royal, Drury Lane, Covent Garden, and Haymarket*, 25 vols. (London: Longman, Hurst, Rees Orme, 1808), XVIII: 5–6.

34. Elizabeth Bonhote, *The Rambles of Mr Frankly. Published by his Sister*, 2 vols. (London, 1772), I: 49.
35. Christopher Leslie Brown, *Moral Capital: Foundations of British Abolitionism* (Chapel Hill: University of North Carolina Press, 2006), 27.
36. Ibid., 205–206.
37. See, for example, an epilogue written for the popular afterpiece *The Padlock* by 'a very worthy CLERGYMAN' and included in *Remarks on the Slave Trade and the Slavery of the Negroes. In a Series of Letters* (London, 1788): 57. The book was published under the pseudonym Africanus.

    > But I was born on Afric's tawny strand,
    > And you in fair Britannia's fairer land.
    > Comes Freedom then with colour? Blush from shame!
    > And let strong Nature's crimson mark your shame.

38. Lawrence Price, *An Inkle and Yarico Album* (Berkeley: University of California Press, 1937) and Frank Felsenstein, ed., *English Trader, Indian Maid: Representing Gender, Race Slavery in the New World: An Inkle and Yarico Reader* (Baltimore: Johns Hopkins University Press, 1999).
39. Famously related in Petronius's *Satyricon*, the story describes a seemingly virtuous woman who, despite her display of excessive grief at her husband's death, is easily seduced by a soldier as she mourns at her husband's tomb.
40. *A Trip to Parnassus; or, The Judgment of Apollo on Dramatic Authors and Performers. A Poem* (London, 1788), 19.
41. On Seeing Mrs Kemble in Yarico:

    > KEMBLE, thou cur'st my unbelief
    > For Moses and his rod;
    > At Yarico's sweet notes of grief
    > The rock with tears had flow'd. [1794]

42. See Wright, *Revels in Jamaica*, 263–265.
43. *American Ballad Operas*, ed. Walter Howard Rubsamen (New York: Garland, 1974).
44. Composer James McConnel created a new score for the opera, which was staged at the Edinburgh Festival in 1999, where it received glowing reviews. His musical version was subsequently staged at the Crampton Theatre and in Washington, DC.

45. John Adolphus, *The Memoirs of John Bannister*, 2 vols. (London: Richard Bentley, 1839), I: 167–168. The manuscript of the play in the Huntington Library (Larpent 782) corroborates this account; the final pages of the manuscript were clearly removed and replaced by a new conclusion. See also Felsenstein, *English Trader, Indian Maid*, 24–26.
46. Raymond Williams, *Marxism and Literature* (Oxford: Oxford University Press, 1977), 129.
47. In *Plays by George Colman the Younger and Thomas Morton*, ed. Barry Sutcliffe (Cambridge: Cambridge University Press, 1983).
48. O'Quinn's use of the Sutcliffe edition, for example, allows him to stress the importance of the martial man (Campley) in the play. But shortly after Colman's play debuted, the roles of both Narcissa and Campley had been cut to the point that Adolphus can refer to 'The very little that is allotted to Narcissa' (*Memoirs of John Bannister*, I: 166). In 'Family Jewels: George Colman's *Inkle and Yarico* and Connoisseurship' (*Eighteenth-Century Studies*, Spring 2001: 207–226), Nadini Bhattacharya, like Felenstein, uses Inchbald's edition, a text that facilitates a reading focusing on Yarico and Wowski as aesthetic objects and on the intersection of race, gender, and taste. In her discussion of miscegenation in *The Limits of the Human: Fictions of Anomaly, Race, and Gender in the Long Eighteenth Century* (Cambridge: Cambridge University Press, 2003), Felicity Nussbaum makes use of the version in *Cumberland's British Theatre* [1827], a nineteenth-century edition of the play that, like Inchbald's, uses a shortened version of the play. In an earlier article on *Inkle and Yarico* ('Performing the West Indies: Comedy, Feeling, and British Identity', *Comparative Drama* 42, no. 1 (2008), 73–88), I relied on Felenstein's edition of the play.
49. Bhattacharya and Nussbaum provide especially cogent readings of Colman's Yarico. In addition to the accounts of the story's history found in Price and Felsenstein, Moira Ferguson provides a useful exploration of the ways in which the tale was represented by women writers (*Subject to Others: British Women Writers and Colonial Slavery, 1670–1834*, London: Routledge, 1992).
50. 'Inkle and Yarico. Or, the Slave Trade Exposed. A Description of the Opera' ([Edinburgh?] [1795?]).
51. Stuart Moncrieff Threipland, *Letters Respecting the Performances at the Theatre Royal, Edinburgh* (Edinburgh, 1800), 228.
52. Williams, *Marxism and Literature*, 132.
53. *The Unsespected* [sic] *Observer, in the Spirit of the Late Martinius Scriblerius. In Two Volumes*. No. 57 (London, 1792), II: 63.
54. Ibid.
55. George Colman the Younger. *Inkle and Yarico: An Opera, in Three Acts. As performed at the Theatre-Royal in the Hay-Market, on Saturday, August 11th, 1787* (London, 1787), 15. All further references to this edition of the play will be made parenthetically.

56. Including the versions in both Inchbald's *British Theatre* and *Cumberland's British Theatre*.
57. In the original production, only Campley, Narcissa, Trudge, Patty, and Yarico sang.
58. *Public Advertiser* (23 October 1788).
59. 'Under the gentle but firm embrace of his father's – and fatherland's – obsession with commerce, Inkle became an exemplar of British mercantile interest, but what should be normative turns out to be monstrous.' Daniel O'Quinn, 'Mercantile Deformities: George Colman's *Inkle and Yarico* and the Racialization of Class Relations', *Theatre Journal* 54, no. 3 (October 2002): 398.
60. Said, *Culture and Imperialism*, xvii.
61. *The Unsespected Observer*, II: 63.
62. Adolphus, *Memoirs of John Bannister*, I: 168. Playbills indicate that by 10 June 1791, Bannister was performing Trudge at the Haymarket Theatre (Harvard Theatre Collection).
63. Ibid., I: 167–168.
64. The only significant omission is that of a potentially controversial song in which Trudge sardonically comments on virtuous 'Christian souls' who drive oxen, skin eels alive, whip horses, hunt cats, and kill flies.
65. *The Monthly Review; or, Literary Journal* 77 (1787): 384–389.
66. Threipland, *Letters Respecting the Performances at the Theatre Royal, Edinburgh*, 228.
67. *The Unsespected Observer*, II: 63–64.
68. Williams, *Marxism and Literature*, 130.
69. Thomas Bellamy, *The Benevolent Planters. A Dramatic Piece* (London, 1789).
70. Huntington Library, Larpent 839.
71. The prologue was published in the *Morning Post and Daily Advertiser*, the *Whitehall Evening Post*, and the *English Chronicle or Universal Evening Post*.
72. *The Benevolent Planters*, 9.
73. Ibid., 13.
74. Ibid., 3.
75. *Inkle and Yarico* was performed at the Haymarket on Thursday, 29 July and Friday, 7 August with Mrs Kemble in the title role (*The Benevolent Planters* appeared on Wednesday, August 5). While we have few details about the play's two performances, we can assume that the mournful song that Mrs Kemble sang in the second scene of *The Benevolent Planters* was popular with audiences as it was pictured on the title page of the published play and anthologized several times. The song appeared as early as 1789 in an edition of *The Songster's Companion: a Select Collection of More Than Two Hundred Songs, Including the Modern. To Which is Added, a Sections of Toasts and Sentiments* published in Coventry. The song, invariably identified as 'Sung by Mrs. Kemble in

The Benevolent Planters', continued to be published through the end of the century, in collections such as *The Muses Banquet, or Vocal Repository* [1790], *The New Vocal Enchantress. Containing an Elegant Selection of all the Newest Songs lately Sung at the Theatres-Royal* [1791], *The Muse in Good Humour; or Momus's Banquet: A Collection of Choice Songs, Including the Modern* [1795].

76. Prologue to *The Benevolent Planters*.
77. Ibid.
78. A similar moment of dissonance would have appeared in the third scene in which the slaves celebrate the yearly day of sport awarded by their owners by engaging in a dance entitled '*Liberty; or, We Slaves Rejoice*' (*London Stage*).
79. David Worrall contrasts the paternalist politics of *The Benevolent Planters* with William Bates's *Harlequin Mungo; or, A Peep into the Tower*, a play staged two years earlier at the Royalty Theatre in London's East End in November, 1787. *Harlequin Mungo* features, among other elements, an interracial marriage as part of its happy ending. As Worrall notes, '*Harlequin Mungo*, with its performances located in London's East End, reflected many of the liberal or radical characters perhaps expected of an audience cut off by distance from the West End royal theatres and otherwise intensely connected to a gradually modernizing world of manufacture, commodity import and dockyard employment.' *The Politics of Romantic Theatricality, 1787–1832: The Road to the Stage* (New York: Palgrave Macmillan, 2007), 105. I would suggest that the composition and popularity of Bates's play was likely influenced in part by the success of *Inkle and Yarico*, staged just two months before *Harlequin Mungo* first appeared.
80. *The Benevolent Planters*, 13.

5 The Moral Muse: Comedy and Social Engineering

1. Richard Cumberland, *The Observer: Being a Collection of Moral, Literary and Familiar Essays*, 5 vols. (London, 1786), III: 31.
2. *St James' Chronicle, or British Evening Post* (8 May 1794).
3. Whereas *Inkle and Yarico* was staged throughout the 1788–1789 season, *The West Indian* was staged only four times during the fall of 1788, and in each case the receipts were notably lower than those received by *Inkle and Yarico* (17 September: £193 10*s*. 6*p*.; October 25: £182 13*s*.; 14 November: £120 5*s*.; 27 November: £63 12*s*. 6*d*. By contrast, during the same period, the receipts for *Inkle and Yarico* ranged from a low of £170 5*s*. on 5 November to a high of £246, on 22 October, the night it premiered. The average take was over £200. After playing Inkle at the Haymarket in summer 1788, Bannister appeared as Belcour in all four performances of *The West Indian* at Drury Lane. All figures taken from *The London Stage*.

4. Daniel O'Quinn, *Entertaining Crisis in the Atlantic Imperium, 1770–1790* (Baltimore: Johns Hopkins University Press, 2011), 281.
5. Elizabeth Inchbald, 'Remarks' on *The West Indian*, in *The British Theatre; Or, a Collection of Plays, Which Are Acted at the Theatres Royal, Drury Lane, Covent Garden, and Haymarket*, 25 vols. (London: Longman, Hurst, Rees Orme, 1808), XVIII: 3.
6. Ibid., 5.
7. Harvard Theatre Collection, shelfmark THE GEN TS Promptbook *Inkle and Yarico* [1819?].
8. Frank Felsenstein suggests that the popularity of *Inkle and Yarico* decreased after Britain abolished the slave trade in 1807. Frank Felsenstein, ed., *English Trader, Indian Maid: Representing Gender, Race, and Slavery in the New World. An Inkle and Yarico Reader* (Baltimore: Johns Hopkins University Press, 1999), 27.
9. Joseph Roach, *It* (Ann Arbor: University of Michigan Press, 2007), 29.
10. Helen Nicholson, 'Emotion', *Contemporary Theatre Review* 23, no. 1 (2013): 20.
11. 'Prologue', *The Jew. A Comedy. Performed at the Theatre-Royal, Drury-Lane* (London, 1794). All further references will be taken from this text and cited parenthetically.
12. *The Fashionable Lover* (1772) concludes with the line, 'By Heaven, I'd rather weed out one such unmanly prejudice from the hearts of my countrymen, than add another Indies to their empire', spoken by Mortimer, the play's moral voice.
13. Michael Ragussis provides an excellent overview of Cumberland's representation of ethnic groups in *Theatrical Nation: Jews and Other Outlandish Englishmen in Georgian England* (Philadelphia: University of Pennsylvania Press, 2010). See pages 104–107 for Ragussis's discussion of *The Fashionable Lover*. Ragussis argues that in this play, the Jewish figure becomes the vehicle used to attack the commercial interests of the English.
14. Richard Cumberland, *The Memoirs of Richard Cumberland*, ed. Richard J. Dircks, 2 vols. (New York: AMS Press, 2002), II: 97.
15. Cumberland, *The Observer*, III: 29–30.
16. Ibid., III: 30.
17. Richard Brinsley Sheridan, *The Duenna*, in *The Dramatic Works of Richard Brinsley Sheridan*, ed. Cecil Price, 2 vols. (Oxford: Clarendon Press, 1973), I. iii:58–59.
18. Ragussis, *Theatrical Nation*, 47.
19. James Thomas Kirkman, *Memoirs of the Life of Charles Macklin, Esq. Principally Compiled from His Own Papers and Memorandums, which Contain his Criticisms on and Characters and Anecdotes of Betterton, Booth, Wilks, Cibber, Garrick, Barry, Mossop, Sheridan, Foote, Quin, and Most of His Contemporaries; Together with His Valuable Observations on the Drama, the Science of Acting, and on various other Subjects: the Whole forming*

a Comprehensive but Succinct History of the Stage; which Includes a Period of One Hundred Years, 2 vols. (London, 1799), I: 259.

20. Kirkman, among others, attributes this comment to Alexander Pope. *Life of Macklin*, I: 264.
21. Cumberland, *The Observer*, III: 31.
22. Ibid.
23. Ibid., III: 32.
24. Ibid., III: 33.
25. Henry Home, Lord Kames, *The Elements of Criticism. In Three Volumes* (Edinburgh, 1762), I: 75.
26. Cumberland, *The Observer*, IV: 235.
27. Ibid., 239.
28. Cumberland, *The Observer*, IV: 264–265.
29. See Frank Felsenstein on stereotypical Jewish appearance. *Anti-Semitic Stereotypes: A Paradigm of Otherness in English Popular Culture, 1660–1830* (Baltimore: Johns Hopkins University Press, 1995).
30. Ragussis, *Theatrical Nation*, 117.
31. In addition to *The West Indian*, extravagant praise for merchants and their role in building the British empire appears in Steele's *The Conscious Lovers* and Lillo's *The London Merchant*, among many others. For a discussion of how the figure of the merchant operates in sentimental drama, see Lisa A. Freeman, *Character's Theater: Genre and Identity on the Eighteenth-Century English Stage* (Philadelphia: University of Pennsylvania Press, 2002), 213–234.
32. [George Daniel], 'Remarks' to *The Jew*, in *Cumberland's British Theatre. With Remarks, Biographical and Critical. Printed from the Acting Copies, as Performed at the Theatre-Royal, London*, vol. 38 (London, 1829), n.p.
33. Inchbald, 'Remarks' on *The West Indian*, XVIII: 4.
34. *The Lady's Magazine*, May 1794. Quoted by Stanley Thomas Williams in *Richard Cumberland: His Life and Works* (New Haven: Yale University Press, 1917), 236.
35. See Ragussis, *Theatrical Nation*, 109–111.
36. *Morning Post* (9 May 1794).
37. Robert Armin, *Sheva the Benevolent* (New York: Moreclacke Publishing, 2012).
38. For more information regarding Hebrew and Yiddish translations of *The Jew*, see Louis I. Newman, *Richard Cumberland: Critic and Friend of the Jews* (New York: Bloch Publishing Company, 1919), 45–46.
39. *Charleston Courier* (Charleston, SC, 23 April 1803). *The Jew* was first staged in Charleston on 20 April 1795.
40. *St James's Chronicle or British Evening Post* (8 May 1794).
41. *Morning Post* (9 May 1794).
42. *London Chronicle* (9 May 1794).

43. *Morning Chronicle* (9 May 1794).
44. Cumberland, *Memoirs*, II: 143.
45. Cumberland did, however, complain rather peevishly that 'not a line did I ever receive from the pen of any Jew' thanking him for his positive representation of Jews through the figure of Sheva (*Memoirs*, I: 97).
46. This sentiment was widely invoked regarding how one should respond to viewing the play. As a letter to the *Morning Chronicle* explains: 'In the Theatre [*The Jew*] becomes more and more popular every night of its performance: a circumstance I am not at all surprised at, because that individual who can witness such benevolence of heart, such rectitude of principle, and such correct consonancy of human character as Mr. Cumberland's Sheba [*sic*] evinces, without being charmed, must not only be devoid of every generous feeling, but cannot have observed mankind with a distinguishing eye, and contemplated the wonderful variety of different singularities that discriminate individuals of all sects, descriptions, classes, and countries.' *Morning Chronicle* (30 May 1794).
47. *St James's Chronicle or the British Evening Post* (10 May 1794).
48. *The Monthly Visitor, and Entertaining Pocket Companion. By a Company of Gentlemen*, vol. I (London, 1797): 55.
49. *Federal Orrery* (Boston, MA: 22 December 1794).
50. Ibid.
51. *Aurora General Advertiser* (Philadelphia, PA: 16 February 1795).
52. A review from the *Charleston Courier* of 23 April 1803 employs a more elaborate, and less agricultural image:

    > To extinguish animosities, to correct erroneous and uncharitable judgments, and to encounter unjust and unfeeling prejudices, may be considered among the most useful and amiable exertions of the human mind. And notwithstanding all his real substantial worth, no biped that ever existed, stood so much in need of correction and amendment in that way, as that same sturdy gentleman call JOHN BULL . . . Certain it is, that the prejudices of the multitude of England were unreasonable, rank and inveterate; and the amiable Cumberland deserves a never fading laurel for having been the first who successfully encountered them.

    More distinctly antagonistic than earlier writers, this author uses the emblematic figure of John Bull to attack what he sees as 'rank and inveterate' national bigotry of the English as a people.
53. Charles Beecher Hogan notes 243 performances of *The Merchant of Venice* between 1751 and 1800, making it the most popular Shakespearean comedy of the second half of the century and the fifth most popular Shakespeare play during that period. Only *Romeo and Juliet* (399 performances), *Hamlet* (343 performances), *Richard III* (323 performances), and *Macbeth* (271 performances) were more popular.
54. Cumberland, *The Observer*, III: 31.
55. Ibid.
56. Ibid., 38.

57. Cumberland compares the passage from *The Unfortunate Traveler* to the conversation between Shylock and Tubal in *The Merchant of Venice*, III.i: 79–130. His attribution is not recognized by modern scholars, who usually trace the story of the pound of flesh to Giovanni Fiorentino's *Il Pecorone* (1558).
58. Kirkman, *Life of Macklin*, 260.
59. Ibid., 264.
60. *St James's Chronicle, or the British Evening Post* (8 May 1794).
61. *Morning Chronicle* (30 May 1794).
62. The Haymarket staged *The Jew* on 17 September, followed by Covent Garden's first productions of the play on 21 and 26 September. Covent Garden added *The Merchant of Venice* on 30 September, followed by *The Jew* three days later (3 October) and *Merchant* again on 7 October. Drury Lane countered with its own production of *The Jew* on 12 October and again on 18 October.
63. 'Mr. Bannister's *Shylock* has very little in it to commend. He can play no part without shewing himself to be a master of his profession, but in *Shylock* he is *impar materiae*.' *Monthly Mirror* (June 1808), 458. Both of his attempts at Shylock were described by biographers and critics as unmistakable failures.
64. John Adolphus, *The Memoirs of John Bannister*, 2 vols. (London: Richard Bentley, 1839), I: 340–341.
65. *Morning Chronicle* (30 May 1794).
66. *The Monthly Visitor, and Entertaining Pocket Companion*, 55.
67. *Nathan the Wise* was first translated into English in 1781 and never reprinted in the eighteenth century. The play is occasionally mentioned in reviews of *The Jew*, in most cases to stress the differences between the plays. The review in the *Morning Chronicle* comments 'the plan of the Piece is to exhibit a benevolent Jew, and this Mr. CUMBERLAND, who we understand is the Author, has succeeded in delineating with great effect. LESSING, the German Dramatist, has a character of the same cast, but the Play before us is not a copy. He has treated his subject after his own manner (*Morning Chronicle*, 9 May 1794). Another refers directly to the English translation, 'Mr. Lessing, perhaps the best dramatick writer of the eighteenth century, produced in Germany, a beautiful and pathetick Drama, called *Hassan*, to correct pernicious prejudices, by impressions directly opposite to those of *Shylock*. A wretched translation of the Drama has appeared in English; without any of the effects produced in Germany on the public mind. Mr. CUMBERLAND, actuated we believe by a similar motive, has entered the lists; and he will derive the best fame from the benevolent and sublime moral, which is the very germ and generating principle of the whole Comedy' (*St James's Chronicle or the British Evening Post*, 10 May 1794).
68. William Cobbett, *Cobbett's Political Register*, vol. 10 (6 September 1806): 404. This claim appears in an article titled 'Jewish Predominance', 403–406. See Ragussis (*Theatrical Nation*, 112–113) for a more extended discussion of Cobbett's response to *The Jew*.

69. The excised passage can be seen in prompt books such as one used in 1824 in Drury Lane (held in the Victoria and Albert Theatre and Performance Collection) and in editions such as that published by Thomas Hailes Lacy, 'Theatrical Publisher' (London, n.d.).
70. It was subsequently published in the transactions of the Jewish Historical Society in London, 1915, 146–179.
71. Newman, *Richard Cumberland.*
72. Ibid., 60.
73. M. J. Landa, *The Jew in Drama* (London: P. S. King and Son, 1926), 139.
74. Bryan Waller Procter [pseud: Barry Cornwall], *The Life of Edmund Kean. With Critical Remarks on his Theatrical Performances* (London, 1835), 15.
75. Procter describes the impact of Kean's performance as monumental:

> When Kean first entered upon the stage, that evening, the spectators saw that something decisive (good or bad) was about to happen ... his fine retort on Antonio, which shames, or ought to cast shame on the Christian merchant,
>
> *'Fair Sir, you spat on me on Wednesday last;*
> *You spurned me such a day; another time*
> *You called me – dog; and for the courtesies*
> *I'll lend you thus much monies –'*

was received with acclamations. . . .He went on, still gaining ground, until he arrived at the scene with Salarino, where those fierce and unanswerable interrogations on behalf of the Jew ('Hath not a Jew eyes,' &c) are forced from him: when knitting himself up, he gave them forth with terrible energy, and drew down a thunder of applause. And in this way he went on, victorious, to the end; gathering glory after glory, shout after shout, till the curtain fell. Nothing like that acting, – nothing like that applause, had, for many previous years resounded within the walls of ancient or modern Drury. It was a new era. (38–39)

Afterword

1. James Boaden, *Memoirs of Mrs Siddons. Interspersed with Anecdotes of Authors and Actors*, 2 vols. (London: Henry Colburn, 1827), I: 329.
2. Daniel Mendelsohn, 'How Greek Drama Saved the City', *The New York Review of Books* 63, no. 11 (23 June 2016): 59.
3. It is worth noting that Jeremy Bentham conceived of his panopticon as being applicable not only to prisons but to a wide range of public moral institutions, including schools. He finishes his final letter on the panopticon by referring to the widespread social benefits of the panopticon:

> What would you say, if by the gradual adoption and diversified application of this single principle, you should see a new scene of things spread itself over the face of civilized society? – Morals reformed, health preserved, industry invigorated, instruction diffused, public burthens lightened, economy seated as it were upon a rock, the Gordian knot of the Poor-laws not cut but untied – all by a simple idea in architecture?

Jeremy Betham, *Panopticon; or, The Inspection-House: Containing the Idea of a New Principle of Construction Applicable to any Sort of Establishment, in which Persons are to be kept under Inspection; and in Particular to Penitentiary-Houses, Prisons, Houses of Industry, Work-Houses, Poor-Houses, Lazarettos, Manufactories, Hospitals, Mad-Houses, and Schools: With a Plan of Management Adapted to the Principle*, 4 vols. (London, 1791), I: 139–140.

4. Raymond Williams, *Marxism and Literature* (Oxford: Oxford University Press, 1977), 132.

Bibliography

Addison, Joseph. *Cato. A Tragedy. As it is Acted at the Theatre-Royal in Drury Lane, by Her Majesty's Servants*. London, 1713.

Addison, Joseph and Sir Richard Steele. *The Spectator*. Edited by Donald Frederic Bond. Oxford: Clarendon Press, 1965.

Adolphus, John. *The Memoirs of John Bannister*. 2 vols. London: Richard Bentley, 1839.

American Ballad Operas. Edited by Walter Howard Rubsamen. New York: Garland, 1974.

Anderson, Misty. *Imagining Methodism in Eighteenth-Century Britain*. Baltimore: Johns Hopkins University Press, 2012.

Armin, Robert. *Sheva the Benevolent*. New York: Moreclacke Publishing, 2012.

Asleson, Robyn, ed. *The Notorious Muse: The Actress in British Art and Culture*. New Haven: Yale University Press, 2003.

'"She was Tragedy Personified": Crafting the Siddons Legend in Art and Life'. In *A Passion for Performance: Sarah Siddons and Her Portraitists*, edited by Robyn Asleson, 41–95. Los Angeles: J. Paul Getty Museum, 1999.

The Attic Miscellany; and Characteristic Mirror of Men and Things. Including the Correspondent's Museum. 3 vols. London, 1791.

Aurora General Advertiser.

Bagster-Collins, Jeremy F. *George Colman the Younger, 1762–1836*. New York: King's Crown Press, 1946.

Baker, David Erskine. *Biographica Dramatica, Or, a Companion to the Playhouse. A new Edition: Carefully corrected, greatly enlarged, and continued from 1764 to 1782*. 2 vols. London, 1782.

Bannet, Eve Tavor. 'Cumberland's *Benevolent Hebrew* in Eighteenth-Century Britain and America'. *Studies in American Jewish Literature* 33, no. 1 (2014): 84–106.

Barbauld, Anna Letitia. *Poems*. London, 1773.

Barish, Jonas. *The Antitheatrical Prejudice*. Berkeley: University of California Press, 1981.

Beattie, James. *Essays on Poetry and Music, as they affect the Mind. On Laughter, and Ludicrous Composition. On the Utility of Classical Learning*. Edinburgh, 1776.

The Beauties of Mrs Siddons: Or, a Review of Her Performance of the characters of Belvidera, Zara, Isabella, Margaret of Anjou, Jane Shore, – and Lady Randolph; in Letters from a Lady of Distinction, to her Friend in the Country. London, 1786.

Bell's Edition of Shakespeare's Plays, as they are now performed at the Theatre Royal in London. Regulated from the Prompt Books of each House by Permission; with Notes Critical and Illustrative; by the Authors of the Dramatic Censor. 9 vols. London, 1773.

Bellamy, Thomas. *The Benevolent Planters. A Dramatic Piece, as performed at the Theatre Royal, Haymarket*. London, 1789.

Bentham, Jeremy. *Panopticon; or, The Inspection-House: Containing the Idea of a New Principle of Construction Applicable to any Sort of Establishment, in which Persons are to be kept under Inspection; and in Particular to Penitentiary-Houses, Prison, Houses of Industry, Work-Houses, Poor-Houses, Lazarettos, Manufactories, Hospitals, Mad-Houses, and Schools: With a Plan of Management Adapted to the Principle*. 4 vols. London, 1791.

Bernbaum, Ernest. *Drama of Sensibility*. Boston: Ginn, 1915.

Bernstein, Robin. 'Toward the Integration of Theatre History and Affect Studies: Shame and the Rude Mechs's *The Method Gun*'. *Theatre Journal* 64, no. 2 (2012): 213–230.

Bethum, John. *A Short View of the Human Faculties and Passions. With Remarks and Directions respecting their Nature, Improvement, and Government*. 2nd edn. Edinburgh, 1770.

Bhattacharya, Nandini. 'Family Jewels: George Colman's *Inkle and Yarico* and Connoisseurship'. *Eighteenth-Century Studies* 34, no. 2 (2001): 207–226.

Blair, Hugh. *Lectures on Rhetoric and Belles Lettres*. Edited by Harold F. Harding. 2 vols. Carbondale: Southern Illinois University Press, 1965.

Blau, Herbert. *Take Up the Bodies: Theater at the Vanishing Point*. Champaign: University of Illinois Press, 1982.

Boaden, James. *Memoirs of Mrs Siddons. Interspersed with Anecdotes of Authors and Actors*. 2 vols. London: Henry Colburn, 1827.

B[ogle], Maria Belinda. *Epistle: From Miss Maria Belinda B–gle; at Edinburgh. To her Friend, Miss Lavinia L–tch, at Glasgow*. In *Edinburgh Fugitive Pieces*, 172–175. Edinburgh, 1791.

Bonhote, Elizabeth. *The Rambles of Mr. Frankly. Published by his Sister*. 2 vols. London, 1772.

Boswell, James. *London Journal, 1762–1763*. Edited by Frederick Pottle. New York: McGraw-Hill, 1950.

Brooke, Frances. *The Old Maid. By Mary Singleton, Spinster. A New Edition Revised and corrected by the Editor*. London, 1764.

Virginia a Tragedy, with Odes, Pastorals and Translations. London, 1756.

Brown, Christopher Leslie. *Moral Capital: Foundations of British Abolitionism*. Chapel Hill: University of North Carolina Press, 2006.

Brown, Laura. *English Dramatic Form, 1660–1760: An Essay in Generic History*. New Haven: Yale University Press, 1981.

Burke, Edmund. *A Philosophical Enquiry into the Origin of Our Ideas of the Sublime and Beautiful*. Edited by J. T. Boulton. London: Routledge and Kegan Paul, 1958.

Reflections on the Revolution in France. In *The Writings and Speeches of Edmund Burke*. Edited by L. G. Mitchell and William B. Todd. 9 vols. Oxford: Clarendon Press, 1989.

Burns, Robert. *The Poems and Songs of Robert Burns*. Edited by James Kinsley. 3 vols. Oxford: Clarendon Press, 1968.

Burroughs, Catherine. '"The Father Foster'd at His Daughter's Breast": Fanny Kemble and *The Grecian Daughter*'. *Nineteenth-Century Contexts* 28, no. 4 (2006): 335–345.

Campbell, Thomas. *The Life of Mrs Siddons*. 2 vols. London: Effingham Wilson, 1834.

Charleston Courier.

Chetwood, W. R. *A General History of the Stage, From its Origin in Greece down to the present Time. With Memoirs of most of the principal Performers that have appeared on the English and Irish Stage for these last Fifty Years*. London, 1749.

Cobbett, William. *Cobbett's Political Register*. London: Printed by Cox and Baylis, 1802–1835.

Coleman, Edward D., comp. *The Jew in English Drama: An Annotated Bibliography*. New York: The New York Public Library, 1943.

Collier, Jeremy. *A Short View of the Immorality, and Profaneness of the English Stage, Together With the Sense of Antiquity upon this Argument*. London, 1698.

Colman, George the Younger. *Inkle and Yarico: An Opera, in Three Acts. As performed at the Theatre-Royal in the Hay-Market, on Saturday, August 11th, 1787*. London, 1787.

Inkle and Yarico. In *Plays by George Colman the Younger and Thomas Morton*, edited by Barry Sutcliffe. Cambridge: Cambridge University Press, 1983.

Cook, William. *The Elements of Dramatic Criticism. Containing an Analysis of The Stage under the following Heads, Tragedy, Tragi-comedy, Comedy; Pantomime and Farce*. London, 1775.

Corneille, Pierre. *Horace*. Translated by Philip John Yarrow. New York: Macmillan, 1967.

Crisp, Samuel. *Virginia. A Tragedy. As it is acted at the Theatre-Royal in Drury-Lane, by His Majesty's Servants*. London, 1754.

The Critical Review.

Cumberland, Richard. *The Fashionable Lover*. London, 1772.

The Jew. A Comedy. Performed at the Theatre-Royal, Drury-Lane. London, 1794.

The Jew. London: Thomas Hailes Lacy, 'Theatrical Publisher', n.d.

The Letters of Richard Cumberland. Edited by Richard J. Dircks. New York: AMS Press, 1988.

The Memoirs of Richard Cumberland. Edited by Richard J. Dircks. 2 vols. New York: AMS, 2002.

The Observer: Being a Collection of Moral, Literary and Familiar Essays. 5 vols. London, 1786.

Timon of Athens, altered from Shakespear. A Tragedy. As it is acted at the Theatre-Royal in Drury-Lane. London, 1771.

The West Indian. A Comedy. As it is Performed at the Theatre Royal at Drury-Lane. London, 1771.

The West Indian. Cumberland's British Theatre. Vol 14. 1829.

[Daniel, George]. 'Remarks' to *The Jew*. In *Cumberland's British Theatre. With Remarks, Biographical and Critical. Printed from the Acting Copies, as Performed at the Theatre-Royal, London*. Vol. 38. London, 1829.

Davies, Thomas. *The Memoirs of David Garrick, Esq. Interspersed with Characters and Anecdotes of his Theatrical Contemporaries. The Whole Forming a History of the Stage, which Includes a Period of Thirty-Six Years*. 2 vols. London, 1780.

Dennis, John. *Appius and Virginia. A Tragedy*. London, [1709].

The Critical Works of John Dennis. Edited by Edward Niles Hooker. 2 vols. Baltimore: Johns Hopkins University Press, 1939.

Dibdin, Charles. *A Complete History of the Stage*. 5 vols. London, 1800.

Diderot, Denis. *Selected Writings on Art and Literature*. Translated by Geoffrey Bremner. New York: Penguin, 1994.

Dodsley, Robert. *Cleone. A Tragedy*. London, 1758.

Doody, Margaret. *Frances Burney: The Life in the Works*. New Brunswick: Rutgers University Press, 1988.

Dunbar, Howard Hunter. *The Dramatic Career of Arthur Murphy*. New York: Modern Language Association of American, 1946.

Durkheim, Emile. *The Elementary Forms of Religious Life*. Translated by Joseph Ward Swain. London: George Allen and Unwin, 1915.

Edinburgh Fugitive Pieces. Edinburgh, 1791.

Edwin's Pills to Purge Melancholy: Containing all the Songs Sung by Mr Edwin, of Covent Garden Theatre, Since his First Appearance in London; And Many Duets Mr Edwin has a Part in. With a Humourous Account of Mrs Siddons's First Reception in Dublin. And a Portrait of Mr. Edwin Finely Executed. The Second Edition, with Considerable Additions. London, 1788.

Ellis, Frank H. *Sentimental Comedy: Theory and Practice*. Cambridge: Cambridge University Press, 1991.

Ellis, Markman. *The Politics of Sensibility: Race, Gender and Commerce in the Sentimental Novel*. Cambridge: Cambridge University Press, 1996.

Engel, Laura. *Fashioning Celebrity: Eighteenth-Century British Actresses and Strategies for Image Making*. Columbus: Ohio State University Press, 2011.

English Chronicle or Universal Evening Post.

An Essay upon the Present State of the Theatre in France, England and Italy, with Reflections upon Dramatic Poetry in General, And the Characters of the Principal Authors and Performers of these Nations. A work absolutely necessary to be read by every Lover of Theatrical Exhibitions. London, 1760.

Federal Orrery.

Felsenstein, Frank. *Anti-Semitic Stereotypes: A Paradigm of Otherness in English Popular Culture, 1660–1830*. Baltimore: Johns Hopkins University Press, 1995.

ed. *English Trader, Indian Maid: Representing Gender, Race, Slavery in the New World: An Inkle and Yarico Reader*. Baltimore: Johns Hopkins University Press, 1999.

Ferguson, Moira. *Subject to Others: British Women Writers and Colonial Slavery, 1670–1834*. London: Routledge, 1992.

Festa, Lynn. *Sentimental Figures of Empire in Eighteenth-Century Britain and France*. Baltimore: Johns Hopkins University Press, 2006.

Fliegelman, Jay. *Prodigals and Pilgrims: The American Revolution against Patriarchal Authority, 1750–1800*. Cambridge: Cambridge University Press, 1982.

[Flitcroft, Henry]. *Theatrical Entertainments Consistent with Society, Morality, and Religion, in a Letter to the Author of 'The Stage the High road to Hell'. Shewing that Writer's Arguments to be fallacious, his Principles enthusiastic, and his Authorities (particularly from the Ancients) misconstrued and perverted.* London, 1768.

The Follies of St James's Street. 2 vols. London, 1789.

Freeman, Lisa A. *Antitheatricality and the Body Politic*. Philadelphia: University of Pennsylvania Press, 2017.

Character's Theater: Gender and Identity on the Eighteen-Century English Stage. Philadelphia: University of Pennsylvania, 2002.

'The Cultural Politics of Antitheatricality: The Case of John Home's *Douglas*'. *The Eighteenth Century: Theory and Interpretation* 43, no. 3 (Fall 2002): 210–235.

Garrick, David. *The Plays of David Garrick*. Edited by Harry William Pedicord and Fredrick Louis Bergmann. 7 vols. Carbondale: Southern Illinois University Press, 1981.

An Ode upon Dedicating a Building and Erecting a Statue, to Shakespeare, at Stratford Upon Avon. London, 1769.

The Gazetteer.

[Gibb, Adam]. *The Players Scourge: Or a Detection of the ranting prophanity and regnant impiety of stage plays, and their wicked encouragers and frequenters; and especially against the nine prophane Pagan Priests, falsely called ministers of the gospel, who countenanced the thrice cursed tragedy called* Douglas. Edinburgh, n.d.

Gildon, Charles. *Life of Mr Thomas Betterton, the late Eminent Tragedian. Wherein the Utterance of the Stage, Bar, and Pulpit, are distinctly consider'd. With the Judgment of the late Ingenious Monsieur de St. Evremont, upon the Italian and French Music and Opera's; in a Letter to the Duke of Buckingham*. London, 1710.

Gilliland, Thomas. *The Dramatic Mirror: containing The History of the Stage, from the Earliest Period to the Present Time; including a Biographical and Critical Account of All the Dramatic Writers, from 1660; and also of the most Distinguished Performers, from the days of Shakspeare to 1807: and a History of the Country Theatres, in England, Ireland, and Scotland. Embellished with Seventeen Elegant Engravings*. 2 vols. London: C. Chapple, 1808.

Goldsmith, Oliver. *The Collected Works of Oliver Goldsmith*. Edited by Arthur Friedman. 5 vols. Oxford: Clarendon Press, 1966.
Gollipudi, Aparna. *Moral Reform in Comedy and Culture, 1696–1747*. Farnham: Ashgate Publishing, 2011.
Gonda, Caroline. *Reading Daughters' Fictions: 1709–1834: Novels and Society from Manley to Edgeworth*. Cambridge: Cambridge University Press, 1996.
Gregory, John. *A Father's Legacy to his Daughters. By the Late Dr Gregory of Edinburgh*. London, 1774.
Gross, Daniel M. *The Secret History of Emotion from Aristotle's Rhetoric to Modern Brain Science*. Chicago: University of Chicago Press, 2006.
Guthrie, William. *An Essay upon English Tragedy. With Remarks upon the Abbe de* Blanc's Observations *on the English Stage*. London, 1757.
Hawkins, William. *Miscellanies in prose and verse. Containing candid and impartial observations on the principal performers belonging to the two Theatres-Royal; from January 1773, to May 1775. Likewise strictures on two favourite tragedies, viz. The ORPHAN and The FAIR PENITENT. Being part of an epistolary Correspondence on those Subjects with a young Lady. With Many other agreeable and interesting Articles, such as Pastoral Songs, Epitaphs, &c. &c.* London, 1775.
Highfill, Philip H., Kalman A. Burnim, and Edward A. Langhans. *A Biographical Dictionary of Actors, Actresses, Musicians, Dancers, Managers & Other Stage Personnel in London, 1660–1800*. 16 vols. Carbondale: Southern Illinois University Press, 1973.
Hogan, Charles Beecher. *Shakespeare in the Theatre, 1701–1800*. 2 vols. Oxford: Clarendon Press, 1957.
Home, John. *Douglas. A Tragedy. As it is acted at the Theatre-Royal in Covent-Garden*. London, 1757.
Hume, David. *Enquiry Concerning the Principles of Morals*. Edited by Tom L. Beauchamp. Oxford: Clarendon Press, 1998.
A Treatise of Human Nature. Edited by L. A. Selby-Bigge. Oxford: Clarendon Press, 1888, repr. 1967.
Hume, Robert D. *The Rakish Stage: Studies in English Drama, 1660–1800*. Carbonsdale and Edwardsville: Southern Illinois University Press, 1983.
Iliff, Edward Henry. *A Tear of Sympathy!!! Or, Striking Objects of Travel, Antient, and Modern! In Italy, Prussia, Spain, Russia, &c. With Reflections Critical, Moral, and Biographical*. London, 1796.
Inchbald, Elizabeth. *The British Theatre; Or, a Collection of Plays, Which Are Acted at the Theatres Royal, Drury Lane, Covent Garden, and Haymarket*. 25 vols. London: Longman, Hurst, Rees Orme, 1808.
A Simple Story. London, 1791.
Such Things Are. A Play, in Five Acts. As performed at the Theatre-Royal, Covent Garden. London, 1788.
Inkle and Yarico. Or, the Slave Trade Exposed. A Description of the Opera. Edinburgh, 1795.
Johnson, Samuel. *A Dictionary of the English Language: in which the Words are deduced from their Originals, Explained in their Different Meanings, and*

Authorized by the Names of the Writers in whose Works they are found. Abstracted from the Folio Edition, by the author Samuel Johnson, A.M. To which is prefixed, A Grammar of the English Language. In Two Volumes. London, 1756.

Johnson on Shakespeare. Edited by Arthur Sherbo. New Haven: Yale University Press, 1968.

[Johnson, Samuel]. *Sensibility. A Poem. Written in the Year 1773*. London, n.d.

Jones, Chris. *Radical Sensibility: Literature and Ideas in the 1790s*. New York: Routledge, 1993.

Kames, Henry Home, Lord. *The Elements of Criticism. In Three Volumes.* Edinburgh, 1762.

The Elements of Criticism. The Third Edition. 2 vols. Edinburgh, 1765.

The Elements of Criticism. 2 vols. Edited by Peter Jones. Indianapolis: Liberty Fund, 2005.

Kemble, Fanny. *Francis the First: A Tragedy in Five Acts. With Other Poetical Pieces by Frances Ann Kemble. In which is Included an Original Memoir and a Full Length Portrait.* New York: Peabody & Co., 1833.

Kirkman, James Thomas. *Memoirs of the Life of Charles Macklin, Esq. Principally Compiled from His Own Papers and Memorandums, which Contain his Criticisms on and Characters and Anecdotes of Betterton, Booth, Wilks, Cibber, Garrick, Barry, Mossop, Sheridan, Foote, Quin, and Most of His Contemporaries; Together with His Valuable Observations on the Drama, the Science of Acting, and on various other Subjects: the Whole forming a Comprehensive but Succinct History of the Stage; which Includes a Period of One Hundred Years.* 2 vols. London, 1799.

Kowaleski-Wallace, Elizabeth. *Their Fathers' Daughters: Hannah More, Maria Edgeworth, and Patriarchal Complicity.* Oxford: Oxford University Press, 1991.

Krutch, Joseph. *Comedy and Conscience after the Restoration.* New York: Columbia University Press, 1949.

The Lady's Magazine.

Lamb, Jonathan. *The Evolution of Sympathy in the Long Eighteenth Century.* London: Pickering and Chatto, 2009.

Landa, M. J. *The Jew in Drama.* London: P. S. King and Son, 1926.

Lansdowne, George Granville, Lord. *The Jew of Venice.* In *Five Restoration Adaptations of Shakespeare.* Edited with an introduction by Christopher Spencer. Urbana: University of Illinois Press, 1965.

Lessing, Gotthold Ephraim. *Emilia Galotti.* Translated by Benjamin Thompson, Esq. London, 1800.

Nathan the Wise (*Nathan der Weise*). Translated by Peter Demetz. New York: Continuum, 1991.

Lillo, George. *Fatal Curiosity: A True Tragedy of Three Acts. As it is acted at the New Theatre in the Hay-Market.* London, 1737.

The London Merchant: or, the History of George Barnwell. As it is acted at the Theatre-Royal in Drury-Lane. By His Majesty's Servants. London, 1731.

Limon, John. *Stand-up Comedy in Theory, or, Abjection in America*. Durham, NC: Duke University Press, 2000.

The London Chronicle.

The London Magazine: Or, Gentleman's Monthly Intelligencer

The London Stage, 1660–1800; a Calendar of Plays, Entertainments & Afterpieces, Together with Casts, Box-receipts and Contemporary Comment. 5 vols. Carbondale: Southern Illinois University Press, 1960.

Macklin, Charles. *Love a la Mode*. London, 1779.

Malthus, Thomas Robert. *T. R. Malthus: The Unpublished Papers in the Collection of Kanto Gakuen University*. Edited by John Pullen and Trevor Hughes Perry. 2 vols. Cambridge: Cambridge University Press, 2011.

Manning, Susan. 'Sensibility'. In *The Cambridge Companion to English Literature, 1740–1830*, edited by Thomas Keymer and Jon Mee, 80–99. Cambridge: Cambridge University Press, 2004.

Marinacci, Barbara. *Leading Ladies: A Gallery of Famous Actresses*. New York: Dodd, Mead and Company, 1961.

Marsden, Jean I. 'Daddy's Girls: Shakespearean Daughters and Eighteenth-Century Ideology'. *Shakespeare Survey* 51 (1998): 17–26.

'Performing the West Indies: Comedy, Feeling, and British Identity', *Comparative Drama* 42, no. 1 (2008): 73–88

'Shakespeare and Sympathy'. In *Shakespeare and the Eighteenth Century*, edited by Peter Sabor and Paul Yachnin, 29–41. London: Ashgate, 2008.

Marshall, David. *The Figure of Theater: Shaftsbury, Defoe, Adam Smith, and George Eliot*. New York: Columbia University Press, 1986.

The Surprising Effects of Sympathy: Marivaus, Diderot, Rousseau, and Mary Shelley. Chicago: University of Chicago Press, 1988.

Matthews, Sean. 'Change and Theory in Raymond Williams's Structures of Feeling'. *Pretexts: Literary and Cultural Studies* 10, no. 2 (2001): 179–194.

McGann, Jerome. *The Poetics of Sensibility: A Revolution in Literary Style*. Oxford: Oxford University Press, 1996.

McPherson, Heather. *Art and Celebrity in the Age of Reynolds and Siddons*. University Park: Penn State University Press, 2017.

'Picturing Tragedy: Sarah Siddons as the Tragic Muse Revisited'. *Eighteenth-Century Studies* 33, no. 3 (2000): 401–430

'Searching for Sarah Siddons: Portraiture and the Historiography of Fame'. *Eighteenth-Century Studies* 33, no. 2 (1999): 281–287.

'Theater Riots and Cultural Politics in Eighteenth-Century London'. *The Eighteenth Century: Theory and Interpretation* 43, no. 3 (2002): 236–252.

'Tragic Pallor and Siddons'. *Eighteenth-Century Studies* 48, no. 4 (2015): 479–502.

Mendelsohn, Daniel. 'How Greek Drama Saved the City'. *The New York Review of Books* 63, no. 11 (23 June 2016): 59–61.

Merry, Robert. 'Ode on the Restoration of his Majesty, Recited by Mrs. Siddons'. In *An Asylum for Fugitive Pieces, in Prose and Verse not in any Other Collection: with Several Pieces never before Published*. London, 1789.

Middlesex Journal and Evening Advertiser.

Monthly Mirror.

The Monthly Review.

The Monthly Visitor, and Entertaining Pocket Companion. By a Company of Gentlemen. London, 1797.

Moore, Edward. *The Gamester. A Tragedy.* London, 1753.

Moore, Thomas. *Letters and Journals of Lord Byron: With Notices of His Life.* 2 vols. London: John Murray, 1830.

The Morning Chronicle.

The Morning Post and Daily Advertiser.

The Morning Post.

Mullan, John. *Sentiment and Sociability: The Language of Feeling in the Eighteenth Century.* Oxford: Clarendon Press, 1986.

Murphy, Arthur. *Gray's-Inn Journal.* 5 vols. London, 1759.

The Grecian Daughter: A Tragedy. As it is acted at the Theatre-Royal in Drury-Lane. London, 1772.

The Muse in Good Humour; or Momus's Banquet: A Collection of Choice Songs, Including the Modern. London, 1795.

The Muses Banquet, or Vocal Repository: Being the Newest and most modern Collection of Song, Duets, Trios, &c. lately sung at the Anacreontic Society, Theatres Royal, Vauxhall, Sadler's Wells, Dibdin's Oddities, Beef Steak Club, Astley's, Circus, And at other Convivial and Polite Assemblies in the Town. London, 1790.

Newman, Louis I. *Richard Cumberland: Critic and Friend of the Jews.* New York: Bloch Publishing Company, 1919.

Nicholson, Helen. 'Emotion'. *Contemporary Theatre Review* 23, no. 1 (2013): 20–22.

Nussbaum, Felicity. *The Limits of the Human: Fictions of Anomaly, Race, and Gender in the Long Eighteenth Century.* Cambridge: Cambridge University Press, 2003.

Rival Queens: Actresses, Performance, and the Eighteenth-Century British Theater. Philadelphia: University of Pennsylvania Press, 2010.

O'Quinn, Daniel. *Entertaining Crisis in the Atlantic Imperium, 1770–1790.* Baltimore: Johns Hopkins University Press, 2011.

'Mercantile Deformities: George Colman's *Inkle and Yarico* and the Racialization of Class Relations'. *Theatre Journal* 54, no. 3 (2002): 389–409.

Staging Governance: Theatrical Imperialism in London, 1770–1800. Baltimore: Johns Hopkins University Press, 2005.

Orr, Bridget. 'The Theatrical Origins of Sentimental Discourse'. In *The Oxford Handbook of The Georgian Theatre, 1737–1832,* edited by Julia Swindells and David Francis Taylor, 621–637. Oxford: Oxford University Press, 2014.

Otway, Thomas. *The Works of Thomas Otway: Plays, Poems, and Love-letters.* Edited by J. C. Ghosh. Oxford: Clarendon Press, 1932.

Perry, Ruth. 'Colonizing the Breast: Sexuality and Maternity in Eighteenth-Century England'. *Journal of the History of Sexuality* 2, no. 2 (1991): 204–234.

Novel Relations: The Transformation of Kinship in English Literature and Culture, 1748–1818. Cambridge: Cambridge University Press, 2004.
Pinch, Adela. *Strange Fits of Passion: Epistemologies of Emotion, Hume to Austen*. Stanford: Stanford University Press, 1996.
Piozzi, Hester Thrale. *British Synonymy; Or an Attempt at Regulating the Choice of Words in Familiar Conversation*. 2 vols. London, 1794.
The Playhouse Pocket-Companion, or Theatrical Vade-Mecum. London, 1779.
Pratt, Samuel Jackson. *Sympathy; Or, a Sketch of the Social Passion. A Poem written at the Villa of a Friend, in his Absence*. London, 1781.
Sympathy, and Other Poems. Including Landscapes in Verse, and Cottage-Pictures. Revised, Corrected, and Enlarged. London, 1807.
Price, Lawrence. *An Inkle and Yarico Album* . Berkeley: University of California Press, 1937.
Proctor, Bryan Waller [pseud: Barry Cornwall]. *The Life of Edmund Kean. With Critical remarks on his Theatrical Performances*. London, 1835.
Public Advertiser.
Raggusis, Michael. *Theatrical Nation: Jews and Other Outlandish Englishmen in Georgian Britain*. Philadelphia: University of Pennsylvania Press, 2010.
The Redresser, Or, Weekly Strictures of Simon Sympathy, Esq. No. 1, Saturday, 25 July 1778.
Remarks on Mrs Siddons, in some of her Principal Characters. Edinburgh, 1784.
Remarks on the Slave Trade and the Slavery of the Negroes. In a Series of Letters. London, 1788.
Roach, Joseph. *It*. Ann Arbor: University of Michigan Press, 2007.
The Player's Passion: Studies in the Science of Acting. Newark: University of Delaware Press, 1985.
'Vicarious: Theater and the Rise of Synthetic Experience'. In *Theorizing Practice: Redefining Theatre History*, edited by W. B. Worthen and Peter Holland, 15–30. New York: Palgrave, 2005.
Robinson, Mary. *The Natural Daughter*. 2 vols. London, 1799.
Román, David. *Performance in America: Contemporary US Culture and the Performing Arts*. Durham, NC: Duke University Press, 2005.
Rowe, Nicholas. *Three Plays*. Edited by J. R. Sutherland. London, The Scolartis Press, 1929.
Russell, Gillian. *Theatres of War: Performance, Politics and Society 1793–1815*. Oxford: Clarendon Press, 1995.
Said, Edward. *Culture and Imperialism*. New York: Knopf, 1993.
St James's Chronicle or the British Evening Post.
Shadwell, Thomas. *Timon of Athens; Or, the Man-Hater*. London, 1678.
Sherbo, Arthur. *English Sentimental Drama*. East Lansing: Michigan State University Press, 1957.
Sheridan, Richard Brinsley. *The Dramatic Works of Richard Brinsley Sheridan*. Edited by Cecil Price. 2 vols. Oxford: Clarendon Press, 1973.
Smith, Adam. *The Theory of Moral Sentiments*. Edited by D. D. Raphael and A. L. Macfie.Oxford: Oxford University Press, 1979.

The Songster's Companion: A Select Collection of More Than Two Hundred Songs, Including the Modern. To Which is Added, a Sections of Toasts and Sentiments. Coventry, 1789.

Southerne, Thomas. *The Works of Thomas Southerne.* Edited by Henry J. Jordan and Harold Love. Oxford: Clarendon Press, 1988.

The Speaker: Or, Miscellaneous Pieces, selected from the Best English Writers, and disposed under proper heads, with a view to facilitate the Improvement of Youth in Reading and Speaking. To which is Prefixed an Essay on Elocution. London, 1774.

The Stage the High Road to Hell: Being an Essay on the Pernicious Nature of Theatrical Entertainments; shewing them to be at once inconsistent with Religion, and subversive of Morality. With Strictures on the vicious and dissolute Characters of the most eminent Performers of both Sexes. The whole enforced and supported by the best Authorities, both Antient and Modern. London, 1767.

Steele, Richard. *The Conscious Lovers.* Edited by Shirley Strum Kenny. Lincoln: University of Nebraska Press, 1968.

The Theatre. Edited by John Loftis. Oxford: Clarendon Press, 1962.

Sterne, Laurence. *A Sentimental Journey through France and Italy and Continuation of the Bramine's Journal.* Edited by Melvyn New and Geoffrey Day. Gainesville, FL: University Press of Florida, 2002.

Stone, Jr., George Winchester. 'Garrick's Production of *King Lear*: A Study in the Temper of the Eighteenth-Century Mind'. *Studies in Philology* 45, no. 1 (1948): 89–102.

Tate, Nahum. *The History of King Lear. In Five Restoration Adaptations of Shakespeare.* Edited with an introduction by Christopher Spencer. Urbana: University of Illinois Press, 1965.

The Theatrical Portrait, a Poem, on the Celebrated Mrs Siddons in the Characters of Calista, Jane Shore, Belvidera, and Isabella. London, 1783.

Thomson, James. 'Rule Britannia'. In *The Complete Poetical Works of James Thomson.* Edited with notes by J. Logie Robertson. Oxford: Oxford University Press, 1908.

Threipland, Stuart Moncrieff. *Letters Respecting the Performances at the Theatre Royal, Edinburgh.* Edinburgh, 1800.

Todd, Janet. *Sensibility: An Introduction.* London: Methuen, 1986.

A Trip to Parnassus; or, The Judgment of Apollo on Dramatic Authors and Performers. A Poem. London, 1788.

Turner, Daniel. 'On Sympathy'. In *The Breathings of Genius. Being a Collection of Poems; to which are added, Essays, Moral and Philosophical. By Elizabeth Gilding, Woolrich, Kent,* 92–98. London, 1786.

The Unsespected Observer, in the Spirit of the Late Martinius Scriblerius. In Two Volumes. London, 1792.

Virginia. A New Serious Opera, in Two Acts. As Performed at the King's Theatre in the Hay-Market. The Music by Signor Angelo Tarchi, a Celebrated Neapolitan Composer. Under the Direction of Signor Cherubini. London, 1786.

The New Vocal Enchantress. Containing an Elegant Selection of all the Newest Songs lately Sung at the Theatres-Royal. London, 1791.

Wanko, Cheryl. *Roles of Authority: Thespian Biography and Celebrity in Eighteenth-Century England.* Lubbock: Texas Tech University Press, 2003.

Wahrman, Dror. *The Making of the Modern Self: Identity and Culture in Eighteenth-Century England.* New Haven: Yale University Press, 2004.

Walpole, Horace. *Walpoliana.* 2 vols. London, 1799.

The Works of Horatio Walpole, Earl of Oxford. 5 vols. London: G. G. and J. Robinson and J. Edwards, 1798.

Webster, John. *Appius and Virginia. Acted at the Duke's Theater under the name The Roman Virgin; or, the Unjust Judge.* London, 1679.

West, Shearer. 'Siddons, Celebrity, and Regality'. In *Theatre and Celebrity in Britain, 1660–2000*, edited by Mary Luckhurst and Jane Moody, 191–213. New York: Palgrave Macmillan, 2005.

Whitehall Evening Post.

Wilkinson, Tate. *The Wandering Patentee; or, a History of the Yorkshire Theatres, from 1770 to the Present Time: interspersed with Anecdotes respecting most of the Performers in the Three Kingdoms, from 1765 to 1795. By Tate Wilkinson. In four volumes. To which are added, never published, The Diversions of the Morning, and Foote's Trial for a Libel on Peter Paragraph. Written by the late Samuel Foote, Esq.* York, 1795.

William Whitehead. *Plays and Poems of William Whitehead.* 2 vols. London, 1774.

The Roman Father. London, 1750.

Williams, Raymond. *The City and the Country.* Oxford: Oxford University Press, 1973.

Culture and Society, 1780–1950. London: Chatto and Windus, 1958.

The Long Revolution. London: Chatto and Windus, 1961.

Marxism and Literature. Oxford: Oxford University Press, 1977.

Williams, Stanley Thomas. *Richard Cumberland: His life and Works.* New Haven: Yale University Press, 1917.

Wilson, Andrew, *M.D. Medical Researches: Being an ENQUIRY into the NATURE and ORIGIN of HYSTERICS in the FEMALE CONSTITUTION, and into the Distinction between that Disease and HYPOCHONDRIAC or Nervous Disorders.* London, 1776.

Wilson, Brett D. *A Race of Female Patriots: Women and the Public Spirit on the British Stage, 1688–1745.* Lewisburg: Bucknell University Press, 2011.

Wilson, Kathleen. *The Island Race: Englishness, Empire and Gender in the Eighteenth Century.* London: Routledge, 2003.

Strolling Players of Empire: Theater, Culture and Modernity in the English Provinces, 1720- 1820. Cambridge: Cambridge University Press, 2019.

Wollstonecraft, Mary. *A Vindication of the Rights of Woman.* In *The Works of Mary Wollstonecraft.* Edited by Janet Todd and Marilyn Butler. 8 vols. New York: New York University Press, 1989.

Worrall, David. *Celebrity, Performance, Reception: British Georgian Theatre as Social Assemblage.* Cambridge: Cambridge University Press, 2013.

The Politics of Romantic Theatricality, 1787–1832: The Road to the Stage. New York: Palgrave Macmillan, 2007.

A Worthy Example of a Virtuous Wife, Who Fed her Father with her own MILK, he being Commanded by the Emperor to be Starved to Death, but afterwards Pardoned. London, 1760.

Wright, Richardson. *Revels in Jamaica, 1683–1838: Plays and Players of a Century, Tumblers and Conjurors, Musical Refugees and Solitary Showmen, Dinners, Balls and Cockfights, Darky Mummers and Other Memories of High Times and Merry Hearts.* New York: Dodd, Mead, 1937.

Zangwill, Louis. 'Richard Cumberland Centenary Memorial Paper'. In *The Transactions of the Jewish Historical Society*, 146–179. London, 1915.

Zwinger, Lynda. *Daughters, Fathers, and the Novel: The Sentimental Romance of Heterosexuality.* Madison: University of Wisconsin Press, 1991.

Index

[Johnson, Samuel]
  Sensibility. A Poem, 13, 174n36

Abington, Frances, 193n33
abolition of slavery, 117, 119, 127, 130, 134, 140
  opposition to, 132
American Revolution, 117
Anderson, Misty, 173n30
anti-Semitism, 141, 164
  and The *Merchant of Venice*, 143, 144, 145, 151
  and Shakespeare, 162
  and Sheridan's *Duenna*, 143
  in Britain, 141, 199n52
  in theatre, 142–145
antitheatricality, 29–31, 178n41
  and John Home, 30
  Scottish, 29–30
Aristotle, 16
  catharsis, 28
  dramatic theory incomplete, 37
Armin, Robert, 155
Arnold, Samuel, 119
arts
  and sympathy, 23–28
  hierarchy of, 28
Asleson, Robyn, 43, 96, 189n65
audience
  and benevolence, 145, 156–157, 158
  and nationalism, 76, 93, 101, 121, 155, 157–158, 162, 168, 199n52
    American, 159
  and sympathy, 9, 16, 24, 25, 28, 35, 39–40, 63, 64, 89, 102, 112, 168
    dangerous, 58
  anti-Semitism, 142–143
  as performers, 6, 14, 40, 148, 159
  communal experience, 2–3, 4, 7, 13, 25–26, 43, 66, 67–68, 140–141, 157–158, 164, 167–168
  emotion
    false, 52, 65, 66
  fainting, 49, 52, 54
  hysteria, 49, 50, 51, 53, 54, 181n22
  response to Sarah Siddons, 7, 43–44, 45–46, 51–58, 59–66, 67–68, 95, 181n22, 182n25
    female, 51–52, 60–61
    male, 54
  satire of, 54
  screaming, 49–50, 51–52
  self-indulgent, 56, 65, 66–67
  tears, 3, 9, 49, 52–54, 140, 156
avarice, 110–111

B[ogle], Maria Belinda, 45, 51–52, 56, 64–65, 181n12
Baddeley, Sophia, 193n33
Baker, David Erskine
  Biographica Dramatica, 79, 82
Ballad opera, 118, 119, 193n44
Ballad operas, Garland edition of, 119
Bannister, John
  and Edmund Kean, 165
  as Inkle, 119
  as Sheva, 155, 161–162
  as Shylock, 200n63
  as Trudge in *Inkle and Yarico*, 126
Barbados, 119, 126
  Inkle and Yarico, 118, 125, 130
Barbauld, Anna Letitia, 109
Barish, Jonas, 177n30
Barry, Anne, 187n43, 188n55
  as Ephrasia in *The Grecian Daughter*, 83
Barry, Spranger, 74, 83, 188n55
Beattie, James, 27, 177n34
  on comedy, 35
  on sympathy, 19–20, 24
Beauties of Mrs Siddons, The, 41, 46, 47, 49, 57, 61–64
  and Adam Smith, 63
Bellamy, Thomas
  Benevolent Planters, The, 130–136, 196n79
    manuscript of, 130, 131–133
    music in, 131, 135, 195–196n75
    prologue to, 130, 134

benevolence, 12
  and empire, 106–107, 112–113, 116
  and slavery, 128, 131–133, 135–136
  and sympathy, 22
  and the audience, 140–141, 156–158
  and theatre, 26
  general
    in drama, 16
  in *School for Scandal*, 12
  in *The Jew*, 151–155
  in *The West Indian*, 108, 110, 112–113, 115, 116
  linked with capital, 110–111, 112, 114
Benevolent Planters, The (Bellamy), 130–136, 195n75, 196n79
Bentham, Jeremy, 201–202n3
  panopticon, 167–168, 201–202n3
Bernbaum, Ernest, 171n23
Bernstein, Robin, 4
Bethum, John
  on sympathy, 19, 175n4
Bhattacharya, Nadini, 194n48, 194n49
Blair, Hugh, 106, 158
  literature and national character, 104–105
Blau, Herbert, 6
Boaden, James, 7, 68, 166, 184n61
  on *Romeo and Juliet*, 190n81
  on Siddons, 44
  Siddons as Britannia, 190n81
  Siddons as Euphrasia, 94–95
Bonhote, Elizabeth, *Rambles of Mr Frankly*, 116
Boston, Massachusetts
  theatre in, 155
Boswell, James, 1, 3, 9, 50
breast-feeding, 84–89, 92, 98–99, 187n42, 189n63
Britannia, 98–100
  images of, 98
  Sarah Siddons as, 99
Brooke, Frances, 74, 78
  Virginia, 78, 82–83
Brown, Christopher Leslie, 117
Brown, Laura, 10, 172n25
Burke, Edmund, 20
  and masculinity, 14, 174n41
  on excessive sensibility, 14
  on sympathy, 24, 42
  Reflections on the Revolution in France, 14, 174n38
  Sublime and Beautiful, 177n24
Burney, Frances, 70, 71, 81, 100, 186n38
Burns, Robert, 118, 193n41
Burroughs, Catherine, 187n42

Campbell, Thomas, 83, 187n47
  on Arthur Murphy, 188n50
  on *The Grecian Daughter*, 84
  Siddons as Euphrasia, 95, 96, 189n69
  Siddons as Isabella, 181n22
capital
  proper use of, 110–111, 114–115
Catholics and Catholicism, 114, 142, 154, 192n29
celebrity studies, 7, 43, 173n30, 180n7
Cerrini, Giovanni Domenico, 84
Charleston, South Carolina
  theatre in, 155, 198n39, 199n52
Chetwood, W. R., 1, 3, 29
Cibber, Colley, 9
Cleone (Dodsley), 57–58, 64, 66
climate
  and benevolence, 112–113
  and manners, 113
Cobbett, William, 164, 200n68
Collier, Jeremy, 29, 30, 36
Colman, George the Younger
  Inkle and Yarico, 117–130
    twentieth-century revivals, 119, 193n44
    female characters in, 120
    instability of text, 119–120
    manuscript of, 119, 120, 194n45
    music in, 119, 124, 137
    reviews of, 119, 120, 124, 128
    sentiment in, 12
    staged in Jamaica, 119
    textual changes, 119–120, 122–124
    translations of, 119
colonies, American, 79, 97–98, 100, 117
comédies larmoyantes, 9
comedy. *See also* sentimental comedy
  and national character, 104–106
  and nationalism, 104–106, 108
  and pathos, 37, 120
  and tragedy mixed, 9, 35, 158
  difficulty of, 102–103
  new forms of, 35
commerce
  and benevolence, 112
  and empire, 107–108, 112–113, 116, 117
  and liberty, 107–108
  and masculinity, 107–108
  in 'Rule Britannia', 107–108
  in the *The West Indian*, 110
Cook, William, 32–33, 36
Corneille, Pierre
  Horace, 77
Cowley, Hannah
  Belle's Strategem, 10
Crawford, Anne. *See* Barry, Anne
Crisp, Samuel
  and Frances Burney, 81
  Virginia, 79–81, 82
Cromwell, Oliver, 110

Cumberland, Richard, 158
  and Jewish community, 164–165
  and Lessing, 200n67
  and Shylock, 160, 200n57
  Fashionable Lover, The, 108, 142, 149, 197n12
  Letters, 109, 191n19
  Memoirs, 103, 109, 142, 149, 157, 191n11, 199n45
  Observer, 142–149
  opposes anti-Semitism, 144–146
  The Jew
    alterations to, 164
    and *The Merchant of Venice*, 159–162, 200n62
    and *Nathan the Wise*, 162–164, 200n67
    Christianity and, 151–152, 155
    in the twentieth century, 155, 164–165, 166
    in America, 155, 158–159, 199n52
    Jewish stereotypes in, 149–150
    merchant in, 152–153
    popularity of, 155–156, 158, 198n38, 199n46
    reviews of, 157, 158–159, 161, 199n46
    translations of, 155, 198n38
  Timon of Athens, 75–76
  West Indian, The
    as outdated, 138–139
    benevolence in, 108, 110, 112, 116
    commerce in, 110
    female characters, 115–116
    loses popularity, 137–139, 196n3
    masculinity in, 115
    nationalism in, 110
    reviews of, 192n27
Cymon and Pero. *See* 'Roman Charity'

dance, 118, 131
daughters
  as patriots, 80, 81–82, 89–92, 97–98, 100
  in fiction, 70–72, 100
  in Murphy's *The Grecian Daughter*, 89–93
  in Restoration drama, 72–73
  in Shakespeare, 73–76
  in Valerius Maximus ('Roman Charity'), 84–85
  in Virginia and Virginius tragedies, 77–80, 81–83
  political implications of, 76–77, 97–98, 100–101
Davies, Thomas, 76
Dennis, John
  Appius and Virginia, 78, 186n30
  views on comedy, 35, 179n56
Dibdin, Charles, 2, 3
Diderot, Denis, 8, 9
Dodsley, Robert
  Cleone, 57–58, 64
Doody, Margaret, 71, 81, 184n5, 186n38
Drama and censorship, 14, 104, 133
drame bourgeois, 9
Dryden, John, 178n45
  All for Love, 34
Dunbar, Howard Hunter, 187n42
Durkheim, Emile, 7

Edgeworth, Maria, 14, 71
Edinburgh Fugitive Pieces, 51, 181n11
  Maria Belinda Bogle, 45
  on fight for theatre tickets, 45
Ellis, Frank H., 11, 172n27
Engel, Laura, 43, 173n30
Ephesian matron, 118, 193n39
Essay upon the Present State of the Theatre in *France, England and Italy*, 32
ethnic stereotypes
  African, 128
  Jewish, 142, 144, 146, 149–150, 151
Euripides
  Hippolytus, 63, 183n48

Fair Penitent (Rowe), 72–73, 78, 183n44
familial relationships
  and empire, 82, 90–91, 93, 97–98, 100–101
  and George III, king of England, 76, 97–100
  and patriotism, 78, 81–82
  as sympathetic, 72
  domestic, 70–71, 72
  in Crisp's *Virginia*, 79–80
  in Cumberland's *Timon of Athens*, 75–76
  in eighteenth-century novels, 70–72, 100
  in *The Grecian Daughter*, 84–93
  in *King Lear*, 73–75
  in Restoration drama, 72–73
  political implications of, 77, 79, 93, 97–98, 100–101
  Spectator 449 70, 72
fathers
  and liberty
    in Virginia and Virginius tragedies, 77–80, 81–83
  feeble, 91
  George III, king of England, as, 76, 97–98
  in *The Grecian Daughter*, 88–93
  in Restoration drama, 72–73
  in Shakespeare, 73–76
  in Valerius Maximus ('Roman Charity'), 84–85
  political implications in drama, 100–101
Felsenstein, Frank, 118, 119, 120, 193n38, 194n45, 194n49, 197n8, 198n29
female body, 91, 189n63
Ferguson, Moira, 194n49

Festa, Lynn, 10, 13
filial piety, 70
  and patriotism, 77, 79–83
  in art, 84–85, 92
  in *The Grecian Daughter*, 85–89, 91–92
  in *King Lear*, 75
  in Virginia and Virginius tragedies, 79–83
  Roman charity, 84–85
Fliegelman, Jay, 97
Flitcroft, Henry, 178n46
Follies of St James's Street, The, 39–40, 41, 43, 65, 67, 68, 180n4, 183n58
Formalism, 10, 39
France
  British attitudes towards, 79, 82, 104, 105
Freeman, Lisa A, 29, 102, 170n5, 172n30, 192n31, 198n31
French theatre
  comédies larmoyantes, 9
  drame bourgeois, 9
  English attitudes towards, 9, 104, 105

Gamester, The (Moore), 39–40, 43, 65, 67, 180n4, 183n58
Garrick, David, 8, 34, 46, 82, 175n42
  adaptation of *King Lear*, 74–75, 185n18
  adaptation of Southerne's *The Fatal Marriage*, 44, 47, 181n14
  and Cumberland's *The West Indian*, 109, 191n19
  and Siddons, 44
  as Hamlet, 178n34
  as King Lear, 1, 3
  Clandestine Marriage, 147–148
  comments on *King Lear*, 74
  Jubilee Ode, 74
generosity, 112
  artificial, 112, 192n26
  in *Inkle and Yarico*, 125
  in *The West Indian*, 111–112
  practised by Jews, 145, 147, 149, 151–153
genre
  blurring of, 35
George III, king of England, 76, 97, 98–100
Gibb, Adam
  Players Scourge, The, 29–30
Gildon, Charles, 186n29
Gilliland, Thomas, 46, 48
Gillray, James, 97, 98, 118
Goldsmith, Oliver, 10, 35–36, 102, 112, 192n26
Gollapudi, Aparna, 11
Gonda, Caroline, 71
Grecian Daughter, The. See also Murphy, Arthur
Gregory, John, 71
Greuze, Jean-Baptiste, 84
Guthrie, William, 32, 33

Hawkins, William, 73, 76
Herder, Johann Gottfried, 20
Hogan, Charles Beecher, 179n54, 185n18, 199n53
Home, John
  Douglas, 30, 34
Hume, David, 42
  and spectatorship, 176n20
  and theatre, 25–26
  Enquiry concerning the Principles of Morals, 21, 25–26, 176n21
  on sympathy, 21, 176n10
  Treatise of Human Nature, A, 21, 176n10
Hume, Robert D., 11, 36

Iliff, Edward Henry
  Tear of Sympathy, A, 176n8
Inchbald, Elizabeth
  British Theatre
    text of *Inkle and Yarico*, 119, 120, 194n48
  on *The Grecian Daughter*, 84, 86, 89, 90, 93, 187n49
  on *The Jew*, 154
  on *The West Indian*, 138, 139
  Simple Story, 70, 71
Inkle and Yarico. See also Colman, George the Younger
Inkle and Yarico (Colman), 12, 16, 104, 117–130, 131, 133, 134–135, 137–138, 139–140, 166, 193n44, 194n45, 195n59, 196n79, 197n8
Isabella, or, the Fatal Marriage. See also Southerne, Thomas; Siddons, Sarah
Isabella, or, the Fatal Marriage (Southerne/Garrick), 38, 44, 46–50, 63, 64, 67–68, 181n14, 181n22, 182n25

Jamaica, 108
  Benevolent Planters, The, 130–132, 134–135
  theatre in, 119, 191n17
Jane Shore (Rowe), 38, 58–64, 183n44. *See also* Rowe, Nicholas
Jew, The. See also Cumberland, Richard
Jewish Historical Society, 201n70
Jews and Judaism. *See also* anti-Semitism
  and Cumberland's *Observer*, 142–143, 144–149
  and Cumberland's *The Jew*, 149–155
  response to Cumberland's *The Jew*, 164–165, 198n38, 199n45, 201n70
  stereotypes of, 142, 143–144, 149–150
Johnson, Samuel
  Dictionary, 13

Johnson, Samuel (cont.)
on Nahum Tate's *King Lear*, 38
on Shakespeare, 38
on tragedy, 177n24
Johnstone, John Henry, 124
Jones, Chris, 14, 174n39

Kames, Henry Home, Lord, 6, 28, 184n61
ideal presence, 8, 23, 24, 103, 171n16
on comedy, 104
on sympathy, 22–23
on tragedy, 37–38
spectatorship and virtue, 88
sympathy and moral action, 23
sympathy and virtue, 27
theatre and sympathy, 27
Kean, Edmund, 165, 201n75
Kemble, Fanny, 83, 187n42
Kemble, John Philip, 44, 45
adaptation of *King Lear*, 74
as African sailor, 130, 134
delivers prologue to *The Benevolent Planters*, 130, 134
in *The Benevolent Planters*, 130–131
Kemble, Mrs Stephen, 118, 130, 134, 193n41
as Yarico, 118, 122
in *The Benevolent Planters*, 130–131, 195n75
Kirkman, James Thomas, 198n20
Memoirs of the Life of Charles Macklin, 144, 160
Kowaleski-Wallace, Elizabeth, 71
Krutch, Joseph, 171n23

L'Heroine Americaine, au Inkle and Zarika, 119
Lady of Distinction. *See Beauties of Mrs Siddons, The*
Lamb, Jonathan, 24, 25, 177n26
Landa, Gertrude and M.J., 164–165, 166
Lansdowne, George Granville, Lord, 144
Larpent Collection (Huntington Library), 119, 120, 132, 194n45
Lawrence, Sir Thomas, 61, 97
Le Brun, Charles, 8
Lessing, Gotthold Ephraim, 20, 186n30
Emilia Galotti, 186n30
Nathan the Wise, 162–164, 200n67
Licensing Act, 14, 104
Lillo, George
Fatal Curiosity, 54
London Merchant, The, 1, 9, 32, 33, 34, 152, 198n31
Limon, John, 170n1
Livy
History of Rome, 77
London Merchant, The, 1, 9, 32, 33, 34, 152, 198n31. *See* Lillo, George

London slums
slavery as solution for, 132–133
Lord Chamberlain, 14, 130, 131
censorship of *The Benevolent Planters*, 133

Macklin, Charles
as Shylock, 144, 159, 160
male hysteria, 54
Marinacci, Barbara, 59, 183n40
Marshall, David, 24–25, 172n25, 177n30
masculinity
and capital, 115
and commerce, 107–108
and nationalism, 109–110
in *Inkle and Yarico*, 120–121, 129–130
mercantile, 122–125
passive
in *The Grecian Daughter*, 86
Matthews, Sean, 170n9
McConnel, James, 193n44
McPherson, Heather, 43, 173n30, 175n42, 180n7, 189n75
Mendelsohn, Daniel, 167
mercantilism, 106–107, 112–113, 115, 116, 117–118, 120–130, 152–153
merchants, 198n31
in *The Jew*, 152–153
in *The West Indian*, 110
Merry, Robert, 99–100
Moncreiff, John, 187n39
Appius, 78, 81–82
Monthly Visitor, and Entertaining Pocket Companion
on Cumberland's *The Jew*, 157–158, 162
on Shylock, 161
Moore, Edward
Gamester, The, 39–40, 43, 65, 67, 180n4, 183n58. *See also* Siddons, Sarah
Moore, Thomas, 50
Murillo, Bartolomé Esteban, 84
Murphy, Arthur, 188n50
Grecian Daughter, The, 83–97, 100–101
and performance, 83–84
breastfeeding in, 85–89
popularity of, 83–84, 89, 187n49
reviews of, 86, 87, 89, 187n47
Siddons in, 93–97
source for, 84–85
Lear as father, 73–74
Muse in Good Humour; or Momus's Banquet: A Collection of Choice Songs, The, 196n75
Muses Banquet, or Vocal Repository, The, 196n75
music, 119, 124, 131, 135, 137, 195–196n75
music and affect, 124, 131, 195n75

Nashe, Thomas
  Unfortunate Traveler, The, 160
national character (American), 159
national character (British), 110, 129
  benevolence, 157
  commerce, 107–108, 110
  fellow-feeling, 157–158
  generosity, 125
  liberty, 104–106, 107, 110, 127–128
  liberty dependent on commerce, 107–108
  masculinity, 14, 108, 174n41
nationalism, 76–77, 81–82
  and comedy, 104–107
  and commerce, 107–108
  and slavery, 121–122, 127–130
  and theatre, 2
  and *The West Indian*, 110
  in theatre, 93, 101, 155, 157–158, 159, 168
Newman, Louis I., 164, 198n38
Nicholson, Helen, 43, 66, 140
Nussbaum, Felicity, 173n30, 194n48, 194n49

O'Quinn, Daniel, 97, 106, 125, 137, 173n30, 190n3, 192n32, 194n48, 195n59
opera, 78, 186n30
Otway, Thomas, 25, 31, 77, 178n45
  Venice Preserv'd, 32, 72, 73

panopticon. *See* Bentham, Jeremy
pathos
  and Samuel Johnson, 38
  and slave trade, 124
  and theatrical repertoire, 38
  embodied by Mrs Kemble, 118–119, 134
  importance of in drama, 37–39
  in *Inkle and Yarico*, 118–119, 120, 140
  in male characters, 38–39
  in *The Benevolent Planters*, 130
  source of in *King Lear*, 73, 75
Perry, Ruth, 70, 71, 100, 189n63
Pine, Robert Edge, 93, 96, 189n65
Piozzi, Hester Thrale, 96, 189n70
Players Scourge, The (Gibb), 29–30
Playhouse Pocket-Companion, The, 36
poetic justice
  defence of
    Samuel Johnson, 38
  rejection of, 37
Pope, Alexander, 198n20
Pratt, Samuel Jackson, 18, 19, 21, 23, 175n7
Price, Lawrence, 118
Proctor, Bryan Waller [pseud Barry Cornwall]
    Kean as Shylock, 201n75
    re Edmund Kean, 165

Racine, Jean, 25
Ragussis, Michael, 144, 149, 154, 173n30, 197n13, 200n68
Redresser, Or, Weekly Strictures of Simon Sympathy, 21, 176n9
Remarks on Mrs Siddons, in some of her Principal Characters, 49
Remarks on the Slave Trade and the Slavery of the Negroes, 193n37
Restoration comedy
  support of, 179n56
Restoration drama
  fathers and daughters in, 73
  immorality of, 31, 35, 36, 104, 179n47
Roach, Joseph, 7, 8, 43, 56, 67, 97, 140, 171n18
Robinson, Mary, 84
'Roman Charity', 84–85, 87, 89, 95
  as dramatized in *The Grecian Daughter*, 87–89
  in art, 84–85, 92
  Valerius Maximus, 84, 188n51
Roman Father, The (Whitehead), 77, 80
Román, David, 43
Rome
  and liberty, 77, 78, 79, 80, 81, 82
  as analogue for Britain, 76–77, 79, 81–82, 100
  in drama, 76–83
Rowe, Nicholas, 78, 178n45
  Fair Penitent, The, 33, 67, 73, 183n44
    fathers and daughters in, 73
    representation of domestic life, 33
  Jane Shore, 38, 58–64
    audience response to, 59–64
    female response to, 60–61
    Sarah Siddons as, 59–65
    suffering of, 59–60, 61–64
Rowlandson, Thomas, 54
Rubens, Peter Paul, 84
'Rule Britannia'. *See* Thomson, James
Russell, Gillian, 172n30

Said, Edward, 106, 125
Scott, Sir Walter, 50, 66, 182n25
sensibility, 11, 13–15
  Age of Sensibility, 13, 40, 67, 68
  and theatre, 14–15, 25–26, 27
  and virtue, 14, 15, 25–26
  artificial, 51–52, 67
  definition of, 13–14
  excessive, 14, 57–58
  feminization of, 14
  in audience, 57–58, 162
  socially directed, 139–141, 149, 158
Sensibility. A Poem [Samuel Johnson], 13, 174n36

sentiment, 11–13, 119, 141, 152, 158
  false sentiment, 13
  verbal nature of, 12, 13
sentimental comedy. *See also* comedy
  attacks on, 35–36
    John Dennis, 35
    Oliver Goldsmith, 35–36, 112, 192n26
    William Cook, 36
  criticism of, 10
  difficulties in defining, 11, 172n27
sentimentality, 13
  as literary device, 13
Seven Years War, 79, 117
Shadwell, Thomas
  Timon of Athens, 75, 185n20
Shakespeare, William
  Antony and Cleopatra, 34
  familial relations in, 34
  Hamlet, 178n34, 199n53
  in theatrical repertoire, 34
  Julius Caesar, 34, 38
  King Lear, 73–75, 100
    adapted by Garrick, 74–75
    adapted by Tate, 74–75, 91
    Garrick as, 1, 3
    Lear as father, 73–74
  Merchant of Venice, The, 144, 145, 159–162, 200n57
    Kean in, 165
    Macklin in, 144, 159, 160
  Othello, 38
  Richard III, 199n53
  Romeo and Juliet, 37, 94, 190n81, 199n53
  Timon of Athens, 34, 75–76, 83, 185n20
    adapted by Cumberland, 75–76
    adapted by Shadwwell, 75
  Winter's Tale, The, 34
Sherbo, Arthur, 10, 11, 171–172n23
Sheridan, Richard Brinsley, 10, 158
  compared with Cumberland, 156, 158
  Duenna, The, 143
    and anti-Semitism, 143
  satire on sentiment, 12
  School for Scandal, 12–13
    validation of feeling, 12
she-tragedy
  in *The Theory of Moral Sentiments*, 25, 179n49
  popularity of, 34
Siddons, Sarah, 43–66, 67–68, 93–100
  as Britannia, 99–100, 190n81
  as Euphrasia in *The Grecian Daughter*, 93–97
  as Isabella, 44, 46–57, 67–68, 181n22
  as the tragic muse, 97
  caricatures of, 52, 97
  early career, 44, 93
  in Edinburgh, 45–46, 51
  portraits of, 61, 96–97
slave trade, 121, 134
  abolition of, 130
  British participation in, 121, 124–125, 127–128, 129–130, 193n37
slavery, justification of, 131–133
slaves and slavery
  and empire, 117–118, 120–121, 125, 129–130
  and paternalism, 116, 131–136
  in *The Benevolent Planters*, 130–136
  in *Inkle and Yarico*, 121–125, 126–130
  in the West Indies versus England, 110, 116
  in *The West Indian*, 110
  London slums, 132–133
Smith, Adam, 28, 33, 38, 40, 42, 66, 147
  and *The Beauties of Mrs Siddons*, 63
  and tragedy, 179n49
  influence of, 20–21
  objects of sympathy, 72
  sympathy
    and moral society, 88
    and morality, 21–22, 112
    operation of, 48, 87
    propriety of, 63, 183n49, 184n9
  Theory of Moral Sentiments, The, 20–22
    and theatre, 25
    popularity of, 20–21
    spectatorship in, 176n15
songs, 2, 124, 131, 135–136, 137, 195–196n75
Songster's Companion: a Select Collection of More Than Two Hundred Songs, 195n75
Sophocles
  Philoctetes, 63, 183n48
Southerne, Thomas, 25, 38, 44, 47
  Garrick's adaptation of, 47, 181n14
  Isabella, or, the Fatal Marriage, 38, 44, 46–58, 63, 64, 67–68, 181n14
    audience response to, 47–57, 58, 63, 64, 67–68
    Siddons in, 46–57
Speaker: Or, Miscellaneous Pieces, selected from the Best English Writers, The, 109–110
Spectator, The, 70, 118, 119, 121
Stage the High Road to Hell, 29, 30, 178n41
Steele, Sir Richard, 119
  Conscious Lovers, 152, 198n31
  fathers and daughters (*Spectator* 449), 70, 72
  Inkle and Yarico (*Spectator* 11), 118, 121, 122
  views on comedy, 35, 179n56
Stone, Jr.,George Winchester, 185n18
Sutcliffe, Barry, 120, 194n48
sympathy, 18–27, 56, 145
  Adam Smith
    Theory of Moral Sentiments, The, 20–22
  and aesthetics, 23–24, 27–28, 31–33, 37–39

and audience response, 4, 16, 42–43, 48
and fiction, 24–25
and forms of drama, 31–36
and moral action, 112
and morality, 19–20, 21–23, 145
and spectatorship, 22–23
and the arts, 23–28
and the audience, 41–42
and theatre, 18–19, 25–27, 37–39
audience response, 102
David Hume, 21, 25–26, 176n20
Edmund Burke, 24, 177n24
ephemeral nature of, 140
Henry Home, Lord Kames, 22–24
operation of, 18–23, 39, 87–89
propriety of, 61, 62–63, 64
publications about, 20–21
theatre and morality, 28–29

Tate, Nahum
adaptation of *King Lear*, 38, 74–75, 91
theatre riots, 45, 175n42
Theatrical Entertainments Consistent with Society, Morality, and Religion [Henry Flitcroft], 29–30, 178n46
Theatrical Portrait, a Poem, on the Celebrated Mrs Siddon, 60–61, 67, 183n44
Thomson, James
'Rule Britannia', 107–108, 116, 131
Threipland, Stuart Moncrieff, 121
Todd, Janet, 14
Tragedy
and comedy mixed, 9, 158
domestic, 33
importance of fellow-feeling in, 32–34
in *The Theory of Moral Sentiments*, 25, 63, 179n49
new forms, 9
Samuel Johnson on, 177n24
subject matter of, 32–33
theories of, 31–34, 37–39
versus comedy, 102–103
Trip to Parnassus, or the Judgment of Apollo on Dramatic Authors and Performers, 118
Turner, Daniel
'On Sympathy', 20, 22, 39, 177n34

Unsespected Observer, The, 122, 125, 129

Valerius Maximus, 84–85, 87, 92, 188n51
Vermeer, Johannes, 84
Virginia and Virginius, 77–83, 186n30
as patriotic fable, 78, 79, 80, 81–82
in drama, 78–83
political implications, 78, 186n31
story of, 77–78
Virginia. A New Serious Opera, 186n30

Wahrman, Dror, 63–64
Walpole, Horace, 102, 103, 158
comedy and nation, 105
on comedy, 102–103, 190n8, 190n5
Wanko, Cheryl, 43, 173n30
Watson, Carolyn (engraver), 96, 97
Watt, Ian, 172n25
Webster, John, 78, 186n29
Wedgewood, Josiah, 97, 117
West Indian, The. See also Cumberland, Richard
West Indies
and slavery, 110, 116, 121, 126–129, 130–136
planters, 116
in Bellamy's *The Benevolent Planters*, 130, 131–133, 134
in Colman's *Inkle and Yarico*, 122–123, 125, 139
in Cumberland's *The West Indian*, 108, 110, 111–112
in London, 108
theatre in, 108, 191n17
West, Shearer, 180n7
Whitehead, William
Roman Father, The, 77, 80
Williams, Raymond, 5–6, 8, 15, 120, 129, 168
Wilson, Andrew, 19
Wilson, Brett D., 2, 11, 76
Wilson, Kathleen, 173n30
Wollstonecraft, Mary, 14
Worrall, David, 196n79
Worthy Example of a Virtuous Wife, 85, 188n53
Wright, Richardson, 119, 191n17

Yates, Mary Ann, 65, 189n76

Zangwill, Louis, 164
Zoffany, Johan, 84
Roman Charity, 85
Zwinger, Lynda, 71